"Do you think I wish you harm?" Cristabel asked.

"I think I wish you trusted me," Magnus said softly, his hand caressing her shoulder.

"I didn't get to my great age by trusting too much," Cristabel said gruffly, trying for a quick retort so he wouldn't guess what his touch was doing to her.

She was hesitant and nervous with him tonight. That was new to him. It was her fierce courage that usually amused and intrigued him. But tonight she was shy and tentative. She stood before him, lithe and perfumed, dressed as a spun sugar lady, and she was everything desirable to him.

"Cristabel," he murmured, her name itself a caress the way he said it in his deep voice. "Ah Cristabel, what are you doing to me?"

He didn't let her answer. His kiss was light, almost hesitant until he felt her lips, soft and surprised, beneath his. Then he took her deep into his arms and with infinite gentleness held her close and hard against him as he kissed her again . . .

Edith Layton

A True Lady

POCKET BOOKS

New York London Toronto Sydney Tokyo Singapore

This book is a work of fiction. Names, characters, places and incidents are products of the author's imagination or are used fictitiously. Any resemblance to actual events or locales or persons, living or dead, is entirely coincidental.

An *Original* Publication of POCKET BOOKS

 POCKET BOOKS, a division of Simon & Schuster Inc.
1230 Avenue of the Americas, New York, NY 10020

ISBN: 0-671-88301-1

First Pocket Books printing November 1995

10 9 8 7 6 5 4 3 2 1

POCKET and colophon are registered trademarks of Simon & Schuster Inc.

Cover art by Danilo Ducak

Printed in the U.S.A.

A heroine for Susie

CHAPTER

1

～

Autumn 1721

Her hair blew around her face like silken streamers, but that was the only thing about her that moved. She stood braced against the wind as she looked out over the sea. Her face was as still as the carved figurehead on the great ship she watched, but the girl was far more beautiful than that wooden symbol of female perfection, and real tears, not just salt spray, coursed down her cheeks as she saw the pirate ship approach. She didn't flinch.

She had watched the battle and never doubted the outcome. And now, as she expected, two ships came sailing into the harbor with black flags flying. The merchantman was too fine a ship to send to the bottom of the sea with its crew, so those who had refused to throw in with the pirates had been overtaken and overwhelmed. The crowd on the dock cheered and jeered, and threw their ragged caps in the air to see the prize being brought to them. The hellish sound rose high in the sweltering air: a chorus of rough voices, a screeching of parrots and donkeys and monkeys and all the denizens of the pirate community in raucous celebration. She only dashed away her tears with the back of one hand and breathed a broken sigh at her show of weakness. Then she squared her slender shoulders, took a deep breath, and waited patiently for her destiny.

The pirates carried the gold off first. Many eager hands made light work of it, though the chests were filled to brimming. Many sharp eyes watched the grubby hands, and the noise fell to a murmur as they did. Nothing was so important to a pirate as gold, so the rejoicing stopped until the chests were safely stowed in the pirate king's own coffers. Then the chests of jewels, the boxes of silks and satins, and the kegs of wine and spices were carted off the conquered ship, along with the cattle, the ducks and chickens. And then last, and certainly least, the wretched humans were unloaded. Some were in chains, some in bloody bandaging, and some were dead. The last man was off, with the captain, and he was definitely the prize. You could see the glee in the pirate king's glittering eyes.

He ignored the weary captain and the officers of the beaten crew and turned his back on the passengers of the ship he'd taken. Prodding this captive in the back with his long, glittering knife, he strolled off the ship. The crowd at the cove grew silent and made a path for the two men as they marched forward to the pirate king's house.

It was a small, ramshackle settlement for a king to rule over, but just as the king was named captain of his ship, so he was considered king of the village where his crew lived when they weren't at their terrible business at sea. There were many fierce-looking men in the little village, a few fierce or sullen-looking women, many children. These people lived in lean-tos and tumbledown shacks and tents, yet in truth, these pirate quarters could hardly be called houses. They were merely places to sleep and to keep out of the rain. None were clean, and all were littered, except for the pirate king's own house.

His home wasn't very grand, but it was finer than any other house in the village. It was small, to be sure, and made of wood, but it was neat, and the flower-filled courtyard was fenced in to keep out the wandering chickens, dogs, and goats. It was there that the crowd congregated.

The king of the pirates was a burly middle-aged man with dark eyes and a great beard, black as his sins. His long, greasy hair hung limp in the humid air. He wore tar black breeches and big black boots, but his coat was as scarlet as the blotches of his victims' blood drying on it, and the ragged lace at his wrists and throat was smeared with the same terrible pigment. When he reached his dooryard he threw open the gate and stopped. His smile was white and crooked and he puffed out his great chest in triumph as he looked down at the beautiful young woman who stood before him.

"Aye. I've gone and done it. So here he be—your future husband," he bellowed, and shoved his captive forward with one callused hand.

The young man staggered, but held his head high and didn't fall at the girl's feet as the pirate had planned. He was a fair-haired, slender young man, dressed in what had once been fine clothes. His face was ashen and his light eyes were wild with anger, but his rage was nothing compared to the woman's. She took in a deep breath and looked the pirate square in the eye.

"Stow it!" she shouted, her fine amber eyes glinting with a fierce light. "Ye be off yer nut if ye be thinking I be mating wi' this . . . this . . . fop! So take him back, or sell him for a fine price, but I'll not be wedded to the likes of him. Never!"

The pirate made a low, threatening sound deep in his throat. Despite his shock, the young man turned to him in surprise; he'd never heard a human being actually growl before. The young woman's face was white, but she stuck out her small, dimpled chin and stood firm.

"Oh, but ye will—because I say ye will!" the pirate bellowed. "And this very day!"

"Never!" she shrieked back.

"Aye, well then," the pirate purred, "too bad for the lad. Aye," he went on, nodding as she bit her lip in the horror of sudden comprehension, "'cause if ye won't take him as yer husband, ye'll have his guts fer shoestrings—and his fingers and toes fer a necklace, and his various manly appurtenances on yer dinner plate fer yer tasty delectation—this very night. And I mean it, Cristabel, ye know I do. I'm all out of patience. Have him as husband, or have him in pieces. It's up to ye!"

"Why him?" she wailed.

"Well, him—or me mate, Bold Black Jack Kelly."

She flinched. "Never!" she cried.

"Aye. Well then, take the lad. He's a high lord, and an English one, too, like ye always be going on about. Real refined. Aye. I be a proper concerned papa after all. I could have brought ye a Spaniard or a Moor, or even a Frenchie. But no, I goes to great pains to get ye what ye always said ye wanted: a fine English gent. Behold: Magnus Titus Snow— the great Lord Snow, of Camden Hall, a nobleman born and bred. And yer new husband, child."

The young man, who until now had remained silent, raised his battered head. "But—no!" he said with sudden hope. "I am Snow, but you've got the wrong one. He was supposed to come, but I took passage in his stead. I am not he."

"'I am not he,'" the pirate echoed in wonder. "Ye see? Talks so fine, you could spread it on bread."

"But I'm not," the young man protested, "really. Magnus is my brother."

"Aye," the pirate said with humor, "and that's why yer chests all have the letters 'M.T.' all over them. Cross-eyed Sweeney, what can read, told me," he confided to his daughter.

"My name is Martin Thomas," the young man insisted. "Magnus is my brother, I vow it."

"Aye, aye," the pirate said with a grin that tilted his hedge of a beard, "to be sure. But ye be vowing something else more important soon as we gets ye cleaned up. Ah—stow it," he said, cuffing the young man lightly. "I can see the profit of staying out of the parson's mousetrap, none better, me lord. But yer caught, fair and square. No sense in a fish arguing when he's beached, hooked, baked, and buttered up ready to serve, eh? No. 'Tis my daughter ye'll be wedding, this very night."

4

"I can explain . . ." the young man said.

"No, ye can't," the pirate roared, silencing him. "Mebbe ye wanted some fine lady, I can see that," he went on reflectively. "But mark ye—ye'll be getting none finer than our Cristabel. She's educated. Can read and write. Sew and sing. Her mama was a fine lady herself, I promise ye. And dowry? Well, don't be worrying none 'bout that. She'll come to you richer than any lord's daughter. Chests of gold and jewels, lad, emeralds and pearls enough to make an emperor slaver. I do fer my own, I do. None can say else. And as fer beauty? Look at her straightly and tell me ye seen better in yer lifetime and I'll know ye for a rotten liar."

Many men, with a sharp knife at their back, would agree, whatever she looked like, but for all he wanted to disagree, the young man couldn't. This girl was a rare beauty. She was as flamboyantly vivid and lush as the tropical isle he now stood upon. Though she was slender, her garish parrot green gown showed a high, full bosom and a tiny waist. She had a fair, fine-featured face with a small nose and delightfully plump, curving mouth. Her eyes were long-lashed, sloed, and the color of raw whiskey; her complexion, smooth and blushed with a faint golden bloom; and her glorious red-gold hair, a mass of thick, windblown silken curls. But her fine eyes held murder as she glared back at him.

"She's lovely," he agreed. "But I swear that I'm not who you think I—"

The pirate removed the knife from the small of his back, and now held it beneath the captive's chin.

"Enough. Whoever ye say ye be," the pirate said quietly, "ye be marrying my daughter this night—or ye be getting her pretty slippers all filled with yer bright blood. Now, ye wouldn't want to be ruining her shoes, would ye?"

The young man swallowed. He could feel the thin, cold kiss of steel when he did.

"No," he said softly.

"Good!" the pirate said happily, "Now, he just proposed. What say ye, daughter?"

She swallowed too. "Rot you," she said. Then she looked at the young man before her. She wilted. "Aye. I will," she sighed.

"Amen," said the pirate. "Congratulations. Now. We get us a minister and do it refined. Right?"

The pirates celebrated the wedding all through the night. They camped on the beach before huge fires and ate roasted meat and fresh fruits, drank rum and wine until they were sick or sleeping. They made loud noise and music and love until dawn. They danced with their wives and mothers, daughters and concubines, slaves and servants, and then with each other, jigging and hopping and whirling until they were so overheated, they had to douse themselves in the sea or with whiskey. There were chanteys and love songs and roundelays sung, and all to the music of squeeze boxes and drums, fiddles and flutes. For once, the night birds and tree toads on the isle were silent, and even the tide went out and came in without notice.

"Aye. There's naught like a wedding to make a man sentimental," the pirate king said with a deep sigh as the rising sun showed a rosy blush on the far horizon. He brushed some crumbs from his beard and gave the sleepy girl lying in his lap a long kiss before tumbling her to the ground. This time he didn't join her there, but rose and stretched deeply. "Done and done," he said with satisfaction, "Now there be practical things to settle."

He stepped over various intertwined bodies and made his way to the edge of the beach, where a young man, his hands and feet bound, stared glumly out at the sea.

"Good morning, m'lord son-in-law," the pirate king said heartily.

The young man looked up. "I am not who you think I am," he said wearily.

"I think ye be me son-in-law, and so ye be. Here's the paper what says it," the pirate chortled, taking a ribbon-tied document from his greasy coat pocket and waving it around. "Now, ye ain't consummated the wedding, I agree.

6

But even I didn't expect ye to get up the wind, what with so many dozen lads all jeering ye on." He grinned, tucking the paper back next to his heart again. "There be a long sea journey ahead of ye, and I expect confinement with such as me Cristabel will do the trick. Yer not made of stone, lad. Nor be ye ignorant of such passions, nor slow to take them up neither, not from what I heared of ye. Yer reputation do ye proud, lad, and I don't doubt ye'll do fer me girl—soon as me back's turned, no doubt. Since there's no way out fer ye, why pass up the treat?" He chuckled again.

"What sea journey?" the young man asked with the first show of liveliness the pirate had seen from him since he'd finally been made to gasp: "I do."

"Why, ye be going home. I didn't wed ye to me lass so she could queen it here, ye know. She's already by way of being royalty here. No, no, I wants her to take her rightful place at yer side in England, me lord. As Lady Snow. Lady Cristabel Eleanora Snow," he said with awe. He paused to blow his nose. After he'd dragged his sleeve beneath his nose, he went on thickly, "Aye. A true lady, just like her mum.

"So," he said more briskly, "I'm sending her with ye on the first fair tide. First to Port Royale, and there on a good stout ship back to England. With a word in all the right places—or better yet, the wrong ones—that it would go ill with Felix Stew, Old Captain Whiskey hisself—at yer service," he added with a great sweeping, mocking bow, "were anyone to interfere with the safe passage of that ship—if ye gets me drift."

"Home?" the young man said with dawning eagerness.

"Aye. But don't be getting no fancy ideas, me lord. There'll be some of me own men with ye on that voyage. And though they can't oblige the hangman by staying on in England, there be men of the brotherhood there to pass the word. Try anything rude with me lass, and I'll hear of it, I vow." He wagged a thick finger. "She be yer lady now, and no two ways about it. Ah, but what's the sense of threatening ye? Twist and turn as ye may, it's done."

He bent and slipped his long dagger through the young

man's bonds, and then helped him to his unsteady legs. Then he wrapped one arm around him and walked with him along the beach. "Now, we gets ye washed and packed, and off ye go," he said.

The young man nodded, not wanting to open his mouth lest he have to breathe in more of his captor's rich odor.

"Ah—but," the pirate said thoughtfully a few minutes later, "better ye don't see yer blushing bride again till ye board the ship. She be . . . shy as ye be. So best ye meet again when there's naught but a cabin, a bed, a closed door, and the two of ye, alone. Aye," he said thoughtfully, "best, that way, I think—I hope."

The bride's trunks were packed, and her father had three more filled with jewels and gold. They were all loaded on top of the carriage as she said farewell to her childhood friends and companions. This took quite some time, for there were so many parrots, dogs, and cats for her to cuddle, pet, and promise to never forget. She wept a little, and her eyes were definitely pink when, holding her head high, she marched up the little stair to get into the carriage. She never shed a tear or uttered a single word to anyone—not even her father—all the rocky way to Port Royale.

Her ship was being boarded at the wharfside. The docks of Port Royale served many vessels and were so crowded with people and animals that even the constant trade winds couldn't keep them cool. Between the brightly dressed natives selling their wares, the prostitutes in their gaudy half-dresses, and the remarkably costumed seamen from many far lands, the gaudy pirates almost passed unnoticed.

Cristabel was dressed in the height of pirate fashion. She wore a low-cut gown of bright apricot silk swagged with lace and brilliants, with a silk shawl of canary yellow draped over her shoulders in spite of the heat. She stood fanning herself, as though alone, ignoring Captain Whiskey as he stood at her side.

The groom—along with his trunks—was already loaded on the ship. Two stalwart pirates had seen him to his cabin and then bolted the door behind him. The bride's belongings were also safely stowed. Although the girl seemed resigned to her fate, her eyes flashed with anger and yet sometimes seemed suspiciously misty. Her lips remained sealed, but just as she turned to board, her father took her hand and held it hard in his own callused one.

"Give us a smile, lass," he said in a soft voice, "I did it all for ye. It breaks me old heart to see ye so," he went on when she didn't speak, "fer it's a strange old world, and ye bound fer halfway 'cross it, and given the times and the road I travel, who knows if I shall ever see ye again? . . . Ah, Crissie, love," he sighed, "I did it all for ye, can ye not see it?"

"Married me at knifepoint to a stranger?" she hissed.

"Aye. But listen, it were a fine English lord ye wanted, weren't it? And where was I to find one, I ask ye?"

"But I didn't want one *kidnapped*, held for ransom, paying for his life by joining with me!" she cried.

"How else were I to nab one?" he asked in exasperation. "How else did I find yer own departed mama, child? And she learned to love me proper," he said with reverence, "afore she left us. I always got ye what ye wanted, since you was a sprat, din't I, lass? That's how ye got such notions in yer noggin in the first place, from all them fine English governesses I got ye, curse their cold hearts."

"Fine English governesses ye got me from the slave block, or the decks of burning ships," she muttered darkly.

"Howsomever, I got them for ye, and got ye an education, too, din't I? And then got ye the notion to wed a fine Englishman, curse the day," he said sadly. "And so when ye refused the finest fellow I knew, Black Jack Kelly, what do I do? Did I force ye to wed him, like a father should? No."

"You tried!" she shouted.

"Aye, but I could have tried harder," he said, holding a finger in the air, silencing her. "No, I didn't," he said virtuously, "Like a daft old fool, I go out and get ye the finest lord I ever heared of, and how do ye thank me? With a nose in the air and not a word of farewell."

"Aye, but I wouldn't have needed no husband did ye not have a hankering to wed again and wanted no shrewish daughter underfoot to spoil yer fun, would I?" she asked venomously.

He looked as sheepish as a large, dirty pirate king could.

"Yer toothsome young Carmen hates me, don't she?" she persisted. "Can't stand the sight of me, wishes me ten fathoms deep, though she quakes and shakes her pretty little arse and pretends to be scared of me, don't she? Ye had to be rid of me, Papa, don't fancy it up none, because it won't wash."

"Aye, there's some truth in what yer saying. But think on, were it all true, I'd have made ye take Black Jack Kelly any which way, and ye know it," he said. "I tried to give ye what ye wanted, give me that, love. And what ye wanted were a fine refined English lord, weren't it?"

"Aye . . . but . . ." she began.

"And they ain't exactly thick on the ground hereabouts, is they?"

"No, but . . ."

"Nor are we by way of meeting up with them anywheres *but* on the deck of a ship we're keelhauling, is we?"

"Aye, that's so . . ."

"And since no one *I* knew, nor one of the fine lads panting after you, was good enough for you—and Gawd above, girl, but you *are* one and twenty!" he bellowed.

She fell still.

"One and twenty and unwed," he grieved. "'Twas unnatcheral."

She looked down to the toes of her red satin slippers.

"But whenever I said anything, you'd be always going on about how no one was 'refined and educated' enough for you," he said mockingly. "So here he be—a lad with more names to him than ye can embroider on his handkerchief, and with blood blue as a squid's ink. You wanted an English lord, you got one. So what be ye kicking fer?"

"Because I didn't want *this* one!" she insisted.

"What's wrong with him?" her father roared. "Got all his

teeth, young and sprightly, nice-looking feller too. S'truth," he admitted, "his reputation be leagues ahead of his performance. The man's made a stunning name for hisself, though it be hard to credit. I heared he had wimmen swooning fer him from one end of England to t'other, and that he accommodated most of 'em too. I grant it don't look possible. Nor be he grand and manly as they said, neither. But ye can't hardly complain on that," he said with more spirit. "Ye didn't want a fine, hardy specimen of a man like Black Jack Kelly . . . Oh aye, don't huff, I'll shut me mug on that.

"There be nothing wrong with this lad," he insisted. "And remember, there ain't that many English lords, and ye know Englishwomen—with the exception of yer departed mama, of course—they don't want much liveliness in their beds. I reckon that accounts for it. Still, who can tell? It's early yet. I'll admit he don't show much fire in his wooing, but give him time. Ye only been spliced a few days, and none of them ones to show a man to his best advantage—unless he be a right old rogue like Black Jack K— Oh, aye—I'm mum.

"So howsabout a lass giving her old father a hug, and a wish that the wind always be in his sails, and his enemies asleep in sharks' bellies, eh?"

"Oh, Papa!" she cried wretchedly, and fell into his outstretched arms. He hadn't been much of a father and they both knew it, but he was the only father she had, and this island was the only home she'd ever known.

"Well, what's done's done, and fer the best, so I do believe," he said somewhat soupily when he finally released her. She was his only legitimate child, and he let her go with what might have been genuine reluctance. He ran his sleeve under his nose before he spoke again. "Ye be happy, lass, y'hear?" he demanded. "No use pleading," he added when he saw her eyes. "I may only be a pirate, but I'm the captain because I be a man of me word, and so I raised ye to be. Ye be wed to that fine lord, and that be the end of it. Ye'll be happy too, lass, see if ye ain't.

"Now," he said with more spirit, "let's see. Got yer steel? Good. And yer pocket pistol? Ah, good. Yer cutlass, I hope, been packed? Fine. And yer wee dagger, and yer bonny gutting knife, and them new cutties I got ye too? Fine, fine. Being a lady is yer concern, being safe is mine. A lass has got to be prepared, right? Now. Godspeed," he said, giving her a little push toward the tall-masted merchant ship that awaited her.

"I be seeing ye again?" she asked in a very small voice, looking back at him tearfully.

"I hope not," he said. "Ye be a true lady now, remember?"

She left, but not without shedding a few tears.

She would have shed many more had she not turned to catch a last glimpse of her father and seen him with a young woman whom he took into his arms as soon as he thought his daughter was out of sight.

They tried to ignore each other, but it wasn't possible in a cabin on a great vessel in the middle of the ocean with the door locked behind them till dawn.

He couldn't have ignored her even if they weren't locked together in a tiny room. Many staggering things had happened to him in the past few days, but this girl was by far the most astonishing. He was stunned by her. She looked like a barbarian princess right out of one of the adventure books of his boyhood. She was so brightly, fiercely beautiful and nothing like any lady he'd ever seen, nor even like the boldest whores in London town. With her sunset hair and bright apricot gown and stunningly yellow wrap, she made his eyes ache—as well as other parts he didn't want to think about. It wasn't only her vivid coloring that made her so exciting, there was a sensationally shapely body got up in bold splendor that swayed to her constant movement, as she paced the cabin like a caged tiger.

It was a well-furnished cabin, and a comfortable one. It had a fine Indian carpet on the floor and room enough for a good-sized bed, a chest, a table, and two chairs. A fair-sized porthole gave them a glimpse of the wide sea they sailed over. In all, it could be a comfortable voyage, he thought— if he were on it with almost anyone else in the world and under any other circumstances. As it was, he felt sick to his stomach. He knew it wasn't seasickness, because sailing never troubled him. But he felt decidedly bilious. And the reason for it was pacing back and forth in front of him.

He sat on the bed and watched her uneasily. She was doing a very good job of ignoring him, and that was unsettling. He was an even-tempered fellow who made friends easily, but he didn't know how to talk to this girl. The fact that there were many important things that he had to say to her agitated him, and the fact that he lacked the courage to even begin speaking bothered him even more.

But he wasn't a coward, and so he finally got to his feet and approached her.

It was like trying to start a conversation with a small whirlwind, because she walked right by him and then turned and paced back. Her pale, lovely face was cast in a mold of suppressed fury, and her hands were clenched in fists by her sides. The breeze from her silken gown swept around her and he caught a faintly pleasant scent. Cinnamon, he thought in surprise, breathing it in, and vanilla and sweet tropical blossoms. It was fascinating, like the aroma of baking flowers: seductive, exotic, delicious—edible. He swallowed hard.

"Ah . . ." he began, and paused. "Mistress," as he was going to say, was inappropriate, "madam" was definitely wrong, and he realized he didn't even remember her name.

"Pardon me," he said, but she just ignored him.

Frustrated, he stood watching her. But then when the sea beneath the polished oaken boards of their cabin suddenly swelled, rising and falling unexpectedly, he staggered. Being a gentleman born and bred, he put out his hands to steady her, too, and found himself facing shining steel, and the glare in her narrowed eyes, which was no less menacing.

"Take yer grubby paws off me," she snarled, holding the knife steady at his breastbone, "or be history, matey."

"I thought you were going to fall," he said, dropping his hands to his sides.

"Hoped is more like it," she muttered, "but I'd no more fall from a sea swell than I would fer yer honied blandishments."

He blinked. "Ah, but I said nothing," he replied cautiously, wondering about this savage pirate princess who not only knew but spoke such words.

"Ye be *thinking* them," she said, still glaring at him.

It was so nearly true, he felt his face flush with guilt. "I have some things I must tell you," he said instead.

She paused, cocking her head to the side. Her face was beautiful, but her smile was not. It chilled him. "Do tell," she purred.

"I don't know what you're angry about. You got what you wanted; I wasn't the one who asked for this," he said defensively.

Her smile disappeared. And his stomach grew even colder. He was an honest man and had to go on whether he wanted to or not. "No one would listen to me then. *Listen?"* he spat out bitterly. "They didn't even let me talk. All they'd let me say is 'I do' and 'I will.' But there's more, much more. Oh Lord," he said.

She watched him closely, her knife still poised and aimed at his chest. He was naturally fair, but now he was almost as white as the powder on his wig. He was dressed in all his finery, but when she'd first seen him, his pale hair had been uncovered and he'd been in his torn shirtsleeves. He was a handsome young man, clean-limbed and tall, with a guileless, even-featured face and candid blue eyes. His clothes didn't exaggerate or flatter him, elegant and obviously expensive, they simply suited him. He wore a fitted coat of corded blue silk with falls of lace showing at the neck and cuffs, tight black breeches that ended at the knee with high white silk stockings, and neat silver-buckled shoes. The only touch of opulence was his long embroidered silk waistcoat of dark green and gold design.

The men whom she was used to all swaggered about in

the colorful clothes of their calling, extravagant finery from the high days of the Brotherhood: flowing shirts and wide, baggy breeches and doublets, long, bright waistcoats and high, soft-cuffed boots, and as many sashes and pendants and earrings and rings as they could muster. But this man was dressed like a modern man of fashion: subtle, subdued, but so elegant, she felt like a peacock compared to him— no, a peahen in peacock feathers, she thought unhappily.

"I have something very important to say," he went on. "You see," he said with a sigh. "Oh Lord," he said, sighing again, "the fact is—the truth of the matter is—that we are not married. No, really, we're not. We cannot be married. Every word I say is the truth. I am *not* Magnus Titus, Lord Snow. I'm not even a lord. He is my brother. My real name is Martin Thomas Snow, and as if that isn't enough," he said in a rush, "the marriage would be invalid even if they'd got the name right, because I'm already married. And happily," he added quickly, tensing for whatever reaction this news might elicit.

She stared at him blankly. He saw exactly when the truth began to dawn in her widening amber eyes. They began to glow like warmed honey. He braced himself, wondering how far in the knife would go before he could pull away.

"Oh," she said. "Oh, thank heavens!" she cried in a clear, cultured voice, as she lowered the knife and clasped her hands together as if in prayer. "Oh, thank you! I am so relieved—oh, my dear sir, you can't possibly know how happy you've made me!"

CHAPTER

2

I don't see why you should be so shocked at my reaction," Cristabel said, hands on hips. "I didn't want to marry you in the first place. Of course," she admitted, "there was no way you could know that. But it was either you or a particularly undesirable crony of my father's. You looked as unhappy as I felt, and that decided it for me. I thought there might be some way out of this mess once we left the island. I didn't expect this! This is beyond wonderful! Thank you, thank you, thank you. You have set me free—freer than you can possibly imagine," she said, as she sat down and looked at him with pure pleasure.

He stood and gaped at her. It took him a while to frame his next words.

"I thought," he said slowly, "I mean, I heard, that is to say—good Lord, what's happening? Why are you speaking differently now?" he blurted out.

"Oh," she said, and a delicate peach color suffused her pale cheeks, "well, you see, I speak one way for my father and the people I live with, and another with people of some . . . education. Well, it wouldn't do fer me to yammer at ye like this, would it?" she asked sharply. "Naw, din't think so. Just think," she said, changing her voice from strident tones to a softer, calmer accent, "how it would sound to the islanders if I spoke to them like this. They'd be as startled and uncomfortable with me as you just were. Two completely different worlds," she said sadly, "and I live in both of them. You see, my mother was a lady, a true English gentlewoman, or so my father always says. And so I grew up with governesses who taught me how to speak and act should I ever get the chance to live in her world. Now you've given me that chance!"

"Yes, I suppose I have. By being a coward," Martin said dully, sinking back onto the bed again. "I should have resisted more—I ought to have sacrificed myself. Death before dishonor, and lying is a dishonor even if it was to save myself. Magnus would never, never, have done it. He would have died rather than submit. But not me. I discovered that I wanted to live and so I went through with it. Please, don't thank me. If you'd skewered me, the way I thought you were going to just now, it would have been what I deserved. Going through that charade of a marriage was wrong. I've no excuse but a failure of courage. I'm ashamed of myself."

"You're also alive," Cristabel said tartly, "which you wouldn't have been if you had refused to marry me. Please don't have any regrets. I don't. Oh," she sighed, as though a great weight had been lifted off her heart, "you can't know how wonderful this is. I can hardly take it all in. I'm free. Really free. Away from the island, away from my father, away from that horrible life—free to live my own life at last.

"When we get to London," she said, sitting up on the edge of her seat, her amber eyes sparkling, "we'll part—never to meet again—unless you want, of course, to raise a glass in fond remembrance. Or not," she said generously, when she saw his startled expression. "Just help me find rooms in a good part of town, and a servant or two—and then farewell to thee, Lord Snow, or Mr. Snow, or whoever you are. I'll be free. Under a new name of my own choice," she said triumphantly.

"Your father . . ." he began.

"Will never find me," she chortled.

"But *I* am a Snow," he said with some pride, "and therefore not hard to find."

"I doubt he'll look," she said airily. Seeing Martin's nervousness, she went on, "You see, I think Papa knows his glory days are almost done. That's why he set out to find me a husband. To get me off his hands, so he could get on with his life. Off with the old, on with the new; it's been on his mind a lot lately. I think it's because he lost so many cronies over the last years, or seen them come to grief. It's been hard times for his sort lately. All his old associates, let's see, there was Captain Vane, hanged; and there was Deadeye John Jarvis, hanged too; Jolly Calico Jack, hanged; and his lady, Anne Bonny—vanished. Captain Kidd, hanged; Captain England, beggared . . . Oh, I could go on and on. So many gone one way or the other. Aye, even the great Blackbeard himself ended with his head hanging from the bow and his body fed to the fishes.

"So many," she sighed, "either blown to bits or hanged by the neck—or other parts—until dead. The golden age of piracy is done, I think. Well, at least for him it is. He's very old for a pirate captain, you know. And since pirate captains are always elected free and fairly—oh yes, 'tis so— I think a younger man will get the nod soon. And so, I believe, thinks he.

"Now that he thinks he's got me settled, he'll close the book and be off under some new name to some other island paradise with his booty. Off to a new life with a new woman—who may well be the first since my mother to actually become his wife. I think he's got a hankering for some legitimate male heirs," she mused, grinning at the shocked young man.

He stared at this girl in all her pirate splendor, sitting primly amidst the shining silks and clashing colors. She spoke like a lady—her voice was modulated, her accents pure and well bred—but what she was saying . . .

"I can't just leave you when we get to London," he said.

"I may have done the wrong thing in pretending to marry you, but I can't compound it. I'm responsible for you."

"In a pig's eye," she said. "I mean . . . not at all. We're not really married, after all—unless . . . Could they be saying you've married me to yer brother by proxy?" she asked in sudden horror, her accent slipping as her fear grew.

"No, no," he assured her, "it's not so simple, otherwise anyone could marry anybody to his brother or father or uncle, or whatever, or claim they themselves were married to anyone they chose, and say it was by proxy. No, it's rare and difficult. You've got to have sworn statements and letters of consent with everything clearly stated, witnesses of high repute, and a lot more honored clergymen present than just the drunken old wreck that performed our ceremony. It's only the prerogative of royalty now, I believe, because I remember we had a wild young cousin whose father wanted to marry her off to a duke in Spain . . . but that's neither here nor there. Trust me. You're not married to anyone. If you are, then I'm a bigamist. And that, at least, I am not!"

His young face grew faintly flushed. "Yes," he said, lowering his eyes, "I was doubly sure to be sly about what I did. I even signed a false name to the document, and scribbled it so badly, no one could read it, anyhow. Even if they could, my own handwriting is particularly neat and clear and so it will never be taken for mine. It may have been cowardly, but it was safely done, I promise you.

"They didn't want me anyway," he said bleakly, "they wanted Magnus. He'd have been a great catch . . . Great? Ha," he said with no humor, "every woman in England has tried for him. He's never been caught yet—heart or hand. I'll bet he'd have found a way to wriggle out of what I got into, but without dishonor—unlike me," he said wretchedly, hanging his head in his hands.

"Well, I don't know how his feet don't hurt from walking on all that water," Cristabel snapped.

When he looked up at her, she continued angrily, "You did the best you could. I think you did quite well—

splendidly, as a matter of fact. Really. And if my papa and the others find out, I think they'll admire you for it—after they get through cursing and snarling, that is. But they'll be impressed by you. Beaten at their own game. I don't know this Magnus, but I'm very glad they didn't catch him. I don't think I could bear being married to such a paragon— or being really married to anyone, for that matter. And now, thanks to you, I'm not!"

She rose and began to pace about the cabin again. "I'm far past my prime and I know it," she said, her eyes on the carpet as she walked. "Aye, twenty-one and never married. A scandal anywhere, but unheard-of on Pirate Cove, where a girl can be a granny by the time she reaches thirty. But I didn't wed because I didn't want to. I only said I wanted an English lord because it was the most impossible thing I could think of. Now I have the best of everything. My father thinks I've married a lord, and I know I have not. All I need to do is to set up my own establishment and I'll never ask for anything more. So, as far as I'm concerned, Martin, you did very well, believe me."

"But I'm responsible for you . . ." he began.

"Fiddle! You are not," she said briskly, stopping and glaring at him. In that moment Martin saw that, though she didn't resemble her father at all physically, her voice had all the command his had when he'd held that knife beneath his captive's throat.

"Well, we'll discuss it later," he said, glancing away. That was when he remembered the bed. "Er, but now we've sleeping arrangements to make," he said nervously. "Perhaps I should tell the captain of this vessel—"

"You'll tell him nothing," she snapped, "nary a word! He and me father be thick as thieves." She closed her eyes and took a deep breath. Then she continued in more cultured tones but with the same determination. "Look you, Mr. Snow. We'll stay locked up in here and pretend we're making the best of it. Now," she went on decisively, "I'll take the bed. You'll take covers and blankets and make a nice little bed for yourself on the floor. We'll muddle through this voyage, and then we'll both be free. And that's the end of it."

The sea rocked her as if in a wooden cradle, and her false bridegroom's light snores were like a lullaby. Cristabel smiled, stretching luxuriously, too content to sleep. She was sailing over the sea to freedom, and her bridegroom lay half the room away from her and would never lie nearer.

Free! Cristabel repeated to herself, completely free! All the walks around the deck and the brisk sea air couldn't put her to sleep these nights. In fact, she fought to stay awake in order to savor it. She lay in the dark, gloating. She was leaving that hell of heat and noise, lush flowers, gaudy colors, strong drink and hot spices, and was on her way to that dear little isle of cool breezes and mists and rich history, that bastion of manners where men ate with knives *and* forks, and spoke softly.

She was going to that wonderful world of proper ladies and educated children—the world all her homesick governesses had never stopped speaking about and remembering with tears. In truth, those poor women had so many things to cry about: being torn from their ships, ravished, and then sold on the block. That was enough to make anyone cry. But they wept more for the lost world of England than for all the other terrible insults they'd endured. That had impressed Cristabel even more than their tales of that vanished world—the world her own beautiful mother had come from; the world from which her father was forever barred. The place where she could live out the rest of her life quietly, coaxing shy blossoms from the soil, making polite conversation, reading good books and sipping tea. A world as far removed from the one she knew as was the moon.

And most important of all, this world was a place in which she'd never, ever, have to take a husband. Never have to tie herself to a cheating, blustering, drunken, domineering, violent, lustful man for life. Never have to brawl all night with him, or put up with his infidelity and cruelties, never have to tolerant blows or amorous advances or sudden rages when he came home shouting drunk to steal from her or give her more babies to care for—like all the married women she'd ever known. No, never. She was actually going to that other world now. And no man would ever dominate her.

Smiling, Cristabel finally fell asleep to dream of mist and cool green grass, and freedom, eternal freedom.

They fought about it all the way across the blue Caribbean and into the wild Atlantic. Cristabel was thrilled.

It was the way he fought. Just the way she'd always believed a gentleman from his blessed isle would fight—with reasoned argument, not shouting, with patient denials, not knives or knuckles. And when he became truly frustrated, he'd only run his hand through his hair or stalk away from her. Martin would never run his fist into her mouth, or his boot into her stomach. They were locked up together for most of the day and all of the night, and they fought like puppies in a box—not the way the men and women she knew did. He was a gentleman, and she was ecstatic. She won every encounter, every time.

She had only to shout, and he fell silent, appalled, or astonished at her fluency with curses. If all else failed, she'd weep. Then he'd redden and look shattered. Of course, they had to promenade on deck beneath watchful eyes each day. The sailors knew their situation, and though they watched her with hot eyes, and priced Martin's clothing enviously, neither of them was ever molested by word or deed, because everyone was afraid of her father. But, all the same, the men watched the newlyweds very closely.

Martin's gentlemanliness made the voyage bearable for her. He was quiet and well spoken, neat and clean. Although being neat and clean was a decided plus, looks didn't matter to Cristabel. She had grown up among men, many with splendid bodies and handsome faces, and hadn't cared for any of them. Martin's kindness and considerateness were astonishing to her. He was nothing like the men she had known on the island. Still, she supposed women might find him attractive. She found him interesting but never thought of him as a man; he simply wasn't a threat.

Martin treated her honorably, respecting her privacy as best he could in such close quarters, turning his back or leaving the cabin when the need arose. Cristabel knew he looked at her as a woman from time to time, though, because sometimes she saw *that* look creeping into his usually candid eyes as he watched her, and he'd blush as if she knew what he was thinking. He amazed her.

They got into the habit of chatting together before they slept each night. Not about her freedom, of course, because that would only lead to a fight. Instead they spoke about neutral things. He was as curious about piracy as she was about England. They seldom spoke of personal things.

"What's your wife like?" she asked him idly one night, as they lay in their separate places, waiting for the ship to finish rocking them to sleep.

"Sophia?" he asked as drowsily as she had. "You'd like her. She's very clever."

"Is she beautiful?"

"Oh, yes. Fair hair, skin. Blue eyes."

"She sounds like you."

"I suppose she does, but she's not. She's tiny. Really little. Got a little nose, too, points up. Always makes me laugh. She's got dimples when she laughs. She laughs a lot. She loves practical joking. She's great fun to be with."

"Such enthusiasm," Cristabel commented with a sleepy giggle. "I ask if she's beautiful and you tell me about her sense of humor."

"Well, we've known each other forever," he said defensively. "It's hard to go into raptures about someone's looks when you know them so well."

"I see," Cristabel said, but she didn't.

"We met as toddlers. Everyone always knew we'd marry, and we did," he explained.

"Oh," she said, digesting this latest piece of information.

"So you were in the same situation I was. So why aren't you more sympathetic to me?"

"I *beg* your pardon?" he asked thunderously.

"I mean," she said, yawning, "they made you marry when you didn't want to, didn't they?"

"They did not!" he declared, sitting straight up in his nest on the floor. "I wanted to marry her. Very much, as a matter of fact; we've cared for each other forever."

"Fine, fine," she said, drawing her sheets up over her ears. "Good night."

But she could still hear him sulking long after the conversation had ended.

Martin mentioned his brother often. Far more often than Cristabel liked. When he wasn't fretting about what Magnus would say, he was remembering what Magnus had said. Magnus was the oldest of seven children, only four of whom survived to adulthood. They all looked up to him, and with reason. Magnus was wise, as well as tall, handsome, and elegant. In the gospel according to Martin, Cristabel thought sourly, his brother Magnus was worshiped by his family and adored by all right-thinking Englishmen. Cristabel, however, was the daughter of an aggressive man in a world of petty tyrants, and she didn't believe in small gods. She hadn't set foot in England yet, but so far, Magnus Titus, Viscount Snow, was the one thing about it she didn't like.

"Give over," she finally said one day as they stood at the rail and looked out over the wide ocean. They reckoned they were halfway between his home and hers now, and had become quite accustomed to each other. Cristabel knew what she was going to do when they landed, and he violently disapproved of her plans. Outside of this small area of discord, they got along quite well.

He was educated, and she wanted to learn more about her future home from him. She didn't want him as a man, but she did need him as a friend. He was only a few years older than she, although she often thought of him as much younger.

Cristabel had never had male friends because the men she met were too impressed with her father, one way or the other, to take that risk. The only man her father approved of was his protégé Black Jack, who was so like him that she'd never desired his friendship. As for female companionship, her governesses had hated their situations and her father so much that few ever tried to be friends. Girls her age had little in common with her, and less when they were married off—which they always were. She had about as much in common with the prostitutes on the island as she did with the pirates' wives. Both classes of women were ill used, and used to it.

No, she wasn't attracted to young Martin, but she did need a friend.

"He doesn't have to find out, you know," she finally said in exasperation. "Yes, yes, yes, your brother Magnus is brave and bold and brilliant, but he can't read minds, can he? Just—don't—tell—him. Don't stare at me like that. It's the only answer, if you just think about it. Why should he think you married again—and a pirate's daughter at that? Would anyone expect you to? No. Of course not. It's absolutely ridiculous, isn't it? So forget it. I shall. Look. You went abroad on family business. Your ship was overtaken. You were taken captive and then released. That's why you're home later than planned. Who could possibly imagine that strange wedding by moonlight? Who ever heard of such a thing?

"It's perfect," she said as she saw him mulling over her plan. "Why, in years to come, even you'll wonder if it ever really happened or if it was some strange vision brought on by too much rum one night—like seeing a mermaid. You don't have to lie to your brother. All you need to do is nothing and he won't be able to disapprove, will he?"

Martin's young face grew fretful, and she saw real sorrow in his eyes as he gazed out to sea.

"I've never lied to my brother," he said softly. "No one does; it's impossible to do."

"There is a difference between not telling and lying," she said in exasperation. "My goodness, do you tell him everything? I hope not; you're a married man now, after all."

She saw a slow flush start on his neck and climb to his cheeks.

"Of course I don't tell him everything," he muttered, growing redder.

She knew Martin loved his brother, but in her experience, no man wanted to always feel inferior to another, no matter how qualified he felt that other to be—or else there'd never be the possibility of mutiny.

"And so," she said slowly, sweetly, twining a strand of her copper gold hair around her finger, trying to look innocent and only succeeding in making him feel guilty, "why tell him about this?"

"But you're my responsibility," he said.

"Never," she said.

She nagged him for the rest of the day, and he kept walking away. But late that night, when he lay on the threshold of sleep, there was no place left for him to walk to.

"Martin?" she asked, and by his silence, knew he wasn't sleeping, "Martin," she said, propping herself up on one elbow and looking in his general direction in the dark, "have you ever gone fishing?"

It seemed a safe enough topic to discuss, and so he gave up pretending sleep, and said cautiously, "Of course."

"Why, then," she went on, "you must have one time or another caught yourself a fish you didn't want. One too small, or one too many?"

"I suppose so," he answered warily.

"Why, so have I," she said with encouragement. "I knew you had too. There are some cruel men who leave the poor things out to die, or slice them through and throw them to the gulls, but I knew you weren't that sort. So then. You know how, when you put the fish back in the shallows, they seem so helpless, almost dead? But then after a second or two, they shake themselves, and right themselves, and then with one slither, they're gone—snaking into the deep water in a wink—as though they'd never been inconvenienced in the least?"

He smiled in the darkness, remembering sun-flecked trout streams, and just what she described. It was as though she heard his silent nod.

"That," she said eagerly, "is exactly how I shall be. Put me down in London town, see me on my way if you must, and then—forget me forever. I'll vanish. You'll never have to see me again, I promise. You don't have to worry about me. There are decent rooming houses in London, are there not? And good places to live outside of London? Of course. If it makes you feel better, you can tell me which districts are respectable and which are not—although I promise you I can trust my own eyes.

"Then I'll take a new name, live out of the common way, and become a new person altogether. I have money enough to do anything I like—and that is what I want. It's my fondest wish. No one will ever have to know. Except us. And you'll know that I'll be forever grateful—a fish put back into the water, to live again. Say yes, Martin, and be done with it. You know very well you don't want me. You don't want all the explanations and excuses, not to mention the responsibility and trouble of sheltering someone who only wants to be free. Of course you don't."

She paused, and then went on in an urgent, breathless voice, "That would be like kidnapping—like what my father did to you. If it was wrong of him, why do the same? Set me free. Say yes, my friend, and do a good deed and the right thing."

She held her breath. Bait the hook, cast the line, and then stay very still—that was a thing her father had taught her about both fish and men.

Martin thought about what she said. How nice it would be to pretend that none of this had ever happened—

27

avoiding explanations to Magnus, and Sophia. And himself. He wouldn't dream of agreeing to such a thing with any other woman, but she was like no other woman he'd ever met. She was lovely enough to make a man's eyes water, but he had no doubt she could be lethal if she chose. She was as resourceful and strong as she looked fragile and vulnerable. And he seriously wondered, could he hold her if she didn't want to stay? Maybe she was right—why should he worry so? Say yes, and it will all be over.

"Yes," he said.

She sighed with relief and said, "Thank you, thank you, thank you, Martin. This was a good night's work."

It was a tall ship and a stout one, but however many tons it was and however many brave sails it sported, it was still only like a teacup bobbing in the wild Atlantic. Most nights Cristabel could hear the creaking of the great ship, the snapping of the sails, the washing of the sea against the hull, and the occasional gruff voices of sailors. But toward dawn a new sound woke her. A wild keening sound. Mewling, screeching cries. She sat bolt upright in bed. Gulls. She couldn't mistake the sound. The thrilling noise told her she was nearing land. She pried the tiny round window above her bed open a crack. It was pitch black outside, but she didn't need to see. Her nose, tuned over a lifetime to the shallows of seaports, told her the rest. They'd be landing soon—she knew it. Her heart soared. Freedom was near.

Martin thought slipping away from the watchful crew would be difficult, but Cristabel made it easy. She nodded farewell to the rogues she knew from her home port, and then, raising her head as they descended the gangplank, never looked back. She wore a long, dark cape with a voluminous hood, and took Martin's arm like a lady as they headed toward a waiting carriage. As soon as they'd been driven out of sight of the wharf, she demanded they be put down. After the carriage drove off, leaving them and all their baggage on the cobbles, she took a long look around the street. Only then did she let Martin summon another carriage to them.

When they were seated inside the second carriage, she laughed. When she threw back her hood, he saw her lovely face flushed with excitement.

"Now. You take me to a decent inn, my lad. And then it's good-bye."

"I won't leave you alone. It's not safe or proper," he insisted.

"Laddie, I be bristling with knives and armory. I be safer than any female you know, and most men!" she said angrily, and then subsided. "Oh aye," she muttered grudgingly, "tell you what. Find me an inn, and take dinner with me. I'll find meself a decent girl in the kitchens or serving at the tables, and hire her to play maid to me till I can find better. Will that suit ye?"

He could tell she was impatient and annoyed by the way her accent slipped as well as by the hectic glitter in her golden eyes. He nodded.

"Done then!" she said gleefully. "Thankee, lad. Ah . . . That is to say, thank you, Martin, that will suit admirably."

And ruined it all by giggling so hard, he had to laugh with her.

He installed her in a respectable inn and engaged a sleepy-looking maidservant to unpack for her. He ordered the girl to wait for her in her room, and then took Cristabel down to dinner in a private dining room.

"I'll look in on you," he said, as he saw their dinner ending.

"You'll look in vain. For I shall not be here. I'm being honest with you," she said seriously. "This is good-bye, my friend."

He frowned. He wanted to leave, he yearned to see his wife and family again, but he worried about leaving her. All his upbringing told him to stay with her, but every instinct told him to leave now, just as she was urging him to.

"It's done, Martin, it's over, and good riddance," she said, echoing his thoughts.

"Then this is farewell," he said, as he rose from the table and took her hand.

"No," Cristabel said, rising with him. She shook his hand firmly before he could raise it to his lips as he would a lady's. "No," she said again, "make no mistake. This is good-bye."

CHAPTER

3

The big man moved quietly as was his habit, though he certainly didn't need to move with stealth tonight. No one could have heard him above the babble of happy voices. The lower floor of the town house was crowded; every man there held a drink, and every woman seemed to be laughing. The only quiet place was the clearing they'd made around the obvious center of attention—a young man flushed with pleasure, his arm around a winsome blond lady who smiled up at him tearily as he spoke to the admiring throng.

". . . and so I hailed a sedan chair because I couldn't *quite* run all the rest of the way from the docks, at least not with my trunk in tow," he said before he drank down the last of the ale in his glass.

"Just like the tale of Robinson Crusoe, I vow!" an elderly woman cried out with pleasure, "So exciting! I begged you to read it after I finished it last year, didn't I, my dear?" she asked the man with her.

"Yes, but now I don't have to—young Martin has told me a better tale, I'll wager," he answered heartily.

"Oh, I don't know," she retorted with a wink to the young man in the center of the room. "Did you have a Man Friday on that desert isle, too, Martin—a savage native who catered to your every whim?"

"So long as it wasn't a Lady Friday he had on that desert isle!" a happy young fellow called out before Martin could answer.

The big man who had just come quietly into the room noted with interest that Martin's face became quite flushed before he answered.

"What? With my Sophia here for comparison?" Martin said after a moment's pause. "No, nor any Lady Saturday, Sunday, or Monday, either!" he added, dropping a light kiss on his young wife's forehead, to the approving applause of the group.

"Pirates and desert isles—cutthroats and narrow escapes. I tell you, my friends, this young fellow has had more thrilling experiences in the past months than I have in all my days!" a heavyset man declared.

"I'll drink to that!" another man called.

"Ah, but, Sir Francis, you'll drink to anything!" Martin answered, and the laughter began again.

"A toast then," the big man said in a deep, soft voice that nevertheless carried to every corner of the room, "to the prodigal returned. Welcome home, brother."

Martin stopped laughing and turned to the speaker, his eyes glowing with real pleasure. But then quickly, so quickly that few in the room noticed, his pleasant face held a fleeting expression of something more than surprise and less than delight. It was gone so quickly that even his brother couldn't be sure he'd seen it. In a blink of an eye Martin was grinning again.

"I came as soon as I heard. Unlike some people, I came running all the way from my house—I didn't stop for a sedan chair," the big man said, taking Martin's hand in a firm clasp.

"You couldn't find one big enough," Martin said, his eyes suspiciously damp.

"We're much too old to be so grown-up," his brother Magnus muttered, dragging Martin forward and taking him in a bear hug. "There," he said with satisfaction when he let him go, as Martin pretended to be breathless in order to hide his emotion, "that's how to greet a fellow lost at sea—and found in his own front parlor. You can't know how glad I am to see you. Sophia," he said, turning to his sister-in-law, "I congratulated this wretch on your wedding day, but I offer my best wishes to you this time. Congratulations on getting the fellow back."

"I shall never, never let him go again!" she declared, her piquant face a study in determination. She was a tiny young woman, with delicate features and some freckles on her little upturned nose that even rice powder couldn't entirely conceal. Her fair hair was powdered and curled in the latest fashion. She had blue eyes and a pink mouth, her cheeks were full as a milkmaid's, and her complexion just as fresh. But there was nothing childlike about her figure in her low-cut, wide-skirted gown.

"Not even if I promise to bring you primrose silk next time?" Martin asked slyly.

She pretended to think about it for a second and then cried, "No!"

"Pity, I found a merchant who could supply it—along with some fine bolts of white striped silk too."

"Well . . . perhaps," she said slowly, to make them all laugh.

Everyone laughed more, and raised more toasts. Then, as often happens during any momentous event, wedding or funeral, or as in this case, a sudden return from abroad, the company began to talk of other things. The men began discussing their new German king's policies, and the women, exchanging opinions on his many mistresses. When a group of women came to gossip with Sophia, Magnus raised an eyebrow at his brother and lifted one wide shoulder, tilting it in the direction of the library. Martin hesitated for a second before he went to the library with his brother and closed the door behind them.

"So," Magnus said, after he'd gone to stand by the fire. "You're back." He raised his eyes from the fire to study his brother. "Tell me all. I missed the first telling of your adventures because I was half-dressed when I heard the news. It took my valet and two footmen to convince me to go back and throw some more clothes on before I went running out in the street to see for myself."

He was dressed impeccably, his brother thought with admiration. He was a tall, well-muscled man, and although he was substantial, there wasn't an extra bit of flesh on him. He had lean flanks and a flat stomach to balance his sturdy chest and wide shoulders. Like many younger men, he wore his thick, long light brown hair unpowdered, tied at the base of his strong neck with a simple velvet ribbon. He had sleepy gray eyes in a big face, dominated by a long nose that was too broad at the bridge for beauty. But women couldn't take their eyes off him, and when those sleepy gray eyes grew sharp and concentrated on anyone, that person felt as though he were being seen more clearly than he'd ever been. Magnus's presence was commanding, and not just because of his sheer size.

Magnus was the tree under which his family sought shelter: a friend to all fair men and women, an appreciator of beautiful women and a challenge to all the others. At thirty he was still a bachelor, but he had more friends than anyone Martin knew, and even more than Magnus was probably aware of.

Cristabel had thought Martin worshiped his brother. He didn't, but only because he thought Magnus wouldn't want him to.

"Yes," Magnus murmured, "I'm fully dressed, but I swear I don't remember doing it, I was in such a hurry to see you. But here I am. Again, brother: Welcome home. You had me really worried, you know."

He gazed at Martin, his gray eyes troubled. "I thought of shipping out to find you myself, and would have, had word not got to us that you were safe and bound for home. 'Ods death, Martin, I finally agree to send you out to deal with spice merchants as I've done so many times, so you can

learn the way of it, and you are the one captured by pirates."
He shook his head again. "Well, done's done, thank God.
Now, out with it. How much is it going to cost us? Not that
any price would be too high, you understand."

"How much will what cost us?" Martin asked, genuinely
surprised. "I offered old Benson the same for his pepper
that you always pay, and Greggson, just the going price for
his sugar, and—"

"No, no. Not the merchants. The pirates; what's their
share?" Magnus asked. "How much shall I send them? . . .
The ransom, lad. What is it?"

Martin stopped breathing—or so it seemed to his brother. Then Martin swallowed, and when he spoke at last, his
face was red. Odd, Magnus thought, his gray eyes
narrowing; only moments before, his face had been a
ghostly white.

Magnus seemed relaxed. He leaned back against the
mantel, his eyes unreadable beneath half-closed lashes.
That, his brother knew with queasy certainty, meant that he
was listening very closely.

"Ah well," Martin said, "but there's no ransom involved."

"None?"

"Ah, no, none," Martin said, and then continued with a
sickly smile, "You see, ahm, when they caught us, they
thought they'd a grand lord on board . . ."

"Yes, so the captain told me," Magnus said. "They
thought you were me."

"Ah. So. You spoke to him, then," Martin said in a ragged
voice. "So why ask me? You must know everything."

"I know they carted you away to their stronghold, sepa-
rating you from the captain and crew. The captain's company came up with their ransom and he sailed for home at
once. He had no idea of what happened to you. That's why I
was making plans to sail to Jamaica myself when word came
that you were released and on your way home."

"Oh," Martin said, thinking furiously. Magnus didn't

know! If this *was* true, then things could go on as Cristabel had said. Martin straightened his shoulders. He'd take a page from the pirate's daughter's book of boldness.

"I told them the truth," Martin said, "and it took some telling, believe me. But in time they knew I was telling the truth, because one of his men had seen you once and supported me. I told them you'd be after them hammer and tongs if they harmed me. And I told them further that if they made you pay a ransom for me, they'd regret it, because you had a way of evening up scores. They believed me."

Magnus listened with undisguised interest now.

Martin's confidence grew as he spoke. What he said *was* nearly true. It was exactly what he would have said if they hadn't terrorized him into marrying the pirate king's daughter first.

"And so—voilà!—here I be, as the pirates would say. Safe, and not sorry, because, after all, I've got years of dinner conversation out of the adventure!"

"And nothing else happened?" Magnus asked quietly, watching his brother closely.

"Nothing worth mentioning. Just some amusing adventures I'm saving to bore you with for years to come," Martin said with a shrug.

"I see," Magnus said.

He didn't believe his brother. Not for a minute. But Martin never lied to him, and so he was at a loss to know just what to do. No matter, whatever it was could keep. There was time. Martin would eventually tell him, and for now, he didn't look for sugar on his miracles—the boy was back, whole and safe. This discussion could wait a day or two.

"Well then," Magnus said, "tell me, what did you think of the tropics? Aside from your unwanted hosts, that is? The fruits, the flowers, the women—were they not just as lush and ripe and fantastic as I promised?"

Martin grew very red. "I . . . I had little to do with

36

them—the women at least," he stammered, thinking of Cristabel in all her lavish silks.

"'Ods blood! I forgot," Magnus laughed. "You're a wedded man now; that's not a thing I'd want you to forget. We take marriage seriously in this family. Well done, lad. So then: the oranges. At least you can tell me about them. Better than the sour ones sold in the theaters here, aren't they?"

"Superior, far superior," Martin said, remembering the tangy sweet fruit of the tropics he'd encountered during his adventure. "Exotic and surprising," he said, and then forced himself to concentrate on oranges and forget the forbidden fruit, so Magnus wouldn't read the truth in his face the way he always did.

People of any means seldom walked London's streets alone, and to do so at night was unheard-of. If they walked at all, they were accompanied by linkmen bearing torches, and sturdy footmen. Because London teemed with thieves, prudent men stayed home at night or hired protection if they had to stray far from their carriages or sedan chairs. But Magnus said good night to his brother and the company, stepped down the stairs of the brightly lit town house, and strolled alone into the night.

The moon shone bright, brighter than the lanterns in each doorway, and the glow made his shadow seem to swim down the deserted streets. The moonlight showed an occasional glint from several watchful eyes that followed his progress. But the wavering shadow walked confidently, with a hand resting on the hilt of a sword. It was a *very* large shadow.

Magnus didn't worry about thieves; he had larger concerns. He was worrying about his brother. His shoulders were wide, and it seemed to him that he had been forever carrying the weight of his family on them. Oldest of all the children, he'd looked after each of them since the day they were born. His greatest regret was that, as hard as he tried, he'd not been able to protect them all. He didn't want to fail again. Martin's life wasn't in danger, but something was very wrong. Every instinct told him that, and his instincts were finely tuned when it came to his family.

Not that his parents didn't take care of their own. They did, or tried to. But his mother's first response to crisis was to weep, and his father's first course of action was to try to calm her. It was as if they stood onshore watching someone drown, unable to plunge into the water because they were too busy trying to comfort each other and give each other strength. He didn't know how his parents would survive if he hadn't been born. Nor did they, or so they always said.

No, Magnus thought with a bemused smile as he strode down the street, he was the one who always came to the rescue—ever since he'd been a boy. His parents turned to him whenever there were difficulties. And now that he was a grown man, they were happy to retire to their country estate and let him run the family.

What was left of it, he thought grimly. All his care and attention couldn't save his poor little sister Elizabeth, who died of a fever at three years of age. Nor did it save his handsome young brother William, who, brought low with a toothache one night, died of a raging infection despite all the bleedings and possets. Magnus blamed himself for his death, for hadn't Will complained of a twinge in that tooth only the month before? But Magnus hadn't insisted that Will see the barber to have the tooth taken out, and he should have. Although he was only fifteen, he'd had the authority to order his younger brother. But he'd been too busy thinking of a new horse, or some other stupid trifle, to nag Will into going. This failure ate at his heart still and kept him awake at night.

And his dearest sister, best friend, and wise counselor, gentle Lucy . . . Only one year younger than himself, and at sixteen the most beautiful girl, with the kindest heart. She should have been wed and with her own babes now, not sleeping in the churchyard with her ancestors. His fault, of course. He should never have let her go to that party in the next county. He knew she always picked up every contagion, and it had been such a cold season, and her friend's house was ancient, cold and drafty—but not so cold as where she was now . . . He never should have let her go, but she'd begged and teased and cajoled and got around him, as she always did. And within two weeks he had to bring her cold body to the family vault, and leave her to lie there always.

Magnus was a big man with an equally big heart, and that had caused him much grief. Thirteen years had passed, but he never forgot the pain of these losses. He hesitated to risk burying half his heart again.

Magnus loved his family very much, but he could never again become so vulnerable. They depended on him, and he had to be strong. He knew he had to wed someday. He would, but it would be done sensibly, and carefully, when he had the need of sons. A nice girl from a good family with a strong body who could survive childbirth. He meant to like her, expected to respect her, hoped she'd care similarly for him, but he didn't know if he would ever love her. Loving his family was the most he could do now; he took responsibility for them and they took it as their due.

His sister Anne had married well, to a good fellow who was also a belted earl, and so she was off his mind most of the time. His sister Mary was spoken for the moment she came of marrying age, and while he privately wondered if young Crewe had staying power, he definitely had money and a title, so that relieved Magnus's mind somewhat.

Magnus also took care of the family finances, and they were well-to-do because of this. He took his profits and made them even more profitable by making wise investments. He wouldn't take the easy course the way others did. That was why he hadn't been ruined when the "South Sea Bubble" investment scheme burst the year before. He personally oversaw all of his ventures, even if it meant an ocean voyage like the one on which he'd sent Martin. When he invested in the South Seas or West Indies, or traded with the colonies, he didn't do so blindly. He always made sure he knew where his money was going, watching carefully to see that it didn't go to the most lucrative trade of all: black ivory. He invested in sugar and spice, cotton and coffee. But not human souls; he'd have no part of slavery or the trade in human flesh.

Some human flesh, that was to say, he reminded himself with a grin, his spirits picking up at last. Though he was against buying it, he didn't mind renting from time to time. The lady he was on his way to visit tonight would be horrified if she knew what he was thinking, that the necklace in his pocket was no different from the coins that most men used to pay females for the same services. Magnus just disliked buying pleasure so openly. An experienced woman of high degree and low morals was exactly what he preferred. It was much more pleasant to make love to an equal, also seeking pleasure, than to someone who was performing the act simply to survive.

And pleasure was what he would have tonight, to celebrate his brother's safe return.

He could finally relax. For the first time since Martin had been reported missing, Magnus was at peace with himself and the world. His worries were behind him and he was enjoying a brief moment of freedom from all of his cares and worries. He wanted to savor this time. He was in a wide, warm bed with a warm and welcoming woman. A fire flickered in the hearth and a cold, jealous wind rattled the window shutters, reminding him of how comfortable he was. As if he could forget. The mattress was all feathers, and the bedcovers silky, but neither were as silky or as soft as the woman in his arms. He reveled in the touch, scent, and taste of the smooth skin beneath his hands, and marveled at the impossibly simple, complex curves of the form he caressed.

He sighed and she took it as a sign of pleasure, which it was, or so he thought. A strange idea came to him—an errant thought that nagged at him even as he approached bliss: What if he loved this woman? What would it be like to love a woman as much as he loved making love to her?

Foolish ideas—pointless, he told himself, and tried to force the thoughts out of his head. It was easier when this beautiful lady offered her lips in such a new, unexpected, and charming way and he inhaled sharply. And yet, he couldn't stop thinking. He wondered why he was such an ingrate, to question such pleasure. He was no Puritan; all his grandparents had been Royalists. He thought he must be getting old—or jaded. He didn't know which was worse and he didn't want to know. He was determined to enjoy this moment for what it was—a true feast for the senses. She twisted and turned in his arms, fretful with rampant desire. What delight! And so what if his heart wasn't involved. Was it needed here and now—as she took him fully and yelped with joy, telling him how good he was, again and again and again?

But the thought persisted, spoiling the aftermath of his pleasure, and, making him anxious to be alone.

"Going? So soon?" she murmured, stretching sinuously and reaching for him again. "Ah no, stay the night, my lord. It's soooo cold."

She was so warm and silky and quite aware that if he stayed the night, everyone would see him leaving in the morning. Although she was a widow and free to do as she liked, his staying would raise certain expectations amidst society. He was many things, but not a liar. He never promised what he had no intention of delivering. He would bring her bliss and expensive trinkets, but not a wedding ring. Staying with her would create certain obligations, and well she knew it.

"No, my dear," he said with genuine regret. "I have much to do in the morning. And if I see you when I wake, I'll do nothing but this . . . and this, and . . . ah, but I will stay just a bit longer, I think."

But even so, he was gone before dawn.

Magnus clapped on his three-cornered hat and stepped

out into the clear, cold night. The watchman softly cried out the hour, for fear of waking the privileged persons on this street. The last of them had toddled home and wouldn't rise till noon. It was too late for servants to still be up and too early for even the humblest of them to wake. Even thieves had to sleep, and they did so at this hour, when anyone with money in his pockets was in bed. Bats and burglars might be stirring, but not cutpurses and street thieves. For that reason, Magnus was unprepared for the sudden blow that came from behind. That and the fact that no thief had ever been foolish enough to attack Magnus Titus Snow.

He soon showed them why.

The first blow landed on his shoulder. The fellow behind him was quite short and his club only reached Magnus's powerful neck. It hurt like blazes. His temper flared up with the pain, and he didn't feel a thing after the initial shock. He wheeled around, his sword drawn and slashing before him. He heard a yelp, and pressed forward. But then one of the assailants—there were two—threw a coat over his sword, snared it, and dragged it down.

It didn't matter. He still had his fists, and he knew how to use them. One man went down without a sound, and another—a third, he realized—made the mistake of coming up behind him just as he'd landed some telling blows on someone else. He ducked and spun, and threw the third man into the second, feeling laughter rising in his throat as he lunged forward—straight into a raised club.

There was a fourth, he realized, just before he hit the ground.

He woke to find the four men sitting on him.

"My purse is in my pocket," he gasped. "You're welcome to it. Get off, and have done with it."

"Thankee fer the kind offer, matey," rasped the fellow lying on his right arm, "but that ain't what we come fer."

"Take this then!" Magnus shouted, lunging up with all his strength—which was so considerable that as he gained his feet, they all fell off him, like so many piglets squealing and scattering in the straw as their mother heaved to her trotters.

But a sharp blow on his head brought him to his knees and then again to his face on the cobbles. There had been five of them, he realized before darkness overtook him.

The voices were not that of the angels. They were worried, rough, and profane.

"Well, y' done him good, y' bloody little mawworm. Kilt him, belike, curse ye."

"I done him so you could get him, is wot I done," a grieved voice answered.

"Yeah. But dead ain't no good to us. Capt'n'll have our gizzards."

"Ain't dead. 'E's bleeding like a stuck pig. Dead don't bleed, y'stupid whoreson."

They were still sitting on him. His first coherent thought was not of pain, but of how stupid he must look, for as far as he could tell, there were five of them lying on him, head and limbs, pinning him to the ground at all points, like a beached starfish. He squinted, barely able to make them out in the waning night. They looked as motley as they sounded. They were dressed in the finery of the last generation—flapping coats over long vests and bloused shirts, wide breeches and high, cuffed boots. He could see glimpses of bandannas tied around throats and heads, and scars, eye patches, and beards. The rising light caught glints from various earrings, pendants, and gold teeth. Since they smelled worse than they sounded, and from what they said, they didn't want him dead, he spoke.

"Off!" he snarled. "Or do you want to go round again?"

His voice sounded weak and he frowned. That was when he felt the blood trickle down over one eyebrow and realized his head hurt like the devil. Even his rage wasn't enough to make him forget the dull, throbbing pain.

"In time," the man at his head said warily, "First, we got to talk to ye. Since ye ain't a man to lissen to the likes o' us, we had to get yer attention first. And truth to tell, ye deserve every hard knock we could give ye. Be that as it may—we be saying our piece and then we be off. Fer the time bein'," he added threateningly. "See, we just got a message fer ye now. A warning, like: Keep yer shoes under yer own bed, me fine lord. Don't go catting round on our Cristabel, hear? Capt'n finds out, it'll be us that suffers, 'cause, bet yer fancy boots, he'll blame us fer lettin' it happen. So stay wi' yer lovely wife. Gawd! It beats all. Ye be wed to the finest female in the land, and wed only weeks, at that. And what do ye do? Come aground, and run around on 'er!"

The other men rumbled various agreements, and Magnus heard a ragged chorus of "'Tis a right shame," and "Shame" from all four sides, as though he were in a nursery again, tended by demented nannies.

His jaw hurt when he spoke, but he was so disgusted, it hardly mattered.

"Idiots. Nodcocks," he said. "You've got the wrong man. I am not married. I don't know your 'Cristabel.'"

They all laughed. It wasn't a merry sound.

"Ye be the Viscount Snow?"

He nodded, and wished he hadn't, because his head was still on the cobbles.

"Magnus Titus, Lord Snow?" another asked, rolling his name like thunder.

"Yes, damn it," he said.

"To be sure," one of his captors said prissily, "ye be damned. 'Cause ye be a double-dyed liar, as well as a cheat. 'Cause ye be wed not three weeks past. So our lads told us afore they shipped back to the islands again."

"Aye, married to the beauteous Cristabel 'erself—the most beautiful female in all the West Indies islands," one of the others said reverentially. "And one of the hardest ter get, 'er bein' Capt'n Whiskey's own dotter, and guarded like the left eye in 'is 'ead."

"Aye, an' locked in a cabin wi' her till ye reached England," another said with less reverence and twice as much envy.

"And then ye leave 'er!" continued another in amazement. "Abandon 'er! Romp off ter play piggies wi' another female the very night ye land! I don't know where ye get the nerve—much less the energy! But ye won't continue to diddle no one else. Nor abandon yer wife. Not whilst the men o' the Brotherhood draw breath, me lad."

The various growls of "Aye" were almost loud enough to wake the watch.

"Married?" Magnus said stupidly, for none of this made sense.

"Aye, as if ye didn't know it," one said scornfully.

"Where?" he asked, afraid to hear the answer.

"In the Indies, in Capt'n Whiskey's own stronghold, when the captain took ye hostage," said their leader, holding on to Magnus's hair. "So we was told by the lads what seen it wi' their own eyes. And we be here to gi' ye the message: The captain's men may have left, but there be enough stout lads in the Brotherhood in England to watch over ye, like he ast us to. We may be few, and hunted men at that, and y'may be a grand lord in this grand city, but we be in every port in every land, and we takes care of our own," he added, with what seemed to Magnus as much hope as bravado.

"Go back to her, me lord," he urged, "and take her up as yer rightful wife in 'er proper place. Or else next time, we comes with six other lads—or howsomever many more it takes. Which is better'n the captain hisself coming. Or wild Black Jack Kelly, who will be glad as the captain be mad about yer deserting her, I'll wager."

There was another chorus of "Ayes" and then they all fell silent. They looked at each other. Magnus heard their leader count to three under his breath. On the count, they rose as one and released him. Before he could rise, they ran off—as best they could with their own injuries—into the night.

Martin's valet woke him and helped him fumble into his dressing gown. He followed a footman down the stair. It was too early for the rest of the servants to be up; he himself had seldom seen this hour of dawn since he'd been a boy. He was sleepy and confused, but all sleepiness fled when he saw who awaited him in the kitchens.

Magnus turned from Martin's worried housekeeper, who was trying to wash his wounds. He took the bloody cloth from her hand, and taking Martin firmly with the other, led him out of the kitchens, through the hall, and into the library again. He closed the door behind them. The light of the brace of candles Magnus held made his shadow leap and grow on the wall behind him. The light, Martin thought, wasn't as ominous as Magnus's expression as he stood staring down at him. The cut over Magnus's brow began to trickle blood again, and he dabbed it with the cloth but otherwise disregarded it. One eye was already swelling closed. But the other eye held gray murder.

Still, Magnus's voice was clear, and cold as steel.

"Now," he said with deathly calm, "what was that 'other little adventure' you were going to get around to telling me someday? I suggest you tell me now. And fast!"

CHAPTER

4

The air was damp and chilly, and a thin wind caught at Cristabel's cloak. Its hem, soaked with icy water from the cobbles beneath her feet, slapped against her ankles as she walked. She almost skipped, she was so thrilled. Her newfound maid lagged three steps behind her, sullen as the sky above her. The girl couldn't understand why anyone would go out on such a day if she didn't have to. On such a day! Cristabel almost laughed aloud. What a day it was for her. She glanced up at the leaden sky and prayed it would snow. Snow—little fluffy white feathers of ice she'd heard and read about—could actually come tumbling down from those dank clouds and cover her at any minute. Or so she hoped. It would be beyond wonderful—as if everything she'd done since she'd arrived in London hadn't already been!

She'd hired the girl herself as soon as Martin left her. Not because she liked the sullen maid—she planned to replace her as soon as she could—but because she knew she had to have a female, any female, accompanying her everywhere for decency's sake. Cristabel's governesses had taught her well. An unescorted woman without husband, father, or family would be considered a whore here just as she would be in the Islands. The difference was that in wonderful

47

England, she didn't have to take on some domineering man as husband or keeper. She could hire a woman as companion and live by herself and still be considered a lady. It was too good to be true, but Cristabel and her maid had indeed walked the streets of London town all morning, and she was amazed that no man so much as looked at her, much less catcalled or accosted her.

Of course, she admitted, it could be because of her new clothes.

A new wardrobe had been her first order of business once she had her maid. Not only were her own clothes, all in hues of green and red and gold, wrong for London, but they were also too thin for England's climate. She bought a thick gown ready-made from a dressmaker near the inn and ordered her to stitch up several more as fast as she could. Her eye had been caught by the shades of cherry red and sea blue, but those days were behind her, she thought resolutely. She was going to be a proper lady now. So she stifled her regrets and bought a black gown and a thick, dark, hooded cloak to cover everything.

She marched through the streets of London in amazement. She'd read that over seven hundred thousand souls lived here! Her mind couldn't take in the number any more than her eyes could. She'd never seen so many people all together. She'd thought the docks at Kingston Harbor the busiest hub of the civilized world, but she was humbled and excited by what she saw now.

She wandered down the shop-lined streets whose big, bright signs advertised their wares to everyone—even those who couldn't read. And for those who didn't want to enter the stores, there were carts on the streets heaped high with everything from oysters to nightcaps, apples to scissors to wigs. The cold air felt warmer because of the delicious smells of soup, baked pastry, and meat being sold everywhere. Vendors blew tin trumpets and rattled pans, criers shouted and sang their wares. They proclaimed the finest fruit, coal, fish, gingerbread—and some things Cristabel never heard of—at the top of their lungs. If that wasn't show enough, there were real entertainers performing in the streets. She laughed at the trained dogs and caught her breath at the dancing bear being led through the streets on a rope. The jugglers were fun to see, but the puppet shows made her stop in her tracks, bemused, until her numbing toes reminded her to move on.

There were tradesmen and chimney sweeps as well as elegant gentlemen with fine coats and wigs crowding the streets. They strolled with fine ladies who were followed by an assortment of maids, footmen, and sometimes—at the very end of the procession—little, brightly dressed black pages, who looked to Cristabel like cheerful parakeets flying down the street.

Cristabel got glimpses of some ladies who looked like royalty to her fascinated eyes. They were jogged through the streets in little gilded chairs mounted on long poles carried by one man in front and another in back. Some of these ladies even had another man running alongside—with a drawn sword. And who were these people who clattered past her in their gilded coaches? She'd never seen such riches on display, not even in the gaudiest pirate stronghold.

She also saw men and women with such terrible scars and obvious diseases that she wondered how they lived to limp through the streets of London. She saw beggars with such awful sores, they made her shiver. They begged alongside ballad singers who sang so beautifully she wanted to sit right down on the cobbles and listen to them for hours. That is, if she didn't mind getting splashed by the sluggish stream of filthy water that flowed in a channel down the center of the street, carrying waste away. She kept walking and staring— one hand on her purse and the other on her dagger, of course, for however excited she was, she'd been raised in interesting places herself, and she was, after all, the daughter of a pirate king.

Although she wanted the day to last forever, she began to notice that the sky was getting darker, and not just with storm clouds. She had one more important errand to take care of before nightfall, and set out to do so.

She found the address as an ominous twilight began to replace the lowering day. It was on a quiet street near the market streets she'd been walking. Although no street in this part of London could truly be called quiet, there were no vendors here. The houses were small and close together, but they were neat, and each front step was freshly scrubbed.

Cristabel raised her gloved hand to the knocker on the door. That small hand was closed into a tight fist from tension. She'd come across two seas and five years to see the person she hoped to find inside. No letter she'd sent here had ever been answered, but the mails between here and the Islands were unreliable—because of piracy, she realized, almost giggling at the foolishness of that thought. Her sudden fit of laughter was as much due to nervousness as anticipation.

She had come to hire a companion. She wasn't a rash young girl; she knew that staying alone in England had its pitfalls, even if she couldn't see any now. She wasn't afraid of being alone—she'd always been alone, even amidst all the people on the island. There were no other educated pirate lasses, and none who remained single after they became women. There wasn't a pirate on earth who believed in being friends with a girl, and her father would never have permitted it. He often sailed off for long months in search of his financial enterprises, and was often gone weeks while he pursued his pleasures. And though he'd fillet any man who said he didn't love his daughter, he paid scant attention to her when he was home.

Cristabel had never been physically alone for longer than it took to go to the privy. The only way to get some privacy in a pirate kingdom was to swim underwater, or read books and pretend not to hear what was going on. She'd done both often enough. No matter how often her father left her to her own devices, the truth was, everyone was always watching her. They knew whose daughter she was, and what price they'd pay if they forgot.

But now for the first time in her life, she was on her own

and unknown. She told herself that this didn't frighten her. She could take care of herself. She fairly bristled with knives, not to mention the armory of weapons in her trunks. She doubted she'd need any of it, for this was a land of civilized people, she reassured herself. She'd be much safer here than at home, she reminded herself. And so far as being physically alone—well, she was going to take care of that right now. She'd thought of it the first night on shipboard and formulated her plan all the way to London. Now it would come true. What a surprise it would be! She grinned, letting her excitement rise.

A maidservant opened the door and squinted into the dying light.

"Is Mistress Elphstone at home?" Cristabel asked, moving aside slightly, so that the maid could see she was a proper lady with a servant behind her. "Mistress Mary Elphstone?" she repeated.

"Aye, come in," the maid said.

It was a neat house but not a fine one. The little hall was cramped and dim. Still, she was here! And so was Mistress Elphstone—the only governess she'd ever had who hadn't hated her, or blamed her too much for her state.

Of course, that might have been because Mistress Elphstone hadn't been abused before she'd been brought to Cristabel. Somewhere along the way her father had realized that a female lately ravished by pirates would not be the best influence on his daughter. He may have also noticed that Cristabel had begun to cringe away from all men because of what her sobbing governesses had confided to her. So, her father set out to find a governess whom his men wouldn't molest. Mistress Elphstone was perfect; she was so ill favored that not even a very drunken pirate would have accosted her.

After all, as her father often said: A pirate didn't actually *have* to raid ships for women. Not when there were so many to be had so cheap in every pirate port. It was just that the pretty ones were too much of a temptation to men who had no self-restraint.

Mistress Elphstone had been governess to a rich family when she was captured off Cape Horn. She survived untouched, through two slave auctions, until Captain Whiskey himself saw her on the block in Port-au-Prince. He'd bought her on the spot and had to put up with much jeering for it. Mistress Elphstone's looks were both her salvation and curse. She was short and squat with whiskers, and being English, looked uncannily like their favorite breed of bulldog. It was impossible to say whether it was her terrible disposition or the disposition of her features that gave her such a bad temper. But when she realized that Cristabel was lonely and hated the pirate life as much as she did, and was desperate to be a lady, Mistress Elphstone softened toward her.

Or so Cristabel had thought, because sometimes Mistress Elphstone spoke to her even after lessons were done. Cristabel had been genuinely sad when her father decided that since his daughter was sixteen and marriageable, she didn't need a governess anymore. With Cristabel's nagging and bullying to force his hand, he freed the governess instead of putting her back on the market, and sent her home with gold in her pockets.

Cristabel thought that that final act of kindness would ensure her a glad welcome now. That, and the remembrance of all those soft, hot nights, when she would beg Mistress Elphstone to tell her stories of her cold little island in order to drown out the sounds of some pirate revel. Then Mistress Elphstone would tell her about King Arthur and Sir Lancelot, and other lordly men and gentle ladies from her homeland, her powerful voice drowning out the usual sounds of music and dancing—and later whooping and screaming—and later still, fighting and grunting and creaking of beds. Surely, Cristabel thought, those must have been times when the governess had appreciated her duties as much as her charge had.

One had been a middle-aged slave, the other like a princess in her own barbaric land. But they had a lot in common. Mistress Elphstone disliked men, Cristabel was leery of them. Mistress Elphstone was disgusted by the pirates' women, Cristabel was worried she would become one. Most of all, Mistress Elphstone was educated, and knew how to eat and walk and talk like that most elusive, magical being: a true lady. Just like Cristabel's departed mother.

Cristabel valued her then, but she needed her now. She needed a companion to lend her respectability. And perhaps, she thought a little wistfully, Mistress Elphstone would chat with her as she had never done: as an equal. After all, they were both grown women now.

The maid trundled off in search of Mistress Elphstone, leaving Cristabel in the entryway. She wondered how much money she should offer her to act as her companion. She decided to let Mistress Elphstone name the sum. Cristabel had enough money to last her all her life and didn't know the going rate for paid companions in London. Aside from a generous wage, she could offer her a better home than she had now. Cristabel thought she'd look London over and find a fine house in a good but inconspicuous part of town. If she got bored with London, she might look at something in a small village outside London's gates: Charing Cross or Soho, or some other rural place near the city. Marylbone or Knightsbridge or such. Wherever she went, she'd have peace. She planned to read and garden and never have to obey any whim but her own. And never have to marry, or pretend to be looking for a husband either.

Her happy thoughts were interrupted by the sound of voices. She recognized one, and her heart leaped—Mistress Elphstone, sounding as out of patience and breath as ever.

"Who?" the nasal voice was complaining as it came nearer. "Oh, no matter, stupid creature, you've doubtless got it all wrong; I don't know any 'Belles,' and why should I? I'll have a look at her, but it's probably the wrong—Ah!"

Mistress Elphstone, only a little shorter, squatter, and grayer than Cristabel remembered, stood stock-still before her, her eyes wide, her hand on her heart. Cristabel smiled and put out her hand.

"Mistress Elphstone! Yes, it is I, after all these years!"

"Oh, my dear God," Mistress Elphstone gasped, her face growing white as she staggered back a step.

"Surprise!" Cristabel sang merrily.

Mistress Elphstone stared. "It's her!" she gasped to no one in particular, looking behind Cristabel as though she expected to see monsters lurking there. Seeing nothing but Cristabel's slack-jawed maid, she recovered herself. "Where is your father?" she demanded. "Well, it doesn't matter, he dare not show his face here. If he does, I'll have the watch—Watch! Ha! I'll have the army down on him in a trice. He'll have his head on a pike or the scaffold before he can whistle."

"He's not here," Cristabel assured her. "I'm on my own, entirely."

"Oh," Miss Elphstone said, her small eyes narrowing, "are you?" Her cheeks bloomed purple and she pointed a shaking finger to the door. "Then be gone on your own too," she cried. "You horrid little witch—this is England. My country, not yours!"

"You don't understand," Cristabel said patiently, "there is no need to worry. I'm alone. I've left home. I've left my father. I'm going to live here now. I have enough money to live in grand fashion, and I'd like you to come live with me. I'm going to buy a fine house; you'll have your own room and a good wage."

"Me, go with you? Are you mad? No amount of money—not all the riches in the world—could pay me to so much as speak to you," Mistress Elphstone cried. "Begone before I call the watch. The daughter of a pirate can hang just as high as her father, I'm sure."

"But, Mistress Elphstone," Cristabel persisted, realizing her old governess still didn't understand, "things are different now. My father doesn't come into it at all. You and I were never enemies. I'm offering you the chance to be my paid companion now. We can get on very well together. I plan to live quietly—"

"If you plan to live—leave," Mistress Elphstone interrupted her in the same tones she had used to order Cristabel to bed at night, "or I'll call the authorities. You and I 'friends'? What a joke. I hated you, as I hated all the scum you lived with."

"You hated me?" Cristabel asked in shock.

"Of course. You were a child, pretty and well behaved, yes. But the daughter of scum is also scum. How could it be otherwise? How could you possibly *think* otherwise? I hated every moment of my captivity and cannot bear anything that reminds me of those horrible years. I cannot to this day smell certain spices without becoming sick to my stomach. I can't even see a sailor without heaving. On certain summer nights I can't help remembering . . . Oh, what's the point? Get out. I won't call the authorities if you leave at once."

"I'm sorry," Cristabel said, drawing herself up, dragging on her hood with trembling fingers, "I had no idea. I thought you liked me."

"If you had not, I might be dead," Mistress Elphstone said bitterly. She stared at Cristabel. "Make no mistake," she said in a cold, even voice, "I hated every second I had to endure with you, and now that I don't have to endure you a moment more, I can tell you how it sickened me to try to educate you as though you were a lady. You, a common little slut. You, daughter of a murderer and worse. I lived for the day I could be free—and free of you. And now I am. This is my house, and my country. Leave both, if you're wise. I never want to see you again."

Cristabel turned blindly, and fled.

"She's vanished the way she promised to," Martin said wearily. "I told you so. She's a remarkable girl, like no other I've ever met. She's clever and resourceful. All she wanted was freedom, and now she's got it. She'll never trouble me again, and all she wanted from me was the same courtesy. She's gone without a trace. Why can't we leave it that way?"

"Because her father's men believe she's married to me," his brother growled as he stalked on down the crowded street.

"But you can protect yourself against them," Martin said breathlessly, trying to reason with his brother and keep up with his long stride at the same time.

They'd been walking since early morning, trying to track down the pirate king's elusive daughter. Now night was coming on. Martin was tired of the chase. For the first time he could remember, he didn't understand his brother. Not that Magnus tried to explain. He'd been in a flaming temper since he'd heard the story. Which wasn't like him either. At least he was talking now, Martin thought, although snarling might be more accurate.

"You don't understand, do you?" Magnus said, stopping and wheeling around to glower at his brother, "Then hear this: Of course I can protect myself against them. That's not the point. The point is that the girl's father believes her to be *my* responsibility. I won't rest until I find her.

"Don't look so frightened, lad," Magnus said, relenting enough to put a hand on Martin's shoulder. "You did the best you could, better than most men could have done, at that. You were very clever, getting out of there without having to pay for your freedom in gold or blood. Only ink. It was well done, paying back thievery with trickery."

"You don't think it was . . . craven?" Martin asked, looking very young.

"Beating Captain Whiskey at his own game? No, why should I?"

"Then why are you angry?"

"It's not your involvement with her that bothers me," Magnus said, "it's the fact that you left her."

"But she wanted to be free. What else was I to do? You don't know her, Magnus, she's very determined."

"She's a young girl, alone in London," Magnus said sternly, "and her father thinks she bears my name."

"But she doesn't, not really, I told you. Don't you believe me?"

"Of course I do. I'm not an idiot, I know she has no claim on me—no legal claim, that is . . ." Magnus sighed. "Trust me, I have no desire to shackle myself in any way to a pirate's daughter—beautiful, clever, and resourceful as she may be. I just have to find her and be sure she's safe. Then I can deal with her father, his men, and anyone else who thinks I'm accountable for her. I'm not, and I'll tell them that. Be sure of it. But I *am* accountable to myself. Do you understand? It's a matter of responsibility."

Martin nodded. He might not agree, but at last he understood. Magnus would never shirk a responsibility. He walked on with his brother, hoping that his boots would last, because he might have years of walking ahead of him. Cristabel was a clever girl, and London was a very big town.

He should never have underestimated Magnus. He never had before, and now he vowed he never would again. Magnus had picked up a word here, a hint there, a confused description somewhere else, and was piecing these clues together into a tight net.

Early that morning the innkeeper at the inn where Martin left Cristabel had said she'd gone, taking a maid with her. When Magnus asked what she was wearing, Martin had been amazed. Surely she'd change her clothing. That would be the first thing any fugitive would do. But Magnus had been very particular. He'd asked about more than the color or style of her clothes—he'd asked what materials the gown and cloak she was wearing were, and when he heard "silk" and "satin," he grinned.

Then, instead of going to nearby inns or coaching stations as Martin would have done, Magnus spent the afternoon going to all the closest dressmakers.

"The cold will slow our fugitive," Magnus had said as he'd hurried out the inn door. "They've no need of warm clothes where she comes from. No doubt our escaped bird is shivering in her shoes. If she's as clever as you say, she'll dress for flight and we'll find her as she picks out her new plumage. Not the filmy tropical stuff she's used to—but fabric made from good stout English sheep."

They went to three dressmakers before they found the one

Cristabel had visited. There they'd gotten a description of the clothes she'd purchased. Women in black and gray wool weren't exactly rare in November in London.

Now, as the day was ending, Magnus was on his way to yet another inn near the dressmaker's. He threw his brother a glance. Seeing Martin's dejection, he smiled. "Not the finest district, but not the worst. And not one where a lone woman with her pockets full of gold would want to stay, I agree. But it *is* the one nearest to the dressmaker's, and she could only wear one gown this morning. She has to pick up the others she ordered before she can move on, doesn't she? Ah. The penny drops. You see what I'm talking about. Yes, she'll stay nearby. We'll find her, brother, and you'll be home in front of your hearth with a nice hot drink in your hand and the lovely Sophia in your lap before you know it."

Martin could believe it, for it turned out that there was a female, accompanied only by her maid, staying at The Bull's Eye, an inn two streets and round a corner from the dressmaker. But the innkeeper said the lady had gone out that morning and hadn't been back yet. Night was falling, and the inn, though not luxurious, was warm and snug, with a private parlor right near the front door. And the landlord knew how to make a hot punch. Martin sat back in a chair, stretched his legs, and grinned up at his brother.

"Stop pacing. We have her," he said triumphantly.

His brother slanted him a cold gray glance. "Do we? 'A fine lady,' the innkeeper said. But all swathed in a hooded cloak. She could be nineteen or ninety. We have to wait and see."

"Come now, Magnus," Martin said comfortably, "Relax. How many fine ladies are there that travel with only one maid? And stay alone in London with only one servant? Or travel at all, for that matter?"

"Perhaps," Magnus said, rubbing his palm over the thick glass at the window to melt the frost so he could peer outside into the growing darkness, "But the innkeeper said 'a fine lady.' We're looking for a pirate's daughter."

"But she is a lady; I told you she is."

"Look lad," his brother said, turning from the window, "a man's perceptions change with his circumstances. When you're in the country, the local squire seems to be a fine gentleman, doesn't he? And he is, compared with the farmers and yeomen who work in the fields. But when he comes to London, it's clear he's a country gentleman and suddenly he seems very rustic compared to what you usually think a fine gentleman is, doesn't he? He hasn't changed. You have. How many fine ladies are there in a pirate's lair? Exactly. No, your pirate lass may have seemed a lady in Port Royale, compared to the native girls, serving wenches, and whores there. But she wouldn't strike a London innkeeper as one, would she? That's what's troubling me."

"You're wrong, and you'll soon see."

"Shall I?" Magnus wondered.

"Well, maybe not soon," Martin conceded. "She may be out till all hours of the night. Why don't we go home and come back in the morning?"

"Yes. To find her gone. Once she's hears someone's asked for her, she'll leave. No, here she may be and here we will stay until we know. All night, if we have to. Send Sophia a note, if you want."

"No need. She's knows I'm with you," Martin said blithely. When his brother looked at him oddly, he laughed. "She thinks no harm can come to me when I'm with you. Don't frown, that's what everyone in the family thinks too. So if I get my throat cut, you'll have a lot of explaining to do."

Magnus laughed. He was about to answer when he heard the inn door open and the landlord greeting a guest. He stepped out of the parlor, and stared at the woman who had just come in.

She was dressed in black from her voluminous hood to the hem of the cape that brushed over her slippers. The cape was an expensive one, and the woman did have a cross and tired-looking maidservant standing behind her. A fine lady indeed. Magnus smiled.

But then he heard her voice.

It was low, and sweet, and she spoke in measured, musical tones. A real lady then, Magnus thought with a sigh, and started to turn away. Whoever this lady was, she was no pirate's daughter.

And then, warmed by the fire that blazed in the hearth, she threw back her hood. Magnus froze.

She was magnificent. She bloomed, he thought, like some rare flower in the midst of London's gray winter. His breath stopped; he thought it might be that his blood did, too, for it certainly was not flowing to his brain. It was all flooding his heart, and other lower parts. He had to remind himself to take another breath when his chest grew tight. He stared at her. He had thought other women beautiful. He had never *felt* it before.

Her silky hair was in disarray from being pent up in her hood, and when she shook it out, he saw it was all the colors that flickered in the hearth: red and bronze and gold, with some strands that were even that astonishing white that's born in the heart of fire. Her face was pale, but her cheeks were flushed to rose with the cold. Her nose was straight, her chin determined, and when she blinked and then turned to stare up at him as if she'd felt his eyes upon her, he saw that her long-lashed eyes were warm and gold. A copper russet lady of fire, he thought, enchanted.

"Cristabel!" Martin said.

Those remarkable eyes widened, she gasped, then turned and raced out the door. She got only so far as the step. Magnus was there first, his big hand on her shoulder. He stopped her by simply touching her and letting her feel the strength of that touch.

"No," he said, "that's foolish."

She stopped, head down, and nodded. "Yes," she said, "you're right. I don't know what I was thinking."

She shook her shoulder gently, as though to dislodge the few water drops that had settled there. He removed his hand and she straightened both shoulders and looked up at him again.

60

"His brother, I suppose?" she sighed. "The famous Magnus?"

He nodded, and bowed. Then he gestured to the door. "Talking is better done inside, and in private," he said.

He was very tall—he must have learned early on how to duck his head when he came in and out of doors, she thought inconsequentially. He'd certainly moved out of the inn door faster than she could have imagined. He was big, even bigger than her father, and lean besides. He had wide shoulders, a trim waist, and long legs. She had learned to evaluate men in a place where men were judged by their size and strength as well as wit. She assessed him to be both quick and dangerous. Those sleepy gray eyes didn't fool her. His brother had been right, this was a formidable fellow—who had every reason to be furious with her. After all, her father had kidnapped his brother, thinking he had kidnapped him.

He was dressed like a fine gentleman, though it wasn't his attire that impressed her; he could have commanded in rags. To call that strong, wide face handsome wouldn't be wrong, but it wouldn't be fitting either; it would be like calling the sun "handsome." He was young, but exuded power by giving off an air of total and complete confidence. This big, elegantly dressed man was as dangerous as any sword-rattling, pirate rogue she'd ever met.

Cristabel was brave, but she'd lived her life among violent and dangerous men. She knew there was no shame in surrender if she was outgunned. She also knew when it was time to stop fighting and start thinking.

She took a deep breath and let her fluttering pulse slow. He was, after all, she told herself, a nobleman and an Englishman besides, and so probably wouldn't do most of the things the men she'd known in her past did when they were angry. Or so she hoped. Other than her days spent with Martin, she had no experience with gentlemen. What frightened her most was the thought that she was more afraid of this calm, elegant man than any pirate she'd ever met.

It made no sense; it was strange and made her feel odd.

After all, they both wanted the same thing. His quarrel was with her father, not her. All he needed from her was what she was anxious to give him: her promise that she had no claim on him, and would never make one. She'd gladly give him what he sought, her admission that he had no responsibility for her at all.

He waited. She nodded, raised her head, picked up her skirts, and swept through the door like a queen—even though she had the strangest feeling that she was stepping off the end of a dock, into the jaws of a waiting shark.

CHAPTER
5

"Wait outside," Cristabel instructed her maid before she entered the private dining room.

Magnus raised an eyebrow. He paused at the door. "Is that wise?" he asked.

"I thought ye said you only wanted to *talk* with me," she snapped, wheeling around to confront him. Seeing his brow go higher, she winced at what she'd said.

"I was thinking of your reputation, not rape," he said as he closed the door behind them.

"Oh, aye," she muttered, so vexed with herself and him that she forgot her ladylike accents again. "Be perfeckly understandable, that: a viscount being careful of a buccaneer's daughter's reputation; makes perfect sense, it do."

She plopped down in a chair, accepted the mug of hot punch Martin handed her, and stared up at his brother.

"Well," she said bravely, "I'll say it straight out, and be done with it. I'm sorry me . . . my father abducted your brother, sorrier than I can say. He knows it, and if he says else, he's a god-rotted liar!" She glared at Martin.

Magnus's lips quirked. He stood by the mantel and looked at her. He felt as though he'd trapped some wild, exotic creature. She wasn't like anything he'd ever seen, but she reminded him of something wonderful he'd seen. That lovely little face belonged on an Italian cameo; her hair was out of a painting he'd seen in a chapel there, and he'd seen statues in Greece that tried to capture the loveliness of her figure, though her wonderful, slender but generous female shape was covered by a fashionable, if drab, gown. The fashionable effect was ruined by the way she sat sprawled with her legs apart, one elbow on each knee as she cradled her cup of punch between them, and scowled at him. A minute ago he had thought she was a lady; now it sounded like he was talking to a sailor. He was as charmed as he was amused. But his face didn't show it.

"Hold your fire, my dear. He doesn't say otherwise," Magnus said calmly.

"Oh," she said. "I apologize, Martin. Well then," she said, staring up at Magnus again, "what do you want from me?"

He couldn't tell her here and now. He was shocked when he realized just what it was that he wanted. Her. And not just in his bed. He wanted to know her, although he felt as though he already did. It was a curious feeling. He wanted to take care of her and ravish her all at the same time, and then talk to her for hours, to find out everything about her. He *would* get to know her, he resolved on the spot. He'd have to be very careful. Not of his heart, which was halfway in her pocket already. But of his head, which he had to keep clear. For now, he meant to enjoy himself by simply watching and waiting. Whatever happened was sure to be worth waiting for. He turned an impassive face to her even though his pulse raced from just looking at her.

"Your father's men discovered me in another lady's chamber, or rather, leaving it," he said, "and then tried to dismantle all evidence of the supposed crime—to wit: me. It was not the lady they were looking out for. It was you. They seem to believe that we are husband and wife." He stopped, liking the way the words sounded.

"Oh!" she said, sitting up straight. "That's terrible. I

hadn't thought—we can't have that. Look," she said, rising and pacing in agitation, "I'll get word to them. Better yet, I'll scratch out a note someone can read to my father—and you get it to them. I'll tell the truth, and there's an end to it. He knows my mark; he'll be vexed at being diddled so neat, but he'll take it like a man."

"That will do, I think," Martin said worriedly, looking at his brother. "Won't it?"

"No," Magnus said.

"Why not?" Cristabel demanded. "A hard man is Captain Whiskey, and none say else. But a fair one . . . in his way," she added honestly.

"I'm sure," Magnus said calmly, "but it isn't your father I'm concerned about." She cocked her head to the side, and he had to wrestle with an urge to kiss that bemused expression off her lovely face. "It's you," he said simply.

"Well, then, there's no problem," she said with relief. "I won't bother you a bit. I know what you must be thinking, me being a brigand's daughter and all. But I assure you I have no designs on you or your brother." She lifted her head proudly. "My mother was an Englishwoman and a lady. A true lady. My father may be many things, but he brought me up in a way to make her proud. And she would be, if she was still with us, that is. So I know the right thing to do, and I'm going to do it. I'm going to live simply and quietly here in England. I won't even tell you where because I mean to never get in your way again, in thought or deed."

"I'm afraid that won't do," Magnus said.

"Don't you believe me?" she cried in a challenging voice.

"Yes, I believe that's what you mean to do," Magnus said. She gazed at him, confused.

"It's not what *you* want to do that worries him," Martin explained. "It's you—being on your own in London and all."

She look so perplexed, so honestly puzzled about why anyone should worry about her, that Magnus felt his heart contract.

"How old are you, my dear?" he asked.

"One and twenty," she said quickly, "old enough to look after myself. And I've got money, heaps of it. So you see, there's no need to trouble yourself over me."

"I see," he mused. "Martin told me you've never left the Islands before and that these are your first days in London. Have you any family here?"

"No," she said.

"What about your mother's family?" he asked.

She stiffened. "My mother left us when I was a tyke. She were—was a fine lady!" she said defiantly, lifting her chin. "Lady Elizabeth Ann Edgerton; a lady, she was. Of a fine old Canterbury family."

"An old Canterbury family?" Magnus asked thoughtfully. "And yet you say you have no relations here in England?"

"Nor do I!" she spat, "Her family were—was so angry at her alliance with a pirate, they dropped her as completely as she did them. Not a word from them when she went neither, nor since, and they knowed—knew she had a babe. Even if I knew who they were, I'd not want to see them."

He looked thoughtful. Then he shrugged. "That's your decision," he said. "You are one and twenty, as you say. But you are also singularly alone. And you plan to go on this way? By yourself? I see. So of course, you have no worries about being a wealthy young woman alone in a strange city in a new land."

"I won't be alone. I'll have a maid with me, and not that sour-faced nag out in the hall"—she paused, remembering how the girl had smirked when she'd heard Mistress Elphstone's tirade—"but another, for certain. And I'll get a companion," she said, her voice growing lower, remembering the companion she wouldn't have. "I'll hire a good one too. So I won't be by myself."

"I see," he said, "so then certainly you'll have no worries about the wisdom of becoming known as a rich, beautiful woman who lives by herself, surrounded only by servants, without a family or a man to protect her? In a city where any man could notice her beauty and accost her, or lie in wait to ravish her?"

"Well, just let him try!" she cried. "I'm as quick with a dirk as any man, and a fair shot too. It would be the last time he'd accost a woman, that I be promising ye. Oh, but I'd like to see him try, I would! But," she said more quietly, seeing a peculiar expression, half smile, half frown, flit over the big man's face, "I doubt I'd have to. This is England, after all. I'm in London at last, and safe as houses." She said that and looked quite pleased with herself.

He thought he would choke on his suppressed laughter, but he knew laughing at this odd, lovely girl would hurt her. His laughter faded when he thought about the other things that could hurt her worse.

"Yes, London," he said sadly, "where half the population is starving and the other half live in terror of the ones who are able to survive. Have you been too busy looking at our landmarks to see what lies in our streets?"

She remembered the beggars and all the thin and ragged men and women who watched the crowds with calculating eyes, as well as the packs of ferret-fast thieving children she'd kept her own eyes open for. But she'd seen worse.

"Yes. But as I said, I'm wide-awake."

"Wide-awake enough to fight off several men?" Magnus asked. "Wide-awake enough to be on guard all the time? And even if you are skilled enough to fight them off, random mischief wouldn't be your only concern."

"Did ye not hear me, man?" she cried in frustration. "This be London town! Not Port Royale or New Providence or Madagascar! There be civilization, morals and laws and such, here!"

"Yes" he said unperterbed, "interesting laws, at that. A rich young woman living by herself, with no male kith or kin to protect her, doesn't have to worry about one man— or even a pack of them trying to ravish her here in London. If you insist. But she might be wise to take a minute to worry about just one of them overpowering her and carting her off to the Fleet Prison, where he could ply her with drink or drugs and then tie her into a quick and unholy marriage. Of course, then she wouldn't have to worry anymore, because he would have absolute control over both her body and fortune—for life.

"Yes," he said, as she stared at him, her golden eyes growing wide, "interesting laws, indeed."

"It's true?" she asked Martin, confronting him. "They can do that?"

"True enough," he agreed, "it's been done. Footmen have married ladies that way. It doesn't happen to wise women, of course. Only those foolish enough to believe a sweet-talking rogue."

"Or ones who have no men to protect them from being forced to it," Magnus added.

"Why didn't I hear of it before?" she wondered aloud. "I was very well educated, and none of my governesses ever told me about such things."

"Most likely they didn't think it would ever be a possible danger to you," Magnus said gently, "or it might be that it was the furthest thing from their minds, for it was the least thing likely to ever happen to them."

She grew very still, thinking about that. Most of her governesses had been abducted and ravished, but not for their money, and certainly not for marriage.

"I'll handle it," she finally muttered, but she said it as though to reassure herself. "I'll hire on a footman, too, maybe a brace of them, seeing as how they're so popular here," she said bitterly.

"Anyway," she continued after another moment, in a softer, resigned voice, "it doesn't matter. I've set my course and I can't turn back. If I go back to the Islands, my father would just find me another unwilling mate. The next one might not be as safe or as kind as young Martin here. There are a few fellows of the Brotherhood who have their eye on me too. I don't want them. Whatever the risks, I reckon I'm safer here than there. So I thank you for your concern, but please let me be now."

"Be what? That's the question," Magnus said gently. "None of the obvious answers pleases me. I'm sorry, my dear, but I can't let you be. My conscience, my honor, and my word as a gentleman prevent me."

She stood facing him, her small hands knotting to fists. Martin spoke up quickly. "See? Just as I said, Cristabel. He thinks he has to carry the world on his shoulders. Listen to him—he's right."

"No decent female is going to call you friend, living alone and unregarded as you will be," Magnus said.

"I'll say I'm a widow," she shot back.

"With no family or relatives to see to you? No, that would never work," Magnus said sadly.

"Then what do you want?" she asked angrily. "To marry me? Don't pity me. I wouldn't have you on a platter, with an apple in yer mouth!"

Martin was astonished. No one ever spoke to Magnus like that. But Magnus seemed to be highly entertained. At least, he was smiling.

"A horrible thought, I agree," Magnus said. "I suggest nothing so drastic as matrimony. We have to find a way to settle you. In the meantime we can give you a home and protection. I say 'we,' although I can't. I have the room but I am a bachelor. Martin has a good-sized house in town. What do you think, lad? You can offer her what I can't because you've got a wife. Will you give the lady house-room?"

"Oh aye, and I'm sure his wife will love that," Cristabel laughed. "Stow it. Here, I'll write the note to my father, and we'll be done with the matter."

"But Sophia would be pleased to have you!" Martin said with a wide smile, as he thought about it. "As a matter of fact, she'd be delighted."

"Well, if she's daft enough to take in a stranger, and a pirate's daughter at that, well, I'm sorry for her. But it doesn't matter what she will or won't do, because I know my own mind. And I won't go with you. Here I am, and here I stay."

She folded her arms across her chest and glared at Martin. He couldn't sway her; she knew how to wrap him around her finger, and had done it often already. But that was Martin without his brother.

She peeked at Magnus, and then quickly looked away. Living with Martin and his young wife would be uncomfortable, but safe. That was true. But she didn't fool herself. It would also mean living in this big, elegant man's care and under his watchful eyes. She was more worried about that than she was of being alone. She'd been a prisoner for too many years, she told herself, and tried to resist the strange lure of this trap by remembering that the tightest traps always had the strongest lures.

"I could make you come, but I won't," Magnus said, "nor will I camp on this doorstep until you agree. You're right. You know the right thing to do, but I can't make you do it, can I?"

Cristabel bit her lip and shook her head, stubbornly keeping her arms folded across her chest.

"So be it," Magnus sighed, picking up his hat from the chair where he'd left it. "I'm considered to be good with a dirk, too, as well as sword and saber. So when your father's men come after me next time . . . and they will, of course, since you'll be somewhere in hiding and I'll be continuing to go out on the town without you. You don't expect me to stay home because of you? No, of course not. But when they come after me next time, I should be able to take care of myself too. I'm sure I can manage. Good night, Mistress Cristabel, and good-bye."

"I'll send a letter," she blurted.

"Yes," he said softly, "so you said. That should do it, shouldn't it? You, disappeared somewhere in England without a trace, except for that letter. And me out every night, enjoying myself as usual. I'm sure your father will understand. Oh, absolutely. Thank you."

He stood and marveled at her creative use of language as she answered him, at length. He didn't know sailors could curse like that—much less lovely young women. The most interesting part of it, he thought as he saw Martin listening slack-jawed, was that it was as if she didn't understand what she was saying. It wasn't profane so much as amazing, like listening to a parrot's recital. When she was finally done, she glared at Magnus.

"Blast ye," she snarled, "I'll come with ye. What can I do? Don't want your bloody big head on my conscience, do I?"

"Don't you?" he asked with great interest.

He was astonished and delighted when she blushed.

"Bugger it," she muttered, and turned away to hide her flaming face. Which was just as well, because if she'd seen the tender look in his gray eyes, she might have changed her mind, courageous as she was.

Cristabel hated to admit it, even to herself, but she'd never been so comfortable in her life.

She was warm and snug. She'd never really understood what that meant. She'd been hot, or merely warm at home in the Islands. Sometimes she'd been cool, once in a while even chilly. But in the week she'd been in England, the land of her dreams, she'd been cold, colder, and icy cold. Truth to tell, the weather had disappointed her. She'd read about English winters and thought of them as invigorating, imagining herself frisking through fields of fluffy snow. She hadn't envisioned the misery of icy water dripping down her neck and into her shoes.

But now she wasn't cold anymore even though the world outside her window was turning to ice. A fire crackled in her hearth; the wind whining outside made her glad to be inside. This, then, was *snug*. It was warm, with alternatives that made her feel lucky to be warm. She liked it.

She'd never been in such a beautiful room before, either. Or in such a grand house. It had ornate ceilings and fireplaces with carved mantels, thick glass windows, and carpets good enough to grace a captain's cabin on every polished floor. On every floor she'd seen, she corrected herself. She'd only had a hasty look at the house by candlelight as she'd been greeted and taken to her room. But what she had seen impressed her so much that she dallied now before her mirror, pretending her hair wasn't right, when she was really just worried that she wasn't right for this fine house.

Not that she wasn't as well-bred as the lady of the house, she reminded herself proudly. Not that she didn't have enough money to buy a string of houses like this if she chose to. And certainly not because there was anything she couldn't face up to, even if she was afraid. Admitting fear was the first step to conquering it—any green cabin boy could tell you that. And conquering her fear was exactly what she was trying to do.

What scared her now was the lady of this house, though Sophia looked innocent as an angel, and she'd never said more than "Good evening" to her uninvited guest. She was small and delicate, beautifully dressed, with a pretty, smiling face. A lady all rosebuds and cream. She made Cristabel feel like a cockatoo next to a white dove. Cristabel herself had been born a lady, or at least half one, but she knew too well that she'd only been raised as half a lady too. The other half felt very out of place here.

Cristabel was determined to stand on her own two feet and walk out of this house as soon as she could. This wasn't her home and she wouldn't rely on the charity of strangers or the goodwill of any man, much less a strange and domineering one. Magnus didn't even live here, and probably wouldn't be downstairs now. That thought made her feel relief as well as a vague disappointment. But it wasn't Magnus she worried about seeing just now.

She found herself more afraid of her hostess's disapproval than she was of the whole new world outside her door. Martin's beautiful wife was everything Cristabel's own mother had been, she was sure of that. And Cristabel wasn't sure if she measured up to that kind of excellence.

"You're awake!" a voice exclaimed, intruding on her thoughts. Cristabel spun her head around to see the lady she was worrying about in the doorway. She wore a long, frilled white morning gown, and her pretty little face was smiling. "Good," she said, "I was afraid you'd be one of those girls who sleep the morning away so I wouldn't be able to talk to you until this afternoon. But Martin said you were always up at dawn, and so I came to peek. Here you are, up and dressed, even without a maid. I'd have sent you my own maid. But how I go on. It's my besetting sin. Martin said you weren't very tolerant of fools—please be patient with me, but your being here is so exciting."

"Exciting?" Cristabel asked in confusion. She'd expected the lady to be hostile or, at the very least, suspicious. She wouldn't have blamed Martin's wife for being jealous of a woman who had traveled across the sea in a cabin with her husband, pretending to be his wife, no matter what she looked like. No doubt she'd been told the truth and many another pretty tale besides. If their roles had been reversed, Cristabel herself would have had the wretched female up against the wall with a knife to her throat, and the whole truth out of her before she could blink an eye. This pretty creature's lack of concern, her sweet acceptance of the awful situation, made Cristabel feel coarse and mean, and even more unworthy. Obviously there was much more to being a lady than being born one. She sighed.

"Of course it's exciting," the lady said eagerly as she came into the room, "I've never met a pirate's daughter before. I mean a real buccaneer's daughter. Martin said you grew up among pirates and savages, and can shoot pistols and throw knives, and curse like a sailor yourself. I've seen the wicked females who are hanged at Newgate, but they're mostly low and ugly creatures who kill when they squabble over a man, or bread, or some other trifling matters. They're vulgar and amusing, nothing more. I did once see a woman who was being hanged for forging a pound note, and I must say she looked most respectable. But here you are, a brigand's daughter, and looking like a foreign princess. It's wonderful."

Cristabel's amber eyes narrowed. She'd been expecting disdain, and had been prepared to humbly accept it. But she never expected this. Being thought of as low is one thing, but being thought *so* low that it doesn't matter what someone says about you is completely another.

"I'm pleased, of course, to please you," Cristabel said in the voice she'd learned from her coldest governess. She stood and turned to face her hostess, holding her head high so she could look down her small nose at her. "How unfortunate it would have been if I disappointed you," she said in a bored, deadened voice that belied the way her eyes flared. "I suppose you'd have me out on the streets if I did. I refuse to put my head in a noose to brighten your day, but let me see, what else can I do to entertain you? Would you like me to run someone through? Or would it be enough to simply tie you to the bedpost and carve off your nose?"

Terror came into the lady's wide blue eyes. She backed up a step. "You don't have to do anything," she said quickly.

Cristabel glowered. This pretty little lady was suddenly no lady in her eyes. Ladies were compassionate and just; so she'd always been told. A pirate's woman—wife, mistress, or child—knew the hard and dark side of life. They never found death amusing; no kin of a pirate could and few pirates did either. Too many of them ended doing the gallows trot to find sport in watching another man die that way. Although they labored under a dead man's flag, it was pure boastfulness, and good for frightening their prey into making foolish mistakes. They considered death to be an occupational hazard and a necessary evil. Putting someone to death could be profitable, and sometimes necessary. Abusing women and tormenting prisoners was one thing, but no pirate ever actually killed for mere amusement, no matter what their enemies said.

"Maybe I won't do that, after all," Cristabel said, as if she was considering it. "Maybe I will . . . I tell you what," she said suddenly, eyeing her hostess, who was cringing back against the door now. "Maybe I'll do nothing at all. Maybe I'll just leave here. Look, lady, I want to be shed of you as much as you want to be rid of me. Help me to find a place to stay—a long way from here—and hire on a decent maid. I'm saying good-bye to the sour wench I have this very day. I'll also need a footman and a companion, and keep your mouth closed about it. You'll never see hide nor hair of me again."

"Oh no!" the lady said, appalled. "I couldn't. Magnus would murder me if he found out! Besides, I'd never be able to keep a secret from him for a minute."

"What about Martin?" Cristabel asked, puzzled.

"He'll feel the same way, too, I assure you."

"No, I know that; what I'm getting at is—you're married to Martin, aren't you? So why are you worried about Magnus?"

"Oh," the lady said breathlessly, "You don't know Magnus."

"Well, I know lily-livered cowards when I see them," Cristabel said in disgust. "You and Martin have the backbones of sea slugs! Why, my father is feared throughout the Caribbean, and I dared to defy him! And you're afraid of a foppish Englishman who can't even keelhaul you. Magnus is nothing but a big blowfish, all prickle and air inside. He blusters and roars, and you tremble in your boots. It's no wonder he thinks he's all-powerful; he's got you all convinced."

"Well, *you're* here now, aren't you? And you didn't want to be, did you? So there," her hostess retorted, stung by Cristabel's criticism.

"It's just that he had a convincing argument . . ." Cristabel replied.

The two women eyed each other. Cristabel felt a foolish smile tug at her mouth, and saw her hostess bite her own rosy lips, trying not to giggle. Cristabel grinned.

"Well," she said generously, "he's persuasive, that's a fact. Come, lady, I cry peace. Truth to tell, I don't want to fight. I grant I was quick to take insult at whatever you said. I'm edgy with you. I thought you'd be armed and dangerous when you heard my father kidnapped your husband, and even meaner when you realized I sailed all the way here locked in a cabin with him."

"Oh, call me 'Sophia,' please do," the lady said, "But why should I be angry at you for what your father did? So far as the journey went—Martin told me everything. You're as blameless as he."

"And you believed him? I mean, that is to say, of course, it's true," Cristabel said, color rising in her cheeks. "Your Martin is a pretty lad but not my sort at all. Even if he was—and I promise you he isn't—I'm a virtuous girl, for all that my father's a blackhearted villain. My mother was a lady, you see. I suppose the fact that my father is their leader helped keep men away from me—and me away from men. But in my experience . . . the plain truth is, Sophia, that I don't know one woman who would believe her husband on such a matter."

"But I know Martin," Sophia said simply, "We grew up together. His estate bordered mine. We married as soon as we were able. He couldn't lie to me, I don't think. He wouldn't. He's a gentleman."

Cristabel sensed a rebuke in Sophia's response and didn't answer. She wouldn't trust any man she knew. It would be foolish. But Sophia was saying that a lady would trust a man—if he were a gentleman. Martin was the first gentleman Cristabel had ever met, and it *was* true that he'd sailed across two seas with her without touching her. Still, she'd been on her guard throughout the voyage, sleeping with one ear and eye open. But he'd given her not so much as a pinch or a tweak or a wink. Only a peek from time to time, for he was a healthy young man. Now it turned out that his wife had expected no less. This England, Cristabel thought dazedly, with its moral, reasonable men and confident, trusting ladies, was like nothing she'd ever dreamed of. She felt humbled.

"And Magnus, even with all his 'bluster,' as you call it," Sophia went on, "is a gentleman, too, I assure you."

Cristabel's head shot up. Her eyes narrowed as she studied her hostess. Of course, she thought, it could also be that the girl was simple.

CHAPTER

6

~

She can't spend that!" Sophia exclaimed. "It would be the talk of the town. She'd attract thieves like flies if she showed it in a shop, wouldn't she? 'Ods mercy! Pure Spanish gold. I've never seen anything like it, have you, Martin? Why, it's not even really gold-colored, it's so deep and rich, it's almost rosy pink, don't you think?"

"Yes, and look, it's soft," Martin marveled as he took the big, flat coin in his hand and ran his fingertips over it. "It gives to the touch too."

"Oh, let me feel!" Sophia cried.

They sat at the table, their breakfast forgotten, examining Cristabel's coin.

"Well then," Cristabel said, flustered, "if it's so startling, give it back. Here's another," she said, fishing another coin out of her purse. "What about this one?"

"Oh, it's beautiful!" Sophia crooned. "It's smaller and darker gold, but look, Martin, there's a lion on it. Isn't it cunning? And a sunburst too!"

"Indian!" he cried. "It's from India. I've heard of such. Lord, it's heavy for such a small thing."

"Let me feel," his wife said, snatching at it.

"Not yet, let me take another look," he said, holding it up away from her, to the light.

"Gold fever," said a new voice, rich in amusement. "Take care, Martin, men have sold out their countries, much less their wives, for just 'another look' at such coins."

"Magnus!" Martin said guiltily, giving the coin back to Cristabel as soon as he saw the big man smiling down at him, "Good morning, brother. I was just looking at Cristabel's coins. She wants to go shopping, but I swear I don't have enough men to protect her if she tries to spend these."

Magnus held out one broad hand, palm up. Cristabel dropped the coin into it without a word. He nodded, and looked at her. She saw the unspoken question in his gray eyes. When she saw the amusement in them too, she flushed, bent her head, and picked out another Spanish coin, a Dutch one, a Danish one, two French pieces, and three coins she couldn't identify, and put them in his hand as well. He stood still, waiting patiently. Finally she put her whole purse in his hand and looked away.

"The English silver and maybe some of the gold might possibly be used," he finally said as he poured the coins back in the purse and handed it back to her, "but I agree with Martin, the rest should never be seen inside a London shop. You've some treasures here, worth their weight in gold and antiquity. But not worth the conjecture they would cause."

"Right," Cristabel said. "I don't want my father finding me."

"He doesn't need these to find you; he knows where you are by now," Magnus said gently. "Nor is it the thieves that worry me. It's the gossip. You want to say you're a lady, from abroad? Fine. But few foreign ladies carry such treasure."

"I *am* a lady from abroad," Cristabel said defiantly.

"So you are," he answered calmly before he turned to Martin. "Aren't you going to ask me to breakfast, brother?"

"Join us, join us," Martin said eagerly as his brother took a seat.

Magnus was dressed in shades of fawn today, except for his white neck stock. His hair was drawn back into a neat queue, his face looked freshly shaved, and the clean, spicy rum and floral scent of him disturbed Cristabel as much as his clear, gray gaze did. He sat across the table from her. Although he claimed to be hungry, he passed up the cold meats and hot pasties and instead only took coffee and bread. He joked with his brother without saying another thing to Cristabel, but she still felt he'd changed their pleasant little breakfast with his presence.

She found she couldn't avoid him even when he wasn't watching her, because she couldn't stop thinking about him. He did have a striking face, she admitted, with its broad, high forehead, mobile mouth, and intelligent eyes beneath thin, elegant brows, but she'd grown up among many handsome men. His voice was exceptional, slow and low and rumbling, resonating through that powerful chest. That was true. But she was a captain's daughter and so she responded to the power in it. That was the *only* thing she responded to, she told herself fiercely. And if she could live with her father and thrive under such totalitarian rule, she could surely learn her way around this man for the short time she would have to stay with him.

But it vexed her that she found everything he did so fascinating. He selected a roll and broke it apart. Surely there were better things to do, she thought, than watch those long, strong fingers butter bread? She forced herself to look away from his hands. She looked up to find his gray eyes, steady and sober, upon her.

"I have other coins like the ones that you say seem safe to use," she said abruptly. "I'll see to getting them. There are things I want to buy today." She rose from her seat.

"Please stay," Magnus said calmly, and she sat, wondering how he could make such a simple request sound like a command. "You haven't finished your breakfast yet. There's plenty of time. Our family credit is good enough to cover your purchases until you find simpler gold or until we can help you convert Spanish coin into coin of the realm."

"I wouldn't take a copper piece from you!" she cried in real alarm. "I've plenty of coins, and if you consider them too odd to use for trade here in London, I've other goods that can be converted to money fast enough."

"Goods?" Sophia asked.

"Ah, well, say 'treasures' then," Cristabel said, suddenly embarrassed, recalling just what sorts of things her father had considered an impressive enough dowry for an English nobleman and wondering what these people would think of the items crammed into her trunks.

"Pirate treasure!" Sophia breathed, clapping her hands together. "Here. Right in this house. I never thought anything could be so diverting. You're so full of surprises. Oh, please, Cristabel, may I see?"

Now Cristabel knew for certain what they'd think of her treasure. She felt her breakfast grow cold and hard in her stomach.

"*Rude* little sister," Magnus chided Sophia, "mind your manners. That's like Cristabel asking you to show her your marriage settlement: acreage, annual income, and all. That's not done among your friends and it's not proper to ask of her."

He was trying to spare Cristabel embarrassment, and it shamed her even more. If he really believed her to be a lady, he wouldn't have to say it. Instead, he was making allowances for her as if she were a savage. Her chin came up again.

"No," Cristabel snapped, "not at all. Pirates *love* to show off. You're invited up to my room as soon as breakfast is done. Everyone," she said with a great show of unconcern, even though she was afraid of what they'd think of 'er pirate booty. Although she was half a lady, the other half of her felt as if she were going to be hanged. Well, she might as well have a proper audience for it.

It pleased her to see them choke down their breakfasts in excitement. All except for Magnus, of course, who ate so leisurely, she thought Sophia was going to bounce out of her chair and run him through with a bread knife before he was finished. But eventually even he was done eating, and Cristabel led them upstairs to her room, her head held high and her heart sinking.

"We could have the servants bring the chests down to the parlor instead of traipsing all the way upstairs to see them," Sophia suggested. "How many are they?"

"Only a few," Cristabel muttered as they walked down the corridor to her room. "Don't come up if you don't want to. It's all the same to me." She was full of conflicting emotions, vaguely ashamed of her great treasure, and proud as well.

"We can bear the exercise," Magnus commented. "There's no sense in having the servants see the contents. They're better off under Mistress Cristabel's lock and key and watchful eye. If she's kind enough to show us, a private audience is best, I think."

But because of the width of the ladies' skirts and Magnus's shoulders, even Cristabel's spacious room seemed small for all four of them. There were five sea chests stacked against the wall. Two were for her clothing. And three for her dowry. Cristabel herself hadn't gone through them, but as she knelt to unlock the first one, she had a fairly good idea of what would be inside. She expected them to be impressed with the worth, if not the choice of items. She didn't expect the sudden silence when she raised the lid.

Sophia was the first to speak. And gasp.

"Oh my," she said.

Well, there was a lot of plate, and it shone in the sunlight, Cristabel conceded. He'd done her proud, all right, but she didn't see anything very different from so many of her father's chests. All the trunks had been crammed so full that they hadn't rattled when they were carried—pirates didn't pack for neatness, but for swiftness and safe transport. Looking up, she saw her three visitors staring in wonder at what lay before them.

Finely wrought platters and dishes, pitchers, tureens, and salt cellars of silver, gold, and bronze lay all in a jumble on top of the coins—and necklaces, tiaras, bracelets, rings, pendants, and combs of silver and gold, tortoiseshell and jet, mother-of-pearl and jade, all set with diamonds, sapphires, emeralds, pearls, rubies, opals, and lesser gems—all glittering and gleaming in a disorderly heap. She was proud of her fortune, but Cristabel suddenly felt embarrassed for the higgledy-piggledy look of it.

"I've read about such things," Martin breathed, "but never seen it."

"Can you *imagine* where all this came from?" Sophia said in wonderment.

"It came from my father," Cristabel spoke up defiantly. "He wanted me to be well off. Well, actually, he wanted to impress Martin," she admitted, "but it's all the same."

"I'm impressed," Martin said. "See what I passed up for you?" he asked Sophia, who was still gaping at the treasure. "A fortune in pirate's loot."

He said it in jest, but Cristabel froze. He made it sound shameful for her to have her treasure. She knew it was wrong, always had, but piracy was her father's profession and she had grown accustomed to it, the way she would if he had gone to sea and returned with fish each night, instead of jewels.

"Me father risked his head each time he went to work. I don't see ye going out and turning yer hand at anything." Cristabel spat, spinning round on her heels and glaring at Martin.

She was hunkered down in front of the chest, highlighted by the sun-drenched treasure. Magnus thought the barbaric beauty of the glittering treasure was no less stunning than the play of light on her radiant hair and in her glowing eyes. She was crouched and at bay, and looked as though she wished she had a knife in her hand. He wished he were alone with her, knife or not. But when he spoke, his voice was calm and low and slow.

"'Ods life, Martin, where do you think we got our fortune from?" he asked in amused tones. "Our ancestors were

Viking and Norman, both prime plunderers. There's little to choose from between Saxon and Spanish loot. Cristabel's father's treasure is merely—fresher."

It was such a nice thing to say that Cristabel couldn't speak. She gazed at Magnus, wide-eyed and amazed. He made her father sound almost as respectable as his own family, though she knew that could never be, no matter how many generations passed. She blinked, on the verge of tears, and plunged her hands wrist-deep into the coins.

"Aye, well," she said gruffly, recovering herself, "that is to say, yes. But you've already plowed your gold into the earth and gotten decent coin from it. What can you do with mine?"

Magnus knelt next to her, and didn't speak at once because the wild, fresh perfumed scent of her overwhelmed him.

"Much," he finally said as though nothing had affected him but the sight of her treasure. "Give me what you will now. I'll have it appraised in places where discretion is assured. Gambling is a disease in London town," he explained. "There are too many gentlemen who don't turn a hand to anything but dice and cards. Noblemen are famous for selling off their family treasures bit by bit when the need arises. I'll say the goods are those of a young acquaintance of mine—which you are. Then we'll dispose of what we can, where we can, for the fairest price. We can't do a century's work in a week, so it will take time. But we'll have you set up with nice, dull currency soon enough. And with a strict reckoning of every pence of it, I promise you."

She stared at him, caught between hope and fear. No one had ever been so nice to her without a reason.

"I do so turn my hand at something," Martin said, cutting into their thoughts. "I wouldn't have been kidnapped in the first place if I hadn't gone abroad to look after our affairs. I go to the office, don't I, Magnus, and I contribute my fair share. Of course, if you don't think I do . . ." he said, and then stopped because he couldn't think of a powerful enough threat, and wasn't sure he wanted to use one even if he could.

"So you do," Magnus assured him. "I know it well. So, what shall we take first?" he asked Cristabel.

"I don't know," she answered, flustered by his nearness and the close scrutiny of those knowing eyes. "You pick. Whatever you think will fetch a handsome price."

"Anything in this chest would do more than that," he answered, lifting a silver chalice and turning it in his hands, "but you have to help me choose. I don't want to take anything that's a particular favorite of yours, anything with sentimental value," he added when he saw her look at him in confusion.

"Sentimental value?" she asked, astonished, "it's merely booty. There's nothing here of mine, nothing I want at all."

"Oh, but, Cristabel!" Sophia cried, sinking to her own knees in front of the chest, like a nun before an altar, "look at this comb! Have you ever seen anything like it? The gold is so buttery, and all these tiny rubies! The design is magnificent. How can you bear to lose it?"

"It goes well with your hair," Cristabel said. "If you like it—'tis yours."

"Truly?" Sophia asked, holding the comb to her breast with reverence.

"Aye, well," Cristabel said, embarrassed, "it's nothing to me. It's like—like if your father were a fisherman—would you fall in love with a porgy? I've no use for jewels and such," she said, remembering all the pirate women and their love of jewels and gems. She'd decided, early on in her girlhood, that if she had to grow to be a woman, she wouldn't make matters worse by decking herself out like a pirate's trollop. Ladies wore little perfume and less jewelry, or so she'd always been told. She still had her mother's pendant. It was simply a pearl set in gold. That was the kind of jewelry a lady wore.

"Thank you!" Sophia said eagerly. "I don't know. It's a cunning comb, to be sure. But I have so many—and just look at this tiara! The diamonds, the way they catch the light—what are you doing?" she shrieked as Magnus lifted the glittering crown from her head.

"Just because our guest is generous doesn't mean that we can take advantage of her," Magnus said. "If she wants to give you a gift, fine. But you wouldn't pick through a friend's wardrobe and take everything that caught your eye, would you?"

"She would," Martin said with a fond grin, "greedy little thing. Remember how she took young Alice's favorite doll all those years ago, Magnus? But really, Sophy, Magnus is right."

"If I want to give my property away, I can!" Cristabel said. Because she knew Sophia *was* being greedy, and would not be if she considered her guest to be a friend—or an equal. This realization hurt, and the only way she knew to stop the pain was to pretend she was rich and eccentric enough to give away anything—so long as she didn't give away the truth of how the rejection hurt her.

"So you can," Magnus agreed, "but in this case it would be like giving a boy enough green apples to give him an aching belly. Accepting your gifts wouldn't be good for Sophia. She has enough baubles. She needs to learn to use discretion."

"I don't know what's wrong with appreciating pretty things," Sophia said angrily, "but now, come to think of it, this tiara is just too gaudy. It's vulgar. It must have been taken from some horrid Spanish creature. The comb too— it was likely ripped right off some sluttish thing's head. It probably has hair still in it, or blood—or lice. Lord knows what a devil of a time one has ridding oneself of them. I don't want either."

"Sophia!" Martin gasped.

"Sophia," Magnus said.

Sophia swallowed. "Thank you for the offer, Cristabel, but I don't think I want any gifts from you," she said, and picking up her skirts, she swept from the room. Martin shot a look of apology to Cristabel, nodded at Magnus, and followed his wife out the door.

"She's used to getting her way. It was amusing when she was a child. Much less so now. I'm sorry if she hurt your feelings," Magnus said gravely.

"Of course not," Cristabel said, her amber eyes growing damp. "How could she? Only ladies have feelings. But," she said, her chin quivering despite all her efforts to keep calm, "I'm half a lady, and so I suppose it bothers me a bit. I'll recover. The other half is just as rough and rude as she thinks, ye see."

She dashed away the gathering wetness from her eyes.

"Don't," he said quickly. "Your tears are more valuable than any of your jewels, and she's not worth one of them."

And then, to her astonishment, as well as his own, he lowered his lips to her, and kissed away the last tear from under her eye. He felt her lashes flutter and the softness of her skin beneath the salty dampness on his lips. Her skin was silken, her scent delicious, her warmth incredible.

She opened her eyes to find herself impaled by his intense gray gaze. His lips had felt so soft, so warm; her gaze slid to that astonishingly strong yet gentle mouth. She suddenly found herself looking higher, and then higher as he rose swiftly to his feet. He held out a hand and she rose to face him, scarcely aware of what she was doing, both eager and afraid to see what he would do next.

"Weeping females quite unman me," he said. "Now, you don't want to see something the size of me cry, do you? Even though you're used to spouting whales? Come, it's not worth the sorrow. Forget it. We'll have a look at this treasure and pick out some stuff that we think can be easily disposed of. Then I suggest you lock the chest and keep the key somewhere safe, and far from the prying eyes of Sophia and the servants."

She silently handed the key to him.

He stared at her. "I trust you," she said simply.

"Thank you," he said, looking troubled.

". . . and I am very good with a knife," she added.

He couldn't concentrate on the treasure, he was laughing so hard.

He had stepped away from her just in time, Magnus thought. It had been a struggle, and he wasn't sure he was glad he'd won. There were so many reasons why it was wrong for him to be wishing he had moved that kiss he'd given the pirate's daughter a bit lower that he couldn't count them all. She was young. She was alone in a strange land. She was under his protection, with no other male to look after her. She trusted him implicitly; he was used to that, many people trusted him. But he wasn't sure he trusted himself with her. To act on his impulses would be to take advantage of his power and position as he had never done before. Although he lusted for her, he didn't know her. And that was the most compelling reason of all.

She'd wanted a kiss on the lips as much as he had. He was sure of it. He didn't know exactly why he was so sure of himself, but he was no fool. Still, kisses too easily offered were too often trouble, and kisses too easily given could lead to even more trouble. Cristabel wasn't just beautiful and seductive. She was an entirely unknown quantity: half pagan, half lady—just as she said.

There was only one thing he was certain of: He was fascinated by her. And as with all rare objects, she required closer study. If he was wise, he reminded himself, he'd be careful of just how close he got.

He didn't have to worry now; there would be no opportunity for more moments of passion tonight. He certainly wouldn't be alone with her again, and whatever his lustful fantasies, he wasn't on his way back to Martin's house now to see her for pleasure. This was strictly a financial visit, he told himself. Soon after he'd left her that morning, he'd sold off a serving tray and a teapot, both of which had sent the jeweler into barely concealed ecstasy. But not concealed enough, because Magnus had noticed this reaction and had gotten a good price for the items. He wanted to deliver the money to Cristabel immediately.

And if he wondered why he was hurrying through the night to Martin's house and why the errand couldn't wait until morning, he told himself it was just to see her pleased and grateful expression. He was also going to protect her from Sophia's avarice and possible spite. What a noble fellow you are, he told himself wryly, moving through London like a juggernaut, sparing the girl a few moments of unease and giving her some spending money—even if she does have a king's ransom in those sea chests.

But when he reached the house and announced his success, showing her the money, she didn't move to take it from him. She closed her eyes for a minute and seemed to be praying. Then she opened them again, and reached out, taking approximately two thirds of the coins from his palm.

"You deserve a fee for fencing them," she said, indicating the ones she'd left. "I couldn't have done it, you see."

Martin's snicker turned into a cough at the look on Magnus's face.

"My dear," Magnus said, "I have enough money, I promise you. This was a favor done for friendship's sake."

"Nobody does something for nothing," she argued.

She was wearing a green gown tonight. Not a brilliant, parrot green like the dresses she'd worn at home, but a deep, magical, woodsy green that bordered on black. It made her skin glow and her eyes look tragic.

"A friend doesn't take payment," Magnus said.

"You've only known me for a day or two," she replied. "How could I be a friend?"

"I'd hardly ask for more than friendship," he said with the first hint of annoyance he'd shown. "You're living with my brother, you know."

Her eyes widened. "What difference does that make?" she demanded. "I could tell you tales of things that go on under people's noses that you wouldn't believe. Why, I've known mothers who would look the other way when . . . Be that as it may," she said hastily, realizing that stories about some of the lower life-forms in the islands where she'd been raised would lower his opinion of her. "Anyway," she added spitefully, "from the way Martin treats you, he wouldn't say a word if you carried me off screaming."

"Of course I would!" Martin said, stung.

"Do you think I would do such a thing?" Magnus asked, his thin brow raised high.

"Of course not," she answered. "I know I'm giving myself airs. I'm probably not good enough for you."

She didn't know why she was fighting with him, all she knew was that she felt much safer keeping him at a distance. Sophia had taken dinner in her room, and Martin had sat at the table trying desperately to be casual about his wife's absence. When Magnus had walked in from the night, glowing with the cold, big, tall, and vital, he'd transformed her evening. Now she found herself resenting that. From his silver-buckled shoes to his three-cornered hat, he was every inch a gentleman. Tonight Sophia's rejection reminded Cristabel of just who and what she was. Magnus's appearance made that harder to bear. She was keeping her head above water by fighting him and she knew it.

But she was a fair fighter, and she knew it was wrong to blame him for her reaction.

"Don't take offense, my lord. Look ye," she said, gazing down at the coins in her hand and not seeing his eyes soften. Her lapse of speech showed him how much she was concentrating on her words. "'Tis simple enough. 'Tisn't you so much. I know ye be a gentleman. But I be needing much money, I think, and so I'll be asking ye to do the same fer me again and again fer so long as I be here. But I can't do it if I feel a burden to ye. So let me pay ye the usual fee for transforming loot into coin, and I be easy with it, ye see? . . . Oh, blast," she sighed, hearing her words.

He didn't pretend to misunderstand.

"Take my advice, my dear," he said gently, "never gamble. You may be able to count any sum in your head and memorize every card in the deck, but if you were dealt a good hand, I'd bet you'd say, 'No more cards, please.' And if you had a bad one, it's likely you'd say, 'Thank ye, but nay, I be set.'"

When she stared up at him, her eyes slowly heating to molten gold, he grinned and went on, "It's just like our cousin Thomas. Only he stammers whenever he gets so much as two kings in one hand. Remember, Martin? We always loved to play cards with him. He's an earl, my dear," he told Cristabel, "and the most honest fellow you could want to know. Now that I think of it, I believe it's only the most honest folk whose speech betrays them. It's as if part of them will always refuse to go along with the wicked notions of the other half. Truly wicked people never seem to have such trouble, do they?

"I think it's charming," he continued in a softer, deeper voice, "and if I smile, that's why. I tell you this because I don't like to smile when you're fretting."

She didn't know how to react to this. She didn't like him saying she had two parts—it was too near to how she thought of herself. But everything else he'd said was so kind and flattering, she didn't know how to respond. She was used to men praising her face and form in outrageous ways. But few had ever told her she was good, or honest, or true. She liked it. She didn't believe it, but she did like it.

"And I don't take commissions for doing a simple favor," he added, "so please take all the money or I'll be forced to become a charitable gentleman, and if that word gets around, I'll have so many beggars on my doorstep, I won't be able to get out in the morning."

She hesitated. Then she took the remaining coins and nodded. "Thank you," she said. And then raised a roguishly grinning face to him and added, "I mean, thank ye, me lord. I be obliged."

He felt as though the sun had come out at night.

He was still smiling when he left for his own house a few hours later. He'd stayed to keep Martin company, and was pleased that his presence, and accepting a challenge from

Cristabel at cards, had lured Sophia downstairs. Sophia hovered around the edges of their impromptu party in the dimmest ring of candlelight, until their laughter had drawn her in. Shamefaced, she apologized to Cristabel. Sophia wasn't the sort of woman Magnus could ever care for—he still saw her as the petulant child he'd always known. But so did Martin, and yet Martin loved her, and if they were happy together, that was fine with Magnus. He didn't have to love his brother's wife. He only hoped she might grow up someday so he could like her. But he wouldn't have her hurting Cristabel in the meantime.

Cristabel had nearly beaten Magnus at cards, she'd made him laugh so much—using pirate accents when she had a terrible hand, to confuse him, speaking like a lady when she was winning—until he saw what she was doing. Then she reversed tactics completely. She was a terrible gambler, but so entertaining, it didn't matter.

"I didn't gamble much at home," she finally admitted. "Gambling's not a game there; pirates take the matter of winning and losing—at anything—much more seriously than most people, you see."

Magnus understood, and didn't like the sad look that came over her when she spoke of her home. "Rest easy, Mistress Cristabel," he said as he took her hand to say good night. "It's only a game with us."

She knew it all too well.

When he left, she said good night to Martin, too, and went to her room. Sophia's maid offered to help her get ready for bed, but she was still too unsure of herself to use a real lady's maid. She thanked the girl but dismissed her, telling her she was used to doing for herself. She could only hope the girl would attribute her refusal to strange foreign customs, and not a lack of breeding.

Weary as she was, she found it hard to sleep.

She kept thinking of Magnus, and that both frightened and dismayed her. She'd promised herself she'd never be fool enough to get involved with any male. She'd seen servitude and despair too often for such folly. She'd seen the pattern again and again: courtship and courtesy in the spring, a full belly and curses by summer. A wise woman was a lone woman. A wise woman was a woman no man could brag over, or cheat on, neglect, or abuse. Men were exciting, handsome, and bold. There was no getting around that. She envied them just as much as she was in awe of them. All that power, grace, and strength astonished and excited her. She had eyes and ears, feelings and desires. She wasn't dead, she reminded herself, only wise.

But Magnus was like no man she'd ever met. She couldn't envision him slapping a woman, or reeling home drunk, or bragging to other men about how good a woman had been to lie with. But maybe he would, or did—how could she know? It was as though he spoke another language. She didn't know enough about this new land yet to judge the men who lived here. But she couldn't stop thinking about him. Or fantasizing about what might have been.

If her mother had lived, she thought sleepily, telling herself a happy tale to lull herself to sleep, she might have reformed her father. She *would* have reformed her father, Cristabel decided, because didn't her father's eyes always mist over when he spoke of his lost lady? Didn't he always look strangely awed and gentle just thinking about her? Hadn't he gone to great trouble to see that his daughter grew up into the image of what her mother had been? No, it was certain; if her mother had lived, she would have worked her gentle, civilizing influence upon him. There was no doubt of it. He would have given up piracy on the high seas.

He would have . . . Cristabel thought, as she sleepily put together her pretty story. He would have taken on a job as a proper sea captain. Yes. And he would have journeyed to England with his wife and child. They would have gotten a home somewhere in the countryside. He would have been very successful, because all his old pirate cronies would leave his ships alone, of course. Then her mother's fine family, seeing how rich and respectable he was, would have acknowledged him. Actually been proud of him. As his wife and daughter would have been.

And she would she been raised as a lady. A true lady.

There would have been no blood on her father's hands or her fortune. No sad, despairing governesses to pity and frighten her, no succession of mistresses to confuse her, no neighbor women and girlfriends to see mistreated. No slaves, no whores, nothing to be ashamed of. Her life would have been refined and civilized and sweet as a dream.

And one day she would have met Magnus. At a party or a dinner or through her many charming friends. And because she wouldn't have known how men forced women, or beat them, or cursed them, or deceived them, or sold them or gambled them away at cards, when she met Magnus there would be nothing to make her afraid of him. And there would have been no reason for him to disapprove of her. She would have curtsied and laughed, he would have been enchanted, and they would have danced and danced the night away, together.

Cristabel frowned. She was half-drunk with sleep, but she realized there was something wrong with her pleasant fantasy. She really didn't know how English gentlepersons lived or behaved. Or at least not enough with which to build a satisfyingly realistic fantasy. She wasn't even sure of how English noblemen and ladies danced. Not the way she'd seen dancing, she was positive of that. Not with the women screeching to the music, wagging their breasts and hips before their men, throwing up their skirts and frolicking barefoot to the pounding beat. Nor would the men be likely to dance with their shirts half-open, sweat running down their tanned chests as they threw back their heads and howled to the music.

But wouldn't Magnus look just lovely if he did? It was an on-the-brink-of-sleep thought, a sudden traitorous, forbidden image, but it came to her clear and strong.

If Magnus were a pirate. Someone her father had brought home. A pirate captain in a billowing white shirt, with his hair flying about his face and shoulders, his broad chest naked to the light, a wide sash around his trim waist, and soft, cuffed boots to his knees. A smiling, gentle pirate. A man she could talk with and not feel inferior to and yet not be afraid of, a gentleman Magnus and a gentleman pirate, all in one. The best-looking, most clever, virile, and exciting pirate in all the Caribbean, in the Indian Ocean, on all the vast deeps of all the world. Magnus the Terrible. The terribly wonderful Magnus, she grinned to herself, as she succumbed to the oncoming sleep that pulled at her like an insistent tide.

And so she fell asleep with visions of this Magnus the terribly wonderful. The man who never was—who would never be. And so, the only man she could ever allow herself to love. Because he didn't exist.

CHAPTER
7

"If it was only summer," Sophia complained, "we'd have so many delightful choices. We could ride on a barge down the Thames, strewing flowers and dancing and drinking and eating the most delicious things you can imagine. There are boats everywhere; you can see everyone because everyone is out during the summertime."

"Yes. If it was summer, you'd really see how beautiful the Thames is," Martin said eagerly. "All the ships from every port of call docked there—it's fascinating. Half the men in London are out fishing along its banks. The river teems with fish: salmon, trout, perch, bream, and more. Even I have luck then. They're delicious and good sport too."

"Or if we didn't feel like going on the river, we could go to Vauxhall or some other pleasure gardens," Sophia went on dreamily, "There are so many you can visit—a different one each night. We could dress up in our finest and hear music and dine out of doors, and dance by torchlight . . ."

"If it was summer," Martin said, "we could go to Southwark Fair, or some other one; there are so many when it warms up. Everyone celebrates in London when the weather changes, from maids to chimney sweeps. You should see the processions in the streets—contests and music too. Such fun! Everyone goes. There are games of chance and skill, acrobats and freaks of nature, the best foods cooked on the spot, and music and dancing. There are bearbaitings and cockfights too, but I don't suppose that would interest you. Still, it's fine sport, and I—"

"If it were summer, dear brother," Magnus reminded him, gently cutting him off, "you wouldn't be here in London. At least I hope not. Because you have to see to your estates now that you're a married man, don't you?"

Sophia made a face. "Well, we'll see that when it happens," she snapped. "As for now—this place offends my nose and my eyes. Can't we go? She's seen the jewels. And the wretched animals. Let's have a look at the Block and then go."

"Cristabel?" Magnus asked softly, "Cristabel?"

She'd been half listening to their conversation until Magnus called her name again. Then she tore her gaze from the lion she'd been staring at. It continued to pace the limits of its dank and filthy cage. Her eyes were misty when she looked up at Magnus.

"Why do they keep him here?" she asked. "He's so sick and old. Look at his ribs and coat. He's used to heat and jungles and grass and sunshine," she said urgently, "and they keep him locked in a dirty cage in the cold and dark. He'll die here, certainly. Why do they do such a cruel thing?"

"They've kept strange animals at the Tower for generations," he explained gently, "because kings and emperors from other lands give them to our kings and queens as gifts. The lion won't die soon. Not it, or the elephant, or the leopards and apes, or any of the other exotic creatures. They adjust to their conditions. They all live a long time because they're fed and cared for, and there're no natural enemies to kill them here."

"Better they be killed!" Cristabel said fervently, watching the mangy lion wearily walk its endless circuit of its little cage.

"But it's educational," Martin protested. "If this lion

wasn't here, the children of England wouldn't know what a lion looked like."

"Let them draw pictures and set him free," Cristabel said, looking up at Magnus with eyes as angry and tawny as the lion's own.

"I don't care what they do with the thing, so long as I don't have to smell it anymore," Sophia said. "Let's see the Block and then go. I heard there are still bloodstains from the last execution there." She shivered deliciously. "Some Jacobite or other."

"The Block?" Cristabel asked, pausing to draw up her hood before they left the menagerie at Tower Hill.

"Execution block," Martin explained eagerly, "Very historic, actually. It's where they took off Charles the First's head, and Mary Queen of Scots's, and Perkin Warbeck's, Margaret Pole's when she was old, and Lady Jane Grey's when she was young, and Raleigh's, of course, and most recently, just last—ah!" He stopped raving about the wonderful beheadings that had been done at the Tower when Magnus's elbow dug deep into his ribs. He was about to protest when he saw Cristabel's face. The last time she had looked at him like that, she'd held a sharp knife pointed at his heart.

She was white-faced.

"*We* are supposed to be the barbarians," Cristabel said through tight lips. "We pirates are supposed to be the ones with bloodlust. But all I hear you praise here in London is the fine sport of hanging and beheading and cockfighting and bearbaiting. But what do we poor pirate folk know? We're like that wretched old lion there—not half so sophisticated as those who caught and caged it. But we only kill for our food—not for the fun of it."

"But we don't profit from such things," Sophia said haughtily. "Occasionally these things are done for sport, as with animals. Animals, after all, have no souls. I don't see why you're making a fuss. If you eat them, you can certainly wager on their deaths before you do so, can't you? As for people—hangings and beheadings and such—if you went to church here, you'd know we must do such things as punishments, to deter crime. Or as a moral lesson. *We* only learn from such public exhibitions."

"All you seem to learn is how to do them more often," Cristabel said as she marched away.

"I suppose this means we're not going to see the Block," Martin said with a sigh, taking his wife's arm and following Cristabel and Magnus out of the menagerie.

Cristabel calmed down as they stepped out of the shadow of the Tower. Magnus could feel her relax. She walked beside him with her hand on his arm, as was proper, and he saw her hand unclench and felt the rigidity leave her body the farther they got from the Tower. It was curious, he thought with a pang, how violently this pirate's daughter reacted to cruelty. It was a paradox, like everything else about her. She came from a violent and vicious people, and yet the only thing he'd seen nearly move her to physical violence was the thought of other people or creatures being hurt.

This behavior was as much a puzzle as were her looks. To see that beautiful face and body, those glowing eyes and that glorious mane of hair—she looked like a siren, and yet . . .

And yet, he realized with quickening interest, he really didn't know how she felt about men. He knew what she said. But in his experience, what a woman said to a man and what she felt were two different things. He didn't know how Cristabel would act if she was alone with a man whom she fancied, or how she had acted in the past. She'd lived with Martin for weeks at sea and lived like a nun, but it was clear that she wasn't attracted to Martin. She treated him with the amused patience she'd show to a younger brother.

But Magnus knew she felt something different towards himself. It was in her eyes, the way she looked away when he caught her staring at him. It was in the way she held herself in his presence. He wasn't a callow young man. He knew women and could feel her response to him shiver along every nerve when they were together.

They'd only known each other for a week, but he'd seen

her briefly each day in that time. He'd gone to Martin's house on a dozen premises, and the feeling of attraction intensified each time he saw her. There was definitely something mutual there. But what did it mean? Did she want a brief liaison? Or to trap him as her father had tried to do for her? Or was she as helpless against the pull of attraction as he seemed to be? In truth he didn't know her well enough to guess.

And what did he want of her? That depended. If she was a lady, he wouldn't doubt she was as prim as she pretended to be. But she wasn't a lady—not really. That made him wonder if she would be like the wild pirate women he'd sometimes met in his travels. The thought excited as much as it dismayed him, for those women were as open and free with their bodily desires as their men were. And as experienced.

Magnus wondered how he could find out the answer to these questions. It would be better for them both if he could learn who and what she really was before he sought to discover how she felt in his arms. He had to know soon, because a man's reason flew out the window when he was in bed with an enticing woman. And Cristabel was very enticing.

"That's a beautiful cloak; is it warm enough?" he asked her, hoping she'd look up at him again.

She did, and he almost didn't hear her answer when he saw her smile.

"Yes, thank you," she said, the small smile curving around her mouth, "and such a lovely color, isn't it? You know," she confided, "I thought that once I got to London, I'd have to dress in black and gray for the rest of my life. And I do so love colors. They remind me of home . . . I don't want to ever go home again, mind. But I don't want to forget it altogether either. Parts of it were very nice: the flowers, the birds, the warmth, the colors of the sea . . . You can't throw everything of your past away just because you don't want it in your future, you know. Well, I suppose you don't know," she said sadly, "because you're very proud of your past—all the way back to those Viking and Norman ancestors you mentioned."

He was as moved that she'd remembered his words so well as he was by her sorrow.

"Anyway," she said more comfortably, looking down at her long, fine woolen cloak, "what a pleasure to find out that ladies in London love colors too. Now I realize since my governesses always wore dark colors, I thought all ladies did so too. But just see! Sophia's dressmaker came to me, and then she and Martin went over each design to be sure it was truly in good taste as well as fashionable before I ordered it.

"And just look at me now. A scarlet cloak! Over a cherry-colored gown," she said with deep satisfaction, "with an embroidered panel, all yellow and gold in front, and three flounces on each sleeve, and petticoats and hoops—I confess, I was determined to be a lady. I'd have worn sackcloth and ashes if I had to. But how much easier it will be now that I know ladies love finery as much as any pirate does.

"Pirates do, you know," she told him seriously, "men as well as the women. I suppose it's the pirate in me that loves the show. I'm so relieved that I can be a lady and colorful too. But I have to get used to you sober fellows here in London."

"Sober?" he laughed. "I'll have you know my waistcoat is as colorful as your gown. My tricorne's trimmed with gold, if you haven't noticed. And please note that my shoes have buckles so shiny, you can comb your hair in their reflection. I refuse to wear a wig except for formal occasions, that's true. That's because I'm eccentric and feel I'm so big, not many people are likely to notice the top of my head anyway. Otherwise, I startle myself sometimes with my splendor," he said with a tilted, self-mocking grin.

"Ah, but pirate men wear scarlet sashes and red breeches, tan boots and blue cloaks, black patches on their eyes and bright bandannas on their hair or round their necks," she said. "They love lace and frills, flounces and jewelry, from earrings to pendants, and mostly in gold, the brighter the better. They like color and ornament and plenty of it on their figureheads, their women, and themselves. They look like rainbows. You look like a Tower raven next to them, I promise you."

"And do you like men to look like that?" he asked quietly.

"I—I remember men looking like that," she answered, dropping her gaze, refusing to continue to look into his deep gray one.

"Ah," he said, resisting the urge he felt to draw her closer into the shelter of his arm, "I see. A politic answer. But I'm content. I really didn't feel like buying myself a patch and red britches."

She laughed. And then she thought of his words and stopped laughing, remembering her fantasy of him as a pirate. She looked up at him, and couldn't look away immediately.

"My lord Snow!" a voice hailed them. "Too well met! And young Martin. And the lovely Sophia. And a fair, fair unknown. I *am* in luck."

Now, here was a gentleman who had pirate tastes, Cristabel thought, seeing who had called to them. She couldn't help glancing up at Magnus to see if he agreed. A bright look from him showed her he'd thought the same thing. She could barely keep herself from giggling aloud.

He was a short man who looked a little taller because of his shoes, which had high red heels and gold buckles. He wore his cape open in spite of the cold day, so everyone could see his splendor. It was considerable. He wore a scarlet long coat with huge cuffs and a stiffened skirt that flared in front. His long vest could be seen beneath, and it was ablaze with silk peonies and poppies laced with gold. There was a fall of old lace at his throat and a white wig on his head so high, he had to carry his tricorne instead of wearing it. The wig ended in a long white ringlet at the base of his neck. The sword at his hip had a hilt so heavily encrusted with filigree, Cristabel was sure he couldn't use it to fence with anything but the side of a barn. And, she realized with appalled fascination, he wore paint on his wrinkled face.

"My lord Hastings," Magnus greeted him, "good morning."

"Give you good day, Hastings," Martin said cheerily, as Sophia curtsied.

"Good morning, my lords, Lady Sophia, and . . . ?" the gentleman said, as he swept into a dazzlingly deep bow, so complex that Cristabel wondered if he'd ever be able to get his legs and knees straightened out of it.

There was an awkward silence.

The truth was that for once, even Magnus didn't know what to say, or how to introduce Cristabel to one of the worst gossips in London. Whatever he might have thought to say died on his lips, because he suddenly realized he didn't know Cristabel's last name. It wasn't "Whiskey," that was certain. But he couldn't remember the famous pirate's real name.

Martin remembered. But he was afraid to say a word with Cristabel there to possibly take exception if he said the wrong one. And Sophia was afraid that if she said what she wanted to, which was something amusing, Magnus would kill her. If Cristabel didn't get her first.

"Ah," the gentleman said, his small eyes sparkling with mischief as he rose from his bow, "Lady No Name. A Lady Incognito in our midst. How diverting!"

"I'm no Lady Incognito," Cristabel said. "I be . . . I am Mistress Cristabel Stew, late of the Indies. It is where I was raised. My father sent me to England to be the guest of the Baron Snow and his good lady. My father is intensely interested in shipping, as are the Snows. He also wished me to visit the home of my late mother. And you, sir?" she asked so haughtily that Lord Hastings's grin slipped off his face.

"Oh. I am Hastings," he said. "Forgive me, it is Lord Harry Hastings at your service, my lady." He bowed again, even lower this time, because if there was anything Hastings appreciated and responded to, it was a good set-down, if only because he gave so many and knew their power.

When he straightened, Lord Hastings was very careful to be polite. He exchanged simple pleasantries, and wished them all a good morning again. But his eyes kept slewing to Cristabel.

"Did you ever?" Martin said excitedly when Lord Hastings left them and was gone out of sight. "Little sneak. He was hunting good gossip."

"And he would have had it," Sophia said, fanning herself in spite of the cold. "A good recovery, Cristabel. But what are we going to do in the future?" she whined, looking at Magnus imploringly. "Do you know what this will do to my reputation if the truth gets out?"

"She said nothing but the truth, and very cleverly too," Martin said, "Your father is 'interested in shipping.' So he is, so he is! I almost cried, I was trying so hard not to laugh. Well done, Cristabel."

"Well, maybe," Sophia snapped, "but it was a narrow escape. We can't let who she really is get out. 'Od's mercy, if it were known that we have a pirate's daughter in our house! Her father would be hanged if he was here, and I don't know if they wouldn't want to clap her in jail too. Well, even so, we'd be ruined if word got out. I didn't think of it until now, but now that I do . . ."

"There's nothing to worry about," Cristabel said, cutting across whatever other complaints Sophia had. "Word won't get out. 'Cause *I* will. I stayed too long as 'tis. I don't know what I were thinking of. Get me a suitable companion and point me to a good house in a quiet part of town and I be gone. If you don't, I'll go anyway, y'know. For I don't like the idea of sneaking round, lying and posing, no more'n you do, Lady Sophia."

She wished she could have said it in proper English, but Cristabel was so glad she'd said it without tears that she was proud of herself.

"And do you like the idea of dancing on my grave?"

Magnus asked Cristabel with a mildness he didn't feel. When she stared at him he said, "Because that's where your father, with all his 'shipping interests,' or more to the point, where all his good friends with shipping interests, would try to send me if you left to live by yourself before we settled this thing.

"And she wouldn't go to jail, sweet, dear Sophia," Magnus went on, with a look that made his sister-in-law pull her hood up over her head like a turtle snapping back into its shell. "She'd probably go to Court instead. The only danger she risks is becoming the toast of society. Cristabel is beautiful and wealthy and new to Town. She's pretty enough to desire, rich enough to envy, and good for hours of gossip—and that's all Society cares about. It would boost your esteem if it was known she was your guest, my dear. I forbid you to mention it unless Cristabel says otherwise. Is that understood?"

Sophia, now very pale, nodded.

"Are you going to forbid me to mention it too?" Cristabel demanded, drawing Magnus's attention away from Sophia. She didn't like the lady, but she felt sorry for her. Instead of growing white and silent, she herself would have flared up like a candle if anyone dared speak to her that way.

"Forbid you anything? What? And lose my ears? Hardly," he said with a little smile.

She found the tenderness in his smile as devastating as the thought of his anger had been. "Well, that's good," she muttered, before she asked, "Can we go home now?"

"You don't want to see anything else today?"

"No, thank you," she murmured. And so the two gentlemen walked two silent ladies home. One brooding, and the other remembering that he had said she was beautiful.

They had dinner, and afterwards, Sophia played the pianoforte for them. But they all were too thoughtful for much gaiety. It wasn't long before Magnus left. He asked for a word alone with Cristabel before he went.

They stood in the dim hall together. The footman there

discreetly left them alone. She didn't know what Magnus was going to say, and hoped and feared it would be that he agreed it was time for her to go off on her own. Today's encounter had frightened her; she didn't know if she was more afraid of what might happen to her if people knew who her father was, the gossipy Lord Hastings, Sophia's spite, or Magnus's opinion of her. She had planned to leave, and live anonymously. It seemed the safest way for all concerned. But it now also seemed to be the hardest thing to do.

"Society *would* accept you, you know," he said immediately. "You should aim as high as you like. You don't have to live in seclusion. What I said was true. There's nothing for you to worry about, Cristabel," he said when she didn't answer. "Sophia's used to being the center of attention. That, more than your father, is what galls her about you. And your beauty and your fortune, of course."

"Oh. I can hold my head high?" she asked bitterly, ignoring the compliment. "Knowing how many ships my father sent to the bottom of the sea? How many men and women he has killed, enslaved, and despoiled?"

"Sophia's father owns slave ships and invests heavily in that trade—or did, until I had a word with him," he said grimly. "Her grandfather was known as the most money-grubbing, close-fisted land holder in the North. And her grandmother played him false a dozen times that I know of. Do you see Sophia shrinking from public sight? Do you think I'd let harm come to you? We can tell the truth or spin a dozen stories and let them take their pick. You're not your father; you have nothing to be afraid of, I promise you."

She wanted to believe him, she yearned to. She also wanted to put her head on his shoulder and feel the strength and warmth of his support. When she looked up at him, she was startled because she almost believed he knew what she was thinking.

He started to speak and then saw her distress. He muttered something, low. And then lowered his head, and brushed his lips across hers. Only that. But it was like a brush with lightning. Her eyes flew wide. As did his. She didn't know which of them was the most surprised when he stepped back.

He stared down at her. He ran his hand through his hair and shook his head. "Good night," he said abruptly, and left her standing there, staring after him.

Martin had gone upstairs, but Sophia was waiting for Cristabel when she came back into the parlor. Cristabel was distracted, thinking about the kiss, and trying not to.

"I'm sorry," Sofia said abruptly. "I didn't behave well at all to you today."

"Is that what Magnus asked you to say?" Cristabel asked absently, "Never mind. I understand."

"Martin asked me to say it. Magnus would have told me," Sophia said. She twisted her fan in her hands.

"It doesn't matter," Cristabel said wearily, "Don't worry. I meant what I said. I'll go as soon as I can. I never meant to impose on you. You must hate having me here; I'm sorry for it. But even so, I won't stand for being mocked because I'm a pirate's daughter."

"You're the one who doesn't understand," Sophia blurted. "That has nothing to do with it. Or maybe it does. Oh, I don't know. I just don't know how you can be the one who's so low-bred and so shocking, and has done such dreadful things, and still they all admire you. You have them under your thumb. Even Magnus. While I—I have everything, and I'm so careful to do everything right, and still I'm nothing compared to you."

"What?" Cristabel asked in surprise.

But by then Sophia had fled from the room, and up the stairs. Since Cristabel could hardly follow her and knock on her bedchamber door for fear of encountering Martin in his nightshirt, she had to let it go until morning. Not that she minded, for all she really wanted to do was be alone and think about what Magnus had talked about.

But she couldn't remember. Not after that kiss.

* * *

Magnus was brooding about that kiss, too, as he walked toward his own house. Not the feeling of it; that would be like regretting the touch of sunlight in a dark place. But the meaning of it bothered him, the loss of control it signified. It should have been nothing. An airy little salute, the merest touch, the lightest, gentlest good night he could manage after looking down at her in that dim hall, feeling her hurt, confusion, and longing. God knew he'd wanted to do more. But he hadn't wanted to frighten her or commit himself to her. All he'd wanted to give her was one sweet, brief kiss to reassure her. To comfort her. And it had turned out to be like none he'd ever known. Fresh and sweet and electric. It had given much more than comfort and it had taken all his control to force himself away from her, and out the door.

Now he walked home without looking; as usual, he was without torch boy to light his way or footman to guard his side. He was still reliving the kiss when he suddenly found his passage blocked. He was surprised because, although deep in thought, he'd been unconsciously minding his back as he walked—the way any sane man walking alone in London at night did, and the way he'd been doing since Cristabel's father's men had attacked him. He hadn't sensed anyone dogging his steps.

The man appeared in front of him, stepping out of the shadows to stand with his hands on his hips before him. When he was sure Magnus saw him, he flung off his cloak. He wore a flowing shirt beneath a sleeveless long vest, and bloused pantaloons tied at the waist with a wide sash. The scant moonlight made a golden medallion glint on his tanned chest, and a diamond winked as it dangled from the lobe of one ear. He wore a tricorne with a proud feather in it on his dark head, and high, cuffed gauntlets on his hands. He held a sword in one of those gloved hands.

"Avast!" the man snarled, raising his weapon. "If you be m'lord Magnus Titus Snow, then draw your sword, man. Because I am your enemy!"

"'Ods teeth," Magnus sighed, reaching for his own sword, "haven't you fellows got the word yet? I am not her husband. Her idiot father married her to the wrong man. I have merely taken her under my protection."

"Aye. I know that," the man said.

"Then what's your quarrel with me?" Magnus asked, even as he stepped into position to parry.

"Just that," the man said. "You are the wrong man. But I am the right one."

CHAPTER

8

"I suppose this means you don't want to name seconds," Magnus remarked as his opponent lunged forward with his sword.

Magnus successfully parried the thrust, and his attacker's sword sizzled down the length of his own weapon with a metallic slicing sound, sparking a brief flash of light in the night.

His opponent recovered and drew back with quick grace.

"Glib and cold, aye, you're everything a cold bastard like yourself is supposed to be," the man muttered. "A fine lord with all the trimmings. Enjoy your jests whilst you have your life. It won't be long."

"Possibly. Your skill is a matter best known to yourself," Magnus said, as he surged forward, forcing his attacker back, "but I wonder about your estimate of me. We haven't met before, have we?"

"Aye, I meet lords and ladies all the time—but briefly," the man snarled, "before I send them to the bottom of the sea. I haven't met you before, m'lord, but I know your kind."

The conversation was halted as the man thrust forward again, his sword meeting empty air where he'd sworn the big man had been but a second before. The attacker's eyes narrowed. The fellow was the size of a full-rigged galleon, but he moved like a sloop on a windy day. He stopped thinking about his opponent's speed and only reacted to it when he saw him lunge. The big man's sword skimmed past his shoulder by micrometers.

"Now, I wonder," Magnus said, his rumbling voice showing neither alarm nor lack of breath as he pressed forward, "why does Cristabel's father want my death now? It was enough to try to beat me senseless the other night. What has upped the stakes?"

"I have!" the man cried, lunging again. And missing again.

The fellow was a good swordsman, Magnus thought, which was no small praise, because he was an exacting judge. But the man was fighting with his heart as much as his mind, and it would defeat him in the end. Magnus hated to see a good swordsman extinguished or crippled, so he decided to fence with words rather than his weapon for a moment. It would be easier for him, too, if he only had to defend himself. He knew he could do that for the rest of the night without strain. But he didn't think it would come to that. He had stamina and a clear mind, and his opponent was almost blind with fury. He had only to make him a little more angry. He thought he already knew the magic word.

"Do you imagine Cristabel will be pleased if you kill me?" Magnus asked, "I doubt it. She and I have come to an agreement . . ."

That *was* the magic word. The fellow snarled and leapt. But swordsmanship was not acrobatics, however pretty it looked. Magnus watched, waited for the precise moment, and then struck. A quick thrust under the fellow's hand as he lunged forward caught his hilt on Magnus's sword tip. Magnus pulled and shoved, and then in one sharp motion he flung his opponent's sword up out of his hand and into the air, spiraling it into the moonlight. It clattered on the cobbles, too far for the man to reach without turning his back on Magnus or retreating to a wall.

Magnus looked back from the sword to his foe, and found him crouched low, circling him with a short, sharp dagger in his hand.

"And when I divest you of that, there'll be a cannon, I suppose," Magnus said wearily. "Do you think we could talk before we go on? I think it would be better for you, at least. You're very angry. I'm not . . . yet. That's not fair. Anger is a man's best ammunition."

The fellow stopped, and looked at Magnus straight on. "No," he said in an odd voice, "you know that's not true. Anger will be the death of me. I'm likely to die this night because I'm so filled with hate, and you're so calm and amused. I'm wondering why you're telling me that if you know that calming me down might even the score."

"*That,* I doubt. I'm very good," Magnus said, but he watched the other man closely and didn't lower his sword as he added, "but I have an aversion to killing strangers. Introduce yourself, tell me your grievance, and then we'll get on with it if you like. I am, as you say, Magnus, Lord Snow. And you?"

"Black Jack Kelly," the fellow said, bowing mockingly, but keeping his dagger clenched in his hand and his eyes fixed on Magnus, "the man Cristabel is going to marry."

"Ah," Magnus breathed, reevaluating the man he faced as best he could in the dim light. Almost as tall as himself, young, with a dark, dashing face, and a long, trim body in his soft pirate clothes. "I see. And she knows this? Odd that she never said a word about it. She spoke of her father and her plans for the future, but never mentioned you at all."

"She has to come round to it," the fellow said, shifting his feet, with the first hint of uneasiness he'd shown, "but she will, she will."

"Oh. I see. I think you had better pull up a curbstone then," Magnus said, "because I think we may be here all night."

* * *

The dark and smoky tavern light flattered the man at the table with him, Magnus thought. Even so, it was a handsome face, scarred in all the right places, with rakish dark eyebrows and a lush black mustache for emphasis. Long, straight, shining jet hair bound with a bandanna added to the look. He was lean and spare and hungry-looking, with long, watchful blue eyes and an infrequent smile that showed sharp white teeth. The man was smaller than he himself was, but not by much. And fit and dangerous. Magnus observed him closely, though only those who knew him well would recognize that his casual, half-lidded gaze was intense. They would have been as surprised as was he by the uneasiness he felt as he studied the man sitting opposite him.

The pirate, Magnus decided, was a formidable opponent. He thought he himself was the better fencer and probably the better man—if only because piracy was, after all, thievery on water. Magnus would never take anything he hadn't earned, and thought he would starve before he would. But no doubt the ladies would love this rakish fellow. He found himself wondering, and to his discomfort, worrying, about how much one particular woman who claimed she was half a lady felt about this pirate.

The pirate had agreed to parley when he'd realized there was no immediate need for him to kill Magnus. That was only after Magnus convinced him that he was neither husband nor lover to Cristabel. It was clear the pirate wanted to be both to her. Now Magnus found himself having a difficult time controlling his own murderous urges.

"I've known her since she was a tyke, and I just a green hand," Black Jack was saying now. "I believe I had me eye on her even then. Well, captain's daughter and all, and I a lad eager to get ahead." He laughed and shook his head. "Had I knowed what she was to grow up like, I'd have stolen her away then and devil take the consequences! So much for currying favor with Captain Whiskey. When it came down to it, I wanted her whatever her pedigree."

He paused to swallow more ale, before he went on, "He promised her to me, y'see. And so when I heared he married her off to you! Well, the lads had to hold me back, for I was all set to jump right overboard and swim to England to get her back. But the lads said what's done's done, and I figured there was no way even me paddling like a fury would win back her maidenhead. What's that to me when all's said? It's her I was after, breached or not. So I set out when I could, determined to make her a widow before I got much older. I mean to have her, y'see, maiden or widow, whichever way. She's mine."

"I see," Magnus said, his voice a low, comfortable rumble, his body relaxed. The only thing to betray his nerves was his big hand, which was tightened to white knuckles on his cup, and the faint flickering of the muscles bunching in his jaw. "But if you are her fiancé, why did her father marry her to another man?"

Black Jack shifted in his seat. "Ah, well, Captain Whiskey be a pirate and a good one, a fair man but a tough one, all to his good, and so say I to anyone. But he's a climber, y'see. Married himself a lady, he did. Wanted a gentleman for his daughter too. I'm his crony, and the best man he knows, but I'm common as the dirt beneath my fingernails, for all that."

"You don't speak like a pirate," Magnus remarked.

"But I ain't a gent. Nay, I wasn't born like Cristabel, her 'half a ladyship,'" Black Jack said mockingly, with such a parody of Cristabel's constant claim that Magnus's jaw knotted tighter. "No. But I ain't nothing, neither. An honest cottager is what I was born. With the soil of Ireland at me feet—and almost over me head before I got much older," he added ruefully, "for we was starving, and that's a fact. I went to sea as a lad, as an honest sailor working for the queen's coin. And by the time we had ourselves a king, I was sailing against him.

"Want to know why?" he challenged Magnus. "Count the stripes on me back, and take a guess. Or the bones in me face, broke by one of His Majesty's fine captains. Say what you will about the Brotherhood—but we don't try to force pretty young lads to our berths if they don't want to play our games. I jumped ship, and found fair employment with the bad lads of the sea. In so doing, I discovered the lot of a pirate: The food's better, the voyages shorter, the companionship closer, and the pay's ten times better than that of an 'honest' seaman."

"And the conscience?" Magnus asked dryly.

The pirate was brought up short. His smile was crooked as he answered, *"That* I'll be telling you, m'lord, when I can afford one."

"You've not shown a profit yet?" Magnus asked, "I'm surprised; I'd assumed you were expert at your profession by now."

"Aye, that I am. But the gold goes fast as it comes in, seeing as how the Brotherhood lives higher than your average man. The gambling, the fancy houses—there's nothing on earth as good as the brothels in Tortuga. 'Cept maybe those in Kingston town. No, I make money the same way I lose it—with pleasure. And I've no regrets . . . save for misplacing me Cristabel. But I'm here to see to that. She'll be the making of me, you'll see. With her in me bed, the gold will stay in me pockets. As to the rest? I be a pirate bold and thank the Lord for it too!"

He raised his voice and his mug in mock salute to Magnus. No one in the crowded tavern even looked up. It was the sort of place where Black Jack was safer announcing his occupation than Magnus was in his fine clothes. But Magnus's size and air of casual confidence—and his sword—gave him safe passage here just as it did everywhere else in London at night.

Magnus's face had gone very still at the mention of the pirate's plans for his bed, but his voice was calm and even when he spoke. "I see," he said thoughtfully. "And so I wonder why Captain Whiskey was so quick to marry his daughter to another."

The pirate's shoulders jerked before he spoke again, trying to sound as casual as Magnus had. But he looked into his mug of ale instead of at Magnus as he muttered, "Like I said, the captain be a climber. When he saw a chance to nab a viscount for her, he tried. Ha!" he said with real enjoyment, meeting Magnus's eyes again. "I'd give three bags of Spanish gold to see his face when he finds out the truth! Imagine! Wedding her to the younger son by mistake. And worse yet for his plans—not marrying her at all! Outsmarted—the fox outfoxed! He'll choke on it, it's so rich. And well he may. Aye, and I'd give another dozen bags of gold to see his expression when he finds out I've wed her after all!"

Magnus's broad shoulders stiffened, as did his hand on his own mug of ale. But his voice remained languid. "Now, that surprises me," he mused, "because she claims to want only her independence. She's accepted my protection because she's wise and has been made to see the need for it—and sees no other course right now," he added ruefully. "But she fought it like a tigress, and I know it rankles still. In truth, I can't see her going off with you, my friend."

"She will," Black Jack promised in a low snarl.

"And," Magnus added, "I have to tell you that I won't see her going off with you if she doesn't want to."

It was only one sentence, but Magnus said it slowly and coldly. Then he was still. The pirate stared at him. Magnus met his eyes with a bland gray gaze.

"Ah. I see," Black Jack said. "I take your meaning. I will consider it. But I'm wondering. You're a gent, true. And so maybe you just feel protective toward the wench. But I'm wondering if there be more to it. There's more to her, to be sure."

"So there is," Magnus agreed, but his face remained impassive.

Black Jack rubbed his jaw as he studied the big man he sat with. "I wonder," he mused. "No nobleman such as yourself wants such as her for a wife. She claims to be half lady, but the other half be pure pirate, and no mistake."

"You don't believe her claim?" Magnus asked quickly.

"Oh, 'tis true enough," the pirate said on a shrug. "It were before my time, but all the lads know it for truth. The great Lady Elizabeth—Captain Whiskey's even got her name tattooed above his black heart, lest anyone forget he once bedded a real lady. He even fitted up a figurehead of her for his favorite ship: a frigate he took off the coast of Spain. The thing has too much in the breast and not enough in the eyes, or so the old hands say, but otherwise ain't a bad representation of her. She looks too saintly for me taste, but Cristabel's said to be her spitting image, and so she must have been a beauty, all right. But the lady is long gone, and Captain Whiskey had the raising of her daughter.

"No, I doubt a gent like yourself wants such a lass to bear his noble name, and his sons," Black Jack went on, "but I tell you, if it's the something else you're after, you're fishing in the wrong waters, m'lord. The Cristabel I know would tear off your face afore she'd consent to be your—or any man's—mistress. Her father, rot him, with his parade of sluttish mistresses and all them poor sad, bedraggled creatures he brought home to teach her to be a lady—and taught her instead to hate men. He near ruined her for men forever."

"Odd. She doesn't seem to hate my brother, or me," Magnus mused.

The pirate slanted him a bright look to acknowledge the slight, but his broad white smile was without humor. "Aye, but your brother was no threat to her, you said—being as he's so young, moral, and married, to boot. As for yourself," he purred, "why, m'lord, it just may be she don't consider you exactly as a man neither, being accustomed, as she is, to pirate folk.

"She's used to men with hair on their chests, like they say," Black Jack chuckled. He seemed amused, but beneath his vest his hand crept to his dagger's hilt as he looked for rage on the big man's face. Seeing nothing but a cool gray gaze, he relaxed, shrugged, and added, "Still, whatever it be, I can tell you this: She's got herself a problem. A famous one. She's one and twenty and never had a man, nor wanted one. In fact, the better-looking the fellow, the more she resists him. I can't remember all the names she's called me in me time! Nor the many ways she's threatened to remove my hand if I lay so much as a finger on her." He grinned, as if in fond remembrance.

Magnus lifted one thin brow. Keeping his temper so firmly in check that he appeared incredibly bored, he asked merely, "Then why do you want her as wife?"

"Use your eyes, just look at her, man! Ah, but it ain't just her pretty face, nor that glorious form. It's her, herself. With all her fears and anger, she's pure fire beneath. It's herself she's fearing as much as any man, I tell you. She feels the lure same as any woman, more than most, in fact. But she don't want to become like none of them poor sad wretches her father or his men ill used. For whether they be married or slave, or freeborn whore, she never met no female at home she wanted to grow up to be."

Magnus nodded. He had sensed the conflict in her too. What bothered him was that this man was also clever enough to have seen it.

"Aye," Black Jack went on, "fire. And the right man can set it free. I count meself to be that man."

"I see," Magnus said again. He let out a long sigh and rose from the table. He put his two hands down flat on the top of it and looked down at the pirate. "I'll take you to see her tomorrow," Magnus told him, "if only to save myself the trouble of preventing you from breaking into the house. But mark me well. You will meet with her. You may speak with her. But nothing else. Not tomorrow. After that it will be entirely her decision. I will abide by it . . . and so will you."

Black Jack studied him for a long moment. Then he, too, rose. He spat in his palm and then thrust out his hand. "Done!" he said.

Magnus took off his glove. They shook hands.

"Ten o'clock then. I'll be here," Magnus said.

The pirate grew a slow, long, and toothy smile, just thinking of how it would look for him to swagger alongside the viscount at ten in the morning, and then go up the stairs to his brother's elegant house in the respectable part of town where he lived. He'd spied the place out when he'd first arrived in England, looking for windows to enter should it be necessary. The thought of a pirate fool enough to show his nose on a sunny morning on such a street in London town almost made him laugh aloud. His smile grew wider. It would be good to take the big fellow down a notch or two, he thought, as he prepared to tell him of the sheer idiocy of his suggestion. *Ten* indeed.

"At night, of course," Magnus added, causing the pirate's smile to fade. "Till then," Magnus said, nodding, and turning on his heel, he walked out.

He left the pirate to stare after him, frowning, reevaluating the big man he'd just fenced with in so many ways, thinking furiously and wondering. And worrying.

There was no one at the table when Cristabel came down for luncheon. There was a footman at the sideboard and another to lay out her plate for her. But there was no sign of Martin or his wife.

"The master has gone out," the butler remarked when Cristabel stood and looked at the empty chairs at the table. She'd never been alone in this room before. "And the mistress has decided to have her meal in her rooms. She suffers from the headache."

Cristabel froze. It might be true, but it was more likely just an excuse. It was terrible to think that her hostess disliked her so much now that she couldn't even bear to sit down to eat with her. If that was so, then she had to leave this place at once. She'd take charity from no man and insult from no woman. But she wouldn't inflict pain on anyone for no good reason either. She hadn't followed Sophia to her room last night for fear of involving Martin, but Martin was gone now.

"Thank you, but I think I'll not eat just now. I feel a twinge myself," Cristabel said.

Sophia's maid's eyes widened when she saw Cristabel standing in the bedroom door. But not as much as

Cristabel's did when she looked into the room beyond her. Sophia wasn't lying down in bed, a victim to the headache—as Cristabel had half hoped she would be. Instead, she was turning this way and that before her mirror, holding a smaller looking glass in her hand so she could see the pretty white wig she wore from every angle.

"Yes, I think this one—with oceans of powder, of course—don't you, Annie? Annie? Oh!" Sophia said, catching sight of who was at her door, dropping her hand and gaping at Cristabel.

"I came to say good-bye," Cristabel said woodenly, although she hadn't. She'd come to thrash the matter out, to find out what exactly she'd done to offend Sophia.

But seeing Sophia as she was now—in a rosy-colored day gown, wearing a charming little ringleted wig on her head— made Cristabel's breath catch. Even half-dressed, Sophia looked like the complete lady Cristabel had always dreamed of becoming. She stood in her ornate room with her hovering maidservant, looking like a china doll in an oil painting that belonged in a wide gold frame. Everything in the room was delicate and tasteful, from the fragile gilded chairs to the great tester bed with its satin coverlets. The wig was the final touch. It was all frothy ringlets, and it sat proudly on that little head.

She didn't have to listen to Sophia. She didn't belong here, and she knew it. "I came to tell you that I'm leaving," Cristabel said, not permitting her voice to tremble, "and to thank you for past favors."

Sophia gaped at her.

"I be gone before you know it," Cristabel said, for something else to say. And turned to go.

"No!" Sophia shrieked. "No, no, no, no, no. You mustn't! Oh please. Oh, what are you gawking at, Annie?" she asked, her distress replaced by a sudden air of cold command. "Go downstairs and get us some . . . tea. Yes, tea. Mistress Cristabel and I shall have tea together. What are you waiting for? Go! Now, Cristabel," Sophia said when the girl disappeared. She marched over, pulled her guest into the room, and shut the door behind her. "What are you talking about? Leaving? You can't."

"I can, and I am," Cristabel said. "You don't have to put up with me for one more minute; that, I promise you. I'd have told you last night, but you'd gone to bed, and I didn't want to disturb Martin. Bad enough to have an unwanted guest," she muttered, as though to herself, "worse to find she's snooping about in your bedroom after dark."

"Well, you wouldn't have bothered him," Sophia said, "because he's never here. He'd be furious if you left, I can tell you. Magnus would kill him."

Cristabel only heard the first words, and they struck her to the heart. "Oh, I'm—I'm so sorry, Sophia; I didn't know," she gasped. "How brave of you not to let on. At home, a wife with such a problem would be screaming the house down."

Cristabel stopped, and winced when she heard what she'd said, damning her reckless tongue again. Her sympathy for Sophia was so intense that the words had just spilled out. Sophia's composure only proved again what a lady she was. A pirate woman whose man rejected her would wail and carry on, or carry on in other ways, with other men, to show she didn't care. But everyone would know the truth, one way or the other. The worst thing that could happen to a woman was for her lover to be untrue. The shame of it was that great. Trust a true lady to know how to deal with shame with such calm fortitude, Cristabel thought sadly, looking at Sophia with awe.

"What? Whatever are you thinking?" Sophia asked curtly.

"You know—Martin not ever being here . . ." Cristabel stammered.

"Of course he isn't. This isn't his bedroom. And—and he doesn't expect to be here," Sophia said, her voice getting a little lower, her face growing just a tint of pink. "We've—we've made other arrangements, you see. How awkward," she murmured. "I didn't think. We should have, I suppose, but after all, you're our first houseguest . . . At any rate, there's no problem. Certainly no need for sympathy. But you can't leave, that's the point. Why would you want to? Is there anything you lack?"

"No, of course not," Cristabel said. "It's just that you hate me so much . . . What kind of arrangement? You've only been married a year. Martin did naught but talk about how beautiful you were, aye, every night, all the way across the Caribbean and into the Atlantic."

"Did he?" Sophia asked, diverted. She patted her wig. "Well, that's very nice of him. Of course, he tells me, too, but it's good to hear that he told others. Especially a girl he slept with every night for a month."

"He did not!" Cristabel shouted. "That, he did not! He slept in *the room* with me. He didn't want else, nor did I. I'd have laid him open from his nose to his toes if he did; that, I promise ye! I'm not his woman. *Ye* be. But now ye be telling me yer not?"

"'Od's mercy!" Sophia said, pacing in agitation. "Look you, Cristabel. Sometimes husbands and wives come to certain agreements, especially here in London . . . Martin and I have known each other forever. We always planned to marry. Neither of us ever wanted anyone else. But when I turned twenty, and he two and twenty, our families got involved. The long and the short of it is that my father said that if I didn't marry by the time I was one and twenty, he'd marry me off, and devil take the hindmost if I didn't like the fellow he picked. The truth is . . ." She hesitated before she blurted, "He had a bosom friend who had a son, and there was just a chance he'd seize the opportunity to please his friend rather than me. So Martin and I agreed to marry sooner than either of us planned.

"Well," she said, "we both were mighty happy being single. Since I had to marry, and since I really don't want babies"—she said the word as if it were "rabies," Cristabel thought—"at least not just yet—I'm so young, and having such fun—we decided to, ah, forgo that part of our marriage, for now. There being no other sure way to prevent them, after all."

"But babies are the best part of marriage!" Cristabel gasped. "They're worth all the rest. They're the only reason I would ever wed. Oh!" she said, her hand flying to her lips and her eyes growing round. "Does that mean you've . . . *never?* You and Martin? Oh. I'm sorry, I shouldn't have asked."

"Of course we have," Sophia snapped. "One has to on one's wedding night, after all. But after that—I'm not shirking my duty. Just delaying it."

"Well, I think that's terrible," Cristabel said staunchly. "Poor Martin. Men have certain needs, you know. Unless—please don't say it's all right with you if he has other women?" She was appalled. Pirate women might be free with their favors. But the one thing they wouldn't tolerate was another woman touching their man. It was the cause of the greatest battles between men and women at home. Of course, it was also the constant cause of them, pirate men being no more faithful than were their women.

"Certainly not!" Sophia said.

"Then it's not fair," Cristabel concluded. "If you're not going to take care of a man's needs, you've got no right tying him up in marriage. It's part of the bargain."

Cristabel stared at Sophia thoughtfully. Even though her hostess was a fine lady, and a married one, they were both about the same age, and neither had any older female relatives nearby. At least, she'd never seen Sophia with any family aside from Martin and Magnus, although it might just be that she didn't want anyone from her family seeing her odd guest. Still, for whatever reason, Sophia didn't seem to have an older woman as confidante or counselor. Nor was she married the way Cristabel thought of being married. In fact, in many ways she was as alone as Cristabel herself. And maybe more vulnerable. It occurred to Cristabel that there might be some things ladies didn't know, because they were ladies. Although she'd learned so much from her governesses, there were some things they would never discuss. She'd had to learn about what went on between men and women from pirate women. And she'd learned a lot.

"Look you, Sophia," she said hesitantly, "I've heard a lot of females talking in my time, and they're freer with their tongues than ladies. From what they say—it's clear that which goes on 'twixt a male and female is a peculiar thing. You can't always judge it right from the first time, they say. That time is like a try cake—just made to make sure the skillet's hot, and better off thrown away and forgot soon after. It doesn't mean the rest of the batch of hotcakes will be bad. Just the reverse, in fact."

"There was nothing wrong with that time," Sophia said at once, looking harried and defensive. But Cristabel was too involved with framing her thoughts to notice.

"Then that's very good, to be sure," Cristabel said carefully, "since it's a thing—well, as I hear tell, it's a thing females either like or they hate. But more than that, for some it takes some getting used to—like sailing," she said with happy inspiration. "Why, the first time my father took me out, I thought I'd leave my gizzards at sea forever, and now I can sail in a waterspout and not turn a hair . . ." She saw Sophia's expression and paused.

"But this I do tell you," she went on with utter sincerity. "For them that like it, it's supposed to be such a wondrous good-feeling thing that they can't ever do without it again. Aye, 'tis that good, 'tis what they say. And so it must be. Else why would sane women put up with philanderers and drunks and bad men like they do? Not just for the babies— it can't be that. No, it must be a wondrous thing indeed. It just takes some getting used to. For women. Men, they say, enjoy it mightily from the first. Think, Sophia. If that's so, why then, 'tis a cruel thing to deprive the man you love, isn't it? Especially if he's an honorable man, who won't seek it elsewhere."

There was a silence when she was done. Sophia stared at her. Then she shook her head. "A fine thing that I should be lectured about the intimate side of my marriage by a pirate's brat! And in my own home at that!"

"I'll be going," Cristabel said.

"No," Sophia yelped. She gave Cristabel an odd look, and

then laughed. "I listened to you, didn't I? And I told you things too. I suppose I wanted you to know, and wanted to know what you thought too. I have my own doubts, sometimes . . .

"But as for you," she said, eyeing Cristabel closely, "I'll be as honest with you as you were with me. I didn't like you being here, that's true. And I certainly didn't like what you just said. But it might be true. And it might be that I needed to hear it even if it isn't. It's certainly true that if you leave, Magnus will be furious. I won't be the reason for a break between him and Martin. Martin adores him, and to cause a rift between them would be very wrong of me.

"English gentlemen are not pirates, Cristabel. An English gentleman will give up his own pleasure for his lady's pleasure. Martin says he doesn't mind, he only wants to see me happy. I know other women who have the same arrangement we do. In fact, many won't let their husbands into their beds ever again after they've given them a handful of children. In fact, it's becoming quite fashionable . . .

"However that may be," she went on, "let's stop fighting, shall we? I need you here. And truly, you're not as bad as I thought you'd be. So please say you'll stay, will you?"

Cristabel nodded. It was a poor apology, but perhaps it was the best Sophia could do. She decided to accept because she didn't really know where else to go. It was a thing she'd have to start thinking about, she decided as she walked back to her own room. She didn't belong here. This incident with Sophia just proved it once again. She felt even more odd and out of place than she had before.

She'd tried to offer sympathy and understanding and had gotten her nose snapped off. And she didn't even know why. Her education hadn't prepared her for this. She didn't understand gentlemen or ladies and didn't know if she ever would, or should. It might be a fashionable thing for Englishmen not to bed their wives, and even though she'd once thought that such an arrangement could only happen in heaven, now she wasn't so sure.

It should have been a fine solution for her. She should

have rejoiced to hear that such arrangements were possible. But now she didn't know if she could ever live that way.

Such a husband would have to be a shadow of a man, one she didn't care for at all. When she thought of a man she'd care for—a tall, strong man with controlled emotions showing nowhere but in those knowing gray eyes—she couldn't imagine living like a nun with him. If he were in the house with her day and night, as her legal husband, with every right and cause to be intimate with her, she'd be tempted to touch those wide shoulders. She'd wonder what it would be like to put her hands on that broad chest and feel that great heart beating beneath them. Simply thinking of those big, long-fingered hands of his made her realize where she'd like them to be . . .

If such a man didn't come to her bed, she'd think that she was repellent.

And if he did come to her, she'd become his slave. A mewling, complaining, eternally unhappy woman, like all the ones she known, giving her heart to a man, allowing him to take pleasure and then discard it. She could not bear it. She would not.

Anyway, she thought as she drew a shaky breath, it would never come to pass. She knew better. And as for him? Well, she was foolish to think he felt anything more than responsibility for her. The thoughts went round and round in her head as she went to her room to pace until dinner, when she would see him again, and perhaps know some answers. Or greater confusion.

Magnus didn't come to dinner, though he had been expected. They sat and listened for the door to open all through the meal, but they went from soup to fish to fowl to beef to puddings and cakes, and still he didn't come.

After dinner, they adjourned to the parlor again. Sophia sat at a small table and played a solitary game of cards without looking to see if she'd won or lost. Occasionally she'd look up and study Martin, frown, and then fiddle with her cards again. Martin sipped port and made desultory conversation, and Cristabel didn't know what she said in answer. She couldn't stop thinking about what she had discovered. These new revelations frightened her, and it wasn't in her nature to be afraid of anything. The only thing that made her feel better was the realization that Magnus was too much a gentleman to take advantage of her. He probably didn't want to, anyway. Which somehow made it worse.

When they heard the door knocker and voices in the outer hall, they all stopped breathing and stared at the door. And when Cristabel saw him standing there, tall and strong and with a slight smile on his bold mouth, she knew, in that one instant, to her shame and her fear and her utter delight, that her life had been nothing until she'd met him, whatever came of it. She rose, with a glad smile on her lips.

His eyes went straight to her. Seeing her expression, he smiled back at her. She opened her lips to speak. And only then saw who stood at his side, dark as the shadows around them, but clear as the nose on her face.

"Damn you for a bleeding Judas!" Cristabel shrieked, louder than all the fishwives in Kingston town on a sunny Friday morning. "Double damn yer black-rotted guts, y' filthy, slimy double dog bastard of a whoreson!"

"Be that me, m'lord," Black Jack Kelly asked on a wide smile, "or you?"

CHAPTER

9

Now, don't draw steel, luv," Black Jack cautioned, backing away from Cristabel's fury. "His lordship brought me meek and mild, and that's how I want it to stay. I come after you, and I want you to hear me out. Devil me if you don't look fine, though! You were an eyeful as a pirate lass, but drop me if you don't take me breath away as a lady."

Cristabel ignored him. She was used to pirates and their flattery. They would tell any woman that she was pretty just to pacify her, and nine times out of ten, it worked. But not on Cristabel.

"*You* brought him!" Cristabel said to Magnus, in a voice filled with astonishment and pain.

"Would you rather I refused him and forced him to climb in one of Martin's windows one night—or worse? The only way to keep him out was to kill him, and I hesitated to go that far," Magnus answered.

"Hesitated?" Black Jack said, scowling. "Now, it never came to that, m'lord, but if you think you can, then—"

"Stow it," Cristabel told him in disgust before she spoke to Magnus again. "I take yer meaning, m'lord, and thinking on, I don't disagree," she sighed. "It were just such a surprise. I mean, it *was* such a surprise—ah, you were right,

128

my lady," she told Sophia. "Just see what having a pirate's whelp as a houseguest nets you—more pirates. Like having mice," she grumbled, and turned away so no one could see the real hurt and distress on her face.

Black Jack was a handsome fellow, but every inch a wild buccaneer. From his black looks to his wild clothes, he personified everything she was trying to forget. She couldn't bear to see Sophia's reaction, much less Magnus's. Had she dared to look, she'd have been surprised. As Cristabel despaired, Sophia was staring at Black Jack with fascination, Martin was smiling—and Magnus looked very worried. By the time she turned around again, Magnus had recovered his cool expression.

"Master Kelly has things to say to you, Cristabel," Magnus said, "and I deemed it better they be said in company, as they would be with any other lady. Unless I misread the situation and you'd rather be alone with him?"

He'd called her a lady. She looked at him with sudden rising joy. Then she calmed herself, clasped her hands, and said with as much calm confidence as she could pretend, "No. You were right. If you've something to say, Jack, I think it ought to be said in front of my friends."

Black Jack gave her a glittering look. "Aye, then," he said on a shrug, "if the fine lady and gentleman don't mind me cluttering up their parlor?"

"Oh no," Sophia breathed as Martin said, "Of course not."

"Aye, then, I'll tell you all," Black Jack said, "since there's nothing in it *I'm* shamed to have anyone hear."

But the whole encounter had already made Cristabel feel ashamed. She could only nod her agreement, raise her head, go with them into the parlor, and wait for Black Jack to have his say—and for them all to see her shameful past put on display.

Sophia was stunned. It was as good as a night at the theater. Cristabel was a pirate's daughter, and she sometimes spoke like one. But this man actually was a pirate, there was no doubting it, and he was in her house as her guest. If he'd been any other man wearing outmoded clothing and speaking in such harsh, uneducated accents, Sophia would have sneered. But he was so exciting, so teakwood-tanned and virile, he didn't look foolish or quaint, even in what looked like his grandfather's clothes. His golden jewelry looked as barbaric as his wicked smile. She gave a delicious shiver. It was terribly dangerous and yet perfectly safe. Her husband and his powerful brother stood between her and any danger. And though it was a little disappointing, in a comforting way, of course, it was obvious the pirate had eyes for no one but Cristabel.

Cristabel sat in gloom. She knew she was entertaining a figure from the past, too, and she didn't like it. Because it was her past.

"I don't think the capt'n knows yet," Black Jack was saying now. "Takes three weeks to cross the sea, and don't I know it, even if they set out the minute they found out and had a high wind behind and no rain afore them. So 'twill be a while yet. But I'd give a hogshead of rum to see his face when he does!"

"There's nothing he can do," Cristabel snapped, "however he feels."

"Oh, I wouldn't say that," Black Jack said. "We're talking *Capt'n Whiskey* here."

"Aye. But Captain Whiskey's *there,*" Cristabel countered. "There's a price on his head here. He won't risk his neck for a mere daughter. Not when he's got a new woman with the promise of sons in her."

She looked at Black Jack in triumph, but then her heart sank, remembering who else was in the room. Magnus may have appreciated her looks. He might admire her spirit. She'd sometimes thought she'd glimpsed other longings in those usually unfathomable eyes. But surely he wouldn't want anything from Captain Whiskey's daughter. Why did life have to keep reminding him of her lowliness? she wondered sadly. Truth was part of life, she concluded, and she was the only one who kept trying to deny it.

"Well, there's that," Black Jack admitted. "She's a planter's widow, and there's rumors he wants to give up the sea for sugarcane and rum."

"Planter's widow?" Cristabel scoffed. "Never. Carmen's a waterfront whore, and everyone knows it."

"Aye. That be Carmen. But the word is, it ain't her—'tis a rich planter's widow he's going to make it legal with. Off island, and a grand plantation, they say it is too. A little thing, she is—a churchgoing lass, but full of scrap. Widowed once and tiptoeing into her thirties. But she don't want to go there alone. She's set her heart on the captain, God help her. They say she's determined to lead him to church and keep him there after the ceremony. 'Tis not a new leaf—'tis a new life he's after pursuing. And who can blame him? He's ancient for a pirate, and wise enough to know it."

"I see," Cristabel said. The truth hurt. "Well then, it makes perfect sense now, doesn't it?" she shot back at him. "How convenient it would be for you to step into his boots with his daughter at your side, so as to keep the lads happy and thinking nothing's changed at all."

"You know that don't matter," Black Jack said calmly. "How long have you been gone, Cristabel? You can't hand down a pirate ship and crew like a king passes on his crown. No, when your father steps down, there'll be blood and battle, and when the smoke clears, it'll be me who has the title 'Captain.' And who's at me side don't make no difference.

"Look you," he said, leaning forward and staring at her. "One, your father ain't gone yet. Two, I want you no matter who he is. And three, you know that's how it'll be and there's no sense running, or playing the grand lady. You ain't no lady, and all here know it. You're just fooling yourself and giving them a laugh. But it doesn't matter to me. Nor will Captain Whiskey care no more. He tried to marry you high, and botched it. He'll be glad for you to take me. And so will you. Come home with me now, lass, and that be the end of it."

Before she could answer, Magnus did.

"No one here is laughing," he said in a voice Cristabel had never heard from him—all the rich humor was gone from it. "Nor will anyone else. Society is like a pirate ship in some ways too: No one will care who boards it so long as she's in the right company. And Cristabel is," he went on in that same deadly cold voice. "Don't doubt it.

"Now, as to her plans? I thought she wanted to make England her home; it's half her heritage, after all. I thought she chose to stay here and get London accustomed to her before she made any further decision to move on. Was I wrong, Cristabel?" he asked, his voice gentling, but his eyes still hard on Black Jack.

"No, you were not," she said. "That's what I thought to do . . . after you convinced me to do it," she told him with a broken laugh. Then she turned serious eyes on the pirate. "I don't want to go back, Black Jack," she told him. "Not ever. If you think it be a joke that a half a lady tries so hard to be a whole one, why then, I tell you it's just as cruel a joke for me to try to be all pirate too. I never felt right at home, Jack. Never. I don't fit in here either, but at least here I think I can live out my life quietly and happily.

"You are a good man," she told the pirate before he could answer, "for all you are a pirate. I never heard of you taking pleasure in killing or torture. Nor were you one to force a woman—I know, I know, you always said you didn't have to, but I know it's a point of honor with you too. You do have honor, in your own way. But otherwise you follow the Code, even though it's a harsh one."

She sighed, "Were I to ever love a bold pirate lad, I suspect 'twould be you. But I can't. I can never be with you—can you not see that? Don't ask me no more, 'cause it pains me to naysay ye, Jack, 'cause you were always fair with me, and kind, in yer way."

She turned her head away, but not before the others saw

tears escaping and running down her cheeks. Magnus handed her his sail-sized handkerchief a second before Black Jack produced his bright bandanna.

"I didn't come to England to make ye cry," Black Jack said gruffly, "so leave off. I'm willing to wait and see. As for now," he said, rising from his chair, "I think I'll have meself a look at London town afore I leave it. I'd best be leaving here just now anyway. It never pays for a fellow in my profession to light too long in any strange spot, not knowing the tides hereabouts and all. We be like gulls in that." He grinned at Martin. "I come by night, but it's never dark enough to suit me, for I don't know which of your fine neighbors might think I'd look prettier on the end of a rope than in your parlor. So you take care, Cristabel," he said, touching her cheek with one long finger, "and I'll see you here and there."

She looked up quickly. "You'll not leave England without saying good-bye?"

Magnus frowned as Black Jack's grin grew wider.

"Not me, lass," Black Jack assured her, "and I'm not so sure I'll ever have to neither."

"I meant," Cristabel said with a sniff, "that you be a friend, and although I'm not casting in my lot with you, I care what happens to you."

"I know just what you meant, lass," Black Jack said happily.

But he said it in such a way as to make everyone in the room wonder long after he left them.

In her brief life, she had faced down the fiercest pirates in the Caribbean, drawn steel against double-died villains who'd lusted for her, sailed halfway across the world on a strange ship with a strange man, and landed to find herself a stranger in a strange new world. She'd done all of this bravely, head held high. She had even dared defy her self-appointed protector: Magnus, Viscount Snow. But Cristabel found herself afraid to descend a staircase now, for there was nothing she feared more on earth than mockery.

She ran her hands over her gown once more. Made of apricot silk, with a tiny pattern of roses, it had a low, square neckline graciously ornamented with old lace, a tight bodice, and the full skirt looked fuller because of the hoop she wore beneath it. She wore her mother's single pearl set in gold around her neck. That part of her attire would pass, she supposed. But her hand strayed to her hair again, and she gave it a tentative pat. It felt so odd, she knew it couldn't look right. But Sophia and her maid had insisted. She wore her hair powdered tonight, like a lady. And felt like a clown instead.

It was such a hearty application of powder, she thought she'd sneeze her eyes out as it was put on. But when they removed the nosecone that was used to shield her face, she stared and stared into the looking glass. There was a mass of white curls high on her head, with long ringlets resting on her shoulders in back. It made her skin look dazzling; her eyes glowed like firestones. She looked nothing like herself. But she *did* want to be a lady, after all. She was afraid and vulnerable as Captain Whiskey's daughter would never be.

She went downstairs with a prayer that no one would laugh in her face.

And forgot all her worries when she saw Magnus standing at the foot of the stair, looking up at her. She almost forgot to take her next breath too.

He wore a dark topaz silk coat, with lace at his broad chest and his sleeves, a long vest of ornate design, and dark silk breeches. The white of his powdered hair made his skin glow gold and set off his long, gray eyes. But all she saw were those fine eyes as he studied her.

They stood and stared at each other, neither seeming to realize it until they heard Sophia's voice coming near. Then Magnus bowed and said, his deep voice fogged and low, "You look beyond lovely tonight, Cristabel."

"But—my hair," she murmured, touching it again.

"Lovely," he repeated, and then added in a lighter tone, "for a change, mind. Beautiful as it looks, I like fire more than ice. I find I miss the bright sunrise in your own hair. For tonight, though, it's perfection."

Cristabel reached the bottom of the stair and gave him a tremulous smile.

"'Od's mercy!" Sophia said as she left the parlor and came into the hall. "Stop fussing with your hair, Cristabel. You'll have all the powder on the floor before you know it and ruin Annie's work. I still don't see why we can't go to the theater first," she complained, resuming her argument with Martin. "The play's been on for a week and is sure to change by tomorrow. Everyone says it's so diverting. Can't we go there first?"

Magnus turned his usual calm face to her. "You may," he said. "Martin too. But I won't go to the theater with you again, Sophia. It never is diverting enough to make you stay past the first act. Martin may not mind leaving without seeing the conclusion, but I do. And don't say you'll stay for my sake: If you do, it will be with so much sighing, squirming to see what the audience is doing, and gossiping, that I'll probably strangle you before the second act. I don't know how Martin puts up with it."

"Well, at least it's cheaper that way," Martin laughed. "Since you don't have to pay unless you stay for the second act, I get to see every play in London and not pay a penny piece to do it."

"And money means that much to you?" Magnus asked cynically.

"No," Martin answered, "but Sophia does."

Sophia looked at him in as much astonishment as his brother did. Then Magnus nodded, a small smile on his lips.

"Touché! Well done, brother," Magnus said in pleased surprise. "Now then, shall we go? If you two want to go to the theater, we'll meet you at the Porters' house later."

"Oh, nonsense," Sophia said, with flustered pleasure, "as if we'd desert you now. Although I don't know why Cristabel is worried. It's only a small assembly, only some two hundred or so guests stuffed into the Porters' house. It's not like it was a grand assembly, or even a masked ball."

"But it's Cristabel's first appearance in London at night," Magnus said, "and it's important to her."

"We really don't have to go," Cristabel said, as she'd been saying since they'd told her about the outing.

"I thought you wanted to learn everything about your new country," Magnus said.

She did, but she didn't want everyone watching her. He understood this and knew she would never admit to fear. Smiling, he held out her cape.

The ladies' gowns were too wide to ride comfortably together in a coach, and so sedan chairs were called for. Each lady was carried in a sedan chair with one bearer at the poles in front, another in back, and her gentleman walking beside it. A torch boy ran ahead of each chair and two footmen trotted behind, but each gentleman walked with his hand on his sword's hilt and his eyes on the darkness beyond the jouncing flares of torchlight. This was London at night, after all.

The lights were blazing from the windows and opened door of their host's home. When it was their turn to enter, the sedan chairs were carried right into the hall of the crowded house and each lady stepped out directly into the throng. As Magnus paid the bearers, Sophia immediately found a friend to exclaim over. Martin was hailed by his friends. And Cristabel stood and stared around herself.

Magnus turned from the sedan men and looked down at her with such a look of tender pride that all eyes went to the lovely girl. Cristabel wondered what she had ever worried about.

She could see a room for dancing beyond the one she stood in, but although music played and the musicians sawed away at their strings, there wasn't even a pretense of dancing going on in there. There was no room for more than swaying. In fact, there were so many people pressed into the house, she could scarcely tell one from another. It was all a welter of fine fabrics and white wigs, wide skirts on the men's coats and women's gowns, powdered ringlets and glittering jewelry. Above all rose the surging sound and smell of two hundred people who had come in from a cold night to be crammed into an overheated house that should only hold one hundred. Cristabel could have come in rags, or tags, or a velvet gown, she thought on a rising giggle—no one would have noticed or cared.

She was wrong. Just as a miser knows to the fivepence exactly how much money he's amassed, the rich and influential people of London knew just who belonged in their gilded circle. Every one of them wondered about the strange and beautiful young woman standing at the Viscount Snow's side—the girl he was looking down at with such a look of fierce and gentle interest.

"Mistress Stew, from the Indies, father in shipping," was the whisper that soon went round with such energy, it nearly caused a draft in the overheated rooms. Rich and beautiful as she was mysterious—and likely to remain so, at least with Snow to stand as her cavalier. Even the worst rakes and fortune hunters didn't dare risk his displeasure. Not that he blocked them. He introduced her here and there with an easy smile and a calm voice. But his possession was clear to see in his stance and in the back of his knowing eyes. "Well, the big man's caught at last," was the next whisper, and they turned with a sigh to see what other gossip they could discover this night.

Magnus led Cristabel into the crowd. She was introduced to so many people, she gave up trying to remember them. She smiled and nodded and didn't get a chance to say a coherent thing to anyone for an hour. By then, some of the guests were beginning to leave.

"Sophia will stay until there's no one left to see or talk about," Magnus told Cristabel as he saw her look longingly at the doors when she felt a cool breeze as they closed behind a departing couple, "but we'll leave whenever you want to."

"Do you want to stay?" she asked.

"'Od's life!" he said with a huge smile. "I didn't want to

come in the first place. I was for going first to a French restaurant that just opened in the Strand, and then to a small gathering at another friend's house. But Sophia said we should take you to the finest private party in London tonight. She said she was going anyway, and then added that you might take it amiss if I didn't take you along too. She said you might think I was trying to hide you if I didn't."

Cristabel put her head to one side as she thought about it, "Aye. I might have," she admitted, "but now that you have, I wish you'd taken me to the restaurant and your friend's house instead. Can we leave soon? It's worse than a pirate's picnic here, I think."

He threw back his head and laughed. "Stay right here, Mistress Stew," he told her. "I'll be back in a moment. I'll say good night to Martin and get a sedan chair for you."

He left her standing in a niche between the ballroom and the hallway, and then disappeared into the crowd. She waited, nodding and smiling automatically as people swam past her. And so she didn't really see who she was looking at until the man stopped in front of her, put his hands on his hips, and gave her a wide, gleaming smile. His handsome, dark, clean-shaven face was enhanced by his snowy white wig. He wore a fashionable scarlet silk long coat with oceans of ecru lace at its heart and sleeves. His shoes were buckled with silver, his vest laced with gold. As that smile slowly grew wider and wider, she began to recognize it and realize this fine gentleman wasn't one of the gallants Magnus had introduced her to.

"Black Jack!" she breathed in startled horror. "What can you be thinking of?" She looked around, her heart thudding and her eyes wide. "Are you mad?" she whispered in fright, "There be a price on yer head, man!"

"On that scallywag's Black Jack's head, mebbe," he answered, "but not so much as a penny to be made on that fine gentleman Master Jarvis Kelly's head, don't y'know? And that's who I am tonight. You almost didn't know me yourself. And why should you? I scarce recognize meself.

Look you: no mustache, not a speck of me beautiful black hair to be seen neither, I'm shorn clean as a lamb, white and gentle as one too. And if you believe that . . ." He grinned.

His smile vanished. "Ah, lass," he said, "forget about me—look about. What are you doing here amidst these foolish fops and fancy molls? Not a grain of sense in their heads, nor one idea neither. Call this having a good time? I know you want to be a lady, but I tell you I can't see it. Why, there's scarcely a female here I couldn't have beneath me in less time than it takes to tell. The only difference betwixt them and an honest whore is that the ones at home charge less, and offer more. You don't belong, lass, no more'n I do."

"You may think what you will," she said proudly, "but this is the world my mother came from. I think I could become used to it."

"Aye, I suppose you could become used to it," he agreed, "but don't fool yourself, luv. They'll not become used to you. Nor are you your mother. You look beautiful, to be sure. But you're standing alone. And if they knew who you really was, so you'd remain. Without the big man at your side, you're no one at all. Even without me, you'd be someone at home. Think on that, lass. Think on it long and well. You'll have the time. I'll wait for you to come to your senses. It won't take long. You're a clever lass, for all your wild dreaming. In the meanwhile, I do believe I'll have me some fun."

"If they catch you . . ." she warned him.

"They won't," he said, grinning, "not if I go off with a fine lady who don't want her husband to catch her—ah, don't fret. No need to be jealous. I said I'd be giving you time, didn't I? I can live like a shipwrecked sailor for a few more weeks—knowing the feast that's to come when you come to your senses. But there's more to life than willing wenches—there's gambling and drinking to be done." He touched a finger to her nose, bowed, and melted into the crowd before she could warn him again.

"What happened?" Magnus asked the minute he returned, his hand going to his sword when he saw her pale face, "Who offered you insult?"

"No one," she said, and was glad the sedan chair only seated one, because she didn't know what to say.

When they were back in Martin's house again and all alone, she told him.

"Don't worry. He's right. He can take care of himself," Magnus said when she was through. He was vastly relieved. He'd known something was wrong—he'd seen it in her face and it had struck him to the heart. But this was something that didn't threaten her—it might, he realized, threaten him.

"You, ah, don't worry about him, do you?" he asked casually.

"Black Jack? Not in the usual way of things," she answered. "He's tough and clever—amidst pirates. I don't know how he'll manage in the social world."

Magnus roared with laughter. Literally. Cristabel and Magnus were standing in the parlor, but it was such a full and merry sound that the footmen in the outer hall grinned at each other when they heard him.

"'Od's teeth, but you're a funny girl," Magnus said, looking down at her with a tender smile, "to worry about the fate of such a black villain at the hands of those fops and their ladies."

"He's not such a villain," she said quickly, "or rather, well, I suppose he is. But not as bad as some others. There's bad, and then there's bad . . . or maybe what I'm trying to say is that there's bad and there's *evil*. Neither he or my father is precisely *evil*, though they do wicked things." She clasped her hands together and gazed up at him as though for confirmation.

"I don't know your father," Magnus said quietly, "but if you love him even though you know you must escape him, then—no, I doubt he's really evil. As for Black Jack—do you love him too?"

He hadn't meant to ask that. He was astonished that he'd

140

blurted it out the way a boy would. But suddenly he had to know.

"Love?" she asked, her eyes searching his. "No," she said, "not in that way. But I wouldn't want to see him come to harm."

"Odd," he said, unable to resist the urge to touch one white curl that lay on her white shoulder, "I find I envy him."

She barely felt the slight touch, but it made her shiver, deep inside. "Do you think I wish you harm?" she asked, growing very still.

"I think I wish you trusted me," he said softly, his hand caressing her shoulder now.

"I didn't get to my great age by trusting too much," she said gruffly, trying for a quick retort so he wouldn't guess what his touch was doing to her insides—she felt as though the sea were getting rough beneath her feet. She loved the feeling.

She was hesitant and nervous with him tonight. Her insecurity was new to Magnus. It was her fierce courage that usually amused and intrigued him. But tonight she was shy and tentative with him. That hurt as well as drew him to her even more. He always responded to the lost and lonely. Tonight she seemed just that—more so because she was trying so hard to be brave. She stood before him, lithe and perfumed, dressed as a spun-sugar lady, and she was so desirable to him. He thought she looked beautiful, but he thought her own radiant hair was magnificent. It was these contradictions—the fire of her own hair beneath the ice white powder, the indomitable spirit beneath the guise of the brittle lady of fashion—that fascinated him, and undid him at last.

"Cristabel," he murmured, her name itself a caress the way he said it in his deep voice, "ah, Cristabel, what are you doing to me?"

He didn't let her answer. His kiss was light, almost hesitant, until he felt her lips, soft and surprised, beneath his. Then he took her deep into his arms and with infinite gentleness, held her close and hard against him as he kissed her again.

She was surrounded by him, his strength and tenderness melting her as no man had ever done. She tasted his kiss and burrowed into his embrace as though she were coming home to safe harbor. He whispered against her mouth and she felt her lips parting just as he asked. She responded to the next question she found on his lips, although she hadn't known the answer until he silently asked for it. Yes, she thought dazedly, of course she wanted his tongue against hers, though it was as strange as it was thrilling. She felt his hands on her back, then gently on her breasts, and shivered at the way they feathered over her, seeking and adoring. It made her weak and strong all at once. Although it felt as though he were shaping her for his pleasure, she was pleased to let him do it.

The pleasure was overwhelming. And it was the pleasure that made her stop—the pleasure she was taking in his touch.

"No, no," she breathed. Although his hand was on her breast and his mouth approaching hers again, he stopped the moment he heard the first word. It gave her time to recover a bit, and that little pause was filled with worry: Would he do this with a lady? She didn't know. Her confusion and desire spoke for her.

"What be I thinking of?" she whispered to herself as well as him. "I kept me virtue in a pirate den. I can't lose it here."

"You won't," he said, still holding her close. "Don't worry. Virtue is never lost, it can only be given. If given to the right man, there is nothing to fear."

She looked up at him with hope and fear. "Ah, my lord," she said in despair, "what be you doing?"

He thought about it, and his eyes widened. He knew the truth then, and it was as if a great weight had been removed from his chest. She needed him as no other woman ever had, and he needed her. He wanted her as he'd wanted no other woman. It was a shame that the circumstances weren't right, but it was time. He knew his mind and knew he was a possessive man; he couldn't let her go on living in his brother's house, so close and so far. He couldn't continue taking her around London, watching men from her past and future vie for her, and not say anything. She wanted to be a lady, she behaved like one, and so she was one in his eyes and heart. He couldn't trifle with her. She had to know as soon as he did.

"What I am doing," he told her with a small, crooked smile, "is wooing you, Mistress Stew. That's what I am doing."

He felt her body tense. She put a hand on his chest and stepped back from him, holding him at arm's length. Her eyes were wide and shocked. "I will leave!" she said, her nostrils flaring as though she scented fire.

"No," he said, his voice gentle, but his hands firmly holding her from fleeing, "no, not for anything would I let my intentions send you running into the dangerous unknown. Hear me, Cristabel. I said I'd woo you, but I'd never harm you, force you, coerce you, embarrass you—or whatever it is you're worried about. Do you understand?"

She bit her lip and nodded, unable to meet his eyes. He could feel her trembling, and his heart sank.

"Perhaps 'woo' is too strong a word," he said, craning his neck, trying to see her expression. "I'll try to become a friend. You can't have too many friends, can you? We'll come to know each other. It may be that when you do, you'll decide you dislike me. If so, I'll bother you no more, I promise. Look you, my dear," he said, and his voice was strained, "I know I'm not to every woman's taste. No man is. As for me, I'm too big, for a start, and I've been told I'm overbearing and pigheaded—just hear Sophia on that subject," he said ruefully. "So if you find you agree with her, just tell me and I'll leave you alone. No man can force affection, and though it would pain me, I'd never persist where I'm not wanted."

She put up one hand to stop him. He clasped it in his own. "No," she said in a small voice, "don't apologize. It's not that. You don't bother me. It's just—it's just that I felt you were mocking me."

"Mocking you?" he asked in amazement. "Why should I do that?"

"Or—trying to get round me." She blurted the worst at last.

"Why, so I am," he laughed. "That's what wooing is. Seriously, Cristabel, my intentions are honorable. I'd never bring anything but honesty to you. Be sure, I'm speaking of marriage, nothing less."

She was more shocked. "That can't be!" she gasped.

"Oh yes it can," he said, drawing her close again. "Your father isn't here to accept my declaration of intent, but I think we can take it as given."

"Don't be a fool, man," she cried. "I be a pirate's lass, and you a great lord."

"I don't know what ideas you have of England, my dear," he chuckled, "but this isn't the kingdom of Good Queen Bess anymore, where the rules of Court are the rules of the land. In fact, there are no more hard rules; we live in a kingdom whose king can't even speak English. And if there's one advantage to being a nobleman, it's that I can marry where and when I please: an earl's daughter or a miller's daughter; it's my choice."

"An earl or a miller, aye," she said sadly, "but never a pirate's. My father's a wanted man."

"And you are wanted by me—a wonderful symmetry, isn't it?" he asked, rubbing his cheek against her hair.

"Nay, you don't understand," she sighed. "It cannot be."

"It almost was, remember?" he said calmly. "And so it will be. You don't have to say yes immediately, though it would be wonderful if you did. I understand. You don't really know me yet. I can tell you I'm clever and bold, brave and rich too." He laughed, but then grew sober as he said, "You delight me, mind and body. I'll hold and protect you for the rest of my life, you have my word on it, and there's no mortal power that can make me break my word. But how can you know that? So. I will play the suitor. I can woo you and find pleasure in that. But I mean to have you as my wife, Cristabel Stew, and before too long. Be warned."

Her eyes were filled with despair. "I be a pirate's daughter," she said again. "It can never be."

"And a lady's daughter," he reminded her, "and so it shall be."

He drew her close and kissed her again, and after one stunned moment, her hand left his chest and slid up around his neck. But there were tears on her lips now.

He stopped and looked down at her. "Is it that you don't think you can ever love me?" he asked seriously.

She shook her head violently, and said, "No, 'tis not that . . ." before he cupped her head in his hands to stop it shaking, and put his mouth over hers to silence her denials.

He let her go because he knew there was nowhere else for them to go tonight.

"I'll leave now," he told her. "And don't worry."

She shook her head again. "You don't understand; I can't do this."

"We'll talk about it again tomorrow," he said. "I promise I won't nag you—but that doesn't mean I won't try to seduce you." He grinned, dropped a light kiss on her lips, and left her.

She stood looking after him for a long time after he'd gone. He'd startled and stunned her, and almost convinced her. But now that he was gone and the force of his personality wasn't coloring her thoughts, she could see she was right and he was wrong, on so many counts. She couldn't marry him. There was a natural order to things. Fish of the same sort swam in the same schools, parrots nested in trees with birds of a feather. There was about as much possibility of finding a shark mating with a tuna as having a marriage between a nobleman and a pirate's daughter. His world would never accept her, and in time, neither would he.

She knew men. They acted irrationally, on the spur of the moment and at the spur of desire. That which made them men often did the thinking for them. "A man's brain be in his breeches," the pirate women said. "Men are governed by their lusts," her governesses had said. It was so. She'd seen it again and again. She'd thought Magnus was above that. Obviously he wasn't. And now, she realized, after knowing his kiss, neither was she.

He desired her, but he was a good man and so would marry her in order to have her. But she was a good woman and knew she couldn't have him, one way or another.

Even though such a marriage might be possible—with Magnus almost anything might be possible—and even if the pirate's daughter *could* become a viscountess—she wouldn't marry him. No matter how she felt about him. If there was one thing she knew, it was that to marry was to become as nothing.

She'd seen it too many times. After marriage, a man's desire was replaced by boredom, his devotion vanished, and deceptions were practiced. Marriage meant being shouted at, lied to, or sneered at. She'd never seen a happily married woman. She'd never seen a man so in love with his wife as was her father—but only because his wife was long gone. She had pride and independence; she couldn't trade that for three or four months of love. She knew her own heart. She could bear to be abused and mistreated, but she didn't think she could bear to live to see her love betrayed.

The sight of Magnus set her heart to racing; the sound of his voice seemed to vibrate through her bones. His touch made her forget herself entirely. If such a man possessed her, surely he would possess her very soul. And when he turned against her, there'd be nothing left of herself. She shivered and wrapped her arms around herself, but the chill came from within. This love, this desire for a man, was the greatest danger she'd ever known. She was smart and brave and bold. But even the bravest left the battle when there was no chance of winning.

Cristabel went to her room to weep. She'd left the Islands in despair, thinking she'd gotten herself married to a stranger. But she hadn't cried anything but tears of vexation

146

then. Then she'd snatched victory from what had looked like defeat, and found herself free as she'd always longed to be. Now she wasn't free anymore. She'd found what she wanted, and needed, and knew she couldn't have it. First she would weep. Then she would decide what to do.

Magnus knew he'd still be there. A determined gossip stayed at a party until its last gasp. Lord Hastings wouldn't leave until the housemaids started sweeping over his feet. Sure enough, when Magnus got back to the party, although most of the guests had gone, the too elegant lord was sitting listening to a drunken fop complaining about his tailor. When he saw the Viscount Snow return to the party, Lord Hastings's eyes brightened and he left the morose fop to come to Magnus's side.

"Ah, Hastings," Magnus said, "well met, sir. I came back to see if I could find a missing buckle, but no luck. It's foolishness itself to wear good silver on one's shoe—so I suppose I deserve the loss. Still, I find you here and that's good fortune. Now that I think of it, you could do me a great service, if you would. You've a head for names and faces, don't you?"

Lord Hastings nodded eagerly. It wasn't often a prime buck like Snow even asked him for the time of day.

"Well, then," Magnus said, "think on, if you please, sir. I was talking with an interesting gentleman when we were separated by the crowd. Then I had to take a lady home. But he was telling something to my benefit about trade in the Islands, a thing to do with investments," he said vaguely. "I'd like to continue our chat but can't recall his name, if I ever heard it right in all the babble."

"Of course, of course, too pleased to be of service. What did he look like?" Hastings asked eagerly.

"Well dressed," Magnus said hesitantly, as though in deep thought, "wearing a white wig, a pleasant-enough looking chap. Wait," he said as Hastings looked chagrined, because he'd just described almost every male who had been there that night, "one thing I do recall. Singular thing, actually. He said his family's lived in Canterbury for generations on end. That, I do remember."

"Ah. Canterbury. Well then," Lord Hastings said, thinking furiously. "Yes, yes, well. That could be young Tilsiter. John Tilsiter, bright young lad. Old family, old-fashioned. Did he have a mole on his chin?"

Magnus frowned. "Not sure," he said.

"Then it could be Sir Francis Raynor. His family's been there for generations too. Did he have a lisp?"

"Ah, might have," Magnus said, thinking deeply.

"The only other person it could possibly have been is FitzWilliams, George FitzWilliams. He's looking for a wife again. Was he tall and thin?"

"That might be he," Magnus said heartily, "Thank you, sir. You don't know what a help you've been."

Lord Hastings preened himself, and was about to start a really interesting conversation about the mysterious glowing girl Snow had brought to the party, but before he could open his mouth, Magnus bowed, turned, and strode off into the night again.

Once there, he chuckled and patted the buckle he'd pulled off his shoe and put in his pocket before he'd gone back to the diminishing party. Grinning, he strode home. Three names of men of Canterbury—where Cristabel's lady mother had come from. All gotten without anyone knowing the wiser. Lord Hastings had helped him more than he knew, and certainly more than he'd ever know.

CHAPTER
10

〰

We have a house in Kent," Magnus was saying, "not too far from the sea. I think you'll like it. It's our principal seat and my favorite house. I hope to take you there soon as the weather's warm enough to make the trip comfortable."

He had an estate in Kent with more rooms than a blowfish had eggs, Cristabel thought glumly, or so Sophia had said. She paced along at his side as they strolled through Green Park.

"Of course, we've also got a snug little place up-country, in a land of lakes and stone circles. It's wild and magical there. Deep summer's the best time to go, but it has its enchantments in winter too; if it weren't such a tedious trip, I'd take you there to see it now. But the inns are as unreliable as the roads are," Magnus said pensively. "Travel's no easy thing in this land, especially in winter."

He owned a mansion on a lake there, as well as half the adjoining town. And his own dairy, greenhouse, and blacksmiths, two coaches, and more horses than she'd seen together in her life. Or so Sophia said.

"Then there's the place in Wales, beautiful and wild, with a waterfall nearby. But that's really remote. That's definitely for another time," he said, grinning just thinking about himself and Cristabel on their honeymoon, alone together in the warm old house set deep in the forest.

"The finest house my father has is a seagoing one," Cristabel told him. "It's the size of a mountain, made from trees from the mountains of the North and fitted out with the best woods from the East besides. His cabin has mahogany floors and a window high as two men and so wide, a child can stretch out to sleep on the ledge in front of it without her feet touching either end. It shows the sea better than the eye of a whale does, far and wide and to the horizon. The sunlight sparkling off the water shows off his beautiful carpets and bed dressings—all silk and damask from every land that touches the sea. He has fine compasses and maps, spyglasses and sextants, globes, and a desk made of solid oak besides there. He won it. It used to be a Spanish ship—it's truly a place fit for a pirate king," she said, her voice growing soft as she traveled back to that magical place in her memory.

"But a ship's no place for children, except for a visit," she went on. "The finest house I ever lived in was in old Port Royale, before the quake. It had five rooms and glass at all the windows. But the *best* place I ever lived was the house I was in when I met Martin. It had two rooms, little green lizards running on the walls, a tin roof, and no glass for anything but holding rum and water. It was surrounded by flowers. It was by the sea, and you could hear it at night like breathing when the tide licked at the shore . . .

"Of course," she said in a suddenly altered voice, "that was when there wasn't a party going on down by the shore. Or when there wasn't a new crop of prisoners to keep fenced in there. On those nights, all you could hear was laughing and screaming, moaning and music."

He stopped and faced her. Her hands were deep in a fur muff she held like a lifeline in front of her. He put his hands lightly on her shoulders.

"My father likes to play chess," he said, looking down at her averted face, "interminable games, some played by post, with men from remote parts of the kingdom. It takes weeks sometimes for him to know his opponent's next move. I never saw anything so tedious in my life, and when I was a child, I could never understood why he got so excited when he received a letter with another move in it. His hands would actually shake. I don't play chess to this day. I can, but I don't."

She realized he was trying to spare her feelings, but her voice was still sad when she answered, "Yes, but I doubt he ever hurt anyone playing chess."

"I doubt *you* ever hurt anyone when your father was holding his revels," he said.

She nodded, conceding the point, and dared to look up into his concerned eyes. "Where does your father live?" she asked in a brighter voice.

He smiled a crooked half smile and she felt her heart turn over. "Very good," he congratulated her. "My father? Why, he lives in Kent. But when we visit, it might be hard to find him because he generally stays in his study."

"And there are about a thousand rooms," she said snidely.

His eyebrows rose. "Ah, Sophia's been chatting with you," he said, taking her arm as they began to walk again. "No, actually there are nine hundred and sixty-five rooms less than a thousand."

She tried to imagine such a huge home and gave up. "Ah, a cottage, I see," she finally said.

They laughed so loudly, they sent a squirrel scurrying up a nearby tree. The park was winter-locked and still, but various hardy people of fashion walked and rode by and bowed to them as they passed.

"When you have a house like that," she said awkwardly, because she didn't know if it was right to ask, but she was curious, "does your whole family live in it together? I mean, you said Martin has to look after his estate now. Does that mean that he and Sophia live there with you and your parents?"

"Worried about my relatives crowding you out of my house?" he asked, and grinned when she looked knives at him. "Don't. The estate in Kent is our principal holding, so it's my father's and one day will be mine—one day a very long time from now, God grant. Martin has his own estate in Surrey and another that was Sophia's portion, in the West country. Don't worry, if you don't care for family, our house in Kent has enough rooms to hide from them in—no lizards, though, I'm afraid. Otherwise I think you'll like it, if you don't feel cramped by my parents. The house in the North and the one in Wales are my own, so you won't have to share if you decide we should live there instead. You don't have to choose right away; we can winter in London until the children come and then make up our minds. Or we could keep traveling between houses like Queen Bess in a bad temper, if you like."

"My lord," she said with warning.

"No joking matter? I agree, we'll be very serious about it. Where do you want us to live?"

He was being impossible, and she knew he knew it by his wide grin. They'd been having such a good time, discussing things that were interesting but not dangerous. Talk about books had led them to the book *Robinson Crusoe,* which they'd both read. That led to talking about the Islands, and then homes, and then he'd started in again about what they'd do when they were wed—as he'd done for the past week since he'd announced his intentions to her. He hadn't kissed her since, but his talk was more and more about their future together. It was all so frightening, tempting, and puzzling. She couldn't marry him. But neither could she leave him—just yet.

She had to change the subject, fast. "Will Sophia go to Surrey with Martin in the spring, or to her own home, or will she stay here, do you think?" she asked.

"Why do you ask? Have you become that attached to Sophia?"

"No, it's just that I don't understand some of the things you noble people do. Since they don't live together, I wondered," she said.

"What?" he asked, stopping in his tracks. "Now you've

lost me. How do pirate couples live together any more than Martin and Sophia do? This sounds promising."

"No, I mean, since they don't *actually* live together the way married folk do, I mean, not sleep together and . . . Oh, damn 'n blast, 'n curse me blasted ruddy tongue," she muttered, running out of words as she read the look of astonishment on his face, and knew she had a lot of explaining to do.

But he didn't say much when she was done with her halting explanation.

"What a fool. Still, Martin acts much younger than he is," Magnus sighed. And Sophia—I might have guessed." He stared down at Cristabel and smiled. "This, my dear, is not what's customarily done in England, I promise you. If it were, we'd have very few Englishmen, and if you'll take a look around, you'll see we have no scarcity. Only a young idiot like Martin, married to a shrew like Sophia, would come to that kind of arrangement. Most men and women find a shared bed a shared joy, Cristabel; it's said to be one of the greatest delights in marriage."

"Well, I don't see what's the matter with what they're doing," Cristabel argued. She'd say anything to wipe that tender, amused, intimate expression from his face. It was too unsettling. "I mean, why should a female have to bear children just to make her husband happy?"

"It doesn't always result in babies," he reminded her. "If it does, it makes her happy too. Or should, if there's love in it. But you know that."

"I know that men use the word 'love' to get women into bed," she snapped, "and I know they find that bed right uncomfortable, since so many are so happy to bounce right out of it again to try for a more comfortable berth in some other woman's bed."

"Cristabel," he said with absolute sobriety, taking her muff in his two hands and sliding his hands inside to hold hers tight there; his hands swallowed hers up. His voice was low enough to chill her, warm enough to make her blush. "This much, at least, I can promise. I'll never deceive you,

Cristabel. There'll be no other woman for me after we are wed. It's not my way. You have my word."

His expression made her want to look away so she could hold on to her composure. But his wide shoulders blocked out the scene behind him. His face was the only thing she really wanted to see anyway, and so she closed her eyes, and hardened her heart. "I won't wed you," she said.

"Ah, the pirate's daughter and the sultan's son thing again," he sighed.

"Earl's son," she corrected him, slipping her hands out of his warm clasp.

"Same thing." He shrugged, and they started laughing again, in spite of how hard Cristabel tried not to.

When the wind picked up, they returned to Martin's house. Cristabel wasn't used to an English winter, and though she said she found the cold invigorating, Magnus noticed she said it through chattering teeth. Sophia was out shopping, so Magnus delivered Cristabel to Martin.

"It's too cold for a troll out there, much less a tropical flower," he told Martin, and then warned Cristabel, "so warm yourself thoroughly this afternoon, and then bundle up again and be ready, because I'm coming back to take everyone out to dine tonight at that new French restaurant in the Strand."

She wanted to say she'd prefer not to, but there was nothing she'd rather do instead. It was dangerous and unsettling for her to continue to stay here and keep seeing him, but the thought of leaving the only house and the only people she knew in London was terrifying. Especially since she knew it wasn't the house or the people she'd miss, but only one man. She could leave, of course, she told herself: She was brave enough to do anything. But she didn't know if she was more afraid of knowing him better or of never knowing anything more about him. The only way to find out was to continue staying until she did know. Somehow that decision, which was no decision at all, pleased her. She nodded.

"Fine. Until then," she said lightly, and turned from him and went to her room.

"Some flower, with steel petals," Martin remarked when she'd gone.

"Yes, but that seems to be the only kind of female we Snows appreciate," Magnus said in a troubled voice.

"Speak for yourself, brother," Martin laughed. "Cristabel looks like an orchid, but she's surrounded by thorns. My Sophia looks like an English rose, but she's more of a tender clinging vine."

"If she has no thorns, then why are you so afraid to get close to her?" Magnus asked.

Martin stared at him.

Magnus thrust his hands into his pockets and shook his head. "Pay me no mind, brother," he said gruffly. "I spoke out of turn."

"Out of your mind, not out of turn. What are you talking about?" Martin said, but his fair skin betrayed a growing flush on his neck.

Magnus jerked his head in the direction of the study, and without a word, both brothers went into the room and closed the door behind them.

"It's not my business," Magnus said immediately, turning to stare out the window so he could avoid his brother's eye.

"Since when has that stopped you from saying anything to me?" Martin asked, but there was more tension in his voice than merriment.

"True," Magnus said gloomily. "''Od's blood! Is it this way with one's children? I treat you like the child you were, but I know you're not one anymore. Yet if I don't, I think I've failed you . . . In truth, Martin, this thing is not my business and yet it is because you're always my business."

"What thing?" Martin said, growing very still.

"If you have a houseguest, you should be sure your house is in order," Magnus growled, "especially if she's always watching everything around her, wanting to learn the ways of a new land and copy them." He ran his hand through his hair, turned around, and glowered at Martin. "I had to tell Cristabel that it is *not* the way of the land. That a man beds his wife in this land . . . if he can. Or else he becomes a monk, or stays a rake. But a wife is not an ornament or a male friend. She's more than that, or should be."

"And if a man wants to spare his wife children?" Martin said through white lips.

"Then he spares her his name, damn it!" Magnus said. "Why marry if you don't want children anyway?"

"I do want children," Martin said, his face reddening.

"And she does not?"

"She does, but not just yet—I don't know why I have to justify this to you," Martin said angrily.

"You don't," Magnus began, but Martin interrupted him.

"It's just that she's so young, she wants some fun before she's encumbered with a baby," he said defensively, "that's all."

"That's a great deal," Magnus said soberly. "Life is very short and uncertain, as we both know too well. We had two sisters and a brother whose children we'll never see. And you and Sophia are no longer children. It worries me. I thought you were too young to marry, but you said you must have her. Now you do, and you don't. You could have remained a friend, but you chose to become a husband. It's just an empty title. Since you're her husband now, I think you'd better start becoming one, or else—ah, Martin, I only tell you this because I worry about you and the bargain you've made. There's a time and a tide in the affairs between men and women, just as the Bard said. There's a danger too. If you play the monk too long, you'll become one in her eyes. Love is in the heart, but desire is born in the eyes. It dies there too. If you treat her like a sister, you may become a brother to her in time."

"Really? That's good then," Martin said stiffly. "It might be for the best. Because I think I need one myself now. A different one."

Magnus raised his eyebrows. "I see," he said. "So be it." He bowed curtly, and left the room, and then the house.

Magnus was very glad he had important errands to do, because he refused to think about what he'd just done. He didn't want to think that once again his love had failed to save someone, and worse—might have actually lost him someone dear.

He strode through the streets of London, his mind focused on his errand. His first stop was at a particular coffeehouse in Pall Mall. A waiter told him that the young man he was looking for was sitting near a window with a paper. He introduced himself and then joined young John Tilsiter, of Canterbury, and had to listen to an hour of foolish opinions on the new king and his consort. But in the course of that hour, by carefully placed, innocent-seeming questions, he learned something that made him spill his coffee across the tabletop. He made profuse apologies for his clumsiness, saying it was because of the size of his hands; and was glad no one he knew was there to see it because they'd know he was never clumsy, hands, feet, or body. But he couldn't afford to let the boy know it was due to his shock.

When Magnus left, he was his usual calm self again, sure that young Tilsiter had gotten the story wrong. It had all taken place before his time, after all, and so surely he had to be wrong.

Then Magnus dropped in for a bite to eat in a tavern in St. James Street, where, as he'd been told he would, he found Sir Francis Raynor with a group of friends. Again he had to make idle chat for another hour, and had given up hope of getting the man alone, when Sir Francis announced he had to go home to change for dinner. Magnus swiftly offered to accompany him. The willowy Sir Francis was delighted to have someone Magnus's size with him as dusk began to fall. They chatted as they strolled, and didn't stop until Magnus stumbled. He regained his balance, and joked about his ridiculous size and gracelessness until he was sure Sir

Francis had forgotten what he'd been talking about when he'd missed his step. But he still couldn't believe it. After all, Sir Francis had been gone from Canterbury for ten years, and what a man doesn't forget in that time, he can muddle.

After Magnus himself changed for dinner, he stopped in at the Beefsteak Club and cornered George FitzWilliams before he got too soused to make sense. This time Magnus didn't drop his cup or trip over his own feet. But only because he was sitting with nothing in his hands.

When he finally left to go collect Cristabel and take her to dinner, he was himself again. But he was also more excited than he could ever remember being—or at least more excited than he'd been since the day that he'd first met her. He believed he had something incredible to tell her, and that it might even be true. And better yet, that it might change their lives for the better.

Cristabel wore thin, lime-colored satin and sheer eggshell lace, and the only warm thing about her was her cheeks, when she flushed thinking of Magnus. She didn't powder her hair because it was so cold out, she was sure that when she took off her hood, it would snow down over her bare shoulders. She didn't know how ladies of fashion did it, and tonight she didn't care. *He* didn't expect her to be a lady of fashion. She wasn't sure just what he expected, but for tonight she told herself she didn't care. Magnus was the first man she could safely dream of desiring. She was sure he was a gentleman, and no matter what he saw in her eyes, he'd always respect anything she said with her lips. She had only to mind herself and she'd be safe.

He hadn't kissed her since that shattering first and last time. Of course, they hadn't been alone since then, either. And tonight, she reassured herself, Martin and Sophia would be there too. Cristabel snatched up a fan, put on her cloak, and headed out the door and down the stair. No one else was there. She glanced up at the clock in the hall.

"Eight bells and no one's here?" she muttered to herself.

But Magnus was due soon. She turned and raced up the stair again, heedless of the way the footmen stared. It would never do to seem to be waiting for him so anxiously, alone by the door. She tapped on Sophia's door instead.

"The mistress isn't feeling quite the thing," Sophia's maid said when she opened the door.

"What is the matter? Is there anything I can do?" Cristabel asked anxiously. "Is she very ill? I have some knowledge of herbs; it may be I can help."

"Of course. I'd forgot. The pirate girl doesn't know a thing about polite excuses; let her in," Sophia called out in a tired voice.

The maid stepped aside, and seeing her mistress wave a languid hand, left the room. Cristabel stepped in to see that Sophia was dressed, formally and beautifully, from her satin shoes to her little powdered head.

"Oh, I see, a joke," Cristabel said in relief. "Well, even though it wasn't funny, I'm glad. I thought you were really sick and I got worried."

"Indeed?" Sophia said in a cold voice. "Then spare yourself. Of that, at least. No, I'm not sick of anything—but you, my dear unwanted guest."

Cristabel stared.

"Here's the truth with no sugar on it," Sophia said, "since I doubt it matters anymore. Martin has broken with Magnus, and now there's no need for me to pretend to like what he laid on our doorstep—especially since you're the reason for that break. Couldn't you have kept it to yourself? I suppose not, I suppose something such as yourself has no idea of discretion. Martin's right, it's not your fault, precisely. I ought to have known. Martin and I had a good arrangement worked out betwixt us; it was none of Magnus's business, but he makes all our lives his business," she said bitterly.

"So be it. I'm not married to Magnus, thank the Lord. Martin and I will get on without him. So fly to Magnus's arms tonight by yourself. I wouldn't go to the door for him now. Martin feels responsible for you, so stay on here if you wish, but expect nothing but houseroom from me from now on."

She unfurled her fan and posed for a moment in the mirror, smiling at the effect. Then she glanced at Cristabel. There was no mistaking the loathing in her eyes. "I'm off to the theater and an assembly. I doubt I'll see you there. Good night," she said, and turned her slender back on Cristabel.

Cristabel fled to her room, and looked around in wild surmise. There was nothing to pack. She'd been living neatly from her sea chests, for a sailor's daughter knew the need for a tidy life. And not being sure of her welcome, she'd never settled in for a long stay. There was nothing to do but decide on a destination now—and fast. She couldn't face Magnus tonight any more than Sophia could.

She knew he could solve all her problems. She knew he'd settle things comfortably for her. Too comfortably. She also knew that she was more susceptible than she'd ever been in her life tonight, and was more vulnerable to a man of decision and power like Magnus than she had any right to be. How easy it would be to say yes to him now, when she was lost and hurting. And how much harder to bear the inevitable loss of his interest and care. It would weaken her forever, because once she'd ceded responsibility for her life to someone, she wasn't sure she could ever steer her own course again.

As she stood and dithered, she heard a light tapping on her door.

"Tell the viscount I'm—I'm indisposed,' she blurted when she saw the servant standing there.

"'Tisn't the viscount, miss," the flustered footman said. "I've a note for you, mistress."

Cristabel snatched up the note and shut the door quickly. She uncurled the paper and read it once, and then over again, both because it was so badly written and misspelled, and because she wanted to delay considering an answer. She closed her hand hard over the note. As a sailor's daughter, she believed in omens and portents; she believed she could read them as clearly as she could predict the weather from gathering clouds and shifting winds.

She took a deep breath and then picked up her skirt and hoop and checked the dagger and scabbard she always had tied high on her hip. Dropping the skirt so fast the hoop bounced, she then ran one hand into the bosom of her gown and fingered the tiny dirk she always hid there. Then she ran to her trunk and plucked up a small pistol and shoved it into her ermine muff. Only then did she gather up her cloak, race from her room, and fly down the stairs. A glimpse at the clock in the hall showed her she had only minutes to spare.

"Get me a sedan chair," she ordered the footman, "an' best make it quick, laddie."

The tavern was in a twisting side alley near the muddiest bank of the Thames, and it was so dark and disreputable that the sedan men hesitated to go down the street that led to it. But their passenger assured them there would be no pay if they didn't. Finally deciding that running for their lives with pay in their pockets was a better choice than simply trying to escape with their lives alone, they sighed and delivered the lady to the weatherworn door of the Skull and Bones tavern. And then were gone into the night a second after she dropped their coins into their shaking hands.

Cristabel had seen worse taverns. At least this one had all four of its stained walls, and a roof. Without flinching, she opened the door and tried to peer inside. She coughed as she squinted through the thick smoke generated by the peaty fire in the wide hearth, complicated by fumes of tobacco, rum, gin, and unwashed bodies. It was dank and dark and smelly inside, but in many ways Cristabel felt more comfortable here than she had at the grand assembly she'd been to the week before. At least she knew what to expect here. Her knife was in her hand as she swaggered in through the doorway.

A sudden silence greeted her: All the masculine guffawing, shouting, and cursing stopped, a trill of women's laughter cut off in midscreech. The patrons of the tavern, ill-assorted seamen and dockworkers, mud larks, prostitutes, and petty criminals, were used to many strange and exotic sights. But not that of a fine lady, and a magnificently beautiful one at that, dressed in a gown so wide, she had to edge sideways through the door of one of the lowest taverns in London town. Others simply gaped because they'd never seen a real lady so close before.

Cristabel remembered how she was dressed a second too late. Her hand grew slippery on her knife's hilt. She almost slashed out at the figure who loomed up out of the murk to stand at her side.

"Avast! Lay down your weapon, Crissie!" Black Jack cried, dancing back a step, his hands high in the air, as though he were doing a jig.

"Black Jack!" she said in relief, sheathing her knife. "Lucky for you your tongue's faster than my hand. I read your note and came right away. What's this about you being in trouble and needing me? For in truth, Jack," she said, her eyes searching his familiar face, "I think I need you more than you could ever need me now, old friend."

"That's lovely," he said happily, as he took her hand in his and pushed past the gaping audience they'd attracted. "Just perfect," he said as he cleared a path to the meager private parlor the Skull and Bones provided. "Because," he said with a flourish of a bow as he closed the door and locked it behind them, "behold! Your kidnapper awaits your every command, me lady."

"What?" Cristabel said, stopping and staring at him, since the room was empty except for themselves.

"You've not got a thing to worry about no more, no more vexatious decisions to be making to trouble your pretty head. It's all out of your pretty hands now. Because I'm kidnapping you, me darling," Black Jack said with a grin, "and not a moment too soon, by the looks of your face."

"You're mad, man," Cristabel said in disgust. "Vexed I

may be, but I'm not leaving England, and never with you, my friend. Not that you're not bonny, mind, nor fun, in your way. But you're not for me, Jack. I be—I am an Englishwoman now, even if some persons don't think me a lady," she said with glittering eyes. "England is where my future is."

"With the big man?" Black Jack asked, and saw her face blanch. "Aye, I thought not. You're pretty enough for his bed, but not for his name; that be the way of all grand gents, luv, and—"

"Stow it!" Cristabel shouted. "He wants to marry me, if you must know. 'Tis I who won't have him. A fine thing, a match betwixt a fine lord and Captain Whiskey's daughter! I know what he'd suffer if that came to pass, even if he don't. Ah, but he's not thinking, he's reacting, is what the problem be. Suffice it to say, Jack, the man's not for me. But this country is."

"This cold, nose-in-the-air town? At least at home the beggars stay warm. You're just upset, lass. You've been turned round one too many times. I'm making it easier for you. I've got a place in Tortuga all set for us—all white wood, with a courtyard full of hibiscus, and it sets on a point overlooking the sea. You can have as many servants at your beck and call as any grand lady in this cold town does, and more: horses, dogs, and a goat besides. Ah, we'll live high, lass, don't you fear."

"We will not," Cristabel said.

"Ah, sure we will. We'll marry, lass; I'll not have you else. And I'll be having you, never fear. You may not think it now, but 'tis a long voyage from here to there, and by the time we make land, you'll be thanking me; that, I promise you." He flashed her a white-toothed smile, and inflated his chest.

"Only one of us will get there alive, Jack; that, *I* promise *you*. Listen, and hear me well: I won't be taken by pirate means. Oh, you could, no doubt, but it won't avail you. Take me by force, and you'll have nothing but hate from me, from now to forevermore."

"Lasses like fire in a man, though their lips say they want a milksop," he said, angling closer to her, smiling all the while.

"I'm not a pirate lass, Jack; I'd never forgive it," she said flatly.

He laughed and reached a hand to her, only to leap back as though stung by a bee, although she only let her knife nip at his shoulder. The bite of it made a tiny pock in his white shirt, and a small wound, so small the blood was slow to well up there. Still, he looked down at his shoulder, frowning fiercely. She paused and craned her head to see if she'd done more damage than she thought. As she leaned forward, so did he. Before she could withdraw, she felt his hand on her wrist. He gave it a quick twist, using only enough strength to make the knife clatter to the floor.

"See? You do care," he cried exultantly, reaching for her, "otherwise you'd have skewered me without a thought."

He danced back when he saw what she drew from her bodice. It was a little dirk, but needle-sharp. She was the one to smile then, but not for long. He snaked out a hand and clasped her at the wrist; twist and turn as she tried, she couldn't get the point of her tiny dirk to reach his flesh.

"Give it up, luv," he said. "I don't want to hurt you, but you see 'tis futile."

She dropped the dirk.

"Now, it don't have to be by force, luv. It won't be," he vowed. "I'll be making it a pleasure for you to agree."

He clasped her to him. She smelled rum and gin, the salt smell of brine, and a dark note of male sweat mixed with the sweet bay rum in his hair. It was the familiar scent of all the males of her childhood. His body was hard and warm against hers. She closed her eyes, and heard him chuckle low in his throat as he stared down at how her low, square neckline showed off her high breasts, lust and tender triumph in his eyes—suddenly replaced by sheer astonishment.

"God's blood, Cristabel!" he cursed, "Where did that come from?" he shouted, so close to her ear, she winced.

"Ye be too busy eyeing the goods, Jack," she said. "Ye should have had a better ogle at the wrappings they was in first. I had it in me muff, Jack, and it be primed and loaded, never fear." She pressed the small pistol harder into his chest to emphasize the point. "Now, it ain't the thing for dueling, but this close, it be good enough to do the job, and well ye know it. I'll do it, don't doubt me. So. I'd hate to get yer blood on me nice new gown, so step back slow and easy, laddie, slow and easy."

He hesitated, because he was loath to release what he finally held in his arms. He had her close in a lovers' embrace. Though she pulled the other way, their straining bodies were separated only by the length of the barrel of her pistol. He weighed his options. He looked down to see her cloak parted to reveal how well her fashionable gown showed off her lovely body. But when he looked up and saw what was revealed in her eyes, he sighed. And then slowly nodded.

But before he could take so much as a step away, there was a loud thump at the door and then another louder one. And then a crash. The door flew open. Both Black Jack and Cristabel froze in place and turned their heads to see who was there.

"A thousand pardons. I'd no idea I was interrupting," Magnus said in a light voice, although his face was grim and cold. "Is this some sort of pirate mating ritual?"

He stood in the doorway, breathing heavily, one hand fisted, the other holding his sword. He stared at Cristabel with such an expression of cold disgust that she felt sick. Until he saw the pistol. Then his eyes widened and he stepped forward—but not as fast as Black Jack did. He seized the pistol from Cristabel's numb hand.

"Tsk!" Black Jack said as he inspected the small, silver-handled pistol. "A lady's weapon. Who would have thought it of you, Crissie?"

She whipped her cape closed tight around her and glared at him.

"*Crissie,* is it?" Magnus echoed, watching them closely. "I see. Or do I? Would either of you care to explain?" He ran a hand through his hair. That was when Cristabel noticed his soft brown hair was disheveled, half out of its ribbon. His coat was open, and she could see how his labored breath caused his big chest to rise and fall rapidly. It was the first time she'd seen him untidy, and she realized he must have been running hard.

"I came to take Mistress Stew to dinner," Magnus told Black Jack, "and found her gone without a word, and by herself—not a happy circumstance for a young woman at night in London, you'll agree. Fortunately, one of the footmen heard where she told the sedan men to take her, although he didn't believe his ears. And no wonder. Is the food that much better here?" he asked Cristabel with heavy sarcasm. "I wish you'd have left word. I could have come here at a more leisurely pace; I really didn't need to tear through town like a madman to build up my appetite. Or would you rather dine with Master Kelly alone? Then I wish you'd have told me that, too, because I hate to impose."

"*That*, you do not!" Cristabel said, her temper flaring. "And it's not true neither! Black Jack here, he—he—" She faltered, looking from one man to the other. They watched each other, tense and taut as a pair of angry tomcats. She hesitated, realizing that if she told Magnus the truth, the two men would probably fight, and she didn't think she could bear to see it.

"Master Kelly here, he was after kidnapping the lass, m'lord," Black Jack said, weighing the little pistol in his hand. "She's here tonight 'cause I sent a note telling her I was in trouble and needed her. Well, so I do, but not in the way she thought. Being a good friend, she come. Then I told her I was taking her home with me, and she . . . ah . . . protested. First with a dagger, then with a little dirk, and then with this here cannon. Was there ever a girl like her, I ask you?" he said with admiration, smiling at Cristabel tenderly.

"So put down your sword, m'lord," Black Jack went on, "'cause I ain't fool enough to fight a battle I already lost.

Though mark me well, 'tis only she that could prevent me. When you come to your senses, luv," he told Cristabel as he handed back her pistol, "I'll be here waiting for you. I'm not sailing until the matter's resolved, y'see."

"Then I suggest you begin to pack, because that may be sooner than you think," Magnus said with pleasure. "I've some news for you," he told Cristabel with barely suppressed excitement lighting his eyes, "but it can wait until we're alone."

He bent and scooped up the dagger and the little dirk he saw on the floor. When Cristabel was done slipping the pistol back into her muff, she raised her eyes to see Magnus offering the weapons to her. "Your cutlery, ma'am?" he asked sweetly. He grinned at the way her color rose as she took them and slid them into her cloak pocket.

"And now," he said, offering her his arm, "to dinner?"

"Oh, don't mind me," Black Jack said sourly. "I've other plans."

"Doubtless," Magnus said, as he walked out the door with Cristabel, "but so do I."

The two men gave each other measured glances. Cristabel's chin came up.

"Aye. And so do I!" she said. And frowned as both men stopped glaring at each other and began to laugh.

CHAPTER
11
〜

Magnus sent for his coach, and he sat with Cristabel as they bounced down the narrow streets together.

"You shouldn't be alone with me," Magnus brooded. "There should be another female here, but I didn't have time to wait for Sophia. I'll send word to her when we reach the restaurant."

"No need, she won't be there. She said she don't want to deal with me no more neither," Cristabel said, so upset that her speech was entirely muddled between pirate and lady now. "Houseroom is all she said she'll give me from now on, and so be it. Well, you gone—you went and told her what I asked you about her and Martin, and she's in a taking. I can't blame her. So best tell the coachman to take me home—nay!" she said, sitting up sharply as she heard what she'd said, "It isn't my home, and never were. I don't want to go there no more neither. Fact is," she admitted in a voice so low and hoarse that Magnus frowned, "I was hoping Black Jack would be nicer—I mean not so ardent—'cause I be looking for a place to stay now. But he's no safe harbor neither, blast and damn him," she said in a hurt voice. Then she was quiet as she accepted the handkerchief Magnus handed to her.

The forlorn little honk she made in it made Magnus

smile, though his heart felt as though she'd twisted it. He didn't know how she could play with his emotions the way she did. He had known he cared for her, but hadn't known the depth of his emotion. When he'd heard that she had left Martin's house alone, he felt as though all the blood had left his head, and all his senses with it. He'd called for a horse and gone racing into the night after her, terrifying passersby—and himself for it was only now that he realized how wildly frightened he'd been. Then when he'd seen the tavern she'd gone to, he thought his heart would burst. When he'd broken the door off its hinges and seen her in the pirate's arms, he'd felt such despair, he didn't know how he stopped himself from howling aloud in anguish. He shook his head. He felt as though he had never loved so much. He didn't know if he liked it. He sighed, wise enough to know he had no choice in the matter.

"Of course you'll stay. If you don't, you'll make it worse. Just think about it," he told Cristabel as she began to protest. "How do you think I'll feel if you feel you're forced to leave them? And do you think I'll be quiet about it with them? Aha. You begin to understand."

"But they hate me," Cristabel said, and was sorry to hear it come out sounding like a wail.

"They'll be too busy trying to work things out for themselves," he said blandly. "Besides, they're much angrier at me than you. They never stay angry very long, anyway. If I send word for Sophia to come as chaperon now, she will and double quick. She can't bear to miss out on anything. Martin isn't angry at you at all. He won't stay mad at me either, because—well, because he's a very good lad, when all's said. He knows I love him."

"Well, I wish you'd kept me out of it," she said petulantly.

"There was no way I could. And there was no way I could let it pass. Whatever I may think of Sophia, I want that marriage to succeed. I didn't want her to start looking to other men for approval. She would have, you know. She might have said she didn't want him in her bed, but I'm willing to wager she wonders why he was so pleased to agree."

"Because she didn't want babies so soon," Cristabel said hotly, "and I think it were—was wonderful of him to oblige her, despite his own needs."

"You think he has needs?"

"Of course, all men do, and she's his wedded wife."

"And so, of course, you wouldn't mind if your husband never touched you?" Magnus asked sweetly. "You'd never wonder if he was so obliging because he had another female in his keeping? You'd never ask yourself if he really found you desirable? You'd never, of course, think even for a minute that there was anything wrong with you? Or his love for you?"

He waited as the seconds ticked by, listening to the sound of the horses' hooves clattering on the cobbles. Then her voice came low and grumbling from the darkened carriage. "I don't know how they stand you, I really don't," she muttered.

"In any event," he said, trying to keep the laughter from his voice, "I'm glad she's not here now. I have to talk alone. I've arranged for a private dining room. I'll send for Sophia or Martin to join us, or a maid if neither of them can be found, so you don't have to worry about gossip. And I'll leave the door open until someone gets here to chaperon you. But we must talk first."

Magnus waited until the proprietor had seen them to their table, poured the wine, taken their orders, and left them alone before he spoke. Then he reached out and took Cristabel's cold hand in his. His eyes were smoke-colored and intense. She waited with growing unease.

"Tell me about your mother," he said.

"She was a lady! A fine lady, Lady Elizabeth Ann Edgerton," Cristabel said defiantly, "and—"

"No, no. I know that," Magnus said, putting his other hand over the one he held. "I know she was a lady. That's not what I meant. But tell me, what did she die of?"

Cristabel blinked. And then lowered her lashes, and looked down at their hands. "I—I never was sure," she admitted. "All I know is my father always said she left us when I was a baby. One day she was there, smiling down at me, the next day she was gone, or so he said, but he never told me more. I thought it hurt him too much to say. We moved soon after that, and then again and again, so there was no one else I could ask. Not that I wanted to, I guess. It would have pained me to know. There are so many things that can kill you suddenly and horribly in the tropics, from something small as a spider, to slipping off a thousand-foot cliff into the sea. There are fevers and agues and such too. Any number of things could have done it," she said sorrowfully.

He shifted in his chair. "Cristabel," he said, "what if—what if I told you that it may be that your mother did not die? That she still lives? That when your father told you she 'left' him, it only meant just that? Do you think it's possible? At least—tell me, is there anything you know that might make it *im*possible?"

She stared, her eyes so wide, he could see the white around the amber centers of them that glowed in the candlelight. The faint color in her cheeks came and went.

"I don't know," she said wonderingly. "I don't know!" she said in sudden glee. "You know? It could be so. Aye, very like Capt'n Whiskey, that'd be! To say she'd gone—not strictly a lie—and never say more because it would be too embarrassing for him to let anyone—even his daughter—know a woman left him . . . but how could she? He runs a right tight ship. But if she did—aye. Oh Magnus," she breathed, her face lit with wild joy. "Oh Magnus, it could be!" Then she looked frightened and her hand tightened around his as she asked tremulously, "But why do you ask? What do you know? Can it be?"

"I've spoken with three men from Canterbury," he said. "Don't worry, I was sly about it. I made sure they weren't sure what I was asking, even though they answered me. I was trying to find out if you still had family there, Cristabel. I mean to marry you. You say you can't because of your father. I wanted to tell you something of your mother's family, maybe even arrange for you to see something of them. If you hadn't wanted to meet them and introduce yourself, that would be fine too. I only wanted you to know they were there, and see for yourself that you were as good as any of them.

"But I heard something hard to believe. When I mentioned the Lady Elizabeth Ann Edgerton, they all spoke of what a beautiful lady she was. Which I expected. But it was only a figure of speech, because they also went on to talk about how charming she is. *Is,* Cristabel. This woman they speak of is the right age, and from what they say, I think she looks very much like you. She's said to be very beautiful, with fiery hair and light brown eyes. One other thing: They say she left the country to visit a cousin in the Indies when she was a girl, and stayed abroad for three years before she returned. But return, she did. I think your mother lives, Cristabel."

She sat completely still, in shock. He wished he could take her into his arms, but at least he held her hand. "There's something else," he said, and saw her break from her trance. Slow sorrow came into her eyes and she nodded like an old wise woman.

"Aye," she said softly, "there it be. There's always something else. No matter, it were a good dream whilst I had it."

"No, no," he said, grasping her hand more tightly, "listen, please: It's all as I said. She lives, she's loved and respected. But the problem is that she's also married." He spoke quickly to get the thing over and done before she could imagine worse, though what he had to say was bad enough. "She returned from the Indies nearly twenty years ago and married a near neighbor, an older man, a baron. She has two children with him. Two sons. There was no mention of her being married before. There's no talk of a daughter, or anything before she married the Baron Batsford."

She thought a moment. Then he was relieved to see a small, sly smile begin to grow on her lips. She nodded, but this time with enthusiasm. "Well, but she's not daft, is she? Who would want to claim a marriage to Captain Whiskey? But this I know," she said with sincerity, looking straight into his eyes. "She *were* wed to him. I saw the marriage lines myself," she said with pride. "He kept them in his sea chest, with the finest of his booty. She was just such a prize to him, you see."

But then her face clouded again. "I can see her leaving him and find no fault in it. And if she managed to do it without his knowing, I'd be proud of her. But . . . why did she leave me?"

"Maybe it was too difficult to take you," Magnus said.

"Maybe," she agreed, "but why not try to tell me? It's been a lifetime."

He ran his thumb over her clenched hand as he sought the words to take the pain from her eyes. "Maybe she did," he said. "We don't know. That's the point. But I know what we can do, if you want. We can go to Bath and meet the lady and find out for ourselves. They winter in Bath. The old baron's bones ache and the waters there help him. It will take us a week by slow and easy stages—much less if the weather holds and we travel light and fast. What do you say, Cristabel?"

She didn't answer right away. "If you don't want to go, that's fine too," he said. "Sometimes it's best to let sleeping dogs lie."

Her head shot up. "Never!" she said. "I'd rather know and be damned than never know and imagine worse. I must go." She bit her lip. "I wouldn't trouble you, but I don't know how to get there. Will you take me?"

"I wouldn't let you go alone," he said.

"Well, but I wouldn't ask if I could do it myself."

"Cristabel," he laughed, "let's fight about something else. We need a chaperon for you. If you travel alone with me, you'll be taken for my mistress." He didn't add that he also worried that if she traveled alone with him, he'd take her as his mistress before she ever became his wife. It wasn't only his response to her that made it a real danger; he saw hers to him every time she looked at him. She might not know what her quickened breath and stolen glances meant, but he did. And he knew that if she was alone and frightened, she'd be vulnerable to affection. He was vulnerable to her; a few nights alone in a place where no one knew them would weaken his resolve as much as it would confuse hers. It would be glorious. But like many stolen sweets, it might have a bitter aftertaste. He didn't want anything to sully their relationship; he wanted her to eventually come to him freely and with love.

"Since we want to keep it close," he finally said, "it'll have to be Sophia."

"Never!" she said, appalled. "She hates me proper; she'd spill it all to get even with me. I'd rather take Black Jack; at least he cares for me."

"Oh, a fine chaperon," Magnus said sourly. "No. Sophia will be perfect because she understands secrecy too well. If she says a word, she can be sure you'll have a word or two to say about her marriage. I know it's underhanded, but though one secret is a weapon, two of them can make a strong pact. Besides, she's terrified of me."

Her expression of concern changed to a grin. She clasped his hand hard. "My lord," she said, "you would have made a wonderful pirate."

"Thank you," he said with sincerity. "That's high praise indeed."

Martin insisted on coming along too. But since he and Sophia weren't talking to each other anymore, and were trying to ignore each other and still watch each other's every move closely, it was as though Cristabel and Magnus were alone together. The ladies rode in a coach, the gentlemen on horseback; there was a maid, two coachmen, and a groom for safety's sake besides. It was as small an entourage as any person of fortune dared travel with. But Magnus also relied on his size and talent for weapons, and Martin's steady hand with a pistol. And, Magnus thought with a smile as he rode beside the lumbering coach, Cristabel's small arsenal that he was sure she'd taken with her.

The women wore traveling clothes, which meant that they left off their hoops. Cristabel sighed with relief, Sophia felt naked, but neither told the other, because they weren't speaking to each other either. Cristabel passed her time reading or looking out the window, hoping to catch sight of Magnus. Sophia slept, or stared into space, or glowered out the window at Martin. Cristabel didn't know what their fight had been about, but she had several good guesses and only felt slightly responsible.

Still, it meant that when they stopped to eat or refresh themselves, it was even more wonderful for Cristabel when she met up with Magnus again, because then she could talk about what she'd seen and thought. And watch his smile, and hear his deep voice, and sit next to him again.

Cristabel was used to traveling by sea; the roll and pitch of a boat took some getting used to, but it was a gentle way to cover miles. She wasn't used to traveling in a bulky coach over rutted roads. Their first night at an inn, she went to bed as soon as darkness descended, and fell into such a sound sleep that Sophia complained loudly to Magnus the next day, saying she wished she herself had such low sensibilities that she could sleep in a low, filthy inn among noisy, raucous strangers. Since that was how Cristabel had slept most of her life, she shrugged it off, only thinking sadly that it was how she would feel, too, if she really were a lady. But Martin laughed.

"Good, then," he told Magnus in a voice everyone could hear, "because if she could sleep, she'd have kept Cristabel up all night with her snoring."

It was very quiet in the coach for the rest of that day.

They made good time, but the next day their travels ended early because of a sudden rainstorm.

"At least it's not snow," Magnus said as he stood by the fire in the private dining room of the inn they'd stopped at for the night. "We should be able to get an early start tomorrow. It won't be much longer, Cristabel," he said, watching her as she stood looking out a window. The rain slashed against the panes. It was so dark outside, he knew all she was seeing was reflected firelight in the pocked and dappled panes of heavy glass.

She nodded. "I don't know if that's good or bad," she murmured, letting the curtain fall back again.

Dinner had been surprisingly good, but Cristabel hadn't seemed to notice. She'd been distracted all through the meal, and once the table was cleared, she'd paced to the window and stared out at nothing. She and Magnus had the room to themselves since Sophia had insisted on taking her dinner upstairs, and Martin started drinking with the local lads in the common taproom as soon as he'd finished eating.

"Sometimes I wonder if I did the right thing," Magnus said softly. Cristabel startled, because he had been by the fire a moment ago and now his voice came from just behind her shoulder. "When I found out about your mother, my first thought was that you should know, because you loved her so. But now I realize that love was given to you by your father—you don't remember her, do you?"

"Perhaps I do," she said sadly. "Sometimes a certain scent, a tone of voice, a flash of color, comes to me and I think of her. But truth to tell, I don't know if it's my memory or his, or my fantasy altogether. I was two when she left. Such a long time—I want to see her as much as I don't; can you understand?"

He had been trying his damnedest not to touch the soft curl of hair that lay on her shoulder, on that smooth white skin, and so was surprised by her question. She took his silence for agreement. She sighed, liking the stillness, the companionable silence between them.

Her mother might be alive, she might soon see her! It was her most secret and beloved dream. She envied Magnus his brother and foolish sister-in-law, his other siblings and his parents. She envied all the world their relatives. The absence of family was the one thing about living the pirate life that she'd most hated. Family didn't mean anything to them: Few pirates spoke of their pasts, and fewer still plotted secure futures.

But to have her beautiful lady mother again! To have a mother at all! She'd have to watch the way she spoke; would the lady like the way she looked? Were her manners good enough, was her voice sweet enough, would the lovely Lady Elizabeth Ann Edgerton be pleased with her? Would her two new half brothers think well of her? Two new half brothers! The thought made her mind reel. What if she displeased the lady? It made her wonder if she should do as she half yearned to: run away and hide and never return to England again. Then she'd never know. And that would mean never seeing Magnus again.

But if she suited her mother and if her new family approved of her, there'd be no reason to fight Magnus anymore. There'd be no more fear of not being enough of a lady for him—and less fear of his domination and eventual betrayal. If she was a lady with a family behind her, then perhaps she could survive; it might be that they could help her. It was a little hope, but she grasped at any ray of sunshine that could light the way down the aisle to him.

"It will be a shock to her," he said, and she felt his breath on her neck as he said it.

"Aye," she said, and felt his finger trace a coil of hair on her neck. She felt her skin tingling all the way down her back.

"Cristabel," he said, and she shivered, "don't set your hopes too high, or low. The lady will be as surprised as you are. I tell you what. If you like, we can observe her from afar first and then you can decide if you want to take the final step and meet her."

Cristabel didn't know what to say. His voice and touch unsettled her, but her future worried her more. A fire crackled in the hearth, the rain made it cozy, and he was with her. It was calm and quiet here, in an inn on the outskirts of Bath on the brink of tomorrow.

"Magnus," she said in a very small voice, "I'm frightened."

He knew what a difficult thing that was for her to say. He was fighting an even more difficult desire. The need to comfort her as well as himself became one yearning. He turned her around and looked down into the depths of loneliness he saw in her eyes.

"Ah, Cristabel," he told her, "never be afraid. Never so long as I live."

But it wasn't enough to say it. He lowered his head and kissed her. He meant to offer comfort and reassurance, but when their lips met he found she offered more. He groaned deep in his throat and pulled her closer and she squirmed in his arms, trying to get closer still. She wasn't a woman who knew half measures in anything she did, and she couldn't give him less than she felt. Which was more than she'd ever known. She'd never willingly come into a man's arms to meet his kiss before, and she discovered she wanted even more than that now. He was warm and solid and his hands and lips sent her mind spinning. It was more than comforting, it was a homecoming. She opened her mouth against his, and the taste of him delighted her. Her hands stroked his wide shoulders, touched his hard chest, felt the strong pulse of life in his neck as his hands caressed her to distraction.

They were alone, and no one would bother them. He had only to bolt the door, Magnus thought dazedly, as his lips feathered down her neck to the sweet, warm skin of her throat, to her breast. She was all willingness, all fire; she twisted and turned in his arms with the same restless desire he felt. Tonight she wore no hoop to hold him off; for the first time he could feel the outline of her whole supple frame as she pressed it against his own. Her breasts were high and hard and sweetly upthrust against his palm; they would be beautiful bared to the firelight. The curve of her waist as it dipped into the swell of her hip was a miracle of grace; her small, round bottom fit into his hand. He would help her from her clothes as she would help him from his. There was a carpet by the fire; he would lower her there, and kiss her and touch her and teach her—that men could not be trusted, he thought with sudden icy clarity.

His mind struggled against everything his body was feeling. But he saw his course of action too plain.

He could have her in glory, in the heat of her confused search for comfort and reassurance. And then she would rise from the improvised bed on the floor to find she would have to take him as husband. She was as impulsive and generous and honest in her emotions as she was in her speech; it was what he valued and worried about most in her. She was a creature of sudden passions and equally sudden remorse. He would marry her; that was a foregone conclusion. If he had to move heaven and earth to do it, he knew he would. And she wanted him now. There was every reason to take this hunger to sweet fulfillment. And every reason not to.

He knew her well—too well, he thought in agonized frustration. Because in possessing her now, he would possess all her free will, and when the heat of passion passed, she'd never forgive him. She would always wonder what her life would have been like if he had offered her only what she needed most tonight: the love of a friend. And so would he.

She wasn't the type of woman to be taken on the floor anyway, if only because she had fled a place where men did just that. That thought alone was as a lifeline to him; he caught hold of it and let it pull him back to sanity. It wasn't easy—he wanted nothing more than to bury himself in her now. But his whole life was dedicated to helping those he loved who could not help themselves. This was no different, only harder than anything he'd known.

He slowed his kisses, letting them trail up from her breast to her neck to her lips, retracing the blazing trail he'd left. He fought for the control to end this moment of dark passion slowly and sweetly so she wouldn't mark its gentle passage back to reality. She trusted him. He could not fail her.

"Tomorrow," he managed to whisper against her throat,

resting his head against her cheek, "tomorrow we must be up early and gone from here. It's late, Cristabel." He used familiar names and humor to try to restore himself, as well as her. "If you get back to your room too late, Sophia will be snoring too loudly for you to get any sleep. I have to go get Martin and pour him into his bed now too."

She stilled in his arms. He felt her give a shuddering sigh, then a shaky laugh, but there was only grief in her voice when she spoke. "What you must think of me," she said.

"I think I was trying to seduce you," he said, "as I promised I would. And I think that was wrong—at least for this place and this time. But hold the thought, please."

She looked up at him, her expression unreadable. Then she threw her arms around his neck and dragged his head down and kissed him so sweetly and soundly that he lost his breath. She released him just as fast as she'd grabbed him.

"You . . ." she said in a broken voice, shaking her head, "you . . . Magnus, you are—you are, oh, thank you, Magnus, you are wonderful."

She gathered up her skirt and fled the room. He stepped into the hall and watched her until she disappeared into her room at the head of the stair. He ached as if he'd run a mile, and there were cramps in parts of his body that he yearned to forget about. But he was grinning ear to ear.

Like Rome, Bath was a city built on hills. Conquerors had used the natural springs they found here to build their baths a thousand years before. The wealthiest Romans had used the hot, sulfurous waters to bathe in; now the noblest English used them to cure themselves. Cristabel decided the Romans probably had the better idea. It looked like it would take more than a glass of steaming sour water to cure most of the old people she saw struggling up and down the tilted streets of Bath. The younger ones were so beautifully dressed that she knew, before Magnus told her, that Bath was also a fashionable spa, a prime place for the rich of England to find mates.

She had to caution herself not to skip as she strolled with

Magnus now. Her spirit was surging: She was really, actually, possibly going to see her mother! She hadn't slept the whole night before just imagining it. But she didn't feel so much tired as she did strange: out of time and place as she searched the faces of passersby, wondering if she'd see someone who looked like herself, a few decades from now. She couldn't look for hair like her own, because most of the ladies wore white powder, and it was hard to see their eye color at a passing glance. So she searched passing faces, seeking what she thought she remembered from her infancy as well as what she'd seen in her own looking glass that morning. Not that she had to. Magnus knew where he was leading her. He'd gone out the day before when they'd arrived, and then again early this morning. When he returned he'd been excited, sober, but smiling. He'd held out a hand to Cristabel. "Ready?" he asked.

She was, and wasn't, but she scrambled into one of her nicest gowns and walked out with him. It was a clear, bright, cold day. They were on the Parade, near the Abbey, one of the few level places at the center of the town where all the best people eventually congregated. Sophia strolled ahead of them on Martin's arm, neither of them looking at each other. Cristabel was gaping at everyone that passed, but she looked up at Magnus when he halted.

"There," he said.

She held her breath, and looked. And then lost all her breath as she saw the woman who had to be her mother. She stared for a long moment, until the lady turned and entered the pump room with an old gentleman being carried in a sedan chair.

"Would you like to follow?" Magnus asked quietly, looking down at Cristabel's suddenly white face.

She shook her head violently. "No, no," she said.

"Then you don't want to meet her?"

"Of course I do," she said, "but on me own terms, in me own time. When I be ready—ah, blast. So I don't do that, you see," she told him, her eyes searching his for understanding.

"An appointment then, of your own choosing."

"Exactly," she sighed, feeling as frightened as she was near to hysterical joy. Because this woman was beautiful and elegant and graceful and assured—everything she had ever wanted her to be. And more than that, everything she herself had ever wanted to be.

It was a beautiful house in the best part of town. Cristabel's gown was the finest one she owned: a pure blue that flattered her skin and hair. She hadn't powdered her hair tonight, although she wanted to look fashionable. It was things like hair and eyes that would call to her mother, and she wanted nothing to disguise them. She couldn't hide her trembling as Magnus lifted the door knocker.

He took her hand as they waited for the door to open. "I'm right here," he reminded her. She nodded, because she couldn't speak. His words, as well as his big frame and strong, warm hand, comforted her, although nothing could stop the way her heart was knocking against her ribs. She felt short of breath and panicky when the door finally swung open. She became light-headed and dizzy when the footman fetched the butler, who went to see his mistress, and then told them to wait in a elegant, airy salon off the front hall. She found she couldn't swallow, much less speak, as she waited for her mother to appear.

Magnus spoke for her when the lady entered the room.

It was like looking at herself in a way, and yet the woman was nothing like her; Cristabel could see that at a glance. It was evening, so the lady's age was hidden and flattered by the candlelight; she wore powder, so her hair color was concealed as well. She had a high forehead and brown eyes, and the same nose Cristabel saw in her mirror every day. But in all, her face, so like Cristabel's was entirely different: beautiful, calm, serene as Cristabel's had never been. She glanced at Cristabel, dismissed her with a placid smile, and then turned her attention to Magnus.

"My lady," Magnus said as he bowed, "thank you for receiving us on such short notice. As my note said, I am

Magnus, Viscount Snow, and I've come tonight because I've something of great import to tell you. My companion here has traveled many miles, crossed the seas, in fact, to find you. And yet I have reason to believe her very existence may be unknown to you. There's no point in me going on and on; the situation will speak for itself. My lady, permit me to introduce you to Miss Cristabel Stew, of the Indies."

Cristabel wanted to rush into the woman's arms as much as she wanted to run away. So she did the only thing a lady could; she blushed and, trembling with anticipation, dropped into a deep, low curtsy. But not so low as the one her mother made. Because the lady faltered and would have fallen if she hadn't caught on to the edge of a table instead. Magnus rushed to assist her, but she sank to one knee and waved him away wildly.

"God in Heaven!" she cried, staring at Cristabel. "Tell me it's not true!"

"I am—I have reason to think that I am—your daughter," Cristabel said hesitantly, "or so, at least, my father always said. But see, he said only that you'd left us, and so I thought you'd passed on—never knowing that you lived. I found out when I came to London last month. My lady, I think it must be so. Not just because of the marriage lines, and all the stories I heard of you, but because you look—I look—it must be so, I think," she finally said, fearful of the look in her mother's eyes.

"Get out!" the lady cried. "Out now! I'll deny it to the skies. I'll swear it's not so. He raped me then, he shall not do so again. I have influence and money, I will not permit it. I escaped him once, I'll do it again."

"But I am . . ." Cristabel began to say, and then stopped, realizing that one phrase had said it all, said everything that pained her.

"I wish to God I could forget it," Lady Elizabeth hissed, "but I can't. You have the look of him, the stink of him. Get out, and never trouble me again. I'll deny you, I'll tell them who your father is. Who would believe you then? He can't prove anything because he's a wanted man; he dare not even show his face in England. Ill-gotten brat of a murderer, leave me now and trouble me no more!"

"I'm glad to leave," Cristabel said, backing to the door. "I'll never come back."

She ran out in the hall before she could disgrace herself by crying. As it was, Magnus caught her by the door and held her close and rocked her until she could stop sobbing, great gulping sobs that tore at her throat and brought tears to his own eyes. When she subsided, she raised her tearstained face to him. "I'm done," she said in a hoarse voice. "I'll never cry no more. Not for her. Take me from here, please."

But before he could leave, a dry old voice called to him.

"My lord," an old gentleman in an invalid chair said, raising a thin hand to hail Magnus, "please wait." He waved the servant who had pushed his chair into the front hall away, and signaled the footmen to leave as well. Then he gazed at Magnus and Cristabel. He was very old, or else moderately old and very ill, because he was thin and blue-skinned, and even his rouged cheeks and high white wig couldn't bring the semblance of health to his cold face.

"Yes," the old man said, staring at Cristabel, "very like. 'Tis a pity. I am Lady Elizabeth's husband, the Baron Batsford, her only legal husband, my dear," he told Cristabel in his thin voice, "whatever any bit of paper your father produces says. I've men at law to back me up on that. I don't know your game, my child, but you'd be advised to give it up. Those years were hell on earth for my dear Elizabeth; she wants to forget them, and who can blame her? You are a mistake, my poor child, a sad mistake born of a terrible crime. One best forgotten by all concerned. There's only hurt here for you. I suggest you let the matter rest and go back to the Islands and tell your father it is useless. She is protected now."

"As is Cristabel," Magnus said in a harsh voice. "She will be my wife. Her father has nothing to do with this. I brought her here in the hopes of bringing her some happiness. She doted on her mother's memory, you see. But don't worry, she'll trouble you no more."

He bowed and, putting his arm around Cristabel, led her out.

"Cristabel," he said when they reached the street, "look at me. I didn't know. I couldn't have guessed. Forgive me please."

Her face was stark and shocked, her eyes wide and filled with hurt as she looked into his. "Oh, Magnus," she whispered, "of course I forgive you. But can't you see? You must forget me, please."

CHAPTER

12

❧

Sophia was furious, of course.

"We just got here!" she fumed as she paced the private dining parlor of their inn. "It took days of absolutely wretched travel to come to Bath. I was very good about it; I hardly ever complained about the poor quality of the roads, the inns, the food, and the company, did I? Now we're here at last and I can see that everyone else is too. I'd no idea. So much to do, so much to see: dinners and balls, and gambling until all hours! There's a subscription ball tonight, but I can get in anyway. Beau Nash *himself* bowed to me at the pump room this morning. I refuse to leave just because *she* doesn't want to stay. Take her and leave me, It's quite all right; I can do with a change of scene."

"We can't travel that distance without another lady accompanying us," Magnus said in a dangerously even voice, "and you know it, Sophia."

"Of course you can; it's not as if she was a *lady,*" Sophia spat.

Cristabel flinched. Magnus didn't grimace or snarl, but his lips thinned and he stared at Sophia with the intensity of a predator about to spring, his narrowed eyes glinting with dark ice.

"Of course, she's right," Cristabel said hurriedly, looking from Magnus to Sophia.

Magnus wheeled around and stared at her. Sophia flushed and fanned herself.

"The matter is settled, Sophia," Martin said quietly. Everyone turned to look at him; he'd been so quiet, they'd forgotten he was there at the table with them. But now he rose from his chair. "I'm returning to London too," he said, "and of course, I want my wife with me."

"But I choose to stay," Sophia said, stamping her foot.

"If you do," Martin said very carefully, "it will not be as my wife. You have a choice, Sophia. Make it. I'll be leaving with Magnus and Cristabel, first thing in the morning."

He threw down his napkin and left the room. Sophia stared after him and then, raising her head, she swept from the room as well, leaving Magnus and Cristabel alone together.

"I didn't mean to cause trouble," Cristabel said miserably.

"If it weren't you, it would be something else," Magnus said. "When an argument's ripe, anything will set it off. But are you sure?" he asked, looking at her with concern. "She may have second thoughts. Seeing you was a shock; she may come around."

Cristabel knew he wasn't talking about Sophia, because she herself had hardly paid any attention to Martin or his wife. All she'd been doing since she'd left her mother's house was holding back tears. Concentrating on that was the only thing that helped her sit through a dinner she hadn't tasted, nodding at remarks she didn't hear. The thought that kept drumming in her head was louder than any conversation around her: Her mother didn't want her; her mother hated her, because she was 'a mistake, a sad mistake born of a terrible crime.' Try as she might, she couldn't forget those words, realizing now that her mother had spent her whole life trying to erase her memory.

She had to be strong; she couldn't break down in front of the world. She had no more claim to being a lady, and now her pride was the only thing she had left to prove her gentility. But the look in Magnus's eyes made her feel weak tears start in her own. She glanced away from him, unable to see his pain for her.

He knew. "Cristabel," he implored her, "please don't lock me out. I know what she said, but she spoke from her own hurt. Give her time. We can stay here; maybe seeing you around town will change your mother's mind."

"Aye, mebbe," Cristabel said, as she stared stonily at the wall. "Likely she'll be so thrilled at what she sees, she'll regret having left me like a bundle of dirty wash over two decades ago; oh aye, there be a real possibility. No, m'lord, I see it clear now. Captain Whiskey took her like a pirate takes any pretty thing he sees and likes. He had her for his own pleasure, and filled her belly with me. Likely then, like all men, he soon found another and left her alone with his folly. So she flitted off soon as she could, leaving me like an accident she had in the night, something dirty she left in her bed 'cause she couldn't help it. So be it, and good fer her, I say."

"Cristabel," Magnus said, taking her in his arms. She offered no resistance, but was stiff and unyielding in his embrace. He offered no more than she allowed; one of his big, warm hands made slow circles on her back, the other held her close. "That's not likely how it was," he said gently, "but what difference does it make? We can never know. He may well have loved her in his way. He may have been faithful to her too. But he may have raped her, or hurt or deceived her too—the point is, we'll never know. It doesn't matter. One good thing came from it, one good, radiant, pure thing that made it all worthwhile: you."

She laughed, or sobbed; he couldn't tell which because she buried her face in his chest. "Aye, such a good thing, she can't bear to look at it," she mumbled.

"She doesn't matter, not really," he said, rubbing his cheek against the soft, fragrant curls piled high on her small head. "She did once, but that part of your life is over. You are loved now, Cristabel."

"I be *wanted* now, m'lord," she said in a gruff little voice after a second's silence. "'Tisn't the same. I expect me mother knows the difference if you don't."

She felt his body stiffen. He tensed and drew back from her, holding her away from him at arm's length, and she knew he would have shaken her if he dared—his anger was clear to see.

"I'm not a pirate, I'm not a rapist, and I am not a liar, Cristabel," he said in a deadly cold voice. "Have I ever given you reason to think so? If you do think it—even for a minute—then leave me now."

She swallowed hard. "No, you haven't," she admitted, and then tried to explain, "but every man I ever knew—"

"You never knew me," he said, and now he did give her a gentle shake so that she would look up at him. "You came to England so you could know a new life. I'm part of it, but . . . damn it, Cristabel, if you don't trust me, then nothing I say matters. If you do, then I don't have to say anything more. Marry me, and soon. I'll be your new family. We'll make one, we'll share one. I want you, not your mother. There are dozens of girls I could wed with the most charming mothers you can imagine; I don't want any of them."

"But why do you want me?" she asked plaintively, and now the tears began.

He wanted to kiss her, but he knew that was the answer that would frighten her most. She understood lust; it was love she didn't know.

"Because you need me," he said honestly, and could have bitten off his tongue when he heard the words and saw her eyes widen. "But it's more than that; no man marries for that reason," he said quickly, "else I'd have married ten times over, years ago. I want to marry you for many reasons; needing is only one of them. You please me, Cristabel, you please me mightily. No woman has ever pleased me as much as you do. Your family doesn't matter. Why don't you ask me if I'm marrying you for your body? It's beautiful. Or your wit? It's considerable. Or your fortune? It's vast enough to embarrass me.

"Cristabel," he said a little desperately, his hands tightening on her shoulders, losing his usual calm confidence as he saw her downcast eyes, "Don't think of me. Think of yourself. Do I please you? Do you like my conversation, my sense of humor, spending time in my company?"

She nodded.

"Does my person offend—is there anything amiss with the smell or feel of me?" he asked, "It's possible. I've known women I've liked until I got a whiff of their perfume and realized it was something in their very scent I'd never be able to tolerate. Once the pitch of a fair lady's giggle made me want to run for my life, when a moment before I'd fought off ten other suitors to have a dance with her. Sometimes a small thing can ruin the whole. Is it that way with me?"

"No, of course not," she said, embarrassed that he might think there was anything about him that repulsed her.

"Then do you react to me the way I do to you?" he asked. "Does my face please you? My scent, my voice? My body? Do you think I can bring you pleasure with it?"

She blushed, but being pirate born, she was honest about passion. "There's nothing amiss with you. Quite the opposite, and ye know it well," she managed to whisper.

"Ah. So then it's not my person or my conversation. So then, Cristabel, what could it be? Is it that you don't trust me?"

She cocked her head to the side as she considered her answer. "I don't know. It's not you," she said hurriedly, "it's just that I'm not in the habit of trusting men, do you see? I think—I think I do trust you, Magnus. I want to, that's sure. But it's too new a thing for me. I can't say that I do. But y'see, I can't say that I don't neither."

"You need time," he said.

"Aye, because . . . ah, Magnus, she were terrible to me. I cannot bear it. I dreamed of having a fine family that you could be proud of. I feel so small in your eyes."

"Small? Oh, Cristabel, you are so large in my eyes, I can't see anything else." He cupped her head in his two hands and stared at her, love in his eyes, and brought his lips to hers. He was unable to say all he felt. But his kiss said it all and more. At first his kiss was solemn, almost chaste. Then he deepened it, and she followed where he led. He let his mouth court hers, his tongue pledging things he was unable to voice, promising a taste of everything that could follow. But he kept his hands deep in her hair on either side of her head. It was both frustrating and gratifying to feel the soft surrender of her mouth under his and yet deny his desire to feel more. The best and worst part of it was that he knew, from the small shudder than ran through her slight body, that she felt exactly the same way.

"To London then," he said with a sigh as he stepped back from her. "Your mother knows where I live; it may be that she'll change her mind."

"Aye," Cristabel agreed with a brave little smile that made his heart turn over, "when me father takes to flying 'stead of sailing."

Their return trip was both slow and silent. Sophia and Martin were still not speaking to each other; Martin was brooding, and Sophia refused to talk to anyone except her maid, and then only when she wanted or needed something. Cristabel hardly noticed, she was so lost in her own thoughts. Magnus tried to cheer her up, but his every remark produced only absent smiles, and he gave up. Instead, he passed his time watching her.

She suffered now that the shock was over. He suffered with her, because there was nothing he could do to help. He couldn't challenge the Baron Batsford to a duel because it wouldn't help matters even if he could fight a crippled old man, nor could he fight or browbeat Cristabel's unnatural mother. There was nothing he could do but yearn to ease her pain. His fierce protectiveness towards her surprised even himself. That, and his equally fierce longing for her, body and soul. The wait to gain her trust was something he could bear. The longing for her body was another matter.

He loved making love to women and had made such

pleasures a natural part of his life since he'd become a man, but these feelings for Cristabel transcended anything he'd ever felt. There wasn't even the possibility of slaking some of his lust with some other willing woman, for Cristabel was the only object of his desire, now and forevermore. There might be more beautiful women, but none for him. As they traveled back to London, he pleased himself by simply watching her as much as he tormented himself by doing so: slender and yet lush, with a spirit that burned bright as her radiant hair; he was wholly captivated by her.

It astonished him how such a valiant spirit could be cased in such a delicate structure. He found himself noting her slender neck and delicate wrists as other men might ogle a woman's shapely ankles; he remembered the feel of her narrow waist as much as the swell of her high, firm breasts. He marveled at the vulnerability of her, and yet he knew women and knew that such delicacy could accommodate even a man as large as himself—more than accommodate. His fragile little lady could satisfy and be satisfied in turn by him. He knew it with a delight that fed his desire.

He rode with her each day and dined with her each night, speaking with her when she seemed aware of him, keeping his own council when she was looking too far inward to see him by her side. He gave her the chaste kiss of a friend on her lips each night when they parted. And then he lay awake each night, schooling himself to patience for the next day.

Still, he was almost sorry when they finally arrived at London's gates. Now the grace period was over. Now he would have to make her give up her mourning and accept the facts. And himself. Because he couldn't wait much longer.

The first thing Cristabel did, of course, as soon as Magnus delivered her to Martin's house, was to ask to leave again. He'd been expecting that.

". . . In fact," he finished telling her the minute she mentioned it, "you'd make matters even worse if you left now. Martin and Sophia have to maintain some semblance of a marriage while you're here. Leave, and I suspect their marriage will fall apart. Of course, if you don't care . . . ?"

"You're as good at getting people to do your bidding with words as my father is with his cutlass," she complained, "You're likely right. But I want to get on with my life."

"So do I," he said seriously.

She had no answer to that comment. She thought that her mother's reaction to her would have ended the matter for him. She was ready to go on alone with her life and live quietly somewhere in England, the way she'd originally planned to do. But somehow, in some magical way, he'd turned the tables and she found herself closer to him than ever. She still didn't think such a marriage was good for him, but she knew he disagreed, and she began to believe him. She didn't want to be a slave to any man, but she began to suspect it was already too late. Still, her independent soul strove for freedom—or was it her cowardly soul? she wondered now. Whatever it was, she couldn't leave him just yet.

"So," Magnus said as he prepared to leave Martin's house for his own, "dinner, tomorrow tonight? Not here; Martin's glum looks would poison the wine, and Sophia's tongue might sour the dessert. But somewhere where we can drink and be merry without feeling as though we're disturbing a funeral?"

"But if we meet friends of yours?" she asked quietly.

"We'll ask them to join us. Nothing has changed. You are still Mistress Cristabel Stew, from the Indies. Your father is still anything you want to say he is. And your mother is still lost to you, isn't she?"

That much was certainly true. She nodded.

"Wear something bright," he said, smiling. "We've had a long enough winter, I think."

Cristabel wore a yellow and gold gown, and threaded a bright gold ribbon in her curls. No powder for her hair, but a dusting of it on her face and dab of color for her cheeks and lips. A touch of flowery scent on the inside of her elbows and between her breasts, and a more liberal splash on her wrists so it would seem like a breeze from the tropics when she used her fan. In some corner of her mind she knew she was dressing like a pirate lass out on the prowl, down to the dagger in her garter above her knee. But tonight she didn't care. He was right; her soul was weary of winter. This was a wonderful land, but she couldn't get used to the gray of it; it was time for spring. She wanted to be glad again. She wanted laughter. She wanted his approval, she wanted to be happy.

She sat down and stared into her looking glass, amazed as the enormity of the situation struck her. All at once she knew the whole truth—it had crept up on her and waited in her reflection, staring back at her. She wanted joy, she wanted pleasure, she wanted comfort after a long, cold time. In short: She wanted him.

She might have always feared a man's domination, but now she admitted she'd also always wanted to know what gave a man that power over a woman. She'd never thought to experience it, but now there was one man in her life who might show her what it was. She'd admired other men, she'd seen more handsome ones, but never one who made her laugh so much or promised to be able to make her cry so much either. She'd only known him a matter of weeks, and yet she already felt incomplete without him.

He'd asked if there was any little thing about him that offended her. She couldn't count the small things about him that delighted her, from the way her hand felt swallowed up in his warm, wide palm, his long fingers locked over hers, to the way his soft, long hair looked drawn back behind his powerful neck. She loved to look at his eyes, and when he caught her staring, she lowered her lashes and watched the slow, steady beat of a pulse in his throat instead. She loved to breathe in his scent: lemon and shaving soap and something bittersweet that was essentially Magnus. There was no way to list it all. She wanted him, in every way. She'd lived with the awareness of passion all her life, and had always been able to channel it elsewhere. But not with this man. This yearning, this trembling in her limbs when he touched her, this shivering and puckering of every sensitive part of her body when she simply thought of him—if it was only the prelude, what must loving be like?

If she let him love her, he would never let her go. She knew it, and knew she'd never be able to go either. The only question that remained was whether she was willing to risk everything for something she'd sworn to avoid. His proposal of marriage was nicely done, but marriage lines meant little to her. She'd seen how little marriage meant to everyone else she knew. If she gave him her body, she would give him her heart, and it would be for an eternity. It was the way she was made.

She didn't know what to do now that she accepted the intensity of her feelings. It might be best to cut line before too much harm was done. Wanting and not having was the story of her life, after all. If she tasted love and then gave it up, she didn't know if she could bear it. And if that love produced a child—she knew too well the pain of being raised by one parent. No, she had to weigh the desires of her heart and mind and body before she would know what to do, because whichever she chose, it would be an irrevocable decision. He was giving her time to make up her mind, and whatever she decided would take courage. But she had plenty of courage.

She smiled at herself in the mirror, feeling naked and vulnerable and daring. And good. As bad as indecision and fear were for her, she knew she was at her best when faced with a challenge. She rose, snatched up her cape, and went out to face the night with a high heart.

What still amazed and delighted Cristabel about London was how it defied the night. Of course, the days were both brighter and longer in the tropics. But when night fell there, it did so literally, with a sudden splash of black. The sun dipped into the sea as if the water extinguished the light. Night fell as day ended in the tropics; it was as simple as that. Bonfires might be lit on beaches and there were taverns where the oil burned late, but *late* in the Islands was not the same as it was here in London. Here men and women stayed up until all hours, gambling, drinking, and dancing, and there was enough light to do it in. Every great house was lit with chandeliers that blazed with galaxies of candles; and the restaurants, theaters, and taverns glowed with candles, lamps, and torches far into the night. Linkboys carried their flaring pitch torches high as they guided adventuresome ladies and gentleman through the streets. Even sober citizens did their bit to repel the night: By law, each house had to have a candle burning brightly by its front door.

But little could be done about the cold. She hadn't gotten used to that yet either, and didn't know if she ever would.

"Cold?" Magnus asked as he felt her shiver. "My grandmother would say you haven't been eating right. Mangoes and bananas and fish make for weak blood; you need good red wine and beef to prepare yourself for an English winter. Won't you let me call a sedan chair?"

"I don't like being carried like an old woman," Cristabel said. "It's only a few streets. I wonder that English ladies still have use of their legs."

Besides, she thought, glancing up at him, *when I sit in a sedan chair, you must walk alongside and I can't hold your arm.* She could swear she felt the warmth and strength radiating from his side as she stepped along close to him. English society had few ways a lady could innocently touch a man; now that she found one, she wasn't going to give it up.

He felt her shiver again, looked down at her and frowned. He paused, held out one arm so he could wrap his cloak around her, and then drew her closer to his side so that she nestled there beneath his cloak. She felt its soft folds envelop her, and sighed. There were great advantages to an English winter, after all.

Magnus was big, well armed, and skilled enough to protect her from any lurking villains, and they were walking in a popular district of taverns, restaurants, and clubs. Still, as they paused at a corner, they formed a small parade. A linkboy led them, and a sweep plied his broom for them at the crossing so that they didn't have to tread in mud, manure, or ordinary offal.

Magnus flipped the sweep a coin when he was done and they stepped off the curb into the street. Even though the sweep had done his best, Cristabel had to raise her skirt and step with care because London's streets were never really clean. She was daintily picking her way along, Magnus holding her arm, when she heard the horse approaching. The streets were always busy by day; at night there was less traffic. Tonight they had seen some coaches, sedan chairs, and pedestrians afoot, but few lone horsemen, and none in such a mad rush.

This rider bore down on them even as they heard him and picked up their heads to look. He was riding hell for leather. He was all in black, cloaked against the frosty night, and his horse was black as the night around them. Magnus drew Cristabel against himself and bellowed, "Ho!" at the horseman, to let him know that they were standing midstreet in case the mad fellow didn't see them. He didn't. Or didn't want to, because he came straight for them.

Magnus picked Cristabel up and leaped to the side with her, and they fell together just as she felt the breeze of the racing horse like a slipstream current pulling at her as it tore by. She landed hard, on Magnus, and lay tumbled and bewildered in the gutter as the horse pounded on down the street. It never even slowed, although the horseman glanced back to see the couple he'd almost trampled. Then he spurred the horse on faster, and head down, disappeared around a corner. Magnus scrambled to his feet and stood over Cristabel with his sword drawn, looking after the horseman and cursing as Cristabel had never heard him do.

"Aye, you'd make a brave pirate, to be sure," Cristabel muttered as she struggled to rise from the dirt. "I never heard a finer tongue-lashing."

He was at her side in an instant, drawing her to her feet. "Are you hurt?" he asked worriedly. "That was quite a fall you took. I'm sorry, but I had no choice; it was a near thing as it was. He was either a madman or drunk with a cruel streak," he said, his eyes narrowing against the dark as he gazed down the street again. "He was heading straight at us and didn't even veer away at the last. Are you hurt?"

"My gown is," she said, looking down at herself, seeing her fine gown torn and muddied, "meself, no." She ran trembling hands down her body. "No, I be only shook. 'Tis you who must have taken the brunt of it. I landed on you and then rolled in the gutter . . . Are you hurt?" she asked suddenly, her eyes searching him fearfully. "Sometimes a fellow don't feel a thing till the shock be gone. Why, I once't heared of a man got his ear blowed clean off and din't know till an hour later . . ."

But he didn't look hurt so much as bedraggled. His tricorne lay in the mud, his hair was loose from its ribbon and flying all about his face, the white linen at his throat was muddied, his cloak was pied with dark stains she didn't even want to think about, and his broad face was streaked with grime. And he was grinning, ear to ear.

"You look a sight," he said. "I'm fine; I've suffered worse for sport. Don't look at me like that—I still have both ears. But unless my eyes are deceiving me, Mistress Stew, you look like a mud lark."

She glanced down at herself, and then up at him again. The fine gentleman she knew was gone. Now he looked more like the men she was used to: ruddy from exertion, disreputable, messy, and virile—and altogether wonderful. She couldn't let him know it.

"Aye, just as me governesses always feared," she said with a sigh. "They always did worry about me winding up rolling in the gutter with a gent."

They stood in the center of the street, with a gathering crowd around them, and roared with laughter. Then he hailed a sedan chair and took her back home again. But not before questioning several witnesses to the incident.

"He saw us," Magnus told her as he walked beside her chair, "but never turned from his course. In fact, some said it looked as though he aimed his horse straight at us. Don't worry, once you're home and you can wash and change your clothes, you'll feel much better. I intend to do the same, although mine will be a very hot bath because I'm having a hard time staying upwind of myself. 'Od's blood, but I never wanted to be so far away from myself as I do right now." He waited for her to stop laughing before he went on, "I'm glad you've recovered enough to laugh at my misfortune, my lady, but I don't think you should venture out again tonight. You may be merry as a grig now, but the bruises and shakes come after. But I hate to miss our evening out together. If you like, I'll bribe Martin's cook into bringing us a fine dinner we can share when I return."

"I like," she said with satisfaction. "Magnus," she said a moment later, "I think he did mean to run us down. But why? Not for profit, surely, unless it's some kind of rig they run here in London."

"Bowling down pedestrians for their purses? No. Don't worry. It was probably just as I said: a madman or a drunken fool."

"Could it have been someone who meant you harm?" she asked.

"I doubt it," he said lightly, too lightly.

"My father's men . . ."

"Your father's men," he said, cutting her off, "are seafarers, not jockeys. They dealt with me directly last time they were displeased with me, not from the back of a horse. Whatever else you think of them, they acted openly. This was a craven deed, if it was on purpose. Besides, there's no reason for them to be angry with me anymore. I was with you tonight, just as they said they wanted me to be. Don't vex yourself. London's a dangerous place, filled with drunkards and idiots. It was an accident. Besides, it was dark as pitch, too dark to be recognized except from up close, and we were the only ones crossing the street just then."

She sat deep in thought as the sedan men bore her back to Martin's house. Once there, she called for a hot bath as Magnus had suggested, and once immersed in the water, she sat back and let it soothe her bruised body. But it didn't soothe her mind, because her thoughts were dark and troubled. No stranger to violence, she distrusted the word "accident." God sent "accidents": hurricanes and fires, tidal waves or a slip on a greasy patch on the floor. In her experience, the only way one man harmed another was on purpose. She was convinced that this accident had been deliberate. Although it had been dark and she had been cloaked and so had Magnus, he was still distinctive. Too distinctive. He was much too big for the horseman to have missed seeing—and much too big to be mistaken for someone else. Few men in London were his height and stature. Anyone looking to harm him would have seen that and known him.

She stepped from the tub, refreshed and resolved. If Magnus had enemies, then they were her enemies. And woe betide her enemies.

CHAPTER

13

At first it seemed an impossible task, but on second thought it was easy enough. London or the Islands, she only had to think of the devious way his mind worked and then about the greed and avarice of all men, and Cristabel knew exactly how to get in touch with Black Jack again. She had to speak to him at once; what she would do after that depended on what he had to say for himself. Though she'd dined with Magnus the night before, she hadn't said a word about her intentions to him because she knew he would think he had to protect her, and she knew nothing she could say would change his mind. The way he felt towards her was flattering and very sweet, she supposed, but totally unrealistic. Someone had to protect him now, and she knew no one better for the job. After all, she was half pirate herself.

That wasn't to say Black Jack had tried to run Magnus down in the street, but she was certainly too wise to say he hadn't. Black Jack wanted her; he'd made that clear. And a pirate took what he wanted, and one of the ways he did that was to eliminate the opposition. She didn't think Magnus would understand that because he lived by the code of a gentleman, and she knew that the code had everything to do with honor. She knew the code of a pirate, too, and it was a strict one. But she also knew that pirates only lived by the code of the Brotherhood when they were on a ship, and that it had nothing to do with honor, and everything to do with good sense if a man wanted to survive a voyage surrounded by men as villainous, vicious, and underhanded as he himself was. Off ship, a pirate survived by any means possible.

"I need you to send me a lad from the kitchen, or a stableboy," Cristabel told an awed upstairs maid she'd called into her room. "He must be a lad who knows his way around the, ah, less wholesome parts of London town. I need someone to take a message to a low and wicked tavern near the Thames and to make some inquiries if the person I seek isn't there. So be sure he's a knowing one. He must be able to take care of himself, too, for I don't want to send anyone into danger, and danger there may be in simply walking such streets. Tell him there's a rich lady who needs him to run an errand and who will pay handsomely for it. Aye, there's good gold in it for him—and for you, if you tell no one else about my message. I didn't ask the butler to do this for me, nor the master or his wife neither. I want it done fast and silent. Mark me well, there's trouble ahead for *anyone* who don't keep his or her mouth shut about this, if ye get my meaning," she added in a low growl.

The little maid nodded. "But I know just the lad and I'll send him to you double-quick. And never fear, mistress, in London half a servant's wages are for what she don't say as much as for what she does for her lady. It's why any one of us would be a lady's maid if she could only have the chance. I can be quiet as a mouse if it's needful, and I'm a fine seamstress and neat as a pin, and I'm a treat with hair, I am," the girl said, dipping a curtsy and looking up again eagerly.

The girl was quick and clever. Cristabel had no servant since she'd let the sour-faced tavern wench go. Now she smiled with pleasure. Not only would her errand be done, but she may have just found herself a lady's maid at last.

The answer to her summons came almost as soon as the girl had scurried away to do her bidding. It wasn't long before the youngest footman was standing shifting from foot to foot in her doorway as he delivered Black Jack's answer to her.

"He says to tell you as to how he'll be by here to see you before the sun rises on another day," the footman whispered to Cristabel. "He says as to how you shouldn't fret yourself," he reported. He concentrated, and then beaming, delivered the last of his message. "And he says it's about time you came to your senses; he's been expecting your summons for days."

That made Cristabel scowl so much, the footman was afraid he wouldn't get his payment. But he left beaming at the size of the coin she gave him, although she continued to frown, thinking about Black Jack's answer. "Came to her senses" indeed, she thought as she paced her room; well, as soon as she saw him she'd set him right about that.

And so she did not know the man who came to call on her an hour later. "A gentleman," was all the butler said, but in this household, and with such a butler, she expected someone on the order of Magnus himself. She worried, hesitant to come down and see the fellow, because she didn't really know anyone in London except for Magnus and Martin. But then a sudden joyous thought came to her: Hadn't her mother married a real gentleman? Maybe Magnus had been right; maybe time had made her existence easier for her mother to accept. So she flew down the stairs to greet the man. And stopped and stared when she saw who was lounging in the front parlor.

The gentleman was young, a tall, lean, fashionable fop, like many she'd seen, though his shoulders were broader. He wore a beautiful brown silk long coat over a tapestry vest and dark brown silk breeches. The lace at his throat was as fine as the lace at his wrists, his white stockings were immaculate, and his brown shoes had golden buckles. He carried a polished walking stick, and his full white wig was carefully curled. She hesitated in the doorway—until he turned to look at her.

"Black Jack!" Cristabel hissed, looking around wildly to

be sure no one was nearby. "Are you mad? 'Tis broad daylight, man!"

"So it is," he said with a familiar leering smile. "What of it? Why, you look like you've seen a ghost, Cristabel my dear. But where's the danger? Do you see any highwaymen hereabouts? Or cutpurses? Or me heavens! Any pirates? No, not a one, do you? Just a gentleman of fashion. Don't fret, lass, I be safe as houses. For I'm a fine gent now," he said, sweeping her a bow, his tanned face now set in an expression of perfectly cool amusement. "Master Jarvis Kelly at your service, just like you asked him to be, m'lady.

"See, I got to thinking, Chrissie," he said merrily, "that if Captain Whiskey's own daughter could be a lady, and make such a fine one at that, and if she had a preference for gentlemen, why then, I could be one meself. For think on it: 'Tis only fine clothes—which I have got me—and manners—which me old mam did once teach me—and gold—which I got for meself in plenty—which makes the gentleman. And so behold: your own Jack, a gentleman to suit you to a nicety. So you don't have to be shamed of me no more. And when you come with me you'll know you're coming along with a gentleman. Y'know, luv? I been having the time of me life as a gent here in London town, going to the finest places and parties. Everybody wants to be me friend—so long as the money in me pockets don't stay there too long. And there ain't a lady who minds being on me arm, so long as that arm be seen in the right company, which it always is. I don't know why I didn't try it sooner. Being a gent is a fine thing."

"Being a gentleman is more than clothes and manners and money," Cristabel fumed.

"Is it?" he asked, arching an eyebrow exactly the way she'd seen Magnus do.

"Aye—it's—it's honor and temperament and control— yes, self-control," she said, thinking of Magnus and the things about him that she'd never found in any other man, "doing without what you want, if it makes someone you care about happier. And it's good taste, and—and kindness to people you don't have to be kind to, and protecting those who are weaker than you, and loyalty and honesty—and bravery too."

Black Jack stopped smiling. "Lass, you should hear yourself. Be this our Cristabel?" he asked in wonder. "Speaking about a man the way her father's women used to prattle on about him?"

"That, they did not!" she shouted, losing her last remnants of fine speech along with her temper. "And well ye know it, blast ye! My father's women talked about his capacity and his size, and the way he tossed around his gold, damn ye. I don't know the man's capacity 'cause he don't get drunk in front of me, and as fer his size—well," she said, her cheeks growing pink, "We don't do that neither. And I got gold enough of me own. But since ye brought the matter up, 'tis about the viscount that I wished to speak to ye. Look ye, Black Jack," she said, pacing the room as he watched her with narrowed eyes, "the viscount be a good man whether ye like it or not. And I'll be the one deciding what me future is with him, whether ye like it or not too. What I want from you is the truth," she said, wheeling around and facing him squarely. "Was it you that tried to do him in last night?"

"Do him in?" Black Jack asked.

"Aye. Be it ye who tried to run him over with a horse in the Strand?"

"What?" he asked, genuinely surprised. He stared at her and whistled. "Nay, lass, 'tis not that I love the fellow, but you should know it isn't me way. I'd do him with fists or sword, pistol or knife. But I'd do it face-to-face 'cause I'd want him to know who done it, you can be sure. You were with him? Aye, that must have been something," he mused, "and you didn't get a glimpse at the scum what tried it? Shame, lass, what were you doing, staring into his big blue eyes 'stead of taking care of business?"

"They're gray eyes, and there wasn't no way I could see in the dark," she snapped. "But this horse came running out of nowhere, heading straight at him. If he hadn't jumped, dragging me with him, we'd both have been for it. I thought of you, Jack, sorry, but I did, because you have no love for him."

"But I do for you," Black Jack said quietly, "so there's no way on earth I'd have put you in danger, and from what you say, you were. Nor would I take him out whilst you was there. I'd do him on the sly, nice and neat, so all you'd know was that he'd been done for. I thought you knew me better than that," he said sadly.

"Sorry," she said, shamefaced.

"Aye, well, you owe me one," he said generously. "But I think I can help you. Might be it was the lads who tried for him again."

"No," she said, "Magnus said they wouldn't 'cause he were with me, and that's all they wanted of him last time."

"Aye, *last* time," Black Jack said knowingly, "but then they thought you two was married. This time they might have been vexed 'cause they found out you wasn't really. Didn't think on that, did he? Ha. He don't know everything."

"Maybe he did," Cristabel muttered. "Maybe he just didn't want to worry me."

"Maybe. But there is something I can do that he can't," Black Jack said proudly. "I can talk with the lads and find out just what's up."

"Would you?" Cristabel asked eagerly. "No—better yet, let me talk with them, too, please. Ah, don't be that way. You ought to know I don't have to be wrapped in cotton wool. Use your head, man. Where's the pirate who don't know Captain Whiskey? Or who don't know of me, by now, at least? I know pirates well too. That's why I need to see their eyes when they answer; it will tell me more than what they say. Ah, please, Jack. Arrange it. Do it for me, won't you?"

"Oh my," Sophia said, pausing dramatically in the doorway, "am I interrupting anything? What is it you wish done, Cristabel dear? And who is this gallant gentleman you are asking it of?" She fluttered her eyelashes as much as her fan as she stared at Black Jack.

"Jarvis Kelly at your service, ma'am," Black Jack said promptly before Cristabel could answer. "We met at the Swansons' soiree only a few weeks past. Do you remember? I hope so, for I can scarce forget."

He put his hand on his heart before he swept Sophia a low bow, and then rose and stood staring at her with deep appreciation. With good reason, Cristabel thought nervously. Sophia was a vision in pink and white: a tiny, pretty lady, demure and just a little flirtatious as she hid her dimpled pleasure at his compliment behind her fluttering fan the way only a fine lady could. And Black Jack, Cristabel thought with real anxiety, looked every inch a gentleman, and more, for now he even spoke like one, his voice smooth and low and filled with the secret knowing amusement that was the mark of a fine gentleman as well as a scamp.

"Master Jarvis is an old friend of mine," Cristabel said at once, "from the Islands."

"My interests lie in shipping, my lady," Black Jack said smoothly, his eyes slewing from one woman to the other, enjoying Cristabel's distress as much as Sophia's attention.

"Aha! Like Cristabel's papa?" Sophia said with a trill of laughter, as though it were wildly funny to even try to imagine this fine gentleman at the helm of a pirate ship.

"Ah—no. Not quite," Black Jack said with a wide grin, as though he, too, found it ridiculous to be compared to a pirate.

Cristabel wanted to slap one of them and kick the other. "Take a better look, my lady; you also met him here in this very parlor the night before that," she said angrily.

Sophia's eyes grew wide as she finally recognized Black Jack. Well, now she'll scream and Jack will have to hop it, Cristabel thought with cynical pleasure. She knew he'd get away in time, because he was as quick as he was bold, and very careful of his neck. But she was afraid for her ears. Sophia might screech the house down once she realized she'd been openly flirting with the ragged pirate she'd watched with so much awed caution before. But she didn't. After an instant of shocked surprise, Sophia's smile grew sly and knowing.

"My compliments," Sophia told Black Jack. "A transformation indeed."

"Ah, no, my lady, not really," he answered, "for a fellow does what he has to in order to get ahead in the world. What are a gentleman's garments, after all, but a disguise for the condition of his heart and his mind? Are there not gentlemen with the hearts of pirates? Aye, and so why not the reverse? Under my rags, my heart was as true to the code of a gentleman as it is now: because I am as pledged to honor, self-control, loyalty, and honesty as ever I was before. Only now I can show it to the world."

He bowed again, but his curling smile was for Cristabel. To her astonishment, it grew wider with her anger. He was a pirate through and through. Not only was he a thieving magpie, plucking a person's words and taking them for his own, Cristabel thought wrathfully, but the rogue could talk straight as she could if he wanted.

Her anger faded to real concern when she saw Sophia's delight. She knew Black Jack for what he was, and Sophia didn't. Sophia was very young for her years, and moreover she was neglected by her husband. And the fact that she had asked him to neglect her hardly mattered. Nor did it make any difference if she really was as captivated by Black Jack as she seemed to be or was just looking for a way to annoy her husband. Jack was too dangerous to use as a toy, as dozens of island girls and scores of more experienced wenches could testify. Cristabel didn't like Sophia. But she didn't wish her any harm either.

"You can show them everything you like except for your name, matey," Cristabel told Black Jack harshly, "less you want your fine gentleman's heart to follow your neck up when it gets stretched by a noose."

"I'm touched by how much you care," he said.

"Blast it, Jack!" Cristabel erupted. "'Tis no joking matter. Nor be it any of your business neither, m'lady," she told Sophia, "so I'll thank you to be leaving us now."

Sophia blinked. "You're asking me to leave you alone with a strange man in my own house? And you an unmarried girl? I'm sure Magnus would be fascinated to hear it."

"Aye, that he would be. And so would Martin, I'd bet," Cristabel spat.

"Ladies, ladies, don't fight over me," Black Jack said in delight.

"Better us than the viscount, or the mob," Cristabel said. Then she sighed. "Look you, Jack," she said, "there's no sense in talking more now anyway. You know what I want. And you know I'll get it even if you don't help me. So if you really do have a care for me, you'll deliver, and soon."

"Aye, there's truth." he admitted. "Tonight then. *Late* tonight." He glanced at Sophia again, but there was no flirtation, only cold calculation in his eyes. "Can you trust the lady to keep her tongue in her mouth about it?"

"No," Cristabel said, "but I'll keep watch over her until then, and I'll cut it out of her mouth if I get even a hint that she's going to spill it to anyone."

"That's good," he said, and Sophia gasped. He clapped on his tricorne, bowed, and was gone out the door.

"I thought he liked me," Sophia said nervously after he'd gone.

"Aye, so he does. But he likes his own self more. Most men do. Remember that now, and forevermore, my lady. There aren't many Martins lying thick on the ground in this world." Nor Magnuses either, Cristabel told herself wearily. So she had to do what she could to preserve them. She hoped what she learned tonight would help do that.

Martin and Sophia were in their separate beds, and Magnus had long since gone after their dinner together, when a footman came and told Cristabel that there were some persons to see her in the kitchens. She hadn't undressed and so she came quickly downstairs, holding her single candle before her. The house was dark and sleeping all around her, but it was very lively in the kitchen.

At first she thought there were over a dozen men there. But once her eyes had sorted out the shadows and the eye patches, the grinning faces and broad shoulders, the bandannas and the gleaming gold teeth, she realized there were only five pirates and Black Jack himself waiting for her there. They were all grinning—and eating and drinking and sitting and lounging all around Cook's clean kitchen, brandishing chicken legs like dirks as they talked, and swallowing down mugs of ale for emphasis. She was met with a murmur of general approval. Quiet approval. Pirates were the noisiest men she knew, as a rule. But they were also very good at holding their breath and moving like cats when they had to, because the sea picked up sounds and magnified them on still nights. Stealth was as much a part of pirating as roaring and cursing was.

"Gentlemen," Cristabel said, nodding at them. Which amused them all no end.

She colored, remembering herself. "Aye, mateys," she said a little more gruffly, "so then, how you be, eh?"

A soft chorus of "fine, fine" greeted her, and she relaxed.

"I asked Jack here to bring you to me tonight, 'cause I got meself a vexing problem," she said, leaning back against a carving block and fingering the edge of a knife she picked up from it. "Seems someone tried to do Magnus, Viscount Snow, last night. I was with him on the Strand when a horseman came straight for us, riding like the wind. The viscount would have been pounded to fishbait, and me with him, if he hadn't moved quick and saved us both. Now, I know you lads had a go at him once before, and I understand why you thought you had to then—although there was no need for it, as you've likely discovered by now. What's done is done and no blame given for misunderstanding, and none taken neither, is me motto and me father's. The same applies here.

"The question be: Who has a quarrel with him *now?*

Speak, and we'll hear it out. Keep it to yerself, and there'll be trouble sure to follow. I am my father's daughter."

"And I am her dear friend," Black Jack said quietly, but menacingly.

"As am I—as well as being understandably especially concerned," Magnus said from the darkened doorway.

They all tensed and turned to look at him as he strolled into the room. He carefully plucked the knife from Cristabel's fingers. "I think I'd best not take any chances with your temper, from the look of things," he murmured to her before he faced the others. "Gentlemen and pirates," he said, a smile twitching at the corner of his lips, "I give you good evening. I knew you were here because I've had the place watched since the episode on the Strand. I didn't expect mayhem, but I refuse to miss out on plotting—fine coat, by the way," he remarked to Black Jack.

"Thankee. You're wide-awake, all right, even though you always look like you're half-asleep," Black Jack said grudgingly.

"You'd be surprised what you can learn if the world thinks you're sleeping," Magnus said, and then added. "But don't give me too much credit; half the time I *am* bored to near oblivion by life. Or was—until Mistress Stew came into mine." He saw her blush, and looking very pleased, he addressed the pirates again. "Now then, I'll repeat Mistress Stew's question, and add only one thing to it: The man who brings me information about the mad horseman will be well paid for his efforts."

Magnus hadn't expected much more than a silent calculated interest in what he offered. He certainly didn't expect the tense, angry silence that greeted his announcement. It was broken by an older pirate, whose one good eye glittered with something less than anger but more than tears.

"Keep yer gold, me lord," he rasped, "fer no man jack of us would take a penny piece for doing a favor fer Captain Whiskey's dotter, we wouldn't. We ain't gents, to be sure," he said, making a mocking bow, "but we be men of honor in other ways. We look after our own, we do."

Magnus look unperturbed. "Well then, I salute you. But do you know who attempted it?"

They eyed each other cautiously, and satisfied by what they saw—or didn't see—the pirates started mumbling and talking all at once. There was a ragged chorus of "no's" and "dunno's" until the older pirate spoke up again. "We dunno, lordship. But we'll find out who done it—'lessen it were just some drunken sprout out on the town with no cares in his fool head, but no malice neither."

"That's what I hope it will be," Magnus said smoothly.

"But there be something else," the old pirate said. "We be sorry fer mixing it up with you when last we met, lordship. But like she says, we didn't know better then."

"Aye," another pirate said with a sharkish grin, "and old Redfish here"—he jerked at thumb at their spokesman, who suddenly looked as embarrassed as a weathered old pirate could—"decided to spend the night playing lift-leg with a bar wench and let us hammer the wrong man."

"I said I were sorry, didn't I?" the old pirate snapped. "Leave it be, or be prepared to show steel, here and now!"

"I were only commenting," the other pirate muttered, subsiding.

"Aye. Be that as it may," the old pirate said, sheathing his knife and turning back to Magnus with exaggerated calm, "there be no question that yer brother fair diddled the captain, and he be vexed, I be sure, but he is a fair man, just the same. He don't hold no grudges; that, I will tell you. Now, we wants to know, so we can tell him: Since she ain't wed, when will she be coming back? It were never his plan to strand his dear dotter alone in London town."

"A lot you know of his plans, Redfish!" Cristabel shouted. "I'll bet he never told you a word of them. Besides, you haven't seen him since I have, and the lads that went back home to report to him can't have returned to London yet unless they rode back on a waterspout. So why are you worrying? Come to think of it, why haven't you gone back neither?"

"Aye, well, but," the pirate said, looking down with

sudden interest at his boots. "See, your father be retiring soon, so to speak, Cristabel, and so we be getting ourselves a new captain soon too . . ."

"Ah," Cristabel said, "I do see. Black Jack," she said angrily, "you tell these lads right here and now, where I can hear and see it, that I be plotting me own course from now on."

Black Jack put his hands in the air. "Got me in your sights, luv? All right. Leave off, men. The lass is to do what she wants. And I have the word of the Viscount Snow here, word of a gentleman, that is—which he holds to be a powerful thing—that he'll be looking after her, and seeing that she comes to no harm, at *anyone's* hands, until she do make up her mind. Don't I, me lord?"

Magnus nodded. "You do," he said.

"That be meaning: not only no harm, but no advantage of any kind be taken of her," Black Jack said carefully.

"Oh, for heaven's sake," Cristabel muttered, turning pink.

"My word on it," Magnus said, and thrust out his hand.

The two men shook hands over the butcher block, while Cristabel muttered words neither of them knew she knew. Then the pirates relaxed, and took some more chickens and hams from the larder, and broke out bottles of red wine. The pirates shrugged out of their long coats, and Magnus and Black Jack took off their coats and loosened their collars. If any servants saw or heard the viscount visiting with his odd company, they were wise enough to keep it to themselves. The men lounged and laughed and talked softly together, telling tales and swapping lies so amiably that Cristabel, sitting and watching them, began to see no difference between the lordly Magnus and the newly respectable Black Jack, and all the pirate crew. That's when she realized how sleepy she was and left them all to go to her own bed. She may have muttered something about a pox on them all when they laughingly bid her good night, but as she left the kitchen, she had to conceal her tender—almost tearful—smiles.

* * *

213

"This time," Magnus said sternly, a few days later, "you will ride in a sedan chair, and you will stay by my side when you get out of it, and you will not stray from me after that, not once. Not even to take care of personal matters, so if there's anything you must attend to, do it now."

"I am not a child," Cristabel said sweetly, drawing on her gloves, "and it's not me that has an enemy—if there is one. So staying at your side might be the death of me."

"No," he said with a tender smile, as he looked down at her, "It's you who will be the death of me, that's certain. But I grant it's an interesting question. If you'd like to debate it, we will. However, if you'd like to go to the theater instead, you'll accept that I've won the debate, and agree to my terms."

He stood and waited for her answer. She longed to argue. But she also yearned to go out with him tonight, and to be easy in his company. He looked so handsome in his new gray coat.

"Oh aye," she muttered, gracelessly, "you win."

When he didn't speak or make a move to the door, she said, growing red-faced, "And I don't have to 'take care of anything else.' But since I'm fairly bristling with knives, I'd think you'd be afraid to have me quite so close to your side," she added saucily, because she hated to give an inch without getting back some of her own.

His lips twitched. "Thank you," he said, "I'll remember not to get too near . . . right away, that is. As I recall, even hedgehogs can get close to each other, once they get the hang of it. And they can get very close, in fact, or else there wouldn't be any more hedgehogs." Then smiling at her blushes, he went to the door and had the footman summon sedan chairs for her and Sophia.

Martin and Sophia went with them, but ahead of them, silent and suspicious of each other, as was usual these days. Cristabel settled herself in her chair and looked out at Magnus, who walked by her side. It was a cold, still night, but clear enough so that the stars were bright above. Cristabel felt a thrill of excitement. It was her first visit to a

London theater. The only plays she'd ever seen had been performed by traveling players in the marketplace, or at night, in loud and smelly theaters lit by flaring torches and punctuated by loud and frequent catcalls and comments from a drunken audience. This promised to be both lavish and civilized. But the prospect of a night at the theater wasn't what pleased her most.

He strode beside her and told her about the play, each word a puff of smoke on the frosty night air. She hardly listened. It was all too good to be true. The scare they'd had last week had come to nothing; neither lord or pirate had discovered anything amiss. But it wasn't just the absence of that fear that was so wonderful, it was the absence of all fears. She was free, and in England, and with him, and she wasn't worried about anything but her appearance tonight. And he had already told her she looked lovely.

The street in front of the theater was filled with people and horses, sedan chairs and carriages, so they had to be let down at the fringe of the mob. Sophia and Martin stood waiting for them at the curb. Magnus helped Cristabel out of her chair, and kept her close as he paid the sedan men.

The man appeared from out of the dark as Magnus turned to take Cristabel's arm. He was cloaked in black, with a black tricorne pulled down over his eyes. But not far enough to blind him. Cristabel saw the glint of torchlight shine on his eyes as he looked at her and Magnus, and then with sudden terrible clarity saw the man's hand come out from under his cloak with a long-nosed pistol in it.

She reached for her own pistol, even though she knew, in that weird slowing of thought and time that happens in moments of crisis, that she would be too late. She thought she screamed a warning. But the sound was drowned out by the roar of the pistol. For a moment she thought she was hit, because of the sudden flash of noise and pain as she stumbled back and the utter blackness that came before her eyes. But then she realized the brief pain was from the shock and the jolt to her body because she'd stumbled when Magnus shoved her out of harm's way and stepped in her place to face the assassin alone. The darkness she'd seen in front of her was only because she'd seen nothing but his broad back as he positioned himself to stand between her and their attacker as he fired back at him. The rest was all confusion until Magnus staggered back a step, swearing beneath his breath, before he wavered and fell to his knees at her feet.

Sophia was screaming and Martin was reaching for his sword as the assassin, a hand to his chest, turned to run. There was another flash of fire and clap of thunder and the attacker kicked forward, before he spun around to stare at Cristabel, openmouthed in surprise. Blood rushed from his gaping mouth, and he, too, fell. That was when she realized she held her own smoking pistol in her hand. It was hot and her hand was numb from the recoil of it, so she dropped the pistol to the street before she fell to her own knees and sought Magnus in the dark.

He lay before her, but he had struggled to an elbow and seen what she'd done.

"Oh, mighty Cristabel," he said in a strained voice, "thank you for disposing of the rude fellow."

"How are you?" she asked in terror, her hands going beneath his cloak, to his hard chest, to his heart—her own heart near stopping when she felt the wetness there soaking through her gloves.

"Fine, fine," he said absently, his face growing paler.

"Why did you do it?" she raged. "I could have stood by your side and taken care of meself."

"Had to protect you," he whispered, as he slid down to the street again and closed his eyes.

"Oh, damn you," she shouted, shaking him, trying to throttle him to consciousness again, "Damn you, blast you, rotten bloody pigheaded villain! Who is going to protect you? All your life protecting others: your sap-skulled brother and all yer blasted sisters and yer hen-witted sister-in-law, and me! Me, a blackguard's dirty daughter, who can protect herself, blast ye! Who is going to protect you, ye great bleeding dumb-ox fool? Did ye think ye were made of wood or steel? No, ye be but a man, a good man, too good, damn ye, damn ye. Who asked ye to carry the world on yer shoulders? Does no one look out for ye? Why din't ye let me? Oh, see what you've done, you great oaf, oh, just see," she wailed.

She sat there grieving, holding him and cursing him and stroking his cold face until they pulled her away, and gently raised him up and carried him off, with her sobbing and running beside him all the way, his cold, limp hand held tightly in hers.

CHAPTER

14

They made her leave the room because she frightened the
doctor so much. They worried about his being able to
get the job done in her presence—it being difficult to
operate on a man while a madwoman holds a pistol to your
head. Or so Martin said.

"He's a good physician, I promise, Cristabel," Martin
said as he stood with his back against the door to the room
Magnus was in. "I can't let you go back in. You'll do no
good in there anyway. Let him work. He has to get the bullet
out and tend the wound, that's all."

"He'll cut too deep, he'll bleed him dry, he'll dose him
too strong, he'll sew him sloppy if he don't have someone
there to see. I don't trust quacks. I seen too many of them
hurt a man worse'n his wounds," she fretted, pacing up and
down, eyeing the door Martin stood before, as though she'd
leap in if he just moved a fraction away from it.

"Yes, but not this doctor. He's no fool. He's not fashionable, just sound. He's used to dealing with more than a
matron's crochets; he knows how to deal with shell and
shot. If it makes you feel any better, he sailed with Her
Majesty's navy as a sawbones for years before he settled
here to practice."

"That certainly don't make me feel no better," she grumbled, but he saw her shoulders relax.

They'd taken Magnus to Martin's house instead of his own because they'd thought he'd have better care from relatives than mere servants . . . if he survived the wound, Martin thought uneasily. But he couldn't let his apprehensions show, because Cristabel was a tinderbox. Sophia was frightened into tearful, prayerful silence, but at least she was calm. Not like Cristabel, who raved and paced and ranted like a vengeful wraith. Surprisingly, Martin found that having to appear confident and dealing with Cristabel's touchy temper helped him cope with his own fears, because he was deeply troubled.

Seeing Magnus lying bleeding and pale had frightened him. Seeing him totally unresponsive had shaken him deeply. Magnus filled his life, he was always there to depend on, to lean on. Even in the depths of his misery in that pirate hell, Martin had found the courage to go through with Captain Whiskey's mad request because in the back of his mind he'd known that somehow Magnus would make it right again. Now, seeing his big brother unconscious and vulnerable was beyond tragic, it seemed impossible.

"You'll do no good in there," Martin repeated. "The bullet will come out, the doctor will leave medicines, and there's an end to it."

It was a bad choice of words; he knew it when he heard them, and winced when he saw her eyebrows go up. But before she could open her mouth, the bedroom door opened.

"If there is a Cristabel on the premises, I believe it would be best if she came in now," the doctor said hurriedly. "He calls for her."

"I'm here," Cristabel said, and ran to the door. But the doctor refused to move out of her way immediately. He studied her closely first. She'd been a wild thing when he'd first come to the house. She was quieter now and he could assess her, even in the dim guttering candlelight.

She saw his appraisal and remembered how she'd greeted him when she'd been distracted. Flushing, she put a hand up to smooth her hair. It was a futile gesture. Her dress was stained with blood and dirt, her face had smudges on it, and her hair was out of its pins and tumbled to her shoulders. She looked tousled and hard-used but nevertheless surprisingly young and lovely, less like a grieving woman than like a maid who'd just been soundly tumbled. But her eyes gave her away. When they met the doctor's steady gaze, he saw determination and a terrible fear quickly hidden by her lashes.

"First," the doctor said sternly, "you go wash your face and hands and see to your hair. If he opens his eyes, I want him to see that you're in control and everything is normal. Go, go," he said a little more kindly. "I took the ball out of his chest and he's in pain, but he has a chance." Her face lit with such sudden radiance, his voice grew softer when he added, "I can't speak of the future with confidence. It depends on many things. His heart's whole, thank God, and his lungs were not touched, but it was a near thing and there was too much blood lost. I can't see beneath flesh and bone, so I can't see what else might have been affected. If he lasts through the night and doesn't take a hard fever, he has a chance for a full recovery. But even then—there are sickbed contagions . . . but he's a strong lad, with a good history of healing. I can't say; no one can. Go, Mistress Cristabel," he said impatiently, "prepare yourself. He asked for you, and from now on the state of his spirit is as important as that of his body."

She fairly flew to her room. When she emerged from it again, she'd combed and pinned her hair into a neat bundle of curls, scrubbed her face, changed her gown, taken off her hoop so that she could have more freedom of movement, and had even added a dab of perfume to her wrists. She was pale but composed, if one did not notice the fine trembling of her hands. Magnus didn't.

She entered his room quietly and went straight to his high bed and gazed down at him. He lay on his back, his chest swathed in bandages. Someone had washed his face and combed back his hair. Cristabel reached out and gently laid her hand on his broad forehead. It was warm, but not hectically so, only as warm as his whole glowing body usually was. And as such, far warmer than her icy hand. But he didn't open his eyes.

She blinked back tears. He looked like a warrior carved on a tomb, such as the ones he'd taken her to see in London's great cathedrals. Even in repose, his strength and power were evident; every line of his body spoke silently of grace, his broad-boned face that of a man of valor. All he needed, she thought with a terrible tearful flash of humor, was a sword at his hand and a dog at his feet—and a marble lady all of his own to lie at his side through eternity. Not a pirate's daughter. Not the ill-gotten wretch whose very presence had made him an enemy who had brought him to this.

It was all her fault, she knew it. He'd had no enemies until she'd been landed on him. As she stood by his side and counted his breaths, she felt almost as bad about who she was as she did about what had happened to him. She would settle the score with the man who had planned this. There was no doubt in her mind their attacker had been paid to do his evil work. He hadn't sought a purse or shouted a complaint when he'd struck. Men who killed silently in the dark were men who did others' work. She'd find the one responsible and deal him what he'd dealt, she vowed. Whether Magnus lived or the unthinkable happened, she'd have her vengeance and leave here, forever.

"Cristabel," Magnus breathed. His eyes were open and he smiled. "Cristabel," he said, "you're all right."

"Aye, and so be—are you," she said with a rising smile. "Fine as fivepence, you are."

His big hand rose from his side and he touched his bandaged chest. His hand fell still when he felt what was there. "Yes," he breathed, "but best make that one pence, Mistress Stew. I've a hole in me the size of a cannonball, I think."

"Pshaw, that's soon mended," she said with awful cheerfulness.

He struggled to sit up and fell back before helpful hands could force him to stop trying. "'Od's life!" he said on a puff of pained breath, his great chest rising and falling with the force of it. "It *was* a cannon, I think. Where's Martin?"

"Here," Martin said, coming to his side and taking his hand.

"Good lad. All's safe then?" Magnus asked, trying to search his brother's face in the dim light because he knew Martin could hide nothing from him.

Martin nodded, then not sure Magnus could see it, added, "Yes, all of us are perfectly safe. All of us but you."

"Too big a target to miss," Magnus said ruefully. "And the villain?"

"You got him, and then Cristabel finished him," Martin said.

"Hasty wench," Magnus said with a weak grin. "A pity, he might have had an interesting song to sing. Still, it's nice to have a Valkyrie on one's side. Tell me, brother—" He winced as he paused to suck in another deep breath and went on, "Since Mistress Stew's determined to be a cheerful nurse, I must ask you. I want truth. What was hit? How will I do?"

Martin nodded at the doctor, who had pushed his way to his patient and was feeling his pulse. "Dr. Fowler says nothing vital was hit. But the recuperation will be—up to you."

"Doctor?" Magnus asked.

"Aye," the doctor said gruffly, "I can't promise anything. I did my best. But the ball was near too many important organs and too much blood was lost for me to be pleased. It's as your brother says: up to you and God now, my lord."

"Well, I'll certainly do *my* best," Magnus said, and laughed. He closed his eyes against the pain of his laughter, and did not open them again.

"Sleeping," the doctor said quickly, hearing Cristabel's gasp and turning to see her face. "You'd best learn the difference between sleep and disaster if you're going to last the night. Here, take this chair, my dear. It will be a long night."

It was.

She sat and watched Magnus sleeping, and stood and waited for him to wake. Sometimes she paced, but never too far to miss hearing his every exhalation. Martin sat with her, servants moved quietly through the sickroom going about their chores, and Sophia stole in every so often, looked at Magnus, raised her handkerchief to her eyes, and fled again. She did it almost every hour. It was the only thing that made Martin and Cristabel smile. Until Magnus groaned, and stirred and opened his eyes again.

"Devilish thirsty," he muttered, his head moving restlessly.

They smiled at each other and helped him to sip some water.

"Ah, I'm a deuced nuisance," he said fretfully.

They denied it gladly.

"'Od's blood, but it's hot in here," he complained. They stopped smiling. Because the room was chill.

His fever grew with the night. The doctor bled him, and would have done it once more if he dared face Cristabel's wrath. As it was, since it had done no good so far, he shrugged and resorted to the other best treatments modern medicine offered. They used cold cloths and soft words, they chafed his wrists and stroked his hair, and still the fever rose. It was a dry heat, a burning thing that made his flesh feel like baked stones. It grew until Cristabel could swear it singed her hands so much that they hurt when she put her fingertips together to pray.

She was a sailor's daughter and knew all the superstitions and true lore of the sea, and so when the night grew hazy gray and started to fade to dawn, she held her breath and prayed as she held his hand tight in her own. She knew that human life had its own tides, and that dawn and dusk were powerful times because human souls sought safe harbor at the margins of the night and day. Every sailor knew those turning times were when life had its most tenuous hold. And so she hung on to Magnus's hand as if she were hanging on to his life—holding it back against the turning tide of night, refusing to let it flow away as night vanished into day.

His hand was so broad and wide, she could only hold it halfway round, but she clutched it tightly, squeezed her eyes shut, and prayed.

"Cristabel," Magnus murmured.

"Aye, here," she said.

"Look you," he said with effort, "I have been thinking. Yes, I can think in this oven. I've been lying here thinking things out as best I can. There's a thing . . . there is a thing you must do for me."

"Anything," she said fervently.

"Don't be so hasty," he said, licking his dry lips. "It won't sit well with you. But it is the only right thing to do. I cannot rest easy unless it's done."

"What?" she asked, her heart pounding with fear because of the way the words "rest easy" hurt her ears.

"Marry me," he said. "Now."

The room grew still. He squeezed her hand to get her attention. "Listen, my dear, it's for the best. You need no mother if you have me. You need no father. Even if I die, you'll have the name. If I don't, you'll have me. That's the only problem for you that I see. I can't rest easy with you this way. I've tried, and I cannot. What say you, Cristabel?"

She was still. But the doctor spoke up. "My lord," he said uneasily, "the fever may be speaking. A man oughtn't to act in haste . . ."

"Doctor," Magnus said with enough of his old power in his voice to quiet the man instantly, "I'm not asking for the first time. Pray be silent, and let pity do what prudence would not let her do." He turned his head to Cristabel, his gaze steady, his voice serious. "If you hate me, then naysay me," he told her, "for I fully intend to recover if God lets me. No—I'd even say that if you only have a mild care for me, you should say no and wait for your one true love to come along."

"You are my own true love!" she cried, the words wrenched from her by fear and terror.

He smiled. "It is decided," he said. "Martin, get us a man of God, and double-quick, sir. If not at the church, then at Fleet Prison, or cross the river at Southwark where they commonly do such things, or wherever you can find a holy man practical enough to do the deed here and now. Tell him a soul hangs in the balance—a soul with money in his pockets." He laid his head back down on his pillow again, clearly exhausted just from the effort of issuing so many orders.

Martin hesitated. Sophia, who had crept into the room again, spoke up quickly. "Stay with him, Martin," she said in a small, tear-filled voice. "I'll see to it. I'll send for a minister. I'll send three footmen in three directions if I have to, I promise. Please, let me do something."

Magnus nodded.

Martin stood and watched his brother as they waited for dawn and a minister—or death—to come to the room. Cristabel clung to Magnus's hand just as stubbornly as he clung to consciousness. He didn't say anything, but she could tell he was awake and aware of her from the way he tried to tighten his hand over hers every so often. Her hand grew hot and damp in that desperate clasp. But she didn't let go until Martin touched her shoulder.

"Look," he said with awe.

In the rising light she saw Magnus's face beaded with dampness, and realized that her hand was slippery in his because the fever had broken. She flashed a glad smile, until the doctor spoke.

"Good," he said, "but it must stay this way."

"Cristabel," Magnus said softly, "go. Put on something pretty for our wedding morning. I'll be here when you return. That, I promise. Now that you've agreed to wed me, you'll really have to use a cannon to finish me off." He managed to chuckle, and took a sip of water the doctor offered him.

Seeing that, she nodded. "But you keep your promise, hear?" she warned him in a thickened voice.

"If you keep yours," he reminded her.

She nodded, and left.

The doctor sighed. "A handful, my lord, but quite a woman."

"Quite a *lady*," Magnus corrected him.

"Ah. Well, I think you'd better drink this potion, my lord. It will help ease you. Drink it all. I should hate to think of what she'll do if you die. Not only to me, my lord. But to you."

Magnus grinned, and took his medicine.

The ceremony took place shortly after dawn. It was irregular, but the parson they had gotten never conducted regular ceremonies, his flock being composed of people willing and needful of paying for instant weddings, strange funerals, and odd christenings. It was all as legally binding as the highest church ceremonies, though, and that was all Magnus cared about. All Cristabel cared about was seeing that her groom lived through the ceremony. He was very pale, and she could feel his hand in hers growing warm again.

Magnus lay with his head propped up against his pillows and repeated the words in a low, strong voice. Cristabel stood at his side and tried to repeat them without crying. She knew she was doing the wrong thing, but she also knew that it was for all the right reasons.

"I do," she said at last. At the vicar's instruction, she bent her head to take her groom's kiss. Only then did she let her salt tears flow, to soothe the scalding touch of his lips. Because he burned with fever again.

"Lady Snow," Magnus said with satisfaction, savoring the words. Then, having won her hand, he lay back and closed his eyes to do battle for his life.

* * *

Cristabel spent her wedding night by her husband's bedside. He woke once and sympathized with her for having such a poor sort of groom. She rejoiced, because it meant that he knew what was happening, even if he could do nothing about it. The second night of her marriage, she dozed in fits and starts in a chair by his bedside, willing him to wake, telling him to sleep, watching to see if his sleep was sleep or death. The third night, he refused to let her stay with him any longer.

"Either you crawl in here beneath my covers with me," he said in a stronger voice than she'd heard from him in days, "and thereby likely kill me—or you take yourself off to your old safe spinster bed and sleep a day or so. 'Od's mercy, but I have married a crone! Look you, Martin; shadows under her eyes, wrinkles on her forehead, and yet I begged her to wed me! It must have been a trick of the light, or the fever, like the doctor said."

"Villain!" she retorted. "It was tending your battered carcass that wearied me, and getting you back to your normal nasty self that deprived me of sleep."

They teased the way an old married couple might, because they'd lived very close in the past days, more closely than many couples ever did. It had been hours since the fever had abated, and it had not returned.

"Sleep, wife," Magnus said gently, laying tender emphasis on the word "wife," "or else we'll have you sick too. Then who would be here to torment me? I'll mend on my own now, thank you. You may leave now, too, Martin. And, Doctor, I thank you for your vigil, but it's no longer necessary. I bloom with health. Seriously, I do well now, and I think I'd like to pass one night without cracking open an eye to see someone hovering."

Cristabel and Martin looked at the doctor. He nodded. "The viscount's on the road to health," he said, and then added, "barring infection, of course, and overwork and—"

"And plague, pestilence, and various acts of God," Magnus interrupted, adding wearily, "I know, Doctor, the flesh is weak and you can give no promises. But I tell you, I'm well. I heal with amazing speed; I'm no delicate flower, sir."

Cristabel bit her lip. It was just that kind of thinking that had gotten him into that sickbed.

Magnus saw her hesitation. "If you have any doubts, post footmen at the doors. Because the only thing that will take me tonight will be an assassin, armed to the teeth," he assured her.

She looked at Martin and they exchanged a silent nod. It was exactly what they would do.

Magnus sighed. "I was only joking," he said, "but no matter. So long as I don't have to see them. Don't I get a kiss good night, my lady wife?"

Cristabel blushed, but obediently lowered her lips to his. And was more than a little shocked at the sweetness of the light kiss she received. Magnus's eyes were dark and sincere as she raised her head. "Yes," was all he said, but it was like a promise.

Cristabel paused outside of Magnus's door and leaned against the balcony stair rail. He was right. She needed rest. She was so weary, so guilty and thrilled and frightened all at once, that she knew she'd have to sleep for hours before she could start to really regret her rash marriage. Even that would have to wait until she could figure out how to protect Magnus from future harm. And that would in turn have to wait until she could offer up prayers of thanks for his recovery. And that would have to wait for her to beg that his recovery was real . . . She put a hand to her forehead—he was right, she had to sleep; she couldn't even get her worries straight anymore.

"Cristabel?" Martin said.

She looked up. They hadn't had a chance for private conversation since Magnus had been shot. But she knew what she had to say.

"Don't worry," she said immediately. "It can be set aside, I'm sure. Or I can go away, make it like I never was here at all, the way I wanted to do when I first got to London—remember? Well, I can do it again, I promise."

"What are you talking about?" he asked.

"The marriage," she said. "I did it because I was afraid not to, but don't worry, you won't have to put up with me long. Just let me stay and be sure he'll be all right and then I'll leave. I'll go back to the Islands, or stay somewhere out of the way in England; you don't have to worry about it . . ."

Martin put his hands on her shoulders and held her until she stopped talking. She stared at him. In all the time she'd known him, he'd never so much as touched her hand. His fair face showed his weariness clearly even in the thin light. He looked much older than he'd been a few days ago, and sounded it too.

"Cristabel," he said quietly, "I only wanted to say thank you—for caring for Magnus, as well as for marrying him. I think you'll be very good for him and for this family. No one ever took care of him before—I see that now and feel shamed about it. But you're just the girl to do it. Besides, you bring youth and vigor and light to us all; even Sophia, if she'd just stop envying you and admit it. And that dowry!" He let go of her so he could kiss his fingers to the sky in a silly gesture. His grin made him seem younger again. "Truly, Lady Snow," he went on in a more serious voice, "it was well done of you—all of it. I thank you. Don't you even think of leaving, you hear?"

"I can only think of sleeping now," she told him honestly.

She left him smiling, and went to her room, where she kept herself from wondering and worrying by simply laying her head down on her pillow.

"So!" Black Jack said with chagrin. "Can't say I wasn't warned. Can't say I didn't expect it neither; the man would have been a fool to let you go."

"The man was a fool to marry me," Cristabel said bitterly.

"Aye, the world's fair filled with fools who'll take beautiful, rich, and brilliant women to wife; more's the pity, ain't it? Get your head straight, m'dear. You be a treasure, and the man knowed it, and more power to him. But have pity on me, 'cause I wanted you, Cristabel, and I would have made you a merry husband, that I would."

"Aye, merry indeed," she said, and smiled a crooked smile at him. They sat in the front parlor and spoke in low voices, because neither Martin or Sophia had discovered he'd come to call yet, and they both had things to say before anyone else joined them.

"No, I mean it, luv," he said sadly, "or rather, I guess it will have to be 'my lady' from now on. But before I treat you like a viscountess, let me talk to plain Cristabel one last time. I'll say it once, and then ne'er bother you with it no more: I would have been proud to have you as me wife; nothing in life I wanted more. But so be it, I be a man grown and can take it like one, no matter how it stings. But hark ye: Be he not what you wanted, do he hurt or insult you ever, you call on me and no matter where I am, I'll see to you. You'll always find safe harbor with me. There's a solemn promise."

"Thank you, Jack," she said sincerely, and then faced him squarely, "but in the same spirit, I ask you plain, just between you and me: Were you responsible?"

"Damn you for a suspicious wench—my lady," he said. "I told you once and I'll say it only one more time. It's not me way! Were I to try for his lordship, I'd do it straight on. Nor would killing be me way neither, for if a fellow has to kill another man to get his woman, it ain't worth it. Love ain't a thing a man can gain by murdering a lover; she'd never be his. And before you can insult me again, I'll tell you, I been talking and seeking and searching since I heard of it, and I'll stake me life it weren't one of the lads, neither. But I'll tell you this: It were a job of work. Aye. That much I did discover. The fellow you put a hole in was a hired hand, a man known to do anything for a pence, and worse for two of them. So far I ain't got a clue as to who hired him, though. But if anyone can find out, 'tis me."

"Aye, mebbe," Cristabel sighed. "Now, I think it would be best that you come up and pay a visit to the viscount before rumors get there first, for he hears of everything going on in the house. And I think you should show him no hard feelings too."

"It galls me to congratulate a man for winning me prize," Black Jack sighed, rising from his chair and slapping his hat against his leg, "but I'm learning the ways of the gentlefolk, so I might as well try to do the pretty."

"Think of putting down anchor in London town, my dear?" Cristabel jested, for it was a mad thought.

"Aye," Black Jack said, and as she stared, he added, "Well, maybe for a time. I'm finding that piracy on the high seas pays better if you have friends in high places, m'dear. Like piracy anywheres. Maybe someday I'll be a gentleman proper, seeing as how the girls seem to like them better than pirates."

"Don't, Jack. I married him because I had to. I thought he was dying, remember?"

"But you're rejoicing for it, lass," he said soberly. "Don't try denying it, for I know you too well."

She paused and then decided to be absolutely honest with him. If she had a true friend anywhere in the world outside this house, it would be this wild and daring pirate. "I'm as scared as I am happy, Jack," she said in a small voice, "and there's the truth."

"Ah," he breathed, "then there goes me last hope. I'm sunk entirely. For you love him, my lady, and *that's* the truth."

She stared at him, her amber eyes wide. He sighed and touched a finger to her nose. "Now, let's go see your invalid afore he clomps down the stairs, grabs a sword, and challenges me to a duel on the spot for ogling you. Because the way I feel now, unfair as it would be, I might just take him up on it after all."

CHAPTER

15

There was more to marriage than a ceremony, and that was the first thing Cristabel thought of when she finally woke up the next morning. The realization came to her as her eyes opened and seemed to sit on her chest like a heavy weight, staring into her eyes until she focused them.

"Oh me Gawd," Cristabel groaned, and turned over and buried her head in her pillow.

Then she thought of her new husband and sat bolt upright in bed.

"Magnus!" she whispered in fear.

She scurried out of bed, washed, dressed, and did her hair with such haste, she had to redo it again so that she was presentable enough to leave her room. She knew that a lady, especially a viscountess, ought to have a lady's maid do such things for her, and resolved to ask Magnus's permission to let the clever little upstairs maid become her personal maid. She didn't know if she should remain Magnus's wife, but for so long as she did, she wanted to be sure she didn't shame him—or so she told herself.

If a little voice whispered *Liar, you never want to be anything else in this life but his wife* as she hurried from her room, she turned a deaf ear to it. She had more important things to worry about now.

That important thing she had to worry about grinned at her as she came into his room.

"Wife!" Magnus said with enthusiasm. "Come sit down, help me with this marvelous breakfast."

There was dry toast and weak soup on his tray. But he had a basket of fresh bread resting on his lap. He was propped up on his pillows, and though the morning sunlight showed him looking thinned and wan, he also looked younger and more carefree than she'd seen him before. She stifled her joy because she was afraid of it. He'd been near death just hours ago; she couldn't celebrate life so soon without superstition throttling such joy. And besides, she wasn't used to being his wife, and didn't know how to react to it.

"Bread?" she asked, lifting the napkin on his basket instead of meeting his eyes. "And a slab of butter? Cheese? And fresh preserves. God save us, if the doctor found out, he'd skin you, and undo all his good work."

"More likely he'd ask to share," Magnus said happily. "Come have some yourself; the strawberry tastes like spring itself. Now, don't look like that. I've been sick before, and tepid broth and weak tea make me sicker, I swear it. I didn't ask for beefsteak because it isn't my house, you know, and the servants here are unimaginative. I had to beg just for this much. But my own staff knows me and knows that once I'm well, I'm well. I've broken bones, and even been shot before, my love, and survived."

"What?" she said, losing her apprehension to fascination, and sinking to a chair by his bed, wide-eyed. "When? How? Don't tell me," she said, glowering. "A duel over some hussy, no doubt."

"No," he laughed, "a hunting accident. Not mine, old Lord Larkin's, whose estate matches mine. I wasn't even hunting. I was out riding one fine autumn day"—he finished slathering a piece of bread with preserves and handed it to her—"and the poor old fool was trying for pheasants. Eat up, it's delicious." He waited until she took a bite, and went on, "Well, he's blind as an owl at noon, and so he hunts by sound. My horse shied at a pheasant rising, and before I knew it, I was a target. It was a good thing he had company, or I'd have been plucked, hung, and spitted before I could call for help. Don't giggle, it was very painful. Would you like to see the scar? You can, you're my wife now."

She swallowed suddenly and began coughing.

"My lord!" the doctor's voice said angrily. He strode into the room, and Cristabel guiltily put her bread down on the tray. "I can't believe my eyes. A weak system must have weak sustenance. It's a primary rule of nature. A log on smoldering fire will put it out; you must feed a feeble flame gently until it thrives. *That* is sound medicine. Who is responsible for this—this feast?" he asked, glaring at Cristabel.

"I am," Magnus said imperturbably, "and I thrive. Come knock on my chest and you'll find solid oak, sir. You did a wonderful job; I feel like dancing." He sat up and swung his long legs around to the side of the bed—only to suddenly grow very pale. Before the doctor could reach him, he lowered himself back to his pillows. "But I'll sit and listen to the music awhile first, I think," he said.

"It wasn't the food," Magnus grumbled as the doctor lifted his breakfast basket. He looked so disconsolate and childish in his disappointment that Cristabel almost laughed. When he'd been well, he seemed like a monolith, the epitome of masculine strength and power. When she thought he lay dying, he'd seemed like a fallen knight to her, majestic and untouchable even in his defeat. Now that he was recovering, and found himself thwarted, he was youthful and peevish. He pleased her in all his aspects.

Although she worried about him and yearned to see him whole again, this new attitude of his somehow made her feel more confident with him. She didn't know how she'd have been able to look him in the face if he'd been as virile and vital as he'd been before, now that she suddenly found herself married to him. This present situation bought her time, which she sorely needed.

"I'll starve," Magnus said plaintively as he raised his

spoon and watched the thin soup dribble back down into his bowl. "A fine job you'll have to brag about then, Doctor, having healed the wound and killed the patient."

Cristabel knew he wouldn't starve, but she knew something about men and sickness too. She had a herb garden at home, as all intelligent women did, and had done her share of doctoring. She'd seen too many sick pirates and their captives to be a stranger to illness, death, and men and their complaints.

"Well, I don't know about English doctors," she said thoughtfully, "but at home in the Islands, where we don't have the advantage of having such learned physicians as yourself," she told the doctor, looking up at him with awe and respect, "we have to make do as best we can. But we have found that a man's best doctor is his own appetite. If a man wants food, we feed him. If he isn't ready for it, he'll give it back. If he keeps it, it will do its work. I don't see what's wrong with some solid food, do you, Doctor? I grant bread may be heavy. And cheese, too fatty, to be sure. But surely, if we make a thin toast of such fine bread? And keep the preserves, because a little sweetness heals a sharp temper as well as a sour tongue?" She winked at him and tipped a shoulder toward his brooding patient. "And perhaps just a wee bit of butter to make it all go down smoothly?" she cajoled.

"Aye, well, perhaps," the doctor said, softening his voice for the charming smile she gave him. "Moderation in all things *is* good medicine. But if you become ill, my lord, you'll have only yourself to blame," he told Magnus sternly.

"Magic," Magnus breathed when the doctor had gone. "I've gone and wedded myself to a enchantress. Pass the butter please; I need more than a wee bit."

"You may get sick, you know," she warned, but passed it to him.

"I won't," he promised, ignoring it and taking her hand in his, his eyes sober and earnest. "I mean to get well soon as I can. I'm a wretched bridegroom, Cristabel, and I'm sorry for it. But I do heal with amazing speed."

"Magnus," she said, pulling her hand from his, "I don't know, I can't believe—Magnus, I married you because—"

"I forced you, yes," he said. "But it's for the best. I know that's what your father said, but in this case it turns out he was right; you'll see."

"No—you see," she said in desperation. "I am Cristabel Stew, daughter to a pirate and a lady—though she despises me. So I can act the lady, yes. But when I get excited, I be every inch me father's daughter. You deserve—ah, my lord, you deserve the very best wife that there is."

"Cristabel, please, no more. We've been through this so many times. I know everything you are, and you delight me."

She dashed her foolish tears aside with her hand and sniffed. "Well," she said, struggling for composure, "there's a good side to this, too, I guess. If it was a pirate who was vexed with you, you should be safe when news of the marriage gets out, right? Aye, and then, too, you'll have someone here to see to you whilst you mend. And best of all," she went on in a stronger voice, as she picked up a piece of bread and vigorously buttered it for him, "there's time. Aye. For when you're better, when you come to your senses, you can have the thing annulled. I'm sure the vicar will take money for undoing what he did. For sure, the doctor will testify to the fact that you were out of your mind. Aye, an annulment would be granted in a wink, I be sure."

She lowered her gaze as she piled preserves on the bread, and didn't see how he stopped breathing when she said the word "annulment." Nor did she see the look that came into his eyes as he watched her sitting by his bed, her long lashes half hiding her topaz eyes, the sunlight fingering her hair and gilding the slight peach down on her cheeks, showing up the purity of her profile, her skin, and her smooth white breast. He caught his breath and sighed. When she looked up, he spread his hands in a gesture of hopelessness.

"A twinge," he said. "Sometimes I forget what I suffered. Don't worry, it's gone already." But the warm and considering look in his eyes stayed long after she had left him to rest after his hard-won breakfast.

He got better faster than anyone thought he would, but it was a fight in more ways than one. He ate and drank things that were strictly against the doctor's orders, getting them by trickery, bribery, and flattery, and sometimes plain sympathy because he was always a favorite with the servants, more so now that he was an invalid. He hated being sick. He was always kind to his many nurses, although it was clear that being at their mercy rankled him. He was restless and impatient with his sickbed, so it was no surprise to anyone that Magnus was out of it before the doctor permitted, and so just as naturally had to go back to it when his body failed him. Though usually sunny-tempered, he growled with complaints when the doctor insisted he obey, worse when his own body betrayed him.

His spirit was willing, but the loss of blood and pain from the wound had cost his body too much for him to recover as quickly as he wished. He complained it was the bed rest itself that weakened him. From the way he sometimes greeted his family in the mornings—pale, damp with perspiration, and breathing hard—they suspected he was getting up before them so he could defy them on the sly. He denied it vigorously. But the chairs and tables he sometimes knocked over on these secret expeditions spoke volumes about his treachery.

"And your slippers are right by the bed," Cristabel said evenly one bright morning well over a week after he'd been shot, "which is odd, since we deliberately had your valet leave them in the wardrobe last night. Cut line, my lord, we have you. You've been sneaking out of bed, and I know it."

"Look at me, wife," he commanded, and she did, without a blink, though she still couldn't get used to the way he used the word all the time now. "I'm in better condition than half the males in London town. The wound is closed, and while it's not beautiful, it's only a memory. I wish to be up and out of here."

"Do you? What a surprise. You ought to have mentioned something about it," she said mildly enough, though the sight of his broad chest beneath his half-buttoned nightshirt made her heart turn over. There was only a light furze of hair on that wide chest, and the muscles beneath the smooth skin bunched and slid when he moved. The nurse had gotten to know her patient; as the bandages had shrunk over the days, exposing more of his chest, she'd gotten used to seeing it. But she still reacted to it.

"Don't gnash your teeth," she said helpfully, as she patted his pillow. "You'll grind them down to stubs. May I remind you of another thing: If you could, you would be out of bed now and we both know it. No doctor on earth could hold you down."

"Perhaps not," he agreed, eyeing her carefully, "but have you considered that it's more than a sawbones keeping me here? It may be that the will of one woman is what's making me so compliant. One frail little piece of baggage may be what's pinning me to this bed."

She turned her head and looked down at him. It was a mistake, for when she saw the look in his steady gray eyes, she didn't know what to say. Before she could stop herself, her hand, as if of its own volition, reached out to smooth back a strand of his long hair. It felt silken and soft beneath her fingers. He took her hand in his and brought it to his lips. When he heard her breath catch, he tugged on her hand, put his other on her neck, and slowly brought her lips down to his. His kiss was a light, sweet question. She didn't know what to answer, but her lips parted in pleased surprise. She felt his breath halt. He sat up higher, and in one smooth gesture pulled her down so that she lay half across his lap. He buried his hands in her hair, devoured her mouth, kissing the sense of all her protests from her.

He slid his tongue across the seam of her lips, and as she opened her mouth to ask why, she felt the strange rough texture of his tongue against her own as he deepened their kiss. She accepted it, wondering at the odd and then wonderful feel of it that made her burrow closer to him, eager to feel more and more. His mouth tasted fresh; his scent was soap and sunshine. She was caught up in a whirlpool of his longing and found herself spinning out of control with him; warm and dizzy, surrounded by the wonderful comfort and power of him. His big hand caressed her back, his lips moved to her neck, to her cheek, up to close her wondering eyes before moving down to plunder her mouth again. His other hand molded her breast, relishing the high, firm contours of it, delighting in the way his lightest touch made her shudder and gasp and cling to him. It was the most delicious feeling Cristabel had ever known, and she squirmed against him, offering him her body and her lips.

She needed to give something back to him—she wanted to learn him as he was learning her. She was tentative as she ventured to open her hand over the hard chest pressed against hers, but then she sighed against his mouth. He was all smooth warmth, satiny steel against her hand, and his nipple beneath her palm was as taut as her own. She heard him murmur encouragement, and dared to move her hand further—and suddenly felt the edge of the rough linen binding his wound. She froze, remembering everything.

He felt her body tense as she pulled back, her eyes wide, her hand flying up to cover the lips he had just savored. He was still an invalid, she thought in shame. It took only seconds for her to remember all the other good reasons why this wonderful lovemaking was such a bad idea. She scurried out of his arms and his bed, and stood staring down at him.

He groaned and laid his head back against the pillow, taking deep breaths.

"Did I hurt you?" she gasped.

"Yes, but it's not the wound that's hurting," he said with a wry smile that became real as he saw her reaction. Although she looked shamed and shocked, she also looked thoroughly loved; her hair was loosened from its pins, her cheeks ruddy from rubbing against his morning stubble. Her gown was half-off her shoulder, and one shapely breast rose from it to taunt him.

"I thought it was going rather well," he said in the calmest voice he could muster. Seeing the new direction of her horrified gaze, he tried to be nonchalant as he draped his bedcovers across his lap so that they merely looked rumpled, not obscene. "We *are* married, Cristabel," he added.

"Aye, but . . ." she said, before seeing the new direction of his heated gaze. She glanced down at herself and gave out a small yelp and spun around and drew up her gown before she said more.

"But it is morning, and anyone could walk in, so I suppose you're right," he said. "But I repeat, Cristabel, you are my wife."

"Not really," she said, turning back to show him a neatly done up gown. Her hands flew to her hair to secure her pins, but nothing could be done about the high color in her face and the redness of her freshly kissed lips. He sighed again.

"Really," he said.

"And you're sick," she said in bewildered shame.

"Not really," he said, with a gleaming look of mischief. "I don't know how you do such things in the Islands, but here in England, when a man says he can make love, we let him. I want to make love to you, wife," he said, suddenly serious.

"You're still sick and things may change. Making love isn't a good idea—I don't think you can get an annulment after you do, leastways not at home, so I suppose not here as well. I'll see you soon," she babbled. "I'll send someone in to see to you. Oh, blast and damn and I'm sorry, Magnus," she said before she fled.

He was sorry, too, and thoughtful. And determined. He had picked out something from the jumble of things she'd said, and immediately resolved to get better even sooner than he'd planned. After a long moment's thought, he rang for a servant to summon his brother to him.

* * *

Cristabel ran to her room and washed her face. *What you almost did!* she breathed to herself as she splashed water on her heated face.

Well, why not? she asked herself, lifting her hands from the basin of cool water she'd plunged them in. Her head came up and the water dripped down her neck, unheeded. *Cristabel Stew!* she told herself, shocked. *A fine question that is. Why not? Have you lost your mind entirely? Why, because . . . because it would be wrong. He's a sick man; you could set him back with such carryings on.*

Forget about his being sick; he be almost entirely well, and well ye know it, another voice reminded her.

And then what, my lady? The pirate's daughter shall be a viscountess? Are you as mad as your evil father? Why, they'll laugh at you both.

Don't be daft. Laughing never killed no one, and he says he wants you. Just look at the man, lass. He knows his own mind. What Magnus, Viscount Snow, wants, he gets, and there's an end to it.

My dear girl, the clear voice of sanity warned her, *what of your bright dreams of independence? You never wanted to marry, never wanted to be at the mercy of any man; have you forgotten so soon the misery of all the women you've ever known?*

Ah, but Cristabel me girl, the other voice argued, *you be his wife already, and you've never known a brighter dream, have ye? Look at the man, ye fool! Is he such a lad as to do you wrong? No, and ye really don't think so fer a minute, do ye? Believe in him, and yerself. For if you don't have faith in yer own self—and yer judgment of him is yer own self—why then, you'll never have nothing in this life. Ye do love him, girl, don't ye? And oh Gawd, girl, think of how it was. It were lovely, weren't it? Purely, purely lovely.*

And so Cristabel Stew/Lady Snow sank down to a chair and sat very still, listening to her two selves as they both argued perfect sense to her.

* * *

"I insist that you go, Sophia," Magnus said. "As you can see—I flourish."

Sophia fidgeted with her fan as she looked at him. It was true he was sitting up in a chair, entirely dressed for the first time since he'd been shot. He was thinner, but he looked fine in his dark gold coat and breeches, and the deep rose-colored tapestry long vest he wore gave color to his face. His hair was tied neatly and he was shaved and scented like any man of fashion. If she hadn't lived through it, she wouldn't have known they'd recently almost lost him.

"You and Martin have stayed home with me long enough; you're getting quite dull, if you want to know the truth," Magnus added. "Martin says the Treadwells are having a dinner. All your cronies will be there; go with a clear conscience. Cristabel will be here with me—unless . . . Do you want to go with them, my dear?"

"Lord no!" Cristabel said, startled. She'd been gazing at him quietly, happily drinking in the magnificent sight of him newly restored to health. Now she looked at him in shock. The idea of going anywhere without him was absurd. As was the idea of going with him. She couldn't show her nose in public until . . . The rest of that thought made her swallow hard. Perhaps, she thought, tonight, alone, and with no fear of interruption, they might finally get the matter of their hasty marriage resolved between them.

It seemed that Martin thought so too. He gave Sophia a significant look, and she colored and nodded to him. It was the first intimate, amicable thing Cristabel had seen pass between them in weeks.

"I'm not a heartless beast, Magnus," Sophia blurted, turning back to face him before she left his room on Martin's proffered arm. "I really did worry about you, you know. The fact that I couldn't do anything for you didn't mean I didn't care."

"I know," Magnus said gravely.

"I care," Sophia repeated. "That's why I'm going now."

Cristabel frowned, puzzling over that as Martin hurried his wife out the door.

"The girl's been in the house too long," Magnus remarked. "I'm glad you decided to stay with me, after all."

"Of course I would," Cristabel said in confusion. "I never wanted to go with them."

"But you're all dressed up," Magnus said, looking his fill at her. Her proud little head was crowned with a high swirl of bright curls. Her figure was shown to high advantage in a gown of gold with a design of tiny pink rosebuds everywhere on its wide skirt. The square neckline was low enough to divert him; the only thing to distract his eye from it was the fact that she wore no jewelry on that lovely white breast. He frowned, remembering that the only jewelry he'd ever seen her wear was a single baroque pearl pendant cased in gold. She had always worn it—it had been her mother's, he remembered sadly. She must have discarded it just as her mother had discarded her. Her own jewelry, given in love, just one more thing he'd have to see to when he could leave this room. Which was tomorrow, he vowed. But not too early, he hoped.

She looked away. "Well, I thought that if you looked so fine, I could do no less," she murmured, hoping he wouldn't realize that she couldn't have known how he'd dressed tonight until she'd come into his room, already dressed herself.

"You do me proud," he said in a deep voice. "I wish I could have persuaded you to let me take you out tonight to show the world how proud I am. As it is, I feel so well, I've ordered up a prodigious dinner—with all the things the good doctor refused to let me eat until I was too old to care: oysters and wine, pheasant, venison and ham, all drowned in the richest sauces the cook could contrive. So we shall dine splendidly together anyway tonight, my lady. I regret, it must be here in my chamber, for I'm not supposed to venture so far as the dining room," he said, hoping she wouldn't notice that it was odd that he would defy all his doctor's orders but that one.

"Good," she said simply, and sat down at the little table before Magnus's chair.

A succession of footmen bore in a dizzying array of dishes and served them quietly, smiling with pleasure at the way the viscount and his bride helped themselves. When they removed the plates, it became quite clear that both the lord and his new lady had merely moved their food around instead of eating it. Neither did either of them drink very much, although they had laughed and chatted companionably all through the meal.

When the last sweet had been removed, the little table carried out, and the last footman had silently left, Cristabel rose from her chair. But she didn't go far. She walked to the fireplace and stood looking down into the heart of the fire. She bowed her bright head and clasped her hands together hard.

"Magnus," she finally said in a small, uncertain voice.

"Yes?" he said, coming up behind her.

She turned, startled, then grinned. "You must be better; I didn't hear you at all, and you didn't stumble once. You're not breathing hard either."

"Oh, but I am," he said, and forgetting all the seductive words and phrases as well as all the neat arguments he'd thought up for her seduction tonight, he caught her up in his arms, drew her close, lowered his head, and kissed her.

She threw her arms around his neck and stood on tiptoe so as to return his kiss with all her heart, and gladly abandoned all thought of the daring, clever things she'd planned to say and do to make him take her in his arms again. All her doubts and fears had been outweighed by the terribly wonderful yearning she had for him. Almost losing him had made her burn for him. She'd realized that she'd made all her plans for her future without counting on Magnus, and her own passions and his ability to fire them. Nothing had prepared her for him—for this. She was his wife now and she wanted to be his wife forever, but since she hardly believed in forever, she was willing to settle for this one night and any she could have after. It sounded right when she'd plotted it, but then she'd lost her courage. It didn't seem possible for her to lack courage, but it was so.

She hardly knew herself anymore, and she was weary of fighting.

Magnus only knew that she wanted him, and the joy of that overwhelmed him.

The clothes they both wore were full and made of heavy fabric, held fast by complicated hooks and tapes and tiny buttons. They would laugh, perhaps, some other time and place, at how they struggled to free each other from them, as though the clothes themselves and not just their bodies were on fire. But tonight was not a time for joking. Tonight they were each too anxious to prevent the other from knowing how awkward the business was, and too fearful of breaking the mood. They'd each dressed to impress the other, but it was astonishing how quickly they managed to undress and still keep their hands and lips busy with each other.

When he finally stood in only his breeches, and she in her shift, amidst a ragged circle of discarded clothes, they stopped and looked at each other. And then they smiled and he picked her up and took her to his bed.

"But your wound . . ." she worried, hiding her face in his neck.

". . . is nothing to my need for you," he said, lifting her head with one hand and kissing her softly.

"Afraid?" he asked, pausing as he unbuttoned his fine silk breeches.

"Oh aye, of course," she said nervously, pulling her shift over her head.

He smiled his crooked smile, until he saw her body emerge from her shift. "Oh Lord, Cristabel," he said on a long sigh, "before God, you are so beautiful."

She gazed at him, in all his sleek muscle and firm flesh, and lowered her lashes over her eyes so she could gaze more without him seeing. Her eyes widened at the sight of him, because she'd never seen a man aroused, and Magnus was a very large man. She looked up and away quickly, and only then saw his wound, unbandaged at last. "Oh, Magnus," she said softly, putting her small hand on his wide chest. "Does it hurt?" she asked, seeing the puckered red scar there.

He shook his head, but before he could answer, she said, "Be ye sure? I wouldn't want to hurt ye."

He kissed her for answer. It convinced her he was well enough. She ran her hand over his chest, reveling in the feel of him. "Oh, Magnus," she sighed, "you be like a great seal, a lion of the sea: all smooth and velvety and strong and supple, all life, my dear, to me."

If he thought it odd to be compared to a seal, he didn't say, because he was speechless as he kissed her again and again. She lay down with him and took his kisses, and squirmed in his arms. She caressed his chest, but her touch was still tentative, and featherlight. Her hand trailed down his body towards that which obviously fascinated her. Then she looked away, and brought her hands up to his broad shoulders again.

"Don't be afraid of me," he said. "I know I'm a big man, but I would never hurt you. At first there may be some pain, but it will soon pass and I—"

"I know that," she said quietly. "I'm not afraid of that. I be pirate-bred; I know what is to come, and even so, I could never be afraid of ye. Truth is, I love the look of ye, and wish to touch ye more, but you been so ill, I be feared of hurting ye."

"Cristabel," he said on a broken laugh, "you're killing me, my love. But please don't stop."

She laughed and turned to him, and he showed her how it felt to be touched in such a place by bringing his hand to her tightly closed thighs and easing them apart to delve into the folds of her own secret yearning. She caught her breath in surprise because she'd only been able to contain her desire by holding herself tightly closed to it. Now she realized she no longer had to contain it, she could give it over to him.

Her scent was of flowers and the sea, her skin was warm and sensitive, her response a delight to him, but her delicacy was that of a virgin and a lady, and he took slow and patient care not to shock or dismay her. But her passion was full blown and as fully fledged as that of a pirate lass, and he found himself swept away by it. He brought her to some peace with his hands, and held himself hard against following too soon as she shivered and gasped with the surprise and relief of it. But with all his control, he was only mortal and he ached for her. He paused, at the last, above her, hesitant, wondering how to approach this final, needful, moment. She gave him no choice. She wrapped her arms and legs around him and welcomed him, and ignoring the pain, smiled with the joy of it as she felt his great body buck and heave in tumultuous release as she brought him safely down from the height of his passion to the wonder of their love.

He never let her go, not even when he lost his senses to pure sensation. Now he held her close beside him as she felt his breathing slow and settle to a normal pace again.

"'Od's life, wife," he said in her ear, "but I do believe you've killed me after all." He chuckled with satisfaction. "But where are my wits?" he asked in alarm, rising to an elbow. "Have I hurt you?"

"No more than was needful," she said, snuggling closer to him.

"Cristabel," he said as he stroked back her hair from her brow, "I have never known anything like this. I do love thee entirely. But tell me something. I thought I was so clever, but which of us seduced the other, do you think?"

"It were all your fault," she said comfortably, and then her eyes opened wide. "Magnus, did you hear? Oh my, I never realized . . . Magnus, when we—when we made love, I spoke like a pirate, didn't I? Oh no, does that mean all my teaching, all my tutoring, was for naught? Is my breeding only skin-deep?" she grieved.

"Passion is deeper than the skin, my love," he said with a tender smile, his big hand cupping her chin, "and thank God for it. I'll take me brave little pirate in me bed any day, and we can leave the lady to the parlor, eh?"

She giggled, and called him a wharf rat and a cod's head, and other pirate-styled endearments, until he took revenge in his own way, a new way, and pleased them both entirely. Although when it was done, she realized he had pleased her more than himself.

"That was wonderful. But aren't we going to—you know—again?" she asked shyly, when she finally came to her wits.

"I know," he said ruefully, "too well. But I'm trying not to remember—until tomorrow, that is. You're warm and welcoming, my love, but there is a difference in our proportions as well as our experience. You need to recover a little. I don't want to hurt you again; there's time."

"I'm ready," she said bravely. She was, and she wasn't just being brave. There was pain, to be sure, but there was something more and she was eager to learn the way of it, for his sake as well as her own.

"Ready isn't enough," he told her. "I want you roaring for me and ready to experience exactly what I do. That takes time, and now we have that."

She wasn't so sure she agreed with him, but she was sure she'd never felt anything so good as this, simply lying deep in his embrace, feeling his heart beat as though it were her own. She fell still, and fell asleep in his arms with her head on his wide, breathing chest, as comfortable as if she were rocked on the breast of the wide sea itself. Before she dropped off, she thought with drowsy satisfaction that whether it was for better or worse, at least the worrying and the wondering were over. It was done. There was much that was still unresolved, but at least she was his at last, and nothing could change that now. She was the luckiest female in all England and the Islands together. Tonight for the first time in her life she could almost believe that she was loved for herself, pirate and lady—whichever she was.

She woke to find morning sunlight on the bed, and only herself in it. She raised her head and looked for him. He was gone from her side and the room, but she heard the house bustling around her. She stepped from the bed, wincing at unexpected pains in intimate places. She marveled at all the unused muscles she never knew she had in her thighs as they complained as she crept to the door and cracked it open. There were many voices downstairs, and Magnus's deep voice rose above them all. He was greeting guests; they had company in the house, and her breath stopped when she realized who it was. His parents and sisters had arrived.

CHAPTER

16

It would be embarrassing to have him come get her and drag her out to meet his family, Cristabel thought nervously, but it would be too horrible to think about if he pretended that she didn't exist. She was his wife now, but the thought of meeting her new in-laws—an earl, a duchess, and Magnus's noble siblings—chilled her. He hadn't sent for her, and so now she wondered if it worried him too. She didn't know whether to stay in the room and cower there, or march out bold as brass, unasked, and announce herself to his family. So she did neither. She busied herself by washing and then dressed herself in last night's cast-off clothing. One good thing came of her waiting: When she realized that the whole household probably knew by now that she'd spent the night in Magnus's bed, her embarrassment was forgotten in the fear of being summoned—or abandoned—by him this morning.

When she'd finished her toilette, she looked in the mirror and realized she couldn't go anywhere but to her own room, no matter what he decided to do with her. A lady of breeding didn't wear an evening gown in the morning, nor a crumpled one at that. A tapping at her door made her turn pale. But she had braved hurricanes and the wrath of her father, and so she picked up her chin and said, "Enter" in as calm a voice as she could summon.

The little upstairs maid she'd once used to send her messages stood in the doorway, grinning ear to ear. "My lady," she said, "the viscount, he told me I should help you dress this morning, if I please you, my lady." She dipped a curtsy and looked up at Cristabel expectantly. "Since you had no lady's maid yet, he asked the staff who did for you. I once did something for you, even if it weren't dressing, so I spoke up fast. I hope you don't mind, my lady."

Cristabel grinned. So he had thought of her! Or maybe he just wanted to get her out of his room, she thought nervously. "I don't mind," she said. "In fact, I was going to ask you myself . . ." *If I stayed,* she thought, and bit her lip.

"Well then, my lady," the little maid said as she bustled into the room and appraised Cristabel with a knowing eye, "there's company downstairs, and while that gown is lovely, truly, I don't think it's right for morning. I took the liberty of looking in your closet before I come here, and there's one there that's much more the thing. Shall I fetch it? I've always dreamed of being a lady's maid, my lady," she confided. "I think you'll be pleased with me; I will try, truly."

And I have always dreamed of being a lady, Cristabel thought, and said, "I'm sure you will. Let's get dressed, shall we?"

Wearing a fashionable soft peach sack gown and with her hair artfully threaded with peach ribbons and pulled into a loose knot on top of her head, Cristabel perched on a chair in her room and waited to learn her fate. She looked lovely, flushed with youth and beautifully gowned as she sat and thought of all the ways she would kill her new husband . . . after she found why he'd done it, she decided. She couldn't understand. How could a man seem to be so much one thing and yet be another? How could he make love to a woman, driving her to near insanity—no, driving her clean through insanity into another world, a world where she gave herself body and soul to him—and then forget her? Or remember to forget her. The slowest hour of her life had passed, and he still hadn't come to see her or called her down to meet his parents. Well, but an earl and a countess meeting a pirate's daughter, after all, she thought sadly . . .

He must have come to his senses, she decided. The sight of his parents, his well-wedded sisters and elegant brothers-in-law, must have made him see his horrible mistake. She'd told him so. And so she'd told herself, too, Cristabel thought with grim triumph.

She wouldn't cry, she knew better. That was why she was so angry. It seemed he'd deserted her, after all. Why was she surprised? Wasn't it just what every man she'd ever known had done to every woman she'd ever known? Except for her mother, of course—who had done exactly that to her husband and her daughter. Well, there's a tear, Cristabel thought, dashing away the glittering drop that rolled down her cheek—it had no business being there. Magnus didn't think so either.

"What is it?" he asked the moment he stepped into the room and saw her. He tilted her head up with one hand as quickly as she'd turned it away from him. "Are you all right?" he asked in alarm, his gray eyes searching her face. "Have I somehow hurt you? 'Od's mercy! Was I too rough with you last night? Ah, damn me for a brute. I should have known. There was pain; I saw blood on the sheet this morning, perhaps too much . . . The doctor," he said with decision. "I'll call the doctor at once."

"That you will not!" she said angrily. "A fine thing that would be: 'Come see me wife and see if me lovemaking's kilt her.' I should die of shame! There was not so much blood; a white sheet makes a speck look like a fountain," she said, blushing at the thought that he'd seen any at all; it seemed too base and mortal to be part of what they'd shared. "Anyway, no need. Nothing hurts now, thank you very much, 'cept for my feelings, and not even that," she said hurriedly, ashamed she'd let it slip, "for I be used to lying, cheating knaves who say one thing and do another."

He checked, his lips curving as a small smile quirked and was quickly repressed. "Ah. And how have I lied, cheated, and said one thing and done another?"

"Well," she said, looking away and twining a hair ribbon round and round her finger, "you kept me out of sight when your family come, that's what. Not that I blame ye," she said quickly, "seeing as how I was the one who volunteered to slip away when you saw what a mistake the marriage was in the first place, remember? But why did you pretend it was all right last night? Just to have me?"

That came out sounding too pitiable to her, so she raised her chin, and before he could answer, she went on defiantly, "There was no need for trickery just to get me in your bed. It's what I wanted. It made me no never mind to me; it was time I learned the way of it. I would—I would have done it just the same," she lied, holding her head high.

"Indeed?" he said gently. "Then I'm very glad I happened to be there at the time. Cristabel, my dear, sweet, idiot wife, you were sleeping when my family arrived, so sweetly that I didn't want to wake you. I slipped down and met them. They'd heard I was shot, and hastened to my side. It took some time to convince them that I was well. Then they heard I was wed, and were on fire to meet you. So I sent for a girl to help you dress, and settled them in their own rooms first. We'll see them at dinner."

"Oh," she said quietly, and fussed with a ribbon of her dress.

"And by the way, we're moving to my house soon after. I love my parents and my sisters dearly, but they're hardly the people I wish to spend my honeymoon with. All right?" he asked.

"Fine," she said, and looked up to see him watching her. She threw her arms around his neck. "Oh, Magnus," she sighed, "I thought the most terrible things about you."

He held an armful of sweetly scented warm and curving womanhood, and she was his wife. He kissed her and then held her at arm's length. "A beautiful lady,—my own willing wife, and a house full of relatives. I have far too much of a good thing. But I think I can manage it if you will just please keep your hands off me, and don't look at me that way—'Ods mercy, wife, certainly not that way!"

Cristabel came down the stairs flushed and rosy and very happy. Magnus came down with her, holding her arm as though she were made of porcelain, though she had just showed him that she was made of warm flesh and blood. It was true, he had stopped before he could find out just how warm, but he'd loved her just enough to give her confidence in herself as a woman and a wife. She needed it, she thought, as she saw the people waiting for her in the hall.

"Mother, Father, sisters, Lords Jameson and Crewe, may I present my lady, Cristabel," Magnus said.

Cristabel curtsied and rose, pale and subdued, her teeth worrying at her lower lip. Cristabel, born *Stew,* she thought uneasily, bracing herself for the next question and the inevitable answer: *Aye, just like the pirate, my lord, aye, happen it's no coincidence, happen he's my father, my lady.* And prayed no one would ask.

"Oh, but she's lovely," a gray-haired woman all in blue said.

"Beautiful; well done, Magnus," a portly man, almost as tall as Magnus himself, said.

Two tall women, one very obviously with child and the other looking much like a child herself, stared at Cristabel. "Welcome to the family," the younger one said shyly, as the expectant one said, "Beautiful, beautiful, Magnus; I can see why you hurried to wed before she changed her mind."

"Well done," a foppish gentleman near the younger woman said as he stared at Cristabel.

"Indeed, indeed, a beautiful lady," a fattish one standing near the taller sister said.

They looked at Magnus with approval. And at Cristabel with awe.

"We never thought he'd wed," the younger sister whispered to Cristabel as they went into the dining room.

"Never so well, at least," the older one remarked.

And then they sat down to dine, and talked about everything else.

When Cristabel got over the shock of it, she started to listen. First, the visitors asked questions.

"How are you feeling, son?" the earl, Magnus's father, asked.

"Have they caught the villain that did it?" his mother asked worriedly.

"Fine," Magnus said, "and yes, he was dealt with and there's no more danger."

"Well, I wonder at anyone wanting to live in such a dangerous place as London in the first place," Magnus's mother said indignantly.

"Too true," one of his brothers-in-law agreed. "I've heard the most hair-raising tales of the goings-on here, shocking. I wonder at what's happening to our society."

"Yes, cutpurses and thiefs, Mohocks and burglars; give me the peaceful countryside anytime," his other brother-in-law put in.

"Anyone who lives in such a dangerous place must be mad!" one of the sisters said, and they all agreed.

"Ah, but we have theater here, and art, commerce, and shipping. London is the heart of England, and so it also beats the loudest here. Sometimes it is dangerous, but so, too, is life," Magnus remarked as he cut his meat.

"That's true," a brother-in-law agreed.

"Very educational place, actually," the other put in.

"If I were young, why, I do believe that's just where I would live myself," the earl said with feeling, and they all agreed.

That having been decided, his father asked Martin if he and Sophia were ready to come home and take up their responsibilities yet. Martin grew red-faced and started to stammer an answer, when Magnus remarked, offhandedly, "But he's young yet, Father, just as you say you once were. I think he has time to make up his mind, don't you?"

"Just so, just so," the earl said, nodding his agreement.

"But no children yet, Sophia?" the countess asked sadly. "Have you seen a doctor, my dear?"

Sophia put down her fork and looked like she wanted to cry, and Magnus said, "Mother, that's hardly a luncheon topic. Besides, her husband has been sailing across the world on business matters lately, and the thing can't be done by letter, can it?"

They all laughed, and teased Magnus for talking so warm, then reminded, started to ask about Martin's Caribbean adventures.

Cristabel stiffened and grew cold. Magnus put his hand over hers and held it tight. He smiled at her with something beyond sympathy. In fact, as the meal went on, she saw him become even more secretly amused.

"Well, so do you think he'll have to travel again soon?" his father asked Magnus when Martin was done with his highly inventive and abridged story of pirates and escape.

"Only if he wishes," Magnus said smoothly.

Satisfied, his visitors stopped asking questions and began to report on what they'd been doing. And asking Magnus's opinion of it.

It wasn't until dessert was being served that Cristabel was sure. Then she turned to Magnus and whispered in chagrin, "You could have married yourself a squid's daughter, and they wouldn't have minded! Anything you do is right to them."

"Yes," he said with unholy amusement at her expression. "How lucky for me that I have better taste than that."

"But you let me wonder and worry," she began to say.

"Never," he said seriously, stopping her. "You let yourself wonder and worry; I told you the truth from the start. I always have and I always shall, Cristabel."

She flushed and looked at him with such love that she didn't notice all conversation at the table had stopped. When she looked around the table again, his whole family was beaming at her, even Sophia.

"Well," Cristabel told Magnus, striving valiantly for control, "that's true—so far, at least."

He laughed. "And so it will go on," he whispered, leaning closer to her as if he were only offering her a spoonful of his trifle. "But now you see why I married you. I had to have someone who fought back." She smiled. "Only please," he added softly, "not later tonight. For once, I'm looking forward to your being as obliging as is my family—in a different way, of course."

So was she. His parents were charming, and she was enormously relieved by their instant acceptance of her— although she was a little disappointed, knowing they'd have accepted any woman Magnus married—but so she, too, wished the evening were over and she were deep in Magnus's arms in his bed again.

She fairly bounded from her chair when her new mother-in-law yawned and started murmuring about how tiresome their long journey had been.

"We shall sleep late tomorrow, to be sure," the countess said as she rose and took her husband's arm, preparing to go up to bed, "but when we wake, I want to have a nice long chat with you, Cristabel, my dear. I'm sorry I have no bride presents for you yet, but this rogue of a son of mine didn't tell us his intentions. No matter, I'll make it up to you. Tomorrow then, my dear, we will get thoroughly acquainted."

"Oh yes," his sisters chorused happily.

"Oh. Yes," Cristabel said.

Being held by Magnus was the last thing she was thinking about as he drew her into his room and closed the door behind them. Feeling the tension in her slight frame, he only held her close, his chin resting on the top of her head.

"I don't blame you," he said on a heavy sigh, after she hadn't spoken for long moments. "She's a fearsome woman, my mother. I'd rather face a mad dog myself."

Now she did move. She burrowed into him as if she could hide there. "Don't joke about it. I'm not a good liar," she said in a muffled voice against his chest. "No, I'm a terrible liar, and well you know it. How shall I tell her? But how can I not? Oh, Magnus," she wailed.

He rubbed his chin on her hair, "She knows," he said simply.

She pushed away and stared up at him.

"Unless you're talking about something else?" he asked quizzically. "If it's only that your father is Captain Whiskey, there's no problem. But if you tell me now that you have leprosy or are given to fits of barking like a dog at the full of the moon . . . No, you can't hit me, I'm an invalid, remember?" he said, dancing away a step and grinning like a boy.

"She knows?" Cristabel asked in astonishment.

"They think it's terribly romantic. Of course, they also think the fact that your father so deeply repents his former life that he's given it up to live alone and anonymously, safely across several seas, in penance, is equally romantic. They think your fortune is more romantic than anything, though.

"Mind, they're not going to go bragging about your father," he added, when he saw her expression, "and it's possible they may never mention him to anyone. But they know, and it doesn't bother them. Ours is a proud family with an old name, but the oldest names have the most blood on them, and my parents know it well. I think even your father would be appalled at the way some of my ancestors got our property—and the way some noblemen are still getting theirs. In fact, it's too bad there's a price on his head, because otherwise, the way things are, your father himself might have been able to buy himself a title.

"You see, dear wife, a reformed villain is acceptable to my family. A reformed villain they'll never have to set eyes on, is doubly so. And having their son marry the beautiful daughter of an incredibly rich, reformed villain whom they'll never have to see is actually the dream of most English parents. No, seriously, my love, they know, and they don't mind. As you might have noticed, they trust my judgment. And they know, because I've told them, that you're the best and only woman for me."

"And about my mother?" she asked fearfully, her eyes searching his.

Now he didn't jest. He held her shoulders and spoke seriously. "They know she was a lady, but that's all. That's all anyone needs to know, unless you choose to say more. As I said: You're my lady now. Anyone talking to you or looking at you would know you're everything a fine lady should be. All right? Now, my fine lady, will you take off all your clothes and do remarkable things with me again? Please?"

"Oh, Magnus," she said, laughing and blotting away glad tears, "what am I going to do with you?"

"This," he said in a deeper voice, as he took her back in his arms and lowered his mouth to hers, "please."

She laughed, she wept, and she helped him help her out of her gown. She heard a tapping on the door just as she was unbuttoning his long vest. He raised his head, thought of telling whoever it was to go hang, and then sighed. He took her hands in his.

"Need must," he reminded her ruefully. "It's not our house."

Rebuttoning the few buttons Cristabel had managed to open, he went to the door. Cristabel darted behind the bed hangings as he cracked the door open and exchanged a few soft words with a footman. When he closed the door and came back into the room, she picked up her discarded gown and held it in front of herself. Lovemaking was clearly no longer on his mind.

"I must go downstairs for a few minutes. There's a visitor there waiting for me," he told her. "He sends word that he regrets the late hour of his call but that he has news for me. A tall, dark fellow, extravagantly well dressed, the footman says: one Master Jarvis Kelly."

"I'm coming," she said, scrambling into her gown.

"No," he said, and before she could protest, he added, as he looked at her longingly. "Even if it were necessary, I'll not have him seeing you as you look now."

"I'll be dressed, ninny," she said as she hurriedly tried to do up her gown again.

He put one big hand over hers, and putting a finger under her chin, tilted her head up to look at him. "For once, clothes don't make the woman," he said in a low voice. "Your hair, your eyes, your mouth—my love, you look like a woman ready for bedding. Any man would know. And don't say you'll lose that look before you come downstairs. And," he said in a lighter voice, with love showing in his eyes, "it would take you so long to get dressed, Black Jack would have half the silver plate in the house spirited away by the time you came down. I'm jesting, but really, there's no need for you to go. I'll be quick as I can, and return to tell you everything."

"Everything? Promise?" she asked, standing absolutely still.

He hesitated. "Yes," he finally said. "But I'll also tell him of my promise to you tonight, and my pledge to keep it."

She nodded, puzzled. It wasn't until he was out the door that she realized what he meant. If Black Jack had anything to tell him that she wasn't to know, he wasn't to tell Magnus tonight. She dropped her gown and kicked it aside as she paced the room. A man of honor was just as tricky as a man without it, she decided angrily. Then she stopped and laughed; now at least she knew she could trust him—but she'd also have to keep a close eye on him, which would be a very pleasant task.

"My lord," Black Jack said, putting down the glass of wine he'd been offered, and swept Magnus a low bow as the big man strode into the parlor. "Sorry to call so late, but there's news."

"Come to me at any time with news," Magnus said, noticing that though the pirate was dressed fine and fashionably, he was all in gray and black tonight, as though to blend in better with night shadows. "What is it?"

"Someone's still recruiting murderers . . ." Black Jack said, his dark eyes on Magnus's face.

"No, wait." Magnus held up a hand and shook his head in annoyance. "'Od's mercy," he muttered to himself, "but a man must remember to be less free with his oaths. Black Jack—Master Jarvis, whatever you wish to be called . . ."

"'Jack' will do," Black Jack said with interest, seeing Magnus's discomfort.

"Well then, Jack, your old friend Cristabel pried a promise from me. I have to tell her all you say to me tonight. So if there's a thing you'd rather she didn't know, it will have to wait until tomorrow, if at all possible. If not, I'll hear it now and have to contend with her . . . I am a man of my word," Magnus explained, annoyed at the way the pirate was staring at him. He was even less pleased by Black Jack's shout of hearty laughter.

"Stave my sides, if that ain't a good one," Black Jack said, wiping his eyes. "Leave it to Cristabel! Got you tied like a longboat to her side already, don't she? I gave you my congratulations already, me lord, though it grieved me to do it, for you've got yourself the only woman I'd ever have made me wife. Aye, but for that reason I'll tell you something else too: I'd never tell you a thing I wouldn't tell her, and well she knows it. We pirates got our own word to keep, you know, and old friends come first.

"Be that as it may, the news ain't fair to neither of you. Someone be trying to hire assassins. That's nothing new in London town, but the word is that when anyone asks who it is they want put down, the name be: Snow. They don't give their own name, neither. But they're offering a lot for a job well done. They have to—seems you've made a grand reputation for yourself, me lord, with the poor as well as the rich. Then there's an extra hazard, seeing how neat you and our Cristabel put away the last wretch that tried to do the job. And you be a lord, and the penalty for trying to snuff one of your kind be wicked. Desperate men don't mind simple death as payment for failure," Jack said, picking up an Oriental figurine and examining it. "It be the extras that give a man pause, and cost more money."

Magnus nodded. He poured a glass of the ruby wine for himself. "Do you think sending someone to pretend to take the job would help to find the one responsible?" he asked as he studied its red depths.

"Aye. So I did. But we tried and it don't work," Jack said. "The man what was doing the hiring that night didn't know the answer neither, and there's truth, for not many men tend to lie with their next to last breath."

Magnus's broad shoulders went tight. "I thank you on our behalf. But your method seems a bit extreme."

"Pirates *be* extreme, me lord," Jack said.

"Just what I was thinking," Magnus said with a frown.

"Then unthink it," Jack said through clenched teeth. "It weren't none of us responsible. No, not even the old captain his own self. I told you, it be not his style."

"Agreed. But it occurs to me that he must know by now that I wasn't the man he married his daughter to. And I doubt he knows that there's no longer any reason to be angry with me about that now."

"Yes," Jack said, looking momentarily disconcerted. "But then, me lord," he said with a curling smile, "there ain't many folks do know, except for those of us most directly involved with you two. Oh, I'll not be saying your match ain't legal as the king's own marriage is. Nor that there weren't a good reason for it to be done so quick and silent at the time. But it were kind of a hole-in-the-corner affair, weren't it? How is the capt'n—or anyone else—to know you really gone and married her, and that it's not all a humbug?"

Magnus put his glass down with a snap and uttered a low oath. "Damn you, Jack, for being right. 'Od's death, but I'm a fool! I was so glad to be wed to her, I didn't think . . ." He brooded for a second before he looked at his visitor with a growing smile. "Well then, my friend, you've just invited yourself to one of the finest weddings London has ever seen. I'll contact a minister related to half the royal family, and have the other half packed into St. George's—maybe even St. Paul's—whichever has the most room to accommodate the most of London. Buy yourself a pair of dancing slippers, Jack. You'll have need of them soon."

"Aye," Jack said, "soonest is best. Good then. I may not approve of the groom, mind, but I think that's the ticket. If someone be vexed about you and her, seeing is believing. Having a grand wedding may end the problem, one way or the other."

"Yes. One way or another," Magnus said thoughtfully. "Thank you for giving me an easy solution to what must be a hard problem for you," he said, extending a hand to the pirate.

"It be for the lass," Jack said gruffly, taking his hand and clasping it harder than he had to as he added, "Now, you take care of her until her second wedding day, me lord. 'Twould be prudent—'cause neither your fine reputation nor your title would stop me from my revenge, if you don't."

"We're getting married," Magnus said as he strode into his bedroom again.

"What?" Cristabel squeaked, sitting straight up in bed.

He paused in undoing his cravat and stared at the shapely breasts that had risen from under the covers. She saw the direction of his gaze, and started to pull the bedclothes up again.

"No," he said, coming to her side and taking hold of her hands, "no need to conceal such loveliness from me." He bent his head and kissed one high breast on its puckered rosy tip, then the other. She quivered and touched his hair gently, but stopped him when he began to do it again.

"No," she said, "tell me first. What are you talking about?"

"Oh, that," he said, casting his coat aside hurriedly. "Well, wife, it occurred to me that we wed like Romeo and Juliet, which is fine, and very romantic, but not practical for our purposes. It was good of you not to complain, but I've come to see that I was selfish. I was so delighted with my bride, I didn't think that the best way to introduce her to my world was to have a wedding they'd all be talking about for years to come. Invite people to something they have to dress up for, feed them until they groan," he said in a muffled voice as he quickly drew his shirt up over his head, "let them dance till dawn at our expense, and they'll bless our marriage forevermore. And that's just what we shall do," he said as he emerged from it, "as soon as possible. They are often dullards, but they can count to nine. Of course, we'll tell them the truth, that we married in haste at my sickbed. But I want them to know we didn't have to."

She gazed at him, watching how the candlelight gilded the play of muscles in his broad back as he bent to remove his shoes.

"Aye, I can see that, but—but if you just tell them we were wed, they won't have to know—this way they'll all know my name is Stew," she whispered fearfully, "and surely everyone in London won't be as accepting as your family is."

"True. But there are other Stews, my lady, just as there are other Snows and Smiths and Joneses, for that matter. What of it? You don't think every man named Marlowe is related to the poet, do you? Or every Kidd, a son of that infamous pirate? Well, then." He shucked his breeches and came quickly up the step to the bed. "Of course there'll be rumors. London lives on rumors," he said as he took her into his arms. "There would be rumors even if your name were Becket and you were the holy man's own daughter. Rumors are like gnats: annoying, but mercifully short-lived."

He laid her down, drew back the covers, and looked his

fill at her, drawing her close. She was warm and fragrant against his eager body. He filled his hands with her breasts, with her hips and then her buttocks, feeling the gently swelling textures and contours of her, and bent his head to let his lips follow where his hands had led him. He groaned. It was hard for him to let go of her even for a minute. But he did, because he felt the tension in her slight frame, and because she didn't throw her arms about him and respond with the wholehearted passion he'd come to expect of her. He sighed. "Now what?" he asked, drawing back a little to watch her eyes.

"What did Black Jack say?" she asked.

"Oh," he said, trying to concentrate on what had happened rather than what he hoped would soon happen, "he said there was a man trying to hire someone to do us harm. I knew that, because I've started some investigations of my own. He regretted that he couldn't find out more than that, or who it was that hired the man to recruit a killer in the first place, although he said he interviewed the man thoroughly—in pirate fashion."

He waited for her reaction and was wryly amused to see her nod with satisfaction and mutter, "Aye, good thing that."

"Then he warned me to be very careful of you, as if he had to tell me." Magnus said, "But I forgave him enough to invite him to our wedding. I thanked him. I gave him a glass of wine. He looked very well. Now what?" he said, seeing her frown.

"Nothing else?"

He thought a minute. "That's the gist of it; I can't repeat it word for word. He said we'll find the villain, as, of course, we will. And he said again that he wasn't responsible, nor were any of your father's men, if that's what you're worried about."

She sighed. Then she drew him back to her. "Aye, that was what I was worried about."

He closed his eyes and breathed in the scent of her, and

ran his hands over her and sighed with pleasure and the anticipation of pleasure as her body rose to meet him and her hands sought him as well.

"Then stop worrying," he muttered against her breast.

"Make me," she told him.

He did.

CHAPTER
17
~

She felt him leave her side and cracked an eye open.

"No," she said, and pulled him back down to the bed.

"Greedy thing. But it's morning," he said with warm laughter in his voice, although he nevertheless put his arms around her and held her close again.

"Doesn't matter," Cristabel mumbled sleepily. "Stay."

"If I stay," he said, dropping a light kiss on the tip of her nose, "I'll do more than stay. It would be delicious, but not wise. It's still too new a sport for you to appreciate that gesture as much as I'd like you to."

She pushed him away and sat up, her eyes wide. "I don't please you!" she said in dismay.

She was rosy with sleep, her mouth still pink from his night kisses, her hair witch-wild from his fingers and lying like spilled sunset on her white shoulders. And beneath her shoulders—he smiled a slow, sensual smile. "Ah, but you please me too well," he said. "Your body more than pleases me. That's the problem."

"Where is the problem?" she asked anxiously.

She remembered the night they'd passed together. He'd brought her to the brink of madness with his achingly slow and steady lovemaking. Then he'd brought her to mindless bliss with his clever hands, before letting himself take his release in her. She loved it when he finally found his ease, thrilled to see him become so abandoned to his pleasure. She was proud when she felt his body moving convulsively in hers, knowing in that instant that she occupied every ounce of his questing mind and had chased every rational thought from it. It was no small thing, for he was the smartest man she'd ever known. Seeing how she moved him and feeling the intensity of his response brought her great happiness.

But she wondered if that was enough for him. Pirate women had told her about this part of marriage; she'd known more than most maidens when she'd come to him. So she also knew a man wanted his woman to move with him and share with him in his final ecstasy. For some women, that took time; for some, it might take an eternity. When Magnus's great body pounded into hers as he approached his release, she felt little soreness—just the wonder and joy of holding him as he came to his pleasure. But she did not find the ecstasy that he found, either. Now she worried that he knew it, and that it might be enough to make him turn from her. The men she'd known had always roamed when they found disappointment in their beds. She wanted to be nothing but pleasure to him.

He studied her face, and frowned when he saw her fear. He touched her cheek. "I only meant that I don't want to overburden you with my desires. You're still new at this; there may still be pain. No? Well then, at least, I'd think there was the fact that you are unaccustomed . . . Look, Cristabel, lovemaking isn't a thing learned in a day, although I do believe the way of it was bred in your bones, and I thank God for it, my little pirate. Some of the pleasure came to you at once, but the rest must come with experience. I don't know why, but that's the way of it for most women. I'm not complaining. There are women who never feel anything. Don't worry about that," he chuckled. "You are fire itself. But the ultimate flame is a slower thing to kindle and flare. Do you see?"

"Show me," she said, her eyes searching his.

His eyes were troubled as he looked at her. "No," he said, caressing her bare shoulder, "lovemaking can't be done to prove anything, except love. Not for us. Take me in love, or lust, or simple merriment, and it will be well. But no other way. You don't have to prove anything to me, Cristabel."

She laid her head on his wide shoulder. "Oh, Magnus," she said in a choked voice, "but I do love you."

She said it as though she marveled at it. Then she said it in grateful recognition. Then she said it against his lips, as she gave him a kiss of simple love. Then he took her in his arms. "Well," he muttered, "we might make something of this."

There were tears in her eyes as he came to her, but he knew she wasn't crying. She didn't think of pleasing him now, nor did she wonder about her response. She only knew she loved him entirely, and his lips, his hands, his body, told her he felt the same way. Eventually, when she felt the strange and yet familiar tightening in her body, and when she heard him urging her in low, tense tones to let it go, she did—and found at last the release that she'd been seeking since he'd first touched her, and found it to be so powerful that she had no words, only small sobs, to greet it.

"There," he said when they were done and she lay replete against his chest, feeling his heart and breath slow to normal. "Well, what do you know? For once, I was wrong. It wasn't such a long wait after all, was it?"

She giggled.

"No, no flowers please. No time for congratulations," he said. "I have a wedding to plan this morning. You have that chat with my mother to endure. And then—and then," he said thoughtfully, as he lay gazing into space, one hand behind his head, the other stroking her, "I think I'll see to our remove from this place. It's very comfortable here, but there are drawbacks. We're expected to emerge from this room and greet the family every so often. Making love at midnight and dawn may be fine for old married folk, but I've a penchant for surprises. Noon is not a time to scoff at either, you know. Oh, you don't? Well, you should. Yes," he said with a pleased grin for the blush that covered her entire body, "I'll think I'll go and get my own house ready for my bride."

"We'll go and get it ready," she said.

"I think it best that you stay here, where it's safe," he said, bracing for her protests. Yes, he knew she was good with a knife and a pistol, too, but no, he didn't want her to have to use them.

"I'm not safe unless I'm with you," she said, and before he could answer, she went on, "I couldn't rest knowing you were alone and in possible danger, and if you don't take me, I'll find a way to follow without you knowing; you know I will and then if I get into trouble, you'll be sorry, so it's only truth when I say that I'm not safe unless I'm with you."

He rubbed his chin and stared at her, thinking deeply.

"And I agree that we should live in your house," she added, "alone with each other, with no one to answer to, and no one to see what we do or when we do it, and the sooner the better, too."

"After you speak with my mother, then," he said with a sigh.

When Magnus came to get Cristabel to take her to see his house, all the women in the room complained loudly. Even Sophia seemed sincerely reluctant to let her go.

"But we were having such a nice conversation," his mother complained, but stopped to smile when she saw Cristabel's face as she rose to greet her new husband. All the women beamed then, even Sophia.

"My pardon, Mother," Magnus said, "but I promised to show Cristabel her new home this afternoon. We can't stay with you forever, Sophia," he said, before she could protest, or pretend to. "You should understand that well enough. You have your own life to get on with. You're fairly newly wedded too."

"Of course, of course," Sophia said nervously, "but still, you're always welcome here."

"I know," he said, "and thank you for it. But it was never

my intention to marry and set up housekeeping in your house." As they all laughed he added, "Now I'll spirit your guest away. We'll see you at dinner."

He offered Cristabel his arm. She moved to his side and walked to the door with him, staring into his eyes without a word. It was only when she got to the door that she stopped, turned around to the company, and blushing, said, "Oh. I'm so sorry. We were having such a good time, and I just walked off—what you must think of me!"

"I think," the countess said with a happy little sigh, "that my son has picked a good wife. Go on, my dear. There'll be other times for us to chat, I'm sure, when you've grown tired of Magnus." But she said that as though she doubted it would ever happen, and all the women laughed. Then they, too, sighed as they watched Cristabel and Magnus leave together.

Sophia stood by the window watching them as they went down the street, an odd sad, twisted expression, somewhere between envy and tears, on her pale face. Because her mother-in-law was from the countryside and frowned on Town fashions, Sophia's little face was free of powder today. All her tiny freckles showed, making her look much less worldly than she usually tried to be. She looked young and lost as she watched Cristabel and Magnus turn the corner, and yet she would have stayed there, staring after them, if her mother-in-law hadn't called her back to herself by asking her a question.

"She was wonderful!" Cristabel chirped excitedly as she walked at Magnus's side. "Your mother was charming and welcoming and kind, and I really think someday she could come to like me for myself, and not just because you married me. I was so afraid of what she'd ask, and if I'd stumble and speak . . . well . . . 'pirateish,' if she stumped me, but all she asked was if there was anything she could do to make me happy. Then she told me a dozen, dozen stories about you. Your sisters were just as nice, and they had their stories too. I know about every friend you ever protected;

why, I think I know every dog you ever saved from drowning. They told me every considerate thing you ever did, and you did so many that if you hadn't come to get me, I'd still be sitting there listening to them singing your praises."

She fell silent, and he raised a brow as he looked down at her. He mistrusted her silence. When she was happy, she laughed, or joked with him, or chattered like one of the bright birds from her islands. "What story upset you?" he asked.

"None," she said, looking up, her face somber. "In truth, Magnus, you are just too good to be true."

He laughed so loudly, he made passersby smile. "Exactly," he said, when he could, "so don't hate me when you come to know me better." He chuckled, but stopped when she spoke again.

"Well," she mused, "the things they liked most about you—the things which are truly wonderful about you, Magnus—are also the things that make me very angry with you too. It's good that you protect everyone around you, but not everyone needs protecting all the time. And your selflessness is very fine, but the fact that you don't have a care for yourself when someone else is in danger is upsetting. I want you to be around for ages, my lord. I'll have to teach you to be a little more selfish and proud."

"Like you?" he asked gently. "I think I'll have to find another tutor."

"Well, look what happened the last time you tried to protect me," she said indignantly.

"Yes, I was able to convince you to marry me," he said. "A bad example, my lady, since I don't regret anything about that night because of it. In fact, I wonder if you'd have married me if the wretch hadn't managed to put a hole in me. No, don't say a word. Remember? You said you were a terrible liar."

She laughed and kept laughing as they strolled to his house, a few streets from where Martin's house was. It was broad daylight, so she didn't have to search the shadows for danger as they walked, even if there weren't two footmen following them discreetly, and three pirate lads on the street whom she recognized as she strolled by them. They were lurking, trying to look like innocent citizens. One of them gave her a weak little wave of a mittened hand before he remembered that he was supposed to be looking natural as he sorted through a dustbin.

She was grinning when she went up the steps to Magnus's house. But then she smiled with pure pleasure. She nodded to his servants as Magnus introduced her, but she couldn't keep from looking around herself in admiration. His house was larger and taller than his brother's, rising a full four stories high, with a garden in back, a coach house, and stables. The house had spacious rooms, each one with a fireplace framed in marble, shining wood floors spotted with bright carpets, beautiful walnut furniture, high ceilings, and new sash windows everywhere. Martin's house had cased windows that stingily leaked in small amounts of sunlight. She hadn't realized how she had missed the light until she saw how much sunlight a London house could have.

"Now, you tell me what you want discarded and what you want to buy, and I get to fight to keep the chair I love best, I suppose," Magnus said with mock glumness as he went up the tall staircase with her.

"Why should I do that?" she asked in amazement.

"Well, because it's what every bride does when she comes to her husband's house, or so I'm told," he said as he opened the door to his bedchamber.

She said nothing. He turned to see her standing still in the middle of his room, her hands twisting together.

"What have I said?" he asked in concern.

"How shall I know what to like or not?" she asked in a small voice. "I lived in two rooms, and thought myself lucky if the roof didn't leak. I had to shoo chickens out of my bedroom, and I thought the grandest place anyone on earth could live would be in my father's pirate ship. I thought Martin's home was grand; this is—this is beyond anything

I've seen. And from the way your mother talks about your home in Kent . . . Oh, Magnus, I don't belong," she said, looking up at him, her eyes glowing bright amber in the wash of sunlight and tears. "In your arms, in your bed, I am home. But everywhere else, I'm in some alien land. I don't want to embarrass you or myself. But I don't know how not to."

"Is liking my home embarrassing?" he asked.

"Is it?" she asked.

He took her in his arms. "You *might* be able to embarrass me if you stood on a street corner and balanced an eel on the end of your nose," he said thoughtfully, "but don't bet on it, because it might enchant me. And of course, if it made people throw coins, I think I wouldn't mind the embarrassment at all. Don't cry. Don't even sniffle. The staff will think I'm being a brute. There, better. Now, I'll show you the other rooms, which we must work diligently to fill up with little pirates and noblemen. Yes, very good. Blushes are much better than tears."

She wandered throughout his house—which he kept telling her was her house, and she almost began to believe it.

"In three weeks," Magnus said with satisfaction after they'd finished touring all the rooms, "we'll move in. First we must buy bride clothes, and have our new wedding. I've set all the wheels in motion. We can hurry the thing through—having a title does have its benefits. Of course, the fact that we're already married helps enormously. High churchmen are more competitive with the low fellows who do the service for a shilling than they'd like us to think."

He said good-bye to his staff and led Cristabel to the door. The last of a rosy sunset showed over the rooftops of London, promising a fair new day and the nearness of spring. They strolled along in silence; he thought it was the silence of contentment until she spoke.

"Who will give me away?" she asked in a small voice. "I've no one. What a strange bride I will be." She shook her head solemnly. "No bridesmaids, no guardian, no family at all. Only Black Jack, who can dress and act the gentleman and give a false name if he wants. And a dozen or so pirate lads, who can't even put their noses into such a grand church. I'll be a most peculiar bride, Magnus. Are you sure you want to go through with this?"

He put his hand over hers where it lay on his arm. "Sophia will stand with you, as will my sisters. Martin will be my groomsman. We can find an upstanding man to give you away, and say he's related. But if you like, we can ask Black Jack to do it. As you say, he's a good mimic, and although it might sting him, I think it would please him very much to know you think so highly of him."

It took her a minute to answer because she was so touched. She finally managed a saucy grin as she said, "Now, all I have to do is to remember not to say 'Aye' when the parson asks me to say 'I do.' But do you know?" she asked consideringly, her head to the side. "I think my speech is improving. I don't lapse so often anymore. It must be the company I keep."

"I'm not so sure it's for the good," he said. "I'll miss my little pirate. But if that's the price I have to pay for having you less frightened and unsure, I'll gladly pay it." He squeezed her hand in his warm one as she smiled up at him tremulously.

Which was why neither of them saw what was coming.

There were three of them this time, and their appearance on this street at this hour was so unexpected that even if Magnus and Cristabel had been paying attention, they would have been surprised. As it was, they were totally unprepared for meeting up with three heavily cloaked and armed, grinning would-be assassins, and that one moment of shock cost them dearly. The three were almost upon them by the time Magnus drew his sword and marshaled his wits. And quick as Cristabel was, she scarcely had her knife in her hand before she was crouching, wondering which of them to protect Magnus from first. She and Magnus stood back to back on one of London's finest residential streets, surrounded by three circling men armed with sword, pistol, and cutlass.

It was a bold move, and Magnus was afraid it was a very good one. No one could have expected assassins in such an open, public place; he didn't know if his footmen were nearby. Even if they were, these men were very near now. Magnus watched them closely, holding his sword in readiness for their next move. He was very good with a sword, and with his fists as well, but the pistol bothered him. He felt Cristabel move at his back and worried more, because he knew she wasn't hiding there. For the first time since they'd met, he wished she were the type to faint, then she'd be well out of it and he wouldn't have to worry about her. He was ready for them, but there were three of them, and they looked hard and desperate. He would fight until he dropped, but his only realistic hope was to protect her before he died.

It was like finding a shark in your bathtub, Cristabel thought in horror, but she was quick to adjust. Her eyes narrowed on one fat fellow, the one with the pistol. Guns made a man overconfident. He looked to be a swaggerer, and already wore a grin. He wouldn't expect a knife in his throat, and never from a woman. She steadied herself and stared at him, hoping Magnus could finish off one of the others quickly, so that together they'd have a chance against the third. If he didn't, she'd give up the fat fellow and go for the one who was giving Magnus trouble.

The three men moved closer, still grinning like death's heads. The air was very still, exactly like the atmosphere before a storm, so it was not so shocking when the roar of thunder finally came—except to the man who held the pistol, as he stood and wavered as his forehead grew a gaping hole in it. He fell before any of them knew from where the bolt had struck. Until they heard the screeches. They were so bloodcurdling, the sound of them made a man's hair stand up on end, and several women in nearby houses said afterward that they nearly fainted when they heard it. But it made Cristabel smile. She was used to a pirate's war cry. It meant her friends were near, and that they were the ones who had already dealt a blow for her.

She relaxed, leaning back against Magnus's own back. Which was a mistake, because her eyes widened as she saw the remaining two men grip their weapons tighter—and run straight for her.

Magnus cursed and spun around. He managed to pierce the arm of the man holding the cutlass, who spun on his own heel and slashed back at his attacker. His attack was sloppy because he was so eager to turn back to his primary target again. That was why Magnus was able to leap out of the way of his glittering blade and fight back. He lunged, striking up and under the man's arm with the supple tip of his long sword, burying it deep in the man's chest. Still, Magnus had to dodge and duck and try to pull his sword out with all his considerable strength, for even spitted as he was, the fellow was slashing back again, as if his brain hadn't yet told his body the fight was over. From the corner of his eye, Magnus saw the man with the sword feint at Cristabel. His heart grew cold because she faced a long sword with a meager dagger, and his own blade was wedged too deep in flesh and bone for him to immediately run to aid her.

He spat a curse and pulled as he ducked, feeling his weapon come free just as the saber hissed past his ear. He turned as his opponent finally toppled—to see the swordsman who was facing Cristabel grow a look of sheer amazement, and crumple to his knees, Cristabel's knife in his neck, blank astonishment as well as death growing in his eyes.

There were three dead men at their feet, and what seemed to be a dozen pirates suddenly surrounding them, knives and guns flashing, still defending them. Magnus looked to see if there were any more assailants, and then his eyes narrowed. He thrust Cristabel into the arms of a startled pirate, shouted, "Hold her fast," and ran off, his bloodstained sword in his hand.

Cristabel struggled to follow, but the pirate held her tight. "'Tis no place fer you, missy," he growled. She didn't show steel because she recognized the lad, and gave up to his superior strength. She didn't argue because she was winded and had no idea of whom Magnus was pursuing anyway. Three men had attacked them, three men lay dead. The street before them had emptied of pedestrians when the fight began, and there was only a carriage standing empty at the far curb, and a sedan chair going down the street.

But it was the sedan chair that Magnus raced after. When he got near enough to see the faces of the men jogging fore and aft of it, he let out a thundering roar: "Hold," he shouted, "or I'll gut the lot of you!"

London's sedan men were a tough and ready-fisted lot, half of them from Ireland and the other half from hell, as the jest went, but their faces went dead white when they turned to see who was chasing them. Magnus's sword was held high, its bloody blade clear to see, and there was blood on his clothes and in his eyes as he neared them.

They stopped and stared at the big man pounding on down the street toward them. Then they dropped the poles supporting the chair. As it fell to the street, they took to their heels, abandoning it. There was a madman after them, and it seemed he was followed by a score of enraged pirates. The passenger in the chair tried to right himself, but by the time Magnus reached him, he was terrorized, crawling on his hands and knees, trying to scuttle away from the overturned chair. He was a well-dressed older man, with snowy hair and a beet red face. It got redder when Magnus knelt, jerked him upright, and held him up by his neckcloth.

"Who?" Magnus snarled. "Damn you, tell me who. And now!"

The man croaked a word, and then another. Magnus scowled and shook him again. "More, damn you," he shouted. The man gasped, and then jabbered and gargled, and his eyes rolled up in his head as he went limp in Magnus's grasp. But Magnus continued to shake him and curse him, until Black Jack came up beside him and put a hand over his.

"Softly, me lord," he said in a curiously quiet voice. "He'll not be saying anything more until Gabriel's horn, methinks."

He didn't try to make Magnus release the man, because he'd boarded ships in his time to find himself fighting like a madman against madmen. He knew when a man was lost in a berserk rage. Magnus's eyes were wild with a killing light. He was a big man, and strong, but now he was even stronger and no longer knew his own strength.

It was a moment or two before Black Jack's words reached Magnus. Then he opened his hand. The man dropped like a stone to the ground. Black Jack knelt beside him. He rose with the man's wallet in his gloved hand. He looked through it with interest as Magnus's breathing slowed.

"Dead. Entirely. His heart guv out on him, belike," one of the pirates announced after checking the man on the ground.

Black Jack nodded; he'd thought as much. His eyes slewed to Magnus as he wondered what he would say.

"Too bad," Magnus said in a bleak voice. "There was much I had to ask him. He watched the whole of it; I saw his face as I was fighting for my life. He was interested, damn his soul, merely interested. I hardly thought of it until I saw him set the men running away when he saw the tide turn. Then I knew. Damn," Magnus said, his hands fisting tightly, "I didn't mean to kill him; there was much more I had to ask him."

"No need," Black Jack said, handing Magnus papers he'd found in the wallet, after he'd counted and pocketed the money.

Magnus glanced at the papers, and nodded sadly. Then he looked over to where Cristabel was watching them. "I know," he said. "It's as I thought. Not a word to her, you hear?"

"Of course not," Black Jack said. "Be you forgetting? I love the lass too."

But Magnus didn't hear; he was walking back to Cristabel. He took her in his arms when he reached her, without saying a word. She went into his embrace silently and he felt her shaking. He wondered if he, too, was shaking. Not from the battle, and not from the shock of it, But from what he'd seen with his own eyes. Looking over Cristabel's head now, he saw Black Jack's grim face.

The men had been after Cristabel. They were trying to kill her—not him. They'd never been after him. They'd tried to murder her, just as the wild horseman had, and just as the other had tried the night he'd been shot, trying to defend her. That was bad enough. Worst of all, he knew who had sent them now.

"Are you well?" Magnus asked her, drawing back and cupping her face in his hands.

She nodded. "But you," she asked anxiously, "your wound—are you all right?"

"I'm fine," he said. "We're lucky," he sighed, and held her close.

"That man," she whispered, "the one you chased. Who was he? Was he the one who wanted me dead?"

She felt his body tense at that dread word, and he hugged her closer. "Later," he said, "For now, I think you should go back to Martin's house. Jack can take you. I have to stay to explain things to the watch, but I don't think he'll want to stay around for that."

"No," she said simply, "my place is with you."

As soon as curious decent citizens began to venture back on the street, the pirates vanished like vapor rising from the cobbles, leaving Magnus to explain the matter to the watchmen. When all questions had been answered, except for Cristabel's own, Magnus walked back with her to Martin's house.

"You say you're well, but I think you should lie down and rest," Magnus told her when they got there.

"You say you're well, too, and you're the one who took a ball in your chest just recently," she said.

He was prevented from answering by Sophia's horrified cries when she saw them standing in the hall, bloodstained and disheveled. The footmen ran for Martin, and when he rushed in, he grew pale.

"Again?" he cried.

"We're not hurt," Magnus told him immediately. "but not from want of trying."

"Thank God Mother and Father and the others went out today to pick out wedding clothes, as you wished," Martin said. "They'd die if they saw you like that. What happened?"

"I'll tell you everything," Magnus said, "but first I'd like to wash and change my clothing, and I think Cristabel should too—and quickly."

Cristabel couldn't argue that, but she frowned. Martin followed Magnus up the stair, and she realized that she really couldn't, if she was to change her clothes. She had to go to her own room to do that, because that was where all her clothing was. Although she and Magnus now shared a bed every night, they had decided to do it so recently and abruptly that she still had her own room, and he had his. That meant that he could talk to Martin without her knowing what was said—and perhaps not knowing what the man in the sedan chair had said. Magnus hadn't spoken to her about it, and now that the shock was over and her wits were returning, she was keenly interested. He'd gotten very grim around the mouth when he left the man, and still hadn't said a word about it. The fact that he hadn't troubled her.

"We'll meet down here directly after we refresh ourselves, not a moment later," she said forcefully, glaring at Magnus, "and best be quick about it, because if I have to wait to find out what I need to know until after your parents and sisters are abed, I'll burst."

He smiled for the first time in an hour. But it was a crooked, tired smile that made her heart clench. "We can't have that," he said. "Exploding pirates are very dangerous things. Agreed then, little madwoman, I'll be down directly after I've changed my clothes. Now, let me tell you how she fought—like a tiger, I swear," he told Martin as he went up the stair with him, making her sound like an Amazon, and talking just loudly enough to be sure she heard him.

She grinned, but when he and Martin went into his room

and closed the door behind them, she couldn't hear another word.

"Quick," she told Sophia, as she hurried up the stair herself. "Call me maid to fetch me a clean gown and some soap and water. I must know all, and soon!"

"But so must I," Sophia protested, picking up her skirt and following her.

Cristabel told her what happened, glad for something to do, if only to talk about what she'd done as she endured being scrubbed and dried and correctly gowned, and then sat impatiently as her maid combed out her hair. As soon as the maid was through, Cristabel broke off her story and bolted for the door. Sophia stopped her by putting a light hand on her arm. Cristabel paused and looked at her. Sophia's eyes were reddened with unshed tears, and her mouth quivered. She looked very young.

"I've been terrible to you," she said, "and I know it. If anything had happened to you . . . Cristabel, if I was ever cruel or rude to you, it's because I envy you so much. I know you can't understand it, but it's so. You seemed to me to live life so fully, you seem to be afraid of nothing, not like me. It makes me more cowardly when I see you, do you understand?"

"I see you need spectacles," Cristabel said in astonishment, "for I'm afraid half the time. Can't you hear it when I speak—switching from being a lady to being a pirate every time I get upset?"

"I didn't know that was what it was," Sophia said.

"Well there's a relief," Cristabel sighed, "for it's fair maddening to me. The only time I'm not afraid is when I'm with Magnus—and aye, some of the time with him too. I'm always afraid of putting a foot wrong, of embarrassing myself or him, of losing him—or myself. Why, I'm the most fearful woman I know!"

"But you don't show it."

"Well, I try not to," Cristabel said. "Go cowering, and everybody steps on you; that's a natural fact. My father didn't teach me much good, but he taught me that. You've got to face up to things you're afraid of, and that's all I do. But that doesn't stop the fear."

"Can you ever forgive me?" Sophia asked tearfully.

Cristabel grew very still. "Depends on what for," she said carefully.

"For not being nicer to you, for treating you so badly," Sophia sniffed.

"Oh, that. Certainly," Cristabel said, losing interest and heading for the stair.

"But what did you think I meant?" Sophia asked.

"I thought you might be apologizing for trying to kill me," Cristabel said, and as Sophia gasped, she added, "Someone sure be trying to, you see."

Cristabel ran light-footed down the stair, but no one was in the parlor. She ran back to the hall, as angry as she was frightened. And then her heart sank.

Magnus was coming down the stairs, with Martin and Black Jack behind him. Which meant that though Magnus had probably kept his word to the strict letter of it, he had outwitted her. They'd obviously already met without her knowing—and that could mean only one thing. They were keeping something from her.

CHAPTER

18

The men paused at the foot of the stair.

"We have to go out for a while, Cristabel," Magnus said when he saw her in the hall, staring at him. "We'll be back before long. There's no danger for us," he said, when he saw her face, "but there is something that we must take care of."

She stood facing him, her head back, her silken curls framing a face that was as still as one of her father's figureheads. Her eyes gleamed with unshed tears. But her voice was clear and cold.

"You leave me now, Magnus Titus," she said, "and you leave me for all time. I am not a fool. I know you go to seek vengeance—on my enemy. Aye, this I know. And I'm thinking it's for one of two reasons. Either you think me such a weakling and a child that you feel you must protect me, even from the truth, or else you think it is man's work entirely, and I am of no account at all. Neither is acceptable to me. I am your wife, and your equal—in danger as well as in comfort. And if ye don't agree, then be damned to ye, me lord. For I am what I am, and twist and turn as I might, I cannot be yer version of a lady. Nor do I want to be."

Cristabel fell still and waited for her husband to speak.

Black Jack was grinning ear to ear, and Martin seemed troubled. But she couldn't read Magnus's face; it might have been carved from stone.

"And if the truth be bitter," he finally asked, "and I wish to spare you that, because I love you?"

"I appreciate it," she said simply, "but I still want to know for myself. Think on—would you like it if I did the same to you? For sure, there'll be times in our lives to come—if we have such lives together—when I'll know a thing that I may fear to tell you. Would you wish me to keep it from you because I was afraid it would pain you? Or would you rather I told it to you and let you take it like a man? I be a woman, but I be no less strong than a man. And if you think so, why, you're not the man for me. But," she said softly, with the first hint of emotion in her voice, "I truly thought you were."

Magnus's big chest rose and fell with the power of his great sigh. Then he nodded, reluctantly, "I'd have you no other way. But I'd give my arm to spare you pain. Come with me, if you wish."

She nodded, and sent for her cloak. Magnus wrapped it around her, and paused, only for a minute, to hold her shoulders hard in his hands. Then he signaled to the others and they went out into the night.

"Be careful," Sophia cried at the door, as they entered the coach Magnus had sent for.

No one answered as the coach pulled away from the door. They rode in silence, each thinking his or her own thoughts, although Magnus held Cristabel's hand in his own warm clasp all the while. There was so much Cristabel wanted to know, and so little she dared ask, that she stayed silent. Not from fear of coming danger, because Magnus was by her side. But from fear of the unknown. She could honestly think of no one who might want to harm her—unless they were trying to get at Magnus. The one man who might be his enemy could never be hers—and would certainly not be Magnus's if he knew they were truly wedded now. To the contrary, he'd be ecstatic. But someone had tried to kill her. It still seemed impossible, though she'd seen it with her own eyes, and had, in fact, had to kill someone to save herself this very day. That was real enough for her.

The carriage stopped on a pleasant street on the outskirts of town, where inns and hotels served travelers newly arrived in London. The men got out silently, and Cristabel took Magnus's arm as she stepped down the stair from the coach to the street. She suddenly didn't want to be there. She didn't know what she'd find, but whatever it was, it wouldn't be good. The only thing she did know was that it was something she had to face. She knew how to do that. At least this time, she thought, she didn't have to do it alone. She held Magnus's hand and went into the inn.

It was a homey place, old as the gate it stood beside that had been built around the city itself. The walls were whitewashed as best they could be over centuries worth of soot from woodsmoke, the floors tilted crazily, and the low ceiling was held up by old, blackened timbers. But the scent of many good suppers hung in the air, a fire roared in the hearth, and the place held the peace that a building earns by simply existing through so much time.

Magnus murmured something to the innkeeper, who bowed and showed them into a private dining parlor. They waited there. Black Jack slipped into the shadows, and stood watching. Martin put his hands behind his back and stood by the fire, waiting. And Magnus held Cristabel's hand hard in his.

When the door opened, they all started. But only Cristabel made a sound. She caught her breath with a small, choked sob, before her hand flew to her lips to hold them still as her heart seemed to be.

The old man was pushed into the room in his wheeled invalid chair. At his brief signal his servant left him there in the middle of the room, with only his wife standing still and straight beside him. She looked at Cristabel once, and then stared away into the shadows, where Black Jack's mocking smile made her shift her feet, and look straight ahead again, her back rigid.

"My mother!" Cristabel breathed. "Why?"

"Indeed," Magnus said harshly, "that is the only question that remains unanswered."

"Rodgers told you, I suppose," the Baron Batsford sighed.

"Yes, but so did the papers he carried in his wallet," Magnus said. "He was your man at law; it would have been an easy guess even if he hadn't damned you with his last breath today. I didn't kill him, by the way. His heart—or his conscience—did. But why did you ask him to see to it?"

The old man looked around the room. "I think I'd prefer it if you would introduce me to these others first. I came because you gave me no choice; your message spoke of many dire consequences. Are any of these gentlemen the king's men? Or simply murderers, like your wife's father?"

"Or her mother's husband?" Magnus asked. "But by all means: Baron Batsford and Madam Stew—for that's still your name," he said as Cristabel's mother gasped, "may I present my brother, Martin Snow, and my good friend, Master Jarvis Kelly—from the Indies. They know everything. And before I go further, I'd add that so do my lawyers and theirs, and that there are letters to that effect in all their possessions now, to be opened and made public immediately should anything happen to any of us tonight—or hereafter. You might as well stop hiring assassins, because all they can kill now is your own future. Now that I've obliged you, I ask you to reciprocate," he said harshly. "No more games, sir. Why?"

The old man spread his hands in a helpless gesture; his smile was cold and bitter. "It's obvious, my lord, is it not?"

"Yes," Magnus said, "but I will have it said."

"Very well," the baron said, shrugging his thin shoulders. "It was there in your introduction. We didn't want it known that this—female—is my wife's daughter. That would lead to questions about her first marriage."

"Which is, of course, I remind you, her only legal one,"

Magnus said harshly, "which leaves you with no legal heirs, doesn't it? Only two bastard sons. There never was a divorce, was there? That's the crux of it. It was never you, Cristabel," he said, turning to her. "Don't listen to his venom. It was always her mistake that he tried to correct, not yours."

"Mine?" Cristabel's mother cried, glaring at him. "Mine? Who do you think got me with her? Who do you think forced me into that vile marriage? Why do you think I birthed this—this creature who calls herself my daughter? And why should that hideous time in my life ruin my dear children's futures?"

"Mind your tongue, Madam Stew. This 'person' is my wife," Magnus growled.

Cristabel's mother grew pale, and even the old man blinked.

"That, I did not know," the baron said in a troubled voice.

"It's true. It will be in the paper tomorrow," Magnus said, "and all London will know in a matter of weeks. They would have known sooner if we'd guessed your intent. But there'll be no doubt this time. We're going to be married again with all pomp and ceremony, since our first wedding was so hastily conducted at what we thought was my deathbed," Magnus said with a twisting smile, "thanks to you."

Cristabel stared at her mother. The woman was still beautiful. But it was an icy beauty, for try as she might, Cristabel could see no remorse, no softness, in her. She wore gray tonight and her hair was powdered white. Only her eyes and her jewelry had color. She could have been the figure that her father had carved of her to put on the prow of his ship for luck, she was so cold, so inhumanly beautiful, stiff and still.

"You were trying to kill me when Magnus was hurt," Cristabel said to her mother, as though she couldn't believe it. One last feeble hope made her ask in a very small voice, "You sanctioned my killing?"

"Why shouldn't I have?" her mother asked bitterly. "It would have righted a terrible wrong."

"Aye, I see," Cristabel said, nodding to herself. "I do indeed."

"You could have legally adopted your sons," Martin blurted. "You could have told your husband the truth—that your first husband still lived. You didn't have to try to kill your daughter!"

"He knew," Cristabel's mother said coldly, not sparing a glance for the old man she spoke about, "he always knew. There was no way to get at my first husband to legally end it. He was at the other end of the world, and his life was forfeit if he ever came to England, so we thought that was the end of it—until she appeared and claimed me as her mother. No one else knew about that marriage; I had put it behind me. The pirate himself seemed willing to forget it; why should it have come to light now? Why should one hideous mistake ruin so many good lives?"

"But I was your daughter," Cristabel said, shaking her head in disbelief.

"I have no daughter," her mother said furiously. "You are a stranger. I avoided the sight of you since the day you were dragged out of me. I left as soon as I could. What more proof do you want of my distaste for you? My daughter? I've only your word for it; you don't even look like me, thank God."

Indeed she didn't, Cristabel thought dazedly, except for her forehead, her eyes, her nose, her size, and her shape.

"Cristabel," Magnus said, despairing, seeing the pain in her glowing eyes, "it doesn't matter. You're everything you thought a lady should be, but she isn't. Not by temperament or spirit. She's your mother in name only, and you should be grateful for it. Forget her. Think of our future, which, God willing, will be bright and long.

"And I remind you," he warned the baron, turning to glare at him, "that only God will be the one to decide that. Do as you like with the matter of your marriage and your sons' legitimacy; we don't care. We won't acknowledge you, nor will we prosecute you for past attempts on our lives, because we don't want notoriety either. But a word of wisdom to you, Baron, and to your woman—or whatever she is now," he said carelessly, to see Cristabel's mother blanch. "I suggest you pray to whatever gods will listen that no accident ever befalls Cristabel, or any she holds dear. Because if one does, or if we even think one has—we'll tell everything, from the first marriage to the false one, from the bastard children to all your attempts at murder. They use a silken noose to hang noblemen and women, but I doubt it's much more comfortable. Everything will be made public."

"If there be any of ye left breathing to hear the news, that be to say," Black Jack said from the shadows, "'cause the Lord Snow and his lady have friends in the Brotherhood, Baron, and I be reminding ye to never forget that."

Cristabel's mother froze, and Black Jack chuckled.

Magnus grinned, but his smile was forced because of the look he saw on Cristabel's face; she was staring at her mother, transfixed by some inner turmoil.

"And I also advise you to tell your sons about their legitimate sister," Magnus went on, "whatever you decide to do about their inheritance. We plan to have many beautiful children. It would be best if your family knows of the relationship so they don't end up falling in love with their own sisters and cousins someday. As for the rest— we'll neither claim relationship nor deny it, right, Cristabel? Cristabel?"

But she wasn't listening to him. Nor was she standing still and shocked anymore. Bright color had flown to her cheeks, and her eyes glistened with fury, not sorrow, now. She strode forward, and they all caught their breaths, because the flickering light glanced off a dagger she suddenly held in her hand. Before any man in the room could stop her, she strode up to her mother and touched the point of the knife to the dimple in her mother's chin. Her mother gasped, but didn't move.

The two women were the same size, and this close, their

resemblance to each other was clear. But one woman seemed made of ice, and the other of fire.

"Remember this, my lady?" Cristabel hissed as she moved the knife lower. "Too bad you can't look under your chin to see. It was my father's favorite knife; its hilt is crusted with topaz. He said it reminded him of your eyes, but he gave it to me as a parting gift. He gave me this, and jewels and gold besides. But he gave me nothing as valuable as his own name, and that, I do see now. He's done many wicked things, but he knew no better. At least he tried to raise me properly. Listen to me, lady," Cristabel went on, as her mother swallowed hard, and stopped, because the motion brought her flesh closer to the knife, "and say not a word, because your voice offends my ears, it does. I lived my life trying to be like you, and that's the only thing I'm sorry for now. For I wouldn't want to be like you for all the gold in Troy.

"I have my father's knife, and aye, his brave heart, too, and I be—I am glad of it now. If ever you speak my name, speak it in a whisper. For I don't want it to be known that I was spawned by such as you. And if you ever even think of doing my Magnus harm, know this—I will slit you from your chin to your toes, and dance on your innards, I will.

"To think," Cristabel marveled, "I wanted to be like you! That I was ashamed of being a pirate's daughter. Now I'm proud of it. Hear this: Forget me. But never dare forget my wrath."

She touched the knife a fraction deeper, not enough to pierce the skin, but to make her point. Then, satisfied by the look in the older woman's eyes, she withdrew the dagger, flipped it in the air, caught it, and slid it back into her sleeve. Then she turned her back, and swaggered back to Magnus.

"I be done, now," she said. "Let's go home, my lord."

They walked out of the inn, and back into the carriage. No one said a word as they drove away, though all the men watched Cristabel carefully. She sat close to her husband,

and seemed to be thinking deeply, reviewing all that had happened.

At last she spoke. She smiled radiantly as she looked up at her husband. "And I scarcely made a slip, my lord," she said triumphantly. "I was maddened to the point that I saw everything as though through a long red tunnel. It was amazing. But I remembered. I wouldn't give her the satisfaction, and I didn't. I spoke like a true lady, didn't I?"

"That's because you are one," Magnus said tenderly.

"Aye," she said comfortably, wriggling closer to him, "that I be!"

The wedding was one of London's most lavish in recent memory.

The bride was magnificent in antique pearls and diamonds, and a gown that seemed made of moonbeams and stars. The groom was well dressed and well liked. There were as many jests about his having been caught at last, and by such a beauty—and an heiress from the Indies too!—as there were comments about how proud he was of her, and rightly so.

The groomsman and his lady wife seemed like a pair of turtledoves themselves, the lady Sophia for once paying more attention to her husband than to her admiring friends. As for young Martin Snow, he was pleased and proud, as if he seemed a little dazed by his lovely wife's attentions. Who wouldn't be?

The strikingly handsome dark man who gave the bride away in lieu of her father—who was, as always, traveling around the world consolidating his fortune, they said—was quite a favorite himself in London these days. Witty and rich, and such a devil with the ladies, it was rumored.

And if there seemed to be a crowd of oddly dressed men at the back of the church during the service, no one took more than passing notice, because who wouldn't want to see such a beautiful ceremony?

The ceremony was so beautiful, in fact, that some lingered, as though loath to leave the scene of such happiness, long after the bridal party had left the church.

One lone woman waited until all the guests had gone before she rose from her seat at the back of the cathedral. What could be seen of her was graceful and lovely, though her hair was covered by her shawl, and she wore her cloak, even in the church. She walked to the aisle, and looked to see if her maid was waiting by the doors, where she'd left her. When she felt a light touch on her arm, she assumed it was the girl. And leapt in her skin and grew deathly pale when she saw who it was.

She recognized him instantly.

He wore a wig, of course, a dark gray one. He was still stocky but dressed as a gentleman now. His beard was gone, and although new wrinkles transformed him somewhat, he couldn't bleach the touch of decades worth of tropical sun from his skin. He was bronzed and clean-shaven, and smelled of bay rum, not sweat and salt, now. But she knew him, of course, the minute she gazed into those dark and glittering eyes.

"You," she said simply, her hand at her breast, breathing hard.

"Aye, 'tis I. Been a long time, ain't it, luv?"

"Long, long, indeed," she said carefully.

"She were a right beauty, our daughter, weren't she?" he sighed. "A lady to her fingertips, and a lady true, it happens now. I made sure of that, in every way I could. What about you, Lizzie? I be damned if I'm going to die to make yer marriage legal, but I wonder how yer handling it. Why'd you marry that old stick anyway? Yer bed must have been good and cold—aye! Good usually is cold, ain't it? There's a jest fer ye."

She studied him. He smiled at her. A small smile came to her own lips. "You're right. It is cold," she said, "but he is a lord. And that's what I wanted. That's what I got. It seemed a fair trade then."

"Hard to believe," he said, scratching himself thoughtfully. "Ye were a rare handful, lass. As hot in bed as ye were hotheaded out of it. Our daughter's very like, y'know."

"I know. She said she'd kill me if I tried to harm her again or anyone she loved."

"Good," Captain Whiskey said happily. "'Twould save me the trouble. For I'd've done for ye meself if ye'd hurt a hair on her head, y'know. Stupid lass to forget that, weren't ye?"

"I suppose," she said calmly, "I acted without thinking. It doesn't matter now. The baron's going to legally adopt the boys, quietly, of course, so there will be no problem with the title or estate. And I shall continue to be his wife to everyone else, whatever that paper you still hold says— unless," she asked sweetly, "you'd care to give it to me? Or perhaps sell it to me? I'm very rich now. Or maybe," she asked, moving closer to him, close enough to touch him, close enough for him to scent the freesia perfume she always wore, "maybe you'd even be willing to . . . trade for it?"

He hooted with laughter. Her face set tight as she watched him wipe his eyes. "Aye, that's me dear Lady Elizabeth, for sure! Tricky, and still pretty, I grant ye. But I got me a truer lady for a wife now, and want no other. We live far from here; she'll never know we be still wed no more than your world will know it. I'll keep it that way, Lizzie, and our marriage paper, too, fer I believe that's the only way to keep me dear Cristabel safe. She's the lady you never were, ye see."

"Is she?" Cristabel's mother asked, her thin eyebrow arching.

"Aye. And ye know it. That's why I wed ye, when I could have just had ye anyway and forgot ye after. But ye were a lady and a wench together, and it fair boggled me. I had to have ye for mine, forever. I were such a fool. But ye were willing enough, remember? Ye come off that ship and into me arms like a shot, when there were that nice young lord could've rescued you. But ye turned yer back on him and come to me. Aye, ye were as hot as yer cold now, me old dear.

"Aye, that were the problem," he said with a trace of an old sadness, before he went on. "I'd've kept ye with me for all time, and loved ye only—like I promised—aye, like I did. Huh. Till ye played me false with every handsome pirate ye could get yer hands on when me back was turned, and I had to send ye away, or kill ye fer it. Do ye deceive the old gent, as well, I wonder?"

"That is my own business," she said haughtily.

"Aye, right, but who cares now?" he laughed, "Well, it were good seeing ye, Lizzie, but I got to go now. I told the happy couple I couldn't stay, but they was so glad I come, they din't mind how fast I had to go. I had to see 'em one last time. He be a fine gent; I couldn't have done better, as it turns out," he chortled. "I be saying farewell now, and I hope we never meet again. I won't wish ye happiness, but I suppose I don't wish ye ill, neither. Oh, and save yerself the trouble of calling the watch down on me now, 'cause I'll be gone afore you can draw breath. Be sure that ye never go near the lass again, hear? 'Cause I be always watching." And then he was gone.

She walked out the great cathedral doors, and saw that all the glad company was still there, cheering and shouting to the departing bridal couple. There was such a crowd in the street that their coach couldn't move, and so the two of them, flanked by their smiling family, were standing waving back to their happy guests and spectators.

They made a remarkably handsome couple. He tall, well set up, wide-shouldered, long-legged, and dressed all in pearl gray to match his eyes. She slender and yet curved, dainty and yet lush, her lovely face radiant with happiness. She whispered something to him. He answered something in her ear, and her face lit up with laughter. He gazed at her, and on an obvious impulse, cupped her head in his two big hands like a chalice and lowered his head so he could sip at those rosy laughing lips.

The lone woman at the top of the cathedral steps looked down at them. In that instant there was a flash of longing in her eyes; a hint of some terrible sorrow flickered in her face.

She closed her hands hard. The bite of her fingernails against her own palms seemed to awaken her. She grimaced, and then shrugged, and then calling to her maid, she turned and walked away from all the joyous company.

The groom stopped kissing his bride. She dragged his head back and kissed him soundly again.

The crowd cheered.

AVAILABLE!

A GIFT OF LOVE

Jude Deveraux
Judith McNaught
Andrea Kane
Kimberly Cates
Judith O'Brien

A wonderful romance collection in the
tradition of the *New York Times* bestseller
A Holiday of Love and the newly released
Everlasting Love, A GIFT OF LOVE is sure to
delight romance fans and readers alike.

**POCKET BOOKS
HARDCOVERS**

1093-02